Swan Place

**Center Point
Large Print**

**This Large Print Book carries the
Seal of Approval of N.A.V.H.**

ॐ श्री गणेशाय नमः

AUGUSTA TROBAUGH

Swan Place

CENTER POINT PUBLISHING
THORNDIKE, MAINE

For all the beloved children:
Sean
Nathan
Evan
Daniel
Brianna
and for the ones to come

This Center Point Large Print edition
is published in the year 2003 by arrangement with
Dutton, a division of Penguin Putnam Inc.

The text of this Large Print edition is unabridged. In other
aspects, this book may vary from the original edition. Printed in
Thailand. Set in 16-point Times New Roman type by
Bill Coskrey and Gary Socquet.

ISBN 1-58547-274-3

Library of Congress Cataloging-in-Publication Data.

Trobaugh, Augusta.
    Swan place / Augusta Trobaugh.--Center Point large print ed.
    p. cm.
    ISBN 1-58547-274-3 (lib. bdg. : alk. paper)
    1. African American women--Fiction. 2. Female friendship--Fiction. 3. Southern
States--Fiction. 4. Teenage girls--Fiction. 5. Stepmothers--Fiction. 6. Large type books.
I. Title.

PS3570.R585 S93 2003
813'.54--dc21

2002031450

Acknowledgments

I feel somewhat deceitful when I see the words, "by Augusta Trobaugh" on the front of a book, because that's far too simple. In truth, many people have provided invaluable assistance to me, and without their help, this story may never have come into being. So, to be completely honest, I need to thank and to acknowledge the help of:

Terry Kay, brilliant writer, true Southern gentleman, and treasured friend,

Harvey Klinger, the very best agent in the world,

The brilliant folks at Penguin Putnam—Carole Baron, Ronni Berger, Carrie McGinnis, Anna Cowles, Lisa Johnson, and Kathleen Schmidt,

Kathie, who—twenty years ago—kept my "house of cards" from falling apart,

Beverly, Kaye, Dorothy, and many more of the bright, professional staff members—far too many to name—at the Athens-Clarke County Library in Athens, Georgia, who encouraged me and listened patiently as this story manifested itself in the imagination,

My business manager, who kept me organized, well-advised, and encouraged,

My three grown children and their spouses, who cheered me on, and

Terry Stewart and Eddie Suttles of the Athens Barnes & Noble bookstore.

Finally, I thank my ancestors for the endless hours of great storytelling and "porch talk" I listened to in my childhood.

Did I tell this story right, Mama?

Prologue

EVERY spring, I watch for the first tender assurances of the earth being born all over again—a particular, fragrant sweetness in the air, the green mist of newly sprouting leaves, a veil of dew on the grass early in the mornings, and the savage, melodious songs of young mockingbirds staking out their territories. And I am always drawn back to one particular spring, starting on an Easter Sunday morning when I was only fourteen years old, when I finally started becoming the woman I was destined to become—when *I* arrived, after a long year of losing and gaining all the strong women who became grafted into my being forever. A year of learning what it meant to *get on with living,* as Aunt Bett always said. But also of discovering that I had a secret place deep inside that was filled with the strength and love that came from that terrible and wonderful year. A year when I lost almost everything I had to lose—but when I finally came to realize that no howling storm of life buffeting me would ever be as ferocious as the throbbing breath of resolve deep inside, leading me, at last, to the song I was created to sing.

Chapter One

I WAS dreaming about Mama as that year started, and in my dream she was dancing all around the living room with her favorite honky-tonk music turned up just as loud as it would go. She was wearing her spangle dress and high heels, laughing and jiggling her head, so that her all-over little golden curls went to dancing, too, and the sequins on her dress sparkling and the rhinestones in her dangle earrings just shining! In my dream, I was clapping my hands to the music and laughing with her, while she danced and danced and danced. Then, a little something or other seemed to happen in the music—a sound that was high, like somebody whistling. And another sound—a fluttering sound, so soft.

Mama must have heard it too, in my dream, because she stopped dancing for a little moment, and then she looked right at me with her eyes all blue and shining.

"Listen, sugar! He's singing for you!"

The honky-tonk music started fading away, and so did Mama, until all that was left of the dream was that high sound and the soft fluttering, them no longer in the dream but outside of it. Outside of my window. Then I knew the coolness of the pillowcase against my cheek.

Somewhere, a mockingbird was singing the most wobbly little song I ever heard. Why, it wasn't even dawn yet, maybe not even close to it, that's how dark it was outside. But still the mockingbird sang. He must have been in the big chinaberry tree in the yard, singing his heart out into the darkness. And the soft fluttering sound was a big moth on my window screen, trying so hard to get inside to where the night-light was glowing.

I turned over onto my back and watched the dark ceiling and listened to the soft puppy-squeak breathing coming from Molly and Little Ellis—my little sister and brother—where they slept together in the bed across the room, and to the crooked notes from the mockingbird. I guess he must have gotten awake too early, just like me. Maybe that's why his song was all wobbly and timid-sounding, like he wasn't sure if it was time to sing. Not so early. Not before daylight.

I knew what Mama would have said if she could have heard that mockingbird singing away in the dark. She would have said he was real young and hadn't quite learned his song yet. And in the center of the dark ceiling, I could see my mama's pretty face, smiling down at me.

The moth fluttered against the screen again, Molly murmured in her sleep, the bird kept on singing, and Mama smiled at me from the ceiling, so that it all came together and made a music of its very own. I tried so hard to hold on to it, because I wanted to stay that way forever and ever, with Mama so pretty and happy. But no matter how hard I tried to keep it all, I felt it just drain away, so slow-like—and what was real took its place: Mama couldn't dance anymore, couldn't even remember how to smile. Her just a little, wasted person not much bigger than me, sitting so still and quiet in the corner of the couch, all drawn up and inside of herself, not seeing or hearing us, looking at nothing, and wearing a blue scarf on her head. Under the scarf, no blond curls anymore.

When Mama first started getting sick, Roy-Ellis—my stepdaddy—told me she was going to be all right. But she just got sicker and sicker—until finally she was so bad off that Roy-Ellis had to take her to the hospital, down in Louisville. He stayed there with her as much as he could, had stayed almost all day long the day before—Saturday—but then he came home late in the afternoon, just after I'd fixed Molly and Little Ellis their supper of grilled cheese sandwiches and saltine crackers and applesauce.

When I heard Roy-Ellis coming up the steps to the front porch, I thought at first that Mama must be getting better, because he was singing "In Your Easter Bonnet," and he came into the kitchen carrying a big paper sack and smiling. I started to ask him about Mama, but when I looked at him, there was something in his eyes that stopped me. So instead, I said to Little Ellis and Molly, "You all eat your sandwiches before they get cold. Roy-Ellis, you want me to fix you a grilled cheese?"

"No, honey. Thanks. I just wanta show you all what I've brought you, though." He started taking things out of the sack: three cartons of eggs from the A & P down at Louisville and a little box with Easter egg coloring-tablets in it and some cardboard punch-out bunnies and chickens, for the eggs to sit in and look pretty and some paper decals to stick on the eggs. After Little Ellis and Molly finished their supper, Roy-Ellis set about helping us to make colored eggs. He burned his fingers pretty bad on the pot of boiling water but made himself say "Shoot!" instead of what he usually said. And he didn't fuss one little bit when Little Ellis almost spilled the whole cup full of purple dye, just trying to see it real good. But he gritted his teeth when all the little paper decals stuck to our fingers instead of on the eggs.

I knew how hard all that was on Roy-Ellis, because he really didn't like fooling around with us kids very much, not even Little Ellis, who was his very own child, and so I figured either Mama was lots better, and he was happy about that, or else he was trying to do something nice for us because Mama was so sick. So I just went along with what Roy-Ellis wanted to do, because maybe I really didn't want to know why he was trying so hard.

Roy-Ellis let me and Little Ellis help him color some pretty eggs that evening, but Molly, who was only a year and a half older than Little Ellis, wouldn't color herself a single egg. She just got up from the table and stood back against the sink and watched us with eyes that looked like they were on fire, sucking her thumb the way she always did, with the thumb deep inside her mouth, her index finger curled around her nose, and her soft, baby-mouth in a pout.

"Come on, sugar," Roy-Ellis coaxed her. "Come on over here and color you some pretty eggs." But she just stood there and watched us the whole time, with those storm-cloud eyes of hers. Oh, I'd seen that look plenty of times before, especially when Mama would finally get out of the bed Sunday afternoon and walk barefooted into the kitchen, still wearing her spangle dress and with mascara shadows under her eyes.

Back then—before Mama got sick—she and Roy-Ellis almost always had their Saturday night fun at a big road-house called Across the Line, because it was just across the Beamer County line. The county we lived in was what they called a dry county, on account of nobody being able to buy beer in it, so they went to Across the Line almost every single Saturday night. After Mama got all dressed up in one of her spangle dresses—just like the dress she had been wearing in my dream—she and Roy-Ellis would go honky-tonking; that's what they called it. And she always looked just like a movie star, with her hair silver-blond and in all-over curls and dangle earrings that sparkled when she moved her head and with her makeup done so nice—

even down to a little dot of eyebrow pencil right beside her bright-red lips. A beauty mark—that's what she said it was.

Roy-Ellis could look right nice himself on Saturday nights, especially after he'd had a good bath and combed his wet hair and then settled his cowboy hat on his head just right. Mama always had a pair of freshly ironed jeans for him to wear and a clean shirt. But it was the cowboy hat and the boots that sure made him look so special.

I didn't mind being left alone to take care of Molly and Little Ellis one little bit, because if honky-tonking made Mama and Roy-Ellis that happy, then I wanted them to have it. Even when they came home real late, they would still be happy as could be and having the best time. Mama always laughed when Roy-Ellis tripped on that broken front step and almost fell down and said bad words and then shouted, "Gotta fix that bugger, one of these days!" And Mama would shush him and laugh some more and then go back to singing a jukebox song real soft-like under her breath.

"Come on, baby," she'd say. "Mama's gonna help you."

But on Sundays—usually in the early afternoon, when us children had gotten back from going to church with Aunt Bett—when Mama would finally get out of bed and come into the kitchen, Molly would stare at her like maybe she'd caught Mama doing something really bad.

"Don't you go giving me that Sunday School–teacher look, missy," Mama would say while she lit a cigarette with shaky hands. "I got a right to have me a little fun once in a while. And Roy-Ellis, too."

I thought so too—what with her working all day long every day in that little air-conditioned room Roy-Ellis fixed up for her on part of our back porch, cutting ladies' hair and giving them permanents and sometimes putting lots of little shiny strips of aluminum foil in their hair. I didn't know what that was for. And Roy-Ellis needed some fun too—after a long week of driving that truck loaded with crates of live chickens back and forth, back and forth to the poultry processing plant and him coming home haggard-looking and smelling of chicken feathers and fear and saying to Mama, "Don't you never put a piece of chicken on this table when I'm sitting down to it. You hear me?"

And Mama saying, "Yeah, I hear you, honey."

The only person besides Molly who thought Mama and Roy-Ellis's honky-tonking was bad was Aunt Bett. She and Mama fussed about that lots of times, with Mama telling Aunt Bett she had a right to live her own life any way she wanted to, and with Aunt Bett crying and saying Mama and Roy-Ellis were gonna burn in everlasting hell-fire if they didn't mend their ways.

Because it wasn't just the beer-drinking that bothered Aunt Bett. What she really hated was that neither one of them would . . . or could . . . wake up on Sunday mornings early enough to take us to church. I asked Aunt Bett about that one time. Asked her why Roy-Ellis and Mama didn't like to go to church. She clamped her teeth together and mumbled something about Mama and Roy-Ellis simply not being churchgoing folks. But it was hard for her to say something that easy-sounding, so she added, "I'll just keep praying for them."

But she did lots more than just praying for Mama and Roy-Ellis—she took it on herself to *raise us right*. She said that maybe she couldn't do a solitary thing to stop all that honky-tonking Mama and Roy-Ellis did, but she could certainly take us to church with her every single Sunday, so we would grow up knowing the difference between right and wrong. So every Sunday morning, she drove up in front of our house and honked her horn, and we children would go running out and crowd ourselves into the back-seat, in and among all our damp, clean, soapy-smelling cousins for the ride to church.

But Easter Sunday was always the best of all, with everything feeling all squeaky-clean, or something like that, and us children being so proud in the pretty clothes Aunt Bett always brought over for us the day before, and the church with all that sunlight streaming in through the windows and the voices singing, "Up from the grave He arose!" And then, "Hallelujah! Christ arose!"

Made me think that any minute, Christ Jesus Himself, *raised up from the dead,* was going to come bursting in through the swinging doors at the back of the church, making them go *bang!* And He'd have strong, brown arms and beautiful eyes and white teeth, and He would grin and wave at us all with those big carpenter's hands and stride mightily right down the aisle to the altar, and we all would jump up and down in the pews, whooping and hollering and clapping and cheering for Him. Why, it gave me goose bumps, just to think of it!

So on that early Easter Sunday morning when Mama was sick in the hospital, I thought that maybe things would be okay, after all. Because even though I couldn't see much in the dark room, I knew that our Easter clothes were hanging on the back of the door. Carefully mended, washed, and ironed dresses for me and Molly—dresses that were of sizes in-between Aunt Bett's own girls—and short pants and a white shirt for Little Ellis, from in-between the sizes of Aunt Bett's boys.

I'd been careful to say thank you to Aunt Bett when she brought over this Easter's clothes for us—mostly to show her that Mama *had* raised me right, even if she didn't take us to church. But Aunt Bett just waved the back side of her hand at me like she always did, and then she got in her car and drove away, still shaking her head. That's the way Aunt Bett always did, every single time she stopped by our house, especially after Mama had to go to the hospital. She'd come by with a big bowl of potato salad or some extra cornbread she'd made for us—or else with in-between clothes and shoes she thought we could use, and she always ended up looking around the kitchen and the living room, rolling her eyes and clucking her tongue at the way me and Roy-Ellis were doing things. Then she'd heave a big old sigh and roll up her sleeves and wash up the sink full of dirty dishes and pick up the empty Spaghet-tiOs can and look at me like I'd done something wrong because I'd heated that up and fed it to Molly and Little Ellis for their lunch, and in general do a lot of things to help us out—but she always ended up shaking her head and clucking her tongue and rolling her eyes again, before she said, "Well, I got family of my own to tend to, so I better be getting on back home." That's what she always said. But her heart was in the right place. I know that for sure. And whenever Roy-Ellis was home when Aunt Bett came, they would go into the kitchen and shut the door and talk real low for a long time. Sometimes, if Molly and

Little Ellis were watching cartoons in the living room or already in bed, I stood real quiet outside the kitchen door, trying to hear whatever they were saying. But I never could make out any of it. Except that they sounded worried. That much I could tell.

So maybe that's why I wasn't really much surprised when, on that Easter Sunday morning, the loud ringing of the telephone broke the silence of the dark living room just beyond my door. Because a phone ringing so early always means that something is wrong, somewhere. And for our house, it could only mean that something had happened to Mama.

My heart started thudding in my chest like a squirrel trying to get out of a cage.

Then the phone rang again, and it sounded even louder.

No! I was thinking. *No!*

I heard Roy-Ellis groan and roll out of bed.

No! Don't answer it!

But I could hear him stumbling across his and Mama's room and bumping his shoulder hard on the door frame as he came out. It rang again, and I felt as if all the breath had gone out of my body. *No! Please don't answer it! If you don't answer it, Mama will be fine, like in my dream!*

But then the light in the living room went on, and I could see a little sliver of the light coming under my door.

"Hello," Roy-Ellis said in a rough-sounding voice. Maybe because of his shoulder hurting him. I held my breath.

"Yeah, this is him."

Then silence. A very long silence.

I could hear Roy-Ellis breathing, because my cot was

16

right up against the wall between the bedroom and the living room. Finally, he said, "She did?" And he sounded almost like Little Ellis, the way his voice tilted up in such a sad way. I felt my heart split in two, right inside my chest!

"When?"

Mama!

Another long silence.

Then, "Yes. I'll take care of it."

The sound of the receiver clicking back into its place and after that, no sound at all. So I could hear what the silence said: *Mama was gone!* I heard Roy-Ellis pick the receiver up again and dial. Then his voice was husky when he said, "Bett? I'm afraid it's bad news." A long pause, then, "Yeah." I shut my eyes tight and stayed just as still as could be, believing with all my heart that if I moved so much as my little finger, my cot would tilt, the whole world would tilt, and I'd fall out of bed and down into some deep, dark far-away place—wherever my mama was, all cold and dead.

Mama!

Then it almost seemed that my cot dropped away from under me, and I was floating up in the air, high above our little gray house and the other ones just like it, all lined up along the silent street, like little shaggy gray ponies waiting for a race to start and falling asleep while they were waiting. And I could look down on the big chinaberry tree in our yard, where the mockingbird curled his toes around a twig and sang his baby-song into the darkness. Slowly I floated back down onto my cot, inside the blue-papered walls of the room in the little gray house, where nothing was ever going to be the same again.

I heard Roy-Ellis hang up the phone and go along the hallway, into the kitchen, where the table was still covered with old, rainbow-colored newspapers and the thick white cups holding all those Easter egg colors—purple and blue, yellow and red, green and orange. And in the refrigerator were the three egg cartons holding all those pretty eggs we were supposed to hunt for in the tall grass in the backyard that afternoon. Only now, Mama was *gone*. And right then and there—in a way I'll never understand—I knew that my path had just split in two *again*, that it had split with that very first ring of the telephone. Just like it split for the first time when my daddy—my real daddy, that is—ran off and left me and Mama when some blond-headed lady in the office of the construction company where he worked asked him if he would drive her to California, and he did. And he never came back.

Maybe I could understand how he could leave *me,* because I was skinny and covered in freckles. I had wild-looking red hair, and my teeth were way too big for my face. But how could he leave Mama, and her so pretty and sweet—and her expecting a little baby any day, a baby that would be Molly, my little sister? That was the first time my path split, and Mama cried on Aunt Bett's shoulder and said she didn't know how we would be able to get along without him—without a paycheck coming in. So I decided I would stop loving him, right then and there. It really wasn't hard, and it made me feel better right away. Now, Mama had gone off and left me and Molly and Little Ellis, and if I could only stop loving her too, maybe I wouldn't hurt so bad.

But then I thought about Mama not going off and leaving me because she wanted to, like my daddy did. So, lying there in the darkness, I figured that I would always love my mama, but that from then on—from that very minute—I wasn't going to love anybody else in the whole world, not ever again. Because if I didn't love anybody, I wouldn't have to hurt so bad.

I heard Roy-Ellis come back into the living room, and his footsteps stopped right outside the door to our room. The knob turned, the door opened, and his voice came over me like a wave, like how I feel when I'm going to be sick at my stomach.

"Dove, honey? You awake?"

"I'm awake."

"Well, come on out here and let me talk to you a little bit," he said.

I threw back the covers and sat up, expecting my cot to tilt. But it didn't, and I went out into the living room where Roy-Ellis was sitting on the couch with his head in his hands.

"You don't have to tell me, Roy-Ellis," I whispered. "I already know." My voice tried to catch, but I wouldn't let it.

"Let's not say anything around the little ones just yet," Roy-Ellis said, and he didn't look at me. Just cleared his throat, got up, and flicked the switch to turn on the porch light. So I figured Aunt Bett was on her way. We sat there without speaking, both of us looking mostly at the floor. Almost like we didn't know each other. I glanced at him once, and he looked so bad, I almost felt like I should say something to try and comfort him. But I didn't.

I don't care how bad you look, I thought. *I won't love you. I won't love anybody.*

Aunt Bett finally came, and she looked all pale and shaky. She and Roy-Ellis locked eyes, and then they both looked at me.

"Dove knows," Roy-Ellis whispered to Aunt Bett, and then he motioned his head toward the kitchen. Aunt Bett hesitated.

"Why don't you go on back to bed for a little while, Dove," Aunt Bett said. "Roy-Ellis and me got some things we got to talk about." So they went into the kitchen and shut the door. But I didn't want to go back into the bedroom, because I was afraid I'd see my mama's face smiling down at me from the ceiling, so I turned off the porch light and went out and sat in the swing on the dark porch and listened to that little mockingbird singing his crooked song.

Chapter Two

A UNT Bett and Roy-Ellis were in the kitchen for a very long time, and I sat there in the swing with a big old war going on inside of me. A war between *Mama's gone!* and *No! She can't be!* When the *Mama's gone!* started winning, I hummed one of Mama's honky-tonk songs. *Why, Mama* can't *be gone!* Because if Mama was gone, then everything in Heaven and earth would have to stop. If Mama was gone, then the dawn wouldn't come at all. So I sat there thinking about that and waiting to see if daylight was going to come, or whether darkness was going to cover the earth forever and ever. And what would happen then? Finally, I started rocking just a little in the swing and listening to the soft *clink* of the chains that held so strong and tight to the big iron hooks, and to the creak of the porch beams. Watching and waiting.

Then a tiny silver color seemed to glow out of the tops of the leaves, and soon, things began to appear out of the darkness—the pink dwarf azaleas around the porch and Little Ellis's tricycle with the dew shining on it, and at the last, golden fingers of sunlight coming through the trees and streaming across the yard. So the world was going to go on. But it would never be the same. Me sitting in the swing in my pajamas, with my mama gone, but life going on anyway.

Finally, I heard the familiar squeak of the screen door, and Aunt Bett came out onto the porch. She sighed and closed the door very gently. No matter what, Aunt Bett wasn't one to ever let a door slam shut.

"You okay?" Her voice floated across the porch, and I was thinking, *No. I'll never be okay again.* But instead, I said, "Yessm." She sat down beside me in the swing and put her arm around my shoulder, squeezing me tight. I thought that maybe she was going to try to talk to me about Mama being gone, and I didn't want to talk about that. It was all too fresh. It all hurt too bad. And when something hurts that bad, I guess there's no way you can put words to it at all. But Aunt Bett merely took in a deep breath and relaxed her hold on my shoulder.

"You're going to be a good woman when you grow up, Dove. A good woman and very strong."

Her words surprised me.

"How do you know?" I asked.

"Well, I can see how strong you're trying to be right now. And I've seen how good you are to Molly and Little Ellis. And you don't fuss with me about going to church," she added. I thought about it being Easter Sunday and about the clothes Aunt Bett had brought over for us to wear.

"Thank you for the nice clothes you let us use," I said.

"Goodness!" Aunt Bett exclaimed. "You're grateful, as well. Yes, you most certainly will be a good woman. A strong woman."

I didn't reply: *My mama did too raise me right! And I'm only being this polite to let you know that. And I won't be strong. I don't know how to be!*

Instead, I said, "Roy-Ellis didn't cry." The words surprised me.

"What?"

"I said, Roy-Ellis didn't cry."

"Well, honey, he's a man. And maybe you don't know much about men yet, but they don't like to let other folks see them like that."

"Did you cry?" I asked, once again surprised by my own words.

Aunt Bett waited awhile before she murmured, "No. I didn't cry."

"Why not?" I really wanted to know, even if I hadn't known I was going to ask.

"I loved her, Dove. Even if we didn't agree on . . . some things. And even though we sometimes fussed with each other." She heaved a deep sigh. "But she was so sick. You know that. She'd suffered through so much, and now there's no more suffering for her. No more pain."

"Is she in Heaven?"

"That's not for me to say. Not at all. That's for Jesus to decide." And with that, Aunt Bett stood up. "If you think you can do it, help Molly and Little Ellis get ready and you all come on and go to church with me this morning, just like always. We need to keep things as normal as possible for the little ones. I can take you all's colored eggs home with me now—I could tell by the mess on the kitchen table that you all did color some last night. After church, we'll have a nice dinner and a little Easter egg hunt at my house."

The thought of trying to make things "normal" was something I couldn't even imagine, but I didn't say anything. Aunt Bett added, "Let's just try to get through today, and tomorrow we'll figure how to get through tomorrow." But her voice was a little bit too cheerful-sounding, like she was trying to convince herself that everything was going to be just fine.

"Then," she added in a more solemn tone, "at some point, I'll tell Molly. Little Ellis isn't old enough to understand."

I was remembering about what Aunt Bett said to Mama about hellfire and honky-tonking, so I said, "I'll be the one to tell Molly. I think she'll take it better from me."

Aunt Bett nodded, obviously relieved. "Well, go on then and get me you all's colored eggs so I can put them in my refrigerator. Did Roy-Ellis fix up Easter baskets?"

"I figured he had too much on his mind what with . . . Mama being sick, so I fixed baskets—little ones—for Molly and Little Ellis."

"Well, get those too, and the children can find them at

my house after church. I'll come back for you around ten-forty-five. Usual time."

"Yessm."

"We just have to carry on, Dove," she added. "We just have to get on with living." Her words repeated themselves over and over while I went into the kitchen to get the eggs out of the refrigerator and the Easter baskets from behind Roy-Ellis's chair, where I had hidden them for Molly and Little Ellis to find. Roy-Ellis wasn't in the kitchen, but I could hear water running in the bathroom. We loaded the eggs and the Easter baskets into Aunt Bett's car, and she looked me full in the face for a moment before she drove off. "We just have to do the best we can. Remember that."

When I went back toward the kitchen, Roy-Ellis was sitting at the table with his elbows resting on the rainbow-colored newspapers. His hair was wet and combed, and he was wearing a clean shirt. I waited in the doorway until he looked up at me.

"You and the children going to church with Bett?" he asked, and that pleased me mightily, the way he separated me from "the children."

"Yessir," I answered. Then we didn't say anything else. I made him a cup of instant coffee and sat at the table with him while he drank it. Every time he took the cup away from his mouth, he stared down at the remaining coffee. Finally, the cup was empty.

"That was good, Dove," he said.

"You want me to fix you some . . . cereal?" I'd started to ask if he wanted some eggs, but then I remembered that I didn't know how to cook eggs. Roy-Ellis shook his head, stood up.

"I have to go . . . take care of some things," he mumbled.

After Roy-Ellis left, I pulled all the old newspapers off the table and jammed them into the trash can on the back porch. The door to Mama's beauty shop was closed, and I didn't want to open it. Instead, I went into Mama and Roy-Ellis's room and opened the closet where Mama's spangle dresses and her beauty parlor smocks were hanging. I ran my fingers across the sequins on her dresses, and I stuck my hand into the pocket of one of her smocks. There were two silvery hair clips in the pocket, and I took them out and pinned them in my hair. On the other side of the closet hung Roy-Ellis's blue work shirts and some of his bright cowboy-looking shirts. And they made me think about how Roy-Ellis always made Mama so happy. He never made her cry, not one single time. That was lots more than I could say about my own daddy.

Because right after my daddy ran off to California, Molly was born, and as soon as Roy-Ellis heard about that, he came right over to our house, and he came again almost every single evening, as soon as he got off work, so Mama could cry on his shoulder. Because Mama and Roy-Ellis had known each other almost all their lives, and when they were in high school together, they'd even been girlfriend and boyfriend, right up until just before Mama met and married my daddy.

I think it was because of Roy-Ellis that Mama got done with all her crying so soon. And he took to fixing up a real beauty parlor on our back porch, so Mama would have a nice place to work, once she got done with her classes at cosmetology school. On the very day Mama graduated and got her license, Roy-Ellis drove up in our yard, took a window air-conditioner out of his truck, and staggered up the steps with it.

"Now, don't you go saying anything about this to your mama," Roy-Ellis grunted to me as he lugged the air-conditioner to the back porch beauty parlor. "It's a surprise for her." I didn't say a single word about the air-conditioner when Mama came home, not even when Roy-Ellis made her close her eyes and led her to the beauty parlor door. I guess she heard the air-conditioner running, though, and probably guessed what it was. Because she smiled. Roy-Ellis opened the door, and a blast of that wonderful, chilled air swept out across what was left of our old porch.

"Oh, honey," Mama breathed. "It's wonderful!"

Yes, Roy-Ellis was always good to Mama. And I liked him right well, even though he didn't pay much attention to me or Molly. When Mama's divorce papers came, it seemed the most natural thing in this world for Mama and Roy-Ellis to get married. On the day before the wedding, Roy-Ellis came sauntering across the yard carrying a big plastic bag full of clothes in one hand and his guitar in the other. After Mama helped him put away his clothes in two big drawers she'd emptied for him, I heard her say real soft-like, "Come on and stay the night, honey."

"Can't do that, sugar," he said in a mournful way. "My mama'd be sure to find out, and she'd get all over me for shaming her like that."

"And there's Bett, as well," Mama agreed.

"Well, between my mama and your sister, we got no choice but to behave ourselves."

26

"Yeah, honey," Mama said.

But Roy-Ellis did stay on for supper with us, and afterward, he sat on the porch and played his guitar and sang songs for us. Some of them were songs I could sing along to, but most were what Mama called love songs. They were soft and slow, and while Roy-Ellis sang, I watched Mama smiling with the tips of her ears turning bright pink. Those love songs made me happy because they made Mama happy, and I figured she deserved that, after what all my own daddy had done to her. That last night before their wedding, Roy-Ellis stayed on the porch with Mama for a long time after Molly and I went to bed, and when I fell asleep, it was to a soft, sweet song with lots of "darlings" in it.

The next day, their wedding day, Mama and Roy-Ellis drove up around Dahlonega so a Justice of the Peace could marry them. I didn't get to go see them get married because they were just going to have the ceremony and then have a one-day honeymoon in a fishing cabin that belonged to someone Roy-Ellis worked with at the poultry plant. So Molly and I stayed with Aunt Bett that day and night, and the next day, Roy-Ellis's truck drove up in front of Aunt Bett's house and Mama and Roy-Ellis got out and came across the yard, holding hands. Mama had wildflowers in her hair, and after they came into the kitchen where Aunt Bett was making potato salad, Roy-Ellis hugged Aunt Bett and spun around with her until she squealed. And he did the same with me. And he held baby Molly in his arms and smiled down into her face. She was only three months old.

Even after Mama and Roy-Ellis were married, whenever he got to looking at Mama, seemed to me his eyes went all soft and so melted-down looking, they almost slid right down his cheeks. He looked at her most of the time—like he just couldn't get enough of her, because Mama sure was nice to look at. Maybe not so much after she got so sick or when she was tired or worried or just waking up from drinking too much beer at Across the Line.

But there was one Saturday night only about a month after they were married when Mama was all dressed up and waiting for Roy-Ellis to get his hat on just right. But she suddenly got a strange, surprised look on her face and ran into the bathroom, slamming the door behind her. Roy-Ellis came out of the bedroom and asked where Mama was, but just about that time, we could all hear her being sick. After a few minutes, we heard the toilet flush and later, Mama came out of the bathroom, wiping her face with a damp rag.

"Honey, what's the matter?" Roy-Ellis asked. "You sick or something?"

"No, honey," Mama said. "I'm not sick. I'm just gonna have a baby, is all."

Well, I never saw anything like Roy-Ellis that night. He whooped and hollered and threw his cowboy hat up in the air, and then he picked Mama up in his arms, like she was a little girl, and he danced all around the living room with her. They didn't get to do much honky-tonking until after Little Ellis was born, but Roy-Ellis said he didn't mind one bit. He was going to be an honest-to-goodness papa, and that's all that mattered.

Little Ellis was born exactly nine months later, and Roy-Ellis passed out cigars with boy-baby-blue bands on them at the poultry-processing plant. But after that, he took to paying no more attention to Little Ellis than he did to me and Molly. But he didn't mean it to be that way—just that I guess he loved Mama so much, he didn't have anything else left over for anybody else. And that was okay with me, because Mama was so happy.

And that's what all I was remembering while I stood in Mama and Roy-Ellis's closet. But then I heard a noise behind me and looked to see Molly standing in the doorway, sucking her thumb. "Lil' Ellis wet," she announced, forming the words around her thumb.

After I got Little Ellis all cleaned up, I fixed cereal for us all. Raisin Bran was all we had left, and I had to help Molly pick all the raisins out of hers before I poured in the milk. We ate silently, and how strange that kitchen did feel! The same kitchen as yesterday, but not the same, in some strange way that I couldn't figure out but that I felt lying so heavy on my heart. I heard the softest little moan, and I didn't even know it was me, until Molly looked up from her cereal and asked, "Dovey? Your tooths hurt?"

"My tummy hurts a little bit," I said. "But it will be better tomorrow."

"You promise?" Molly's eyes were suddenly darker.

"I promise." And what I didn't say out loud was this: *I promise, Mama. I promise to take good care of Molly and Little Ellis for you. You don't have to worry about them.*

After breakfast, I sent Molly and Little Ellis into the bedroom, and I washed Roy-Ellis's coffee cup and the cereal bowls and wiped off the table. *We just have to carry on the best we can.* Soon, we were all dressed in the clothes Aunt Bett had brought to us and sitting in the porch swing, waiting for her. When I thought about how I had been sitting in that very swing so early in the morning, it seemed to me as if that was something that had happened a hundred years ago. We heard Aunt Bett's car rattling and coughing down the road before we could even see it, and my heart gladdened. Maybe Aunt Bett was right about keeping things as normal as possible. Maybe even I could pretend this was just another Easter Sunday morning. But when we got into the car, our cousins were quieter than usual and looking at us in a funny way. So I guess Aunt Bett had told them about Mama. And I could almost hear for myself what she must have said to them: "Not a word! Do you all hear? Anybody says a single thing, you'll be in the woodshed with me and my switch before you can even blink!"

So the ride to church was quiet—not the usual giggling and laughing we used to do. At the church, Aunt Bett and I took Molly and Little Ellis and Aunt Bett's two youngest—Jack and Jessica—to the Sunday School section, and then the rest of us pushed open the heavy swinging doors and went into the big, cool sanctuary. The deep red carpeting, the polished brown pews, and the high, soaring white ceiling were a comfort to me. And the flowers! Why, there must have been a hundred Easter lilies banked around the choir loft and the pulpit. After we sat down, Aunt Bett reached over and patted my hand. I wanted to smile at her, but somehow or other, my mouth just wasn't working right. Then all the singing started, the Easter hymns I loved so much. Starting out so slow and mournful-like!

"Low . . . in . . . the . . . grave . . . He . . . lay, Jesus . . .

my . . . savior!"

So sad! So sad!

"Waiting . . . the . . . Coming . . . day, Jesus . . . my . . . Lord!"

A pause—a long pause, and then the organ and the choir and all the people roaring forth: *"Up from the grave He arrroossee! With a mighty triumph o'er His foes!"*

Oh, that music was really something to hear, and I wanted so bad to sing too, but there was some kind of a tight place in my throat that I knew wouldn't let the singing come. So I just stood there and listened and looked at all the beautiful flowers and the sunshine streaming through the windows, and I tried not to think about Mama.

Bang! went the swinging doors at the back of the church, and all the hairs on my arms standing straight up! I turned my head and there He was, just as I had imagined.

"He arose! He arose!" The choir was shrieking.

And I saw Jesus—tall, handsome, and strong— swinging his arms and smiling and taking giant strides down the aisle! And skipping along with Him, holding His hand and wearing one of her prettiest spangle dresses and her dangle earrings was . . .

My mama! My very own mama. And not all thin and pale and hurting so bad, but Mama like she was before she got sick—young and oh so beautiful! I knew Aunt Bett's mouth was going to be hanging open when she saw just how fast Jesus had forgiven Mama's honky-tonking, but when I looked at Aunt Bett, she was still singing along like nothing had happened. Then I looked around at the other people, and not a single one of them seemed to have noticed that Jesus Himself and my very own mama had come into church! And when I looked back at the aisle, no one was there. Not Jesus. Not Mama. And the doors at the back of the church were closed. I sat down and my breath went out of me in a whoosh. Aunt Bett leaned down and put her hand on my shoulder. "Dove?" she said over the sound of the singing. "You okay, baby?"

"Yessm," I managed to breathe.

So she straightened up and went back to singing, but she kept her hand on my shoulder. Me sitting there thinking I must have had a dream! But I was awake, and that didn't make a bit of sense! The more I thought about it, the more I remembered how beautiful and happy Mama looked. No more pain. No more sadness. And her holding His hand. I stood up, and I could sing, sure enough, because whatever had been so hard and tight in my throat was *gone,* and in that one instant, all my bitter-sad turned right into sweet-sad. Just like that.

"He arose! He arose! Hallelujah! Christ arose!"

After services, Aunt Bett and I went and collected the younger children. As we came back down the long hallway, Aunt Bett stopped a few times to speak to her friends and to whisper in their ears. Her friends looked at me and Molly and Little Ellis, so I knew she'd told them about Mama. Some of the ladies patted my shoulder and some stroked Little Ellis's head, but no one tried to touch Molly, because she was wearing her storm-cloud face. I guess Molly was a lot like springtime, with beautiful sunshine and singing birds one minute and a terrible, sudden storm the next.

The ride back to Aunt Bett's was a quiet one, with our

unusually solemn cousins watching us and then turning their eyes away if we looked back at them. So I just held Little Ellis on my lap and watched through the window as our little town went by. The big flour mill and dirt roads that went off through tall grass, the grocery store all closed up because of it being Sunday, and at last, the familiar road and Aunt Bett's little gray shingle house. The minute we came inside, we could smell the wonderful Easter ham she'd left roasting in the oven, and our cousins chirked up a bit.

"All you children get in there and change your clothes," Aunt Bett ordered, putting her purse and gloves on the hall table and heading for the kitchen.

"Darlene?" she called over her shoulder. "You find some shorts and shirts for Dove and them. You hear? And make sure you come help me get dinner on the table."

"Yessm," Darlene answered, and she smiled at me.

"Don't you just hate being the oldest?" she asked, as we steered the children toward the bedroom.

"I guess so," I said, but it wasn't true. The truth was that I had never even thought of such a thing. So I didn't really know whether I minded it or not.

"Believe me," Darlene said, perhaps sensing my lack of real feelings about being the oldest. "One of these days, you'll know what I mean. You'll get tired of wiping their noses and their bottoms and having them around all the time. You'll want nothing more in this world than to have some private time, just for yourself. And you probably won't get it, just like I don't get it."

"I won't?" It still seemed inconceivable to me that I would feel that way about Molly and Little Ellis. To my mind, there were just things to be done, and I was the one to do them.

"You'll know what I mean, one of these days," Darlene assured me, and with that, she led me to Aunt Bett's famous "Closet,"—more than a closet, because it was lots bigger than any closet I'd ever seen before—big enough to have its own window and with shelves that went almost to the ceiling and that were loaded down with clean, folded clothes of all kinds. And three shiny racks on wheels, all jammed tight with hanging clothes, and a big basket full of matched socks. Aunt Bett had more children's clothes in that one room than they had down at the department store on Main Street, but I knew for a fact that she hadn't bought any of them new. The piles of shirts, shorts, and jeans, she had gotten from her friends whose children had outgrown them. And she didn't pay any money for them either, but traded big jars of her good homemade pickles for them. Most of the hanging clothes—the dresses, at least—were homemade, mostly by Aunt Bett herself, but a few were homemade by those same friends, and she paid lots of jars of pickles for them.

Darlene lifted some neatly folded shorts and shirts from a shelf and looked at the labels to see the sizes. "These should fit Molly and Little Ellis," she said. Then she moved down to another shelf, where she found a pair of shorts for me. But for my shirt, she went back into the bedroom and took a bright blue, new-looking shirt out of her own bureau.

"Here," she said, holding the shirt out to me. "You can wear this one today. It's my favorite, but I don't mind." Her eyes told me what she meant. She was trying to be extra nice to me, because of Mama. I got Molly and Little Ellis changed into their shorts and shirts and hung up their good clothes, just like Aunt Bett said. And then I changed my own clothes and hung up my church dress. When I pulled Darlene's blue shirt over my head, I could smell the fine freshness of it and like always, I did wonder how on earth sunshine could have its own sweet smell. Darlene was watching me, and I smiled at her. That favorite shirt of hers did make me feel better. We herded the children into the living room and got them settled. Then we went to the kitchen to help Aunt Bett with Sunday dinner. The smell of that good ham in the oven made me feel sparkles under my tongue.

"Darlene, get the potato salad and deviled eggs out of the refrigerator and put them on the table. Then put on plates and silverware." To me, Aunt Bett said, "It's okay, Dove. Me and Darlene can take care of things."

"But I want to help," I protested.

"Well . . ." she considered. "Are the children all in the living room?"

"Yessm."

"Then why don't you go in there and tell them they can look for their Easter baskets. But they are not to eat a single bite of candy until after dinner."

"Yessm."

In the living room, our cousins were lined up on the big couch like they were waiting for a bus. Molly and Little Ellis were sitting together in a chair, each one leaning over an arm and silently enduring the solemn stares of their cousins.

"Now listen," I said. "When I count to three, you all can

go find your Easter baskets." The faces brightened, and a few of the cousins broke into grins. "But you are not to eat a single bite of candy until after you have your dinner. Do you all hear me?" Faces fell just a little, but heads nodded in agreement.

"Okay then. *One, two . . . three!*"

The cousins lifted off the couch like a bunch of birds flying off a telephone wire and scattered in all directions. Molly and Little Ellis didn't move.

"Wait a minute." I went back into the kitchen, where Aunt Bett was lifting a big roasting pan out of the oven. Her hair was hanging in her face, and her cheeks were pink from the oven's heat. But oh, the smell of that ham! A red, juicy smell and with clove-spice perfume and a bittersweet smell from the pineapple slices toothpicked all over it. She put the roasting pan on a wooden cutting board on the counter and wiped her face on her apron.

"Aunt Bett?" I whispered. "Where'd you hide Molly and Little Ellis's baskets?"

"Back porch," she whispered back. We could hear happy cries and laughing coming from the hallway and the bedrooms, as the cousins found their baskets. I went back into the living room, where Molly and Little Ellis were waiting.

"Come on," I said. "Let's go find your Easter baskets. Let's look on the back porch."

When we did find their baskets—one behind the washing machine and the other behind a big basket of clothes waiting to be washed—Molly and Little Ellis were so happy and excited. And I could see why. New things, things I didn't buy for them, were in the baskets. Jelly-beans in all kinds of colors were scattered over the green paper grass, and little chocolate cookie-candies all covered in tiny, white candy dots, and in the center of each basket, a chocolate Easter bunny with round, white candy eyes that had no eyelids.

The children all gathered back in the living room, showing each other their candy treasures and doing some swapping—a red jellybean for a green one and ten jelly-beans for the ears off someone else's chocolate rabbit. But no one took a single bite, not even Little Ellis, who was too young to understand but seemed to know the rule anyway.

"Wash your hands and come on to the table," Aunt Bett called.

We came into the dining room to find the table loaded with food. There wasn't room for even one more small dish, and no room around the table for one more chair. Besides the wooden chairs that matched the table, there were three kitchen chairs, as well. For a moment, we all just stood there, staring at the table. There was a big platter of sliced ham with the browned pineapple slices all around the edge, a bowl of potato salad, a dish of Aunt Bett's famous pickles, a plate full of deviled eggs, a big bowl of coleslaw, a glistening bowl of Jell-O salad, and a basket piled high with biscuits. Aunt Bett even had fig preserves to put on the biscuits.

"Dove, you sit here and we'll put Molly and Little Ellis on either side of you, so you can help them with their dinner. The rest of you sit in your regular places." So we all finally managed to get into our right chairs, even though they were packed so tight together, and join our hands for the blessing.

"Lord," Aunt Bett began. "We thank you for your risen Son this Easter Day. Make us truly grateful for all we receive from You, and especially the food You have put upon this table. Bless all who are here and make us thankful for each other. And bless those who have gone ahead . . ." I kept my eyes shut tight, but I was once again seeing that dream I'd had, with my mama strong and healthy again and her going along so happy, holding the hand of the risen Lord. ". . . In Jesus' name, amen." As soon as Aunt Bett said amen, we all started in to serving ourselves and the little ones. And I don't know when I've enjoyed a dinner so much, even with my stomach hurting about Mama. We all ate and ate, and Aunt Bett would look around the table at us having such good appetites, and I could tell how pleased that made her.

After dinner, Aunt Bett, Darlene, and I cleared the table of the dinner things and Aunt Bett brought out a high, white coconut cake for dessert. By the time we had each had a slice, there wasn't room enough left for a single piece of Easter candy.

"Darlene, you and Dove go put the little ones down for a rest, please. And then come help me with the dishes." The children were so stuffed, they followed us gladly into the bedrooms, where Darlene and I pulled back the bedspreads, stripped the children of their shorts, and helped them get settled on the cool top sheet. Even Molly didn't complain, and Little Ellis was almost asleep when we tiptoed out and closed the door. Then we did as we were supposed to do and went to the kitchen to dry and put away all the dishes. We were almost done when Aunt Bett said to

Darlene, "Honey, would you leave me and Dove alone for a little bit? We need to talk about . . . things."

"Yessm." Darlene glanced at me before she left the kitchen. Aunt Bett kept washing the last few dishes, and I kept drying. When the last plate was washed, she rinsed it and handed it to me. Then she leaned up against the sink and looked out of the window. "I don't know why, maybe it was all that good singing at church this morning, but I was thinking about the time our mama—your grand-mama—sent me and your mama to take piano lessons with old Miss Eunice. Lord have mercy on her soul!"

Aunt Bett motioned to me to come sit at the kitchen table with her. I guess she remembered how much I liked it when she talked about her and my mama as children together. Mama never would tell me things about that, but I don't know why. Too, Aunt Bett was seldom in a mood to tell me stories about the olden times. She was usually too busy making pickles and washing and ironing clothes, and cooking for her big family. It was nice to see her in a mood to talk, for a change.

"Why, we were scared to death, honey. Because neither one of us had ever touched a piano, and we didn't even *have* a piano in our house, but our mama had decided we would learn how to play anyway. And when Mama spent good money on something, she expected the very best. So we knew we had to do very, very well. I was around nine and your mama was only six years old. And I remember how we held hands as we walked all the way to the very end of Stone Street and then followed a dirt road on for nearly a quarter of a mile, and it nothing more than two hard clay ruts between fields of tall, dry grass where crickets chirped and little creatures we couldn't even see scurried away and made such a fearsome noise in the weeds. We had to walk all that way before we came to Miss Eunice's house—a big, old place with peeling paint standing way back from the road. Funny thing was, there wasn't a tree on the place, and that day—that hot July day—we could smell the tar from the roof. Miss Eunice must have been watching from the window, because we saw the curtains move a little and then she came and opened the door, just as we got to the front steps. And what a sight she was! Such a stout lady and her wearing a white dress with hundreds and hundreds of bright lavender bows printed on the fabric." Here, Aunt Bett paused, looked at me, and smiled. "Honey, she had a bosom like nothing I ever saw in my life! Just like two big old rattlesnake watermelons, and those shiny little buttons on her dress just straining, what with trying to keep it all inside!"

Aunt Bett laughed out loud. "And her hair was salt-and-pepper gray and standing up a little in the back, from where her head had been resting against the back of a chair. And her eyes tiny and just as shiny as the buttons on her dress. Like I said, your mama and I were both scared to death, but we knew if we went back home without having our lessons, we'd get a switching. So we went inside to where it was dark and cool, and when our eyes got used to the dimness, the first thing we noticed was that the entire ceiling of the hallway was gone. We could make out some jagged edges left of what had been the floor of the second floor above it. I'll never forget that, how that ceiling just went up and up and into some kind of a deep and hot darkness, way up there under the roof, where there was no light. When Miss Eunice saw us staring up, she said, 'Oh, don't you pay no mind to that. Whole floor from upstairs fell one summer a long time ago, and after I got that mess all cleared away, I found it made the whole place a lot cooler just to leave it like that. Hot air rises, you see.' "

I had goose bumps on my arms, from imagining how that house must have looked. And Aunt Bett's eyes were moving around the perfectly normal ceiling of her own kitchen, all those years later, but she was really seeing Miss Eunice's house. I waited for her to go back and finish her story, but she just sat there.

"Did you and Mama learn how to play the piano?" I asked, hoping to get her going again. She glanced at me as if she had forgotten I was there.

"Oh, we learned some little songs. Not much, but enough to satisfy your grandmama. But your mama never did like to play the piano. In fact, come to think of it, there wasn't much she ever enjoyed," Aunt Bett admitted, drawing her eyebrows together. Then she made a little huffing sound and smiled. "Except for going dancing with Roy-Ellis," she added, nodding her head.

"Was that really bad, Aunt Bett?" I asked her, wishing with all my heart she could have seen mama holding hands with Jesus.

"Well, it wasn't good, that's for sure," Aunt Bett said. "But God is merciful, and I believe He will have mercy on your mama—mainly because of how well she bore all that sickness and pain, I expect."

"I'm sure He will," I added. "I'm truly sure He will."

Because I didn't need to wonder about it. I *knew.*

While the children were still asleep, Darlene and I went outside and hid all the colored Easter eggs, and when the children waked up, we helped them get their shorts back on, and then we all went out into the yard to watch the fun. Such shrieking and laughing! Little Ellis kept stepping on eggs, and every time he did, we all laughed. When everyone else went back inside, to have a treat from their baskets and to put their eggs back into the refrigerator, I saw Aunt Bett standing on the steps, watching me help Molly sort out the crushed eggs from the good ones. When I looked at Aunt Bett, she pointed to Molly and nodded her head. So it was time for me to tell her.

"Molly, come over here under this tree and sit with me a little bit," I invited, and she came, squirming and nestling against me so that I could feel her hot little body and breathe the perfume that was Molly.

"Honey, you remember that old cat Roy-Ellis brought home that time? The one he found beside the road, and it was sick and hurt?" Molly sat up a little and looked at me with burning eyes.

"I 'member." Then she settled back down against my shoulder.

"It couldn't get well, no matter what we tried to do to help it," I reminded her. "And finally, it died. Do you remember that?" I felt Molly's head nod. My throat tried to go tight on me, and I made myself see Mama again—healthy and happy—and with Jesus. That helped.

"Well, honey—Mama was so sick and so hurt, nothing could make her better." There—the words were said. They

42

were said. There was no response from Molly, so I went on. "But now, she's with Jesus, and she isn't sick or hurt anymore. She's healthy and happy—so happy, she's just dancing around!"

"Her is?" Molly asked.

"Oh yes."

"Her go to Jesus?"

"Yes."

"Her coming back?"

"No."

"*You* go to Jesus, Dove?"

"Me? No. Not for a long, long, long time, anyway."

"Don't go."

"I won't."

When we went inside, Aunt Bett looked at me questioningly, and I nodded my head. Molly put her eggs in the refrigerator and stood there with the door open for a little while, but Aunt Bett didn't say a thing to her about it, and when Molly finally shut the door and came to me, she asked "Her happy?"

"Yes. Very happy."

"Oh, okay."

When it was time for us to go home, Aunt Bett said, "You all just leave your Sunday clothes here. I'll freshen them up for you. You'll be needing them for . . ." She stopped and our eyes met.

"I know what it is we'll need them for, Aunt Bett. And there's no need for you to drive us home. We can walk."

Darlene motioned me into the bedroom. "I'm glad my shirt looks nice on you, Dove, but let me get you another

43

one for going home in." She disappeared into "The Closet" and came out with another shirt. After I had taken off her favorite shirt and put on the new one, I saw that on the front was printed MAMA'S BIG GIRL and under that in smaller letters: FT. LAUDERDALE, FLORIDA. Darlene and Aunt Bett didn't seem to notice that, and I decided I wouldn't let it bother me. Besides, it was true. I most certainly was my mama's big girl. And I always would be. Aunt Bett sent us off down the road with a basket loaded with ham wrapped in wax paper and a big jar of potato salad and some of her good biscuits—in case Roy-Ellis was hungry. He was home, but he was sitting in his chair, drinking a beer and watching the wrestling matches on television. His eyes were tired-looking, and I knew he wouldn't be able to pretend that everything was okay.

"Aunt Bett sent over some ham and potato salad for you," I told him. "I'll put it in the refrigerator."

"Thanks, honey," Roy-Ellis mumbled. But I don't think he even heard me. So I took care of Molly and Little Ellis until it was time for them to go to bed. As soon as they were asleep, I went to bed myself, because there didn't seem to be anything else I could do. And when I crawled into my cot that night, it felt like a hundred years ago that the telephone had started ringing in the early morning darkness.

Chapter Three

BY Monday morning, all Mama's beauty parlor customers had heard about what happened, and they started coming up our front steps loaded down with food for us, and the folks Roy-Ellis worked with at the poultry plant did the same thing. Right after noon, Aunt Mee came up on the back porch and knocked on the kitchen door. Her house was a little gray shack just behind our house, and we shared an overgrown area with old pecan trees in it with her. Of course, folks like us didn't get to know folks like Aunt Mee real well, because we didn't have maids or anyone to help with the cleaning. Aunt Mee and all the other colored women like her really didn't know many white people, except the ones they worked for. The ones who lived in the big houses on the other side of town.

But sometimes, when I sat out on the back porch rocking Little Ellis to sleep, I could see the light on Aunt Mee's back porch far away through the old, dead trees, and it always comforted me, in some strange way. I even liked thinking of her as a real aunt, just like Aunt Bett, but Mama told me one time that the only reason people in our town called black women "Aunt" was something left over from a long time ago, maybe even back as far as slave times, when some slaves were almost like members of a white family—but of course, not members at all. And now, I went to the door and saw her dark face through the screen.

"Hi, Aunt Mee," I said. "Won't you come inside?"

She held out a towel-covered pan and studied my face. "Honey, I'm so sorry to hear about your mama," she said, still looking so hard into my eyes. "Are you going to be all right?"

"Oh yes," I answered, but what I really wanted to do was put the pan down and move into her arms and have her hold me close and say that everything was going to be all right. "Won't you come in?" I asked instead, taking the pan she held out.

"No, honey. Not right now. I'll come back later on and help you all."

I knew exactly what she meant, because Aunt Mee always showed up to help in a house that was full of sad people. Anytime somebody died, Aunt Mee just came in through the back door, wearing a clean, carefully ironed, white apron, and she took over all the dish washing and refilling the trays on the dining room table, and just moved in and out like a dark shadow, doing for folks. When she went to help folks in the big houses, they had to call her to come, and they had to pay her, as well. But when black folks or even poor white folks had their sorrow, she came without anybody calling her or giving her a thing for it. I don't know why.

By afternoon, all the ladies from Aunt Bett's church started arriving, and one went into the kitchen with me and helped me sort out what all had to go in the refrigerator and what could be stored on the counter. There was so much food, we had to rearrange everything in the refrigerator, and the whole time we worked, she kept making some kind of clucking noises. Sounded just like a hen. But she was a nice lady, and before she left, she said for me to call on her if I needed anything. I thanked her and said I would, but of course, I didn't even know her name.

On Tuesday, Aunt Bett came over and brought our Easter clothes, all freshened up and looking nice. She worked at rearranging the refrigerator, as well, and when she shoved Roy-Ellis's beer bottles out of the way, she snorted. After pushing them this way and that, she finally took all but one of the beer bottles out of the refrigerator and stored them in the bottom cabinet. But she handled them with only the tips of her fingers, and after she had moved them, she washed her hands. In the afternoon, Roy-Ellis and Aunt Bett said they needed to talk again, so Roy-Ellis gave me some money, and I walked with Molly and Little Ellis to town, where we got Popsicles at the little grocery store, and we ate them while we sat on a bench in the tiny park right in the middle of town. Then we went in the dime store, and I let Molly and Little Ellis look at all the toys. And everywhere we went, folks smiled sad smiles at us and clucked their tongues behind our backs.

When we came home, Aunt Bett and Roy-Ellis were sitting at the kitchen table, so I knew they had been talking again about "making arrangements." I think Aunt Bett probably did most of the talking, because the next day, Wednesday, Mama's funeral was held at Aunt Bett's church. The lady who kept the nursery on Sundays even came in that afternoon so that Little Ellis and Molly and Aunt Bett's little ones could stay with her, while the rest of us went into the sanctuary.

I didn't like seeing Mama's casket, but it was a right pretty one, and besides, I knew she wasn't in it. Well, I mean that poor sick body was, but Mama wasn't. And the whole time the preacher talked, I could almost hear her humming one of those honky-tonk songs I liked so much. I looked at Roy-Ellis, wishing he could hear it too, but he was just sitting there all stiff and miserable like if he moved so much as a single muscle, it would hurt him so bad he wouldn't be able to stand it.

Once the service was over, I figured out some of what

Roy-Ellis and Aunt Bett must have been deciding at the kitchen table. Because Roy-Ellis wanted the graveside service to be private—with just him there. We had already said our good-byes, and I guess he just wanted to have her all to himself one more time. I could tell Aunt Bett wasn't too happy about that, but she must have finally agreed. We went along the hallway toward where the lady was taking care of the little ones, and I knew that I had to ask Aunt Bett a question. I wasn't quite sure of how to ask it, but I meant to know.

"Aunt Bett, what kind of dress did my mama get buried in?"

She stopped walking. "How come you to ask such a thing?"

"I don't know," I answered. "I just wondered."

But she looked so sad, I said, "I'm sorry. Maybe I shouldn't have asked."

"It's okay, honey." She sighed. "You're her very own daughter, and you should know. But I don't want it to make trouble between you and Roy-Ellis."

"What do you mean?"

"Dove, I went out and bought a beautiful white batiste nightgown with lace at the throat and wrists, and I paid a lot of money for it, but when I showed it to Roy-Ellis, he said he wasn't about to send her off wearing a nightgown."

"Then what did she wear?"

"Love have mercy!" Aunt Bett's eyes filled up. "Roy-Ellis took one of those awful, honky-tonk, spangle dresses over to the funeral parlor, and my baby sister has gone to eternity dressed like that! Like a tramp or something!" Aunt Bett's face had gone a deep red, and her chin was shaking.

I patted her arm. "It's okay, Aunt Bett," I tried to comfort her. "I'm pretty sure Jesus won't mind one little bit about the dress."

And I didn't let her see me smile.

Aunt Bett dropped her own children, and Molly and Little Ellis as well, off at her house, with Darlene to watch after all of them. "You all get out of those good clothes right away, you hear me? And hang them up! Darlene, you get some things out of the closet for Molly and Little Ellis."

Aunt Bett was driving off, but with her head still out of the window, yelling her instructions to the children. Looking back, I saw Darlene laughing. On the way to our house, Aunt Bett said, "We have to hurry getting the food all set out. Folks will be coming any minute, I expect."

"I think Aunt Mee may come to help," I said.

"Aunt Mee! Why, I haven't seen her in years." Aunt Bett's eyes went soft, and the corners of her mouth turned up just a little. So I figured she was remembering Uncle Frank who'd gotten himself killed by a runaway tractor when he was working old Mr. Carter's land, way out on the Waynesboro Highway. I'd seen that same soft look and tiny smile once in a while when she looked at any of her children, and I knew she was seeing something of Uncle Frank in them—in the tilt of their ears or the line of their jaws. Because any time Aunt Bett thought of Uncle Frank, it was a beautiful thing. She didn't seem to mind one little bit that he left her with nothing to help her in raising all those children. But she was doing all right. Because of her being so frugal and all.

When we got home, I found out just how right I had

been about Aunt Mee. As soon as we came into the living room, we could smell the good food she was heating up. She had found a good tablecloth and had put it on the dining room table and had even put a platter of deviled eggs right over that blackberry jelly stain Mama had never been able to get out.

Not only that—Aunt Mee must have been watching and waiting for us to leave for the funeral, because she'd had time to run the vacuum cleaner and dust the furniture, and when Aunt Bett and I went into the kitchen, we could smell pine oil in addition to the good smells of the hot food. Aunt Mee was at the sink, with her arms in hot, soapy water almost up to her elbows. She turned and looked at us. "Good service?"

"Yes," Aunt Bett answered, looking around admiringly at that perfectly spotless kitchen.

"Well, why don't you ladies go lie down for a little minute. I'll call you when folks start coming." Why, Aunt Mee was treating us just like we were folks from across town and she was our maid. And her calling the both of us ladies had my mouth hanging open.

After a brief, startled moment, Aunt Bett said, "Thank you," and without another word, she put her hand on my shoulder and guided me out of the kitchen. To my great surprise, she led me to the bedroom, where we saw that it, too, had been cleaned and dusted, and fresh sheets were on my cot and on the bed Molly and Little Ellis shared.

"We really gonna lie down?" I whispered, thinking that neither Aunt Bett nor I would be able to bear rumpling those crisp, spotless sheets.

"Of course not!" Aunt Bett snorted.

Because we both knew that to "lie down," even for a "little minute" was something rich, pampered folks did. Not people like us, who knew all about working hard and keeping on with it, even if you were tired to death. So we stood in the room, not really knowing what to do.

"What are we doing?" I finally whispered.

"Heavens, child! I surely don't know," Aunt Bett confessed. Then she added "Doing whatever Aunt Mee said to do, is all." So there we stood, not wanting to sit on the beds, and not wanting to go against what Aunt Mee had said for us to do. At last, we heard a car door slam, and Aunt Bett looked out of the window.

"They're here," she announced, and so we went into the living room, to greet the first arrival of Aunt Bett's church people and Mama's beauty parlor people, and Roy-Ellis's chicken plant people, all coming to comfort us.

All during the time of visiting, Aunt Bett kept looking around for Roy-Ellis, even asking me if I had seen him one time. But I hadn't. There were so many people and so much going on, I didn't have time to think of Roy-Ellis. I must have said thank-you a hundred times to good folks who wanted to tell me how sorry they were about Mama. And I heard all kinds of comments when folks didn't realize I was around:

"What's going to happen to the children?"

"Roy-Ellis certainly can't take care of them and work too."

"I'll bet you anything in this world that Bett will take them in. Her own sister's children!"

"Bett's already got enough to handle, what with trying to raise her own."

It was late in the afternoon before everybody finally left, and when Aunt Bett and I went into the dining room, all the food had been cleared away. The kitchen itself was spotless, and the dishes we had to return to folks were all clean and shining and neatly set aside. The sink had been scrubbed, and in the refrigerator, the leftover food was neatly packaged and marked with little strips of masking tape that said what was in the package. Aunt Mee was gone.

We heard the screen door close in the living room, and in a few moments, Roy-Ellis came into the kitchen.

"Roy-Ellis!" Aunt Bett said. "Where *have* you been? We had folks here who wanted to give you their condolences, and you weren't even here." Roy-Ellis didn't even answer. He just sat down at the kitchen table with a groan.

"You want some iced tea?" Aunt Bett asked him, her voice lots softer than it had been.

"No, Bett," he moaned. "I don't want *tea,* for goodness sake. What I really want is a cold beer."

"Don't you go talking like that around *me,* Roy-Ellis!" Her face was bright red. "I won't stay under this roof and see one drop of that nasty devil's brew go down your throat!"

Under her fury, Roy-Ellis's face had turned a deeper red than Aunt Bett's.

"Now do you want some *iced tea?*" she repeated.

"Yes ma'am," Roy-Ellis murmured.

"Dove, you get changed out of that good dress and then walk on down to my house and get Molly and Little Ellis,"

Aunt Bett said. And then she added, "And be sure to hang the dress up."

"Yessm."

To Roy-Ellis she said, "Now let me get you a nice glass of tea and then we'll just sit here and figure out what we're gonna do." So I went into the bedroom to change out of my good dress, but I could still hear every word Aunt Bett and Roy-Ellis were saying in the kitchen, because they hadn't shut the door this time.

"Well, what *are* we gonna do about the children?" Aunt Bett asked right off. So maybe she had heard some of those comments herself.

"Children?" Roy-Ellis sounded like he'd forgotten we were even in this world.

"Yes," she said slowly, giving him some little bit of time to remember about us. "The children," she finally urged.

"What about them?"

"Why, who's gonna look after them?"

"Oh."

"Who's gonna look after them, Roy-Ellis?" she pressed.

"Well," Roy-Ellis heaved a sigh. "They done all right while their mama was so sick. Dove done okay, her taking care of the little ones."

"Dove's just a baby herself, Roy-Ellis. Sometimes I think you forget that," Aunt Bett said. "And besides, how can she take care of Molly and Little Ellis when she's got to go to school?"

I felt my face go all hot when Aunt Bett said I was a baby, because I was *not* a baby, for Heaven's sake! Why, I was going on fourteen, and I knew how to take care of Little Ellis and Molly too, and myself. I'd been doing a good job of it for a long time, even before Mama got sick. Because Mama said we mustn't come into her beauty shop while she was working. So I'd learned how to mix up Kool-Aid and make pimento cheese sandwiches, and slice up a tomato without cutting myself, and get Molly and Little Ellis to take their naps. But Aunt Bett was right about school. I couldn't miss school!

"I'd take them home with me, if I could," Aunt Bett said.

"Lord have mercy, Bett!" Roy-Ellis interrupted. "You got plenty of your own need tending to. You surely don't need no more."

"But my own sister's children . . ." Aunt Bett went on but there was a relieved sound in her voice.

"I'll find a woman to come in," Roy-Ellis said. "I'll bet I can sure find us somebody good. Hey! How about Aunt Mee?"

Aunt Bett thought hard for a few moments. "Aunt Mee's getting on in years, Roy-Ellis," she finally pronounced. "And besides, she's worked for old Miz Stone, across town, for years. I don't know that she would leave her." Silence. So I went back into the kitchen. Roy-Ellis and Aunt Bett looked up at me.

"I thought I told you to change out of that good dress," Aunt Bett said. Then she added, "Dove, honey, when I bring you dresses to wear, you gotta take good care of them. You're more'n welcome to the clothes, because you're of a size right in between my Darlene and my Cassandra. But I gotta have those dresses back in good shape, for passing along to Cassandra." I didn't mind Aunt Bett telling me all that again, even though I'd heard it so many times. Every single time, in fact, that she handed down anything of Darlene's for me to borrow.

"Yessm," I said. "In just a little minute, please?"

She looked resigned. I looked right at Roy-Ellis, saw the misery in his eyes, and how his hair was hanging in his face, and him holding that glass of iced tea and knowing how much he wanted a beer.

"Roy-Ellis," I said so careful-like. "You don't need to find anybody to take care of us. I can do it. You know I can do it. 'Cause I been doing it all along. All the days when Mama was doing hair—"

"But she was *here,* if you needed her all of a sudden," Aunt Bett interrupted.

"But she wasn't here on Saturday nights," I explained to Aunt Bett, and then I looked right at Roy-Ellis and added, "And you weren't either, and I did just fine, all by myself."

Aunt Bett looked away. Roy-Ellis's eyes went dark and sad, probably because he was remembering Mama's spangle dresses and her laugh and how she sang honky-tonk songs.

"I can do it," I whispered to him, like maybe my saying it louder would hurt him too much in that bruised place behind his eyes.

"Well," Aunt Bett relented after a minute or so. "Maybe she could, Roy-Ellis. At least until you find somebody. I can take Molly and Little Ellis while Dove's in school, and she can get them on her way home in the afternoons." She looked me up and down, as if she was measuring how big I was. "And I'm just down the road such a little piece, she could practically holler to me from your own front porch, and I'd hear her. Like if she got scared or something."

Me? Scared? That's what I was thinking, but I didn't

say a single word.

"Thanks, Bett," is all Roy-Ellis said, and I knew I'd won.

"Now you go on in there and take off Darlene's dress and be sure you hang it up," Aunt Bett said to me. And I hummed Mama's honky-tonk song while I did exactly as Aunt Bett said.

Chapter Four

ROY-ELLIS went back to work on Thursday morning, and I walked Molly and Little Ellis down to Aunt Bett's before I went back to school. And I guess it felt good to do something completely usual, like going to school. Of course, everybody knew about my mama passing on, and all my teachers—especially Miss Madison, my English teacher—were even nicer than usual to me. I really didn't expect any of the girls in my school to be nice to me, ever. Because our town had only one school for everybody, and girls from the other side of town—where the houses had real lawns and perfectly painted front porches with matching rocking chairs on them—mostly stayed together and didn't pay much attention to any of us from the far side of town, the ones who lived in houses where the gray paint was wearing off, and the front porches mostly had begonias growing in rusted cans. So those girls from the nice side of town just clumped together, sitting together at lunch, and walking around with their arms around each others' waists at recess. Sometimes they all gathered in the shade of a big tree and squatted together, whispering and giggling. But the girls like me mostly didn't talk much to each other, and we certainly didn't draw attention to ourselves. We just sort of blended into the background and avoided having anybody notice us, in particular.

But in my secret heart, I really wanted to be like those other girls, because they were so pretty and wore such nice clothes. They liked each other and chattered and giggled together, and they were always spotlessly clean and nice-smelling. Like maybe they used perfumed soap or something like that. Sometimes, when I felt especially lonely at school, I'd imagine what their rooms were like, in those big houses. For one thing, I bet they all had their own rooms, and didn't share with brothers or sisters. And frilly curtains at the windows, and a maid to dust and clean and cook for them. I guess I wanted so much to be like them, only not mean or cold to girls like me.

But Miss Madison made up for the way those girls treated me. I'd always liked her, ever since the first day of school. Miss Madison was young and pretty, and the first thing she wanted to know was what books we had read during the summer. One boy answered, "Comic books," and everybody laughed. But Miss Madison didn't get mad.

"Well, that isn't what I had in mind," she smiled, and that smile is what lifted my hand right up into the air. "Yes?" She looked at her roll book. "Yes, Dove?"

"I read *A Tree Grows in Brooklyn.*"

"Very good," she beamed. "And what did you think of it?"

"I loved it," I said simply. "I read it twice, and I'm going to read it again."

"Why did you love it?" she pressed. I had to stop and

think about that for a moment.

"Well," I started, still thinking. "It was about a family that had a hard time. And after the father died, things were even harder. But they made it through. And it had a girl in it I really liked—Francie—and it was about living in a real city."

"Fine," Miss Madison said, nodding her head. "Now try this, Dove. Go back and tell me again, but this time, put everything into the present tense."

"Present tense?" I wanted to be sure I heard her right.

"That's right," she smiled back at me.

"Well, the book *is* about a family that's *having* a hard time. The father *dies,* and things get harder. But in the end, they all *make* it through. I *like* Francie, and the story *is* about living in a real city."

"Good! Now, do you know why we talk about books and the action in them in the present tense?"

"No, ma'am," I said, and I knew she was going to tell me, and I couldn't wait to find out.

"Because the story happens again and again and again, every time we read it. When you talk about what happens in a story, you speak as if it's happening right now. Because it is. Every single time you read it."

"Oh." I wasn't sure I understood, but I figured I'd better not ask any more until I got that straight in my head. But maybe it did make some sense, because when I'd look up from reading, sometimes I'd realize that I'd been living another life. In another world.

Later that first day, when I was almost done with my lunch, some of the girls in my class—girls who lived in those big, white houses way on the other side of town from our little house on a dirt road—whispered "Teacher's Pet" real loud at me, but I didn't care. I liked talking about interesting things. Those girls wouldn't even sit at the same table with somebody like me, so I sat all alone, eating my sandwich and thinking about how Francie felt . . . *feels* . . . when she visits her old neighborhood.

Then Michelle—who was absolutely the worst of the snooty girls—came close to where I was sitting, and in a loud, mean whisper, she said, "Dove wears old clothes nobody else wants!" But I didn't care, because I was absolutely certain that Francie wouldn't have cared about that, either.

But that had all been a long time ago, and I thought maybe I wouldn't have any more trouble with Michelle. I was wrong. My mama had died, and that made all the big-white-house girls notice me again. And I should have known that getting noticed was going to lead to trouble, but I didn't. I was still hurting too bad about Mama to look out for anything like that. But that first day back at school after spring holidays, Michelle came up right behind me at lunch time, with one of her big-white-house girlfriends in tow and said in a loud voice, "Dove's aunt gives her Darlene's old clothes to wear." I didn't turn around. So she added, "And the aunt is so poor, she can't even pay good money for clothes. She has to trade *pickles* for them!" I turned and stared at Michelle, but I said not one single word and I didn't look at her funny-like or anything.

But Michelle didn't stop there. She went around telling everybody that all my dresses were the very same ones Darlene wore last year and that we were all so poor, we couldn't afford our own clothes—but had to borrow clothes from other folks. I'm not sure of why it hurt me so bad, but it did. Maybe it had something to do with my mama and Aunt Bett—like everybody was laughing at how hard Aunt Bett tried to help me and Molly and Little Ellis. So when we were lining up to go back inside after recess, I walked right up to Michelle and stuck my face into hers and bored my eyes into her startled ones.

"You shut up, Michelle. You just shut up. You hear me?" My voice was so strong-sounding, it almost surprised me. Then I turned on my heel and walked away. But when we got into the classroom, Michelle went up to the teacher's desk and told her something. We had a substitute teacher that day, and that was unlucky for me. The teacher looked at me, and then she wiggled her finger for me to come to her desk, too.

"Dove," she whispered. "Michelle says that you cursed at her during lunch time. Is that true?" I looked at Michelle, and she had the meanest, happiest look on her face I have ever seen.

"No, ma'am," I said. "I'm not allowed to use curse words."

"She did!" Michelle shot back, and then she went back to wearing that same look.

The teacher looked back at me, and I blinked at her with my face as open and honest as could be. But I could tell she had already made up her mind.

"Dove, you go down and see Miss Frazier." And that was the way she dismissed me, and I found myself sitting in the principal's office. Miss Frazier was a heavyset person, and that day, she was wearing a dress with tiny purple bows in the fabric. Made me think of Aunt Bett's story about her and my mama taking music lessons. But I knew better than to smile. I'd never been sent to Miss Frazier's office before, and I sat real still, trying to decide if I was mad because of Michelle lying about what I said or if I was scared to death. Miss Frazier closed my file and put her hands together on top of it.

"You've never caused trouble before, Dove. Now I know about your losing your mama so recently. Is that why you're causing trouble?"

"No, ma'am." I met her gaze without blinking.

"So what happened that you used curse words to Michelle? You hear that kind of talk at home?" I thought of Roy-Ellis and how sometimes he used bad words. But when he'd burned himself on that boiling water when he was helping us dye Easter eggs, he'd stopped himself from saying those words around us. And I hadn't heard him say anything bad since then.

"No, ma'am," I said. "But Michelle was saying bad things about my clothes, and I had to tell her to shut up. I *did* tell her to shut up, but I didn't use any curse words. And that's the truth. And it doesn't have anything to do with . . . Mama," I managed to add, but then I knew I had to stop talking or I was going to cry. Miss Frazier studied me hard, and I sat there running my hand across the hem of Darlene's last-year dress.

"Are you telling me that Michelle lied?" The question was sent at me just like a spear.

"Yessm," I gulped. "I guess I am."

She leaned back in her chair and sighed.

"Dove, Michelle's father is an outstanding member of this community. He has raised Michelle right, and I'm sure

61

she doesn't lie."

"But I've been raised right too, and *I'm* not lying, Miss Frazier," I said in all honesty.

"Well, I want you to stay away from Michelle altogether. I don't want you to say *anything* to her. Do you understand?"

"Yessm." And I certainly did understand. Miss Frazier believed Michelle and not me.

"You may go now, but remember what I told you," she warned.

"Yessm."

Going back to my classroom was awful hard to do, because when I came in, everybody looked at me, especially Michelle, who smiled and tossed her head, as if to say "See what I can do?" I wanted to run, but I didn't. I walked to my desk and sat down, and I didn't even look at her again. That was the longest day of school I ever lived through in my whole life, and I couldn't keep my mind on much of anything except what had happened. And what did her daddy being such an important person in our little town have to do with anything? Michelle out-and-out lied, but Miss Frazier believed her anyway. *Why?* I just couldn't make any sense of it.

I was so glad when it was time to go home, and as I went up the steps to Aunt Bett's house, my eyes started trying to sting. Aunt Bett was standing at the door, and Molly and Little Ellis were standing behind her.

"You sure you can manage all right with Molly and Little Ellis until Roy-Ellis gets home?"

"Yessm," I said. And Aunt Bett studied me hard.

"Is everything all right?" she asked, and I managed to

nod my head. I didn't dare try to say a single word, my heart was hurting so bad. So Molly and Little Ellis came with me and we walked home.

But the next day, I found out that Michelle wasn't through with me yet. After recess, she told the teacher I'd stuck out my tongue at her, and Michelle's friend confirmed the lie, so I wound up in Miss Frazier's office again. This time, I was in tears, and there wasn't a thing I could do about it.

"Dove, what have you done?" Miss Frazier accused, and I didn't say a word, because I knew she wouldn't believe me anyway. "Well, you will have to stay after school today. If you bother Michelle again, I'll have to take stronger measures to get you to straighten up and behave yourself."

So that second day back at school after spring holidays, I had to stay after school for a whole hour, and of course, I missed the bus and had to walk all the way home. When I got to Aunt Bett's, she was standing out on the porch.

"Where have you been?" Aunt Bett demanded, but I was already so miserable, her angry tone didn't bother me. "I was worried when I saw that you weren't on the bus."

"I had to stay after school," I mumbled.

"What?"

"Just what I said. I had to stay after school." Aunt Bett's mouth was hanging open, and I wanted so bad to defend myself, but I had to be careful about not saying anything that would hurt her. But all of a sudden, my throat got so tight, I couldn't speak. And a flood of water got in my eyes and all the blinking in this world wouldn't take it away. Aunt Bett sat down on the top step and reached out for my hand.

"Talk to me, Dove. What's wrong?" she asked, but I still couldn't speak. And yet I knew the time had come to talk to somebody, anybody, because it was too much for me to carry all by myself. And I had no idea of how to put a stop to Michelle's meanness.

So I told Aunt Bett about what Michelle was doing, but I said not a single word about what Michelle said about Aunt Bett's trading pickles for clothes. I just said that Michelle was telling lies about me. I talked through hiccups and a runny nose and water rushing out of my eyes. Aunt Bett listened with her eyebrows drawn together. I finished up by telling her about how I had to stay after school. And for something I *didn't* do. Why, I felt like throwing back my head and howling like an animal! Because what on earth was to be done about it? Michelle could go on lying and lying about me, and every single time, I would get into trouble.

Aunt Bett pulled a handkerchief out of her apron pocket and gave it to me. And she sat right there and looked at me for a long time. When she finally spoke, it was in a very low voice—almost a whisper.

"I guess there's always someone like Michelle in every class in school," she said. "But this is going beyond foolish teasing and the way almost all little girls pick on somebody or other at some time."

"Did you ever have someone like that in your school?" I asked.

"Of course," she said. "But it was just some harmless teasing me about my freckles, and it only lasted a little while."

"What did you do?"

"I didn't do anything. And I think that's why it didn't last long."

"Huh?"

"When I told my mama about it, she said that if I didn't pay any attention at all, the teasing would stop. I guess it's only fun if the person getting teased acts upset about it."

"That makes sense, and I can ignore it. But what can I do about Michelle lying and getting me in trouble? How on earth can I stop her?"

"You tell the principal the truth," Aunt Bett said.

"That won't help. She doesn't believe me," I said miserably.

"Why not?"

"I guess it has something to do with Michelle's father being so important, or something."

Aunt Bett sighed, and a bitter little look of some kind flickered through her eyes.

"Well, then. We've bumped into that 'them' and 'us' thing, I guess. So what we have to do is make sure you're someplace during lunch where you have a witness who can testify that you didn't do or say anything to Michelle. Then the principal would have to believe you."

Why, that was nothing short of brilliant!

"Wow!" I said, and Aunt Bett blushed a little.

"Do you have a favorite teacher?" she asked me.

"Oh yes—Miss Madison," I answered. Aunt Bett brightened visibly.

"Well then, why don't you go see her tomorrow—and ask her if you can eat your lunch in her room. That way, you don't have to go outside or be around Michelle at all.

And if she tells any more lies about you, Miss Madison will be your witness." Aunt Bett looked at me hard.

"But this is only for a little while, Dove. You can't let Michelle make you hide forever. And when you're around her again, no matter what she says and no matter how much it hurts you, you just pretend you didn't hear her. If you don't act upset, she'll lose interest pretty soon and start picking on somebody else."

"That's a good idea, Aunt Bett," I said. "A very good idea." We sat in silence for a few minutes, and I could tell that Aunt Bett was proud of herself for coming up with such a good idea.

"Sometimes I think the boys have things easier," she added. "They have trouble, they just settle it with their fists. But girls can't do that." I was surprised to see that she had tears in her eyes.

"I'm sorry this happened to you," she added, simply. I saw that bitter little look flicker through her eyes, and I thought once again about what terribly mean things Michelle had said about her. It almost broke my heart. Took me a few minutes to realize that it was just love hurting me again! Would it never stop?

The next morning, I got up real early and took Molly and Little Ellis to Aunt Bett's so I could walk to school and get there ahead of classes. I was praying that Miss Madison would be there early too, so I could talk to her without anyone else being around. I got to school before anybody, and I was sitting and waiting in the back row of seats when she came into her classroom.

"Dove!" she said, surprised. "Is anything wrong?" I got

up and followed her to her desk and while she put her papers into her drawer and took off her sweater, I told her everything about what Michelle was doing. When I came to the part about Miss Frazier, I was very careful. I knew better than to speak ill of a principal to a teacher—any teacher. And I told her about what Aunt Bett had suggested and why I wanted to spend my lunch times in her class-room. She listened like she was taking in my words through her very pores. And when I finally stumbled to a stop, she said, "Well, of course, you may spend your lunch time in my room. But . . ." I held my breath. Miss Madison just *had* to help me, and whatever I had to do, I would do it.

"Surely, you understand that you can't hide from Michelle forever. That way, you let her win. At some point, you have to learn to ignore children like her." Oh, how I did like Miss Madison grouping Michelle in with "children"! "And if you want to be in my classroom for your whole lunch time, you will have to put your time to good use."

"I will!" I agreed, with relief. She opened a bottom drawer of her desk and took out a new Blue Horse note-book.

"When you finish your lunch, you will write in this," she said.

"Write what?" I asked, while she put the new notebook on her desk and pushed it toward me.

"Anything you want to write."

"Anything?"

"Yes. Will you do that?"

"I will," I promised, and just then, some of her early stu-dents came into the room, talking and laughing.

"Then I'll see you at lunch time," she said. And I could hear the gentle dismissal in her voice.

I was ever so happy in all of my morning classes, knowing that I had the new notebook and that I didn't have to worry about Michelle and her lies about me. Lunch time came, and I had a nice, long drink from the water fountain before I went into Miss Madison's room. When I went in, she was at her desk, writing. She looked up at me, nodded her head, and went back to her work. I sat down in a desk in the back row, put my books away, and left only three things on the desk: my sandwich, the new notebook—open to that first pure, blank page—and my pen. I looked up at Miss Madison. She had a sandwich too, and while I watched, she unwrapped it, took the half in both hands, and bit down on it—all the while still looking at whatever she had been writing. So I did the same thing, only the page I looked at was absolutely blank—except for all those perfect, pale blue lines, waiting to be filled up. I looked up again. Miss Madison was dabbing her mouth with a paper napkin. So again, I did the same, with the sheet of paper towel that was my napkin. When she started on the second half of her sandwich, so did I. And when the sandwiches—hers and mine—were gone, she wiped her hands, gathered the waxed paper and the napkin together, and tossed them into the trash can. But I didn't have a trash can to throw things in, so I wadded up my waxed paper and paper towel and stuffed them into my pocket.

And I waited and watched. Miss Madison was still looking at a page of her notebook. But then she picked up her pen and started writing. I picked up my pen, too. But that beautiful, blank page seemed to look back and me and to say *What now? What a good question!* I thought. And what was it Miss Madison had said to me that morning when I asked about what I should write? *Anything you want.* I sat and sat and thought and thought. What did I want to write about? That was a hard question! But then I got to thinking about Mama and her honky-tonk songs, and I knew right away that was something I could write about. So I started writing and all of a sudden, my pen seemed to fly across the page. Why, I was so surprised when I heard Miss Madison's voice suddenly jumping into the middle of my story about how Mama was so very, very beautiful and how she sang those sweet-sad songs.

"Lunch time is over, Dove," the voice said. "Go on to class and I'll see you tomorrow at the same time." But coming up out of the writing was like heaving myself out of a pit of deep mud that kept trying to hold on to me. That was another surprise, and when I looked up at Miss Madison, I could feel it was the same way for her. Like her hand hated to put down the pen, and her eyes wanted to stay looking at the paper. Finally, we both got free from it, but when I left the room, I suddenly realized that while I had been writing about Mama, it was almost the same thing as having Mama right there again with me. Then I remembered what Miss Madison had said about always talking in the present tense and how a story happened over and over again, every time you read it. Yes, it was almost as good as really having my mama there with me. So I went about the rest of my school day with a gladdened heart.

During math class, Michelle went up in front of the classroom to sharpen her pencil. When she passed my desk, she whispered, "I don't know where you're hiding, but I'll find you!" I wanted to tell her that I wasn't *hiding* at all. But I didn't, because right then and there, I started practicing what I knew I had to do. I completely ignored her.

"I'll find you!" she hissed, but I pretended that I didn't even hear her.

Every day at lunch time for that whole week, I went to Miss Madison's classroom, ate my sandwich, and wrote about my mama until Miss Madison would tell me the time was up. Sometimes, I hated to go to my other classes, because I really wanted to keep writing. But I always did as Miss Madison said.

On Friday morning, when I got to school, the homeroom teacher told me that Miss Frazier wanted to see me. I didn't even feel the least bit alarmed, because I knew for a fact that I hadn't said or done anything that Michelle could twist around and use against me. So I went right down to Miss Frazier's office. When I opened the door, Michelle and the same friend of hers that had lied about my sticking out my tongue were sitting in chairs in front of Miss Frazier's desk. Miss Frazier's face was like a stone, and Michelle smiled at me just the least little bit. The mean smile. Her friend was looking a little nervous.

"You wanted to see me, Miss Frazier?" I asked, keeping my voice calm. She didn't invite me to sit down.

"Dove, Dove, Dove . . ." she moaned.

"Yessm?"

"What do I have to do to make you see how serious this is becoming?"

I didn't know what to say. So I asked, "What's this about, Miss Frazier?"

"You know good and well what it's about," Miss Frazier's voice was rising. I stayed as calm as possible.

"No ma'am, I don't," I insisted.

"You've said nasty things to Michelle *again*," I looked at Michelle and her friend. Michelle wasn't smiling that mean smile anymore, and her friend was blinking her eyes and biting her lip.

Michelle spoke. "You know good and well, Dove Johnson, that you called me a . . . a witch with a capital B."

"When?"

"At lunch time yesterday." Michelle turned to her friend. "Isn't that right? Didn't you hear her call me that?"

The friend hesitated and then nodded her head the least little bit. I turned to Miss Frazier and took a deep breath.

"Miss Frazier, I have not spoken a single word to Michelle, and I have spent every single lunch time sitting in Miss Madison's room, doing some extra work." Miss Frazier's eyes went wide and locked onto Michelle.

"You can ask Miss Madison," I concluded. Michelle's face was as white as milk, and her friend had turned beet red and was starting to cry.

"Dove, you may go," Miss Frazier said, still with her eyes locked onto Michelle. And so I did, but not before I gave Michelle a mean smile of my own.

That afternoon, when I got Molly and Little Ellis from Aunt Bett, I told her all about how the plan she made up had worked. She nodded and smiled, but then she said, "Now, Dove, the weekend is here, and you'll have Molly and Little Ellis all by yourself, you sure you can

71

handle everything?"

"Yessm," I assured her. And I had absolutely no doubt in my mind at all that I was equal to the task.

Chapter Five

THAT first Saturday, I made believe to myself that Mama was working in her little beauty parlor, so that taking care of Molly and Little Ellis and the house felt real natural for me. Felt just like something that had been that way for a long time. And it had, of course. But Aunt Bett called to check on us every hour or so, until around noon, when I told her I was getting ready to fix lunch and put the little ones down for their naps. Around two-thirty the phone rang again. It was Darlene.

"Mama said for me to find out if you all are okay. She's on the back porch trying to fix the belt on the washing machine."

"We're fine, Darlene. And tell Aunt Bett our machine is working fine, if she wants to come over and use it." So around three o'clock, Aunt Bett drove up and came in with a big basket of dirty clothes and a box of detergent on top.

"Dove, I'll have to use you all's washer." She went toward the back porch, but her eyes were darting this way and that, taking in the picture books spread out all over the couch and the Kool-Aid glasses on the coffee table, and the lunch dishes in the sink. While she was loading clothes into the washer, I stacked the books, pushed Little Ellis's yellow truck behind the couch, took the Kool-Aid glasses into the kitchen, and started washing up the lunch dishes. Aunt Bett came into the kitchen, opened the refrigerator, and started counting Roy-Ellis's bottles of beer.

"We can bring the clothes down to you, soon as they're done," I offered, trying to keep her from getting all riled up about Roy-Ellis's beer.

"No, honey. Thanks. I'll wait on them." Then, "What are you all having for supper?" she asked, and I could tell that she was trying to make her voice sound cheerful instead of worried. I thought for a moment. "I was thinking about hot dogs and beans."

"Well, when you heat the hot dogs, make sure you use a back unit on the stove, so there won't be any chance of Molly or Little Ellis pulling that hot water down on themselves."

"Yessm."

"Now if you'll get me your canned beans, I'll show you how to fix them up a little bit." I got the cans and opened them. Aunt Bett emptied them into a bowl and then she added some mustard and ketchup and brown sugar. She stirred it all together and gave me a spoon to taste it.

"Oh, that's better than just plain beans."

"Now what you do is this," she went on. "Empty these seasoned beans into a baking dish and put some raw bacon slices on top and bake it until the bacon's done."

"Yessm."

"You'll learn, little by little, and one of these days you'll be a good cook," she pronounced.

"Like you," I said, and she blushed.

By the time Aunt Bett took her basket of clean clothes home to hang on her own clothesline, she had helped me to make a cottage cheese and canned peaches salad and a chocolate sauce out of cocoa powder, sugar, and canned milk for putting on ice cream for dessert. The next week, Aunt Bett got a new belt for her washing machine, and Roy-Ellis put it on for her on Sunday afternoon, so she didn't have to carry her laundry down to our house. But she took me to the grocery store with her every week and taught me lots of things, like how to give Molly and Little Ellis slices of apple with peanut butter on them, instead of so many cookies; how to mix dry milk half-and-half with real milk so that it tasted just fine and was cheaper; and how to find day-old bread at a better price than fresh.

At school, Michelle stayed away from me and even though everything was fixed, where Michelle was concerned, I kept on spending every lunch time in Miss Madison's room. I loved doing that so much that I almost hated for school to be over. But I made up my mind that I was going to get me some notebooks and keep on writing about my mama.

So I guess we spent the rest of that springtime and the first few days of summer doing what Aunt Bett said we would have to do—just carrying on the best we could, just doing what had to be done and not thinking much about it. Roy-Ellis worked lots of extra shifts, because we needed the money so bad, so he came home late almost all the time. Most of the time, he was too tired to have any supper at all, so he just had a cold beer and went to bed.

Then something happened right in my own backyard at the end of May that made that summer such a happy one for me, in spite of everything. Because even though we had an electric clothes dryer on the back porch, I always hung our sheets out, where they got all crisp-like and smelled like sunshine and were ever so much nicer to sleep on. And besides, running the dryer made the electricity bill way too high.

So that day, I washed a load of sheets while Molly and Little Ellis were having their lunch, and when they went down for their naps, I took the sheets outside in a big basket to hang them on the line. The sun was high in the sky, and the earth was just roasting under its heat. Even the little bit of grass in our backyard sounded crispy when I walked across it in my bare feet. I wasn't thinking about anything at all, that I knew of. Just making sure to get all the wrinkles out of the sheets before I clipped on the clothespins. So I'm not sure of when I first noticed a scurrying sound in all the tall weeds under the dead pecan trees farther back in the yard. The part that we shared with Aunt Mee.

She had come and knocked on our back door about once a week or so, to check on us and see if we needed anything. I always invited her in, but she smiled and shook her head. Except for once, when she came into the kitchen to help me figure out if a moldy piece of cheese was still any good.

"Oh sure, honey," she had said. "This cheese is fine. Just you trim off the moldy part, and the rest is fine." But I hadn't seen her recently, so maybe that sound I heard that afternoon was her coming to see about us.

"Aunt Mee?" I called, and the sound stopped right away. No answer.

"Aunt Mee?" I called again. "Is that you?"

I heard a giggle and then more scurrying sounds in the weeds.

"Who's there?" I called, suddenly feeling prickly all over. Another giggle, and I knew at once there was nothing about that silly little sound to be afraid of.

"Okay," I said, trying to sound impatient. "Who's there!"

"Me!" A high-pitched voice. Then another giggle. I walked toward the tall weeds, and suddenly, a face appeared through them. The funniest face I have ever seen in my life. It was a girl, maybe about my age. Maybe a little younger, but it was hard to tell because the face was scrunched into shut-tight eyes, pouting lips, and a wrinkled nose. While I stood there, she stuck out her bright pink little tongue at me. I laughed.

"Who are you?" I asked.

The eyes popped open, big and brown, and the face unclenched itself—a face the color of coffee with lots of milk in it. A deep smile carved itself right in front of my eyes, in between two deep dimples like I'd never seen before, except on a store-bought doll.

"I'm Savannah," she said. "I been watching you hang out sheets, and I wondered if you wanta play."

"Play?"

"I have a checkers game," she said, tilting her head toward Aunt Mee's.

"You staying with Aunt Mee?" I asked.

"Just for a while." She paused and the face went solemn. Just like somebody had blown out a candle. "'Cause my mama died. And now folks in her family have to decide who's going to take care of me." The back of my neck prickled.

"Your mama died?" I breathed. She nodded a few times,

but then she ended up her nodding with her chin very high in the air and a determined look in her eyes.

"My mama died too," I said, holding my chin exactly like hers. We stood there for a long moment, looking right into each other's eyes.

"Well, do you wanta play?" she asked, at last.

"I . . . don't think I have time. I have work to do. And my little sister and brother to take care of," I answered.

She brightened. "Children? Oh, can I see them?"

"They're asleep."

"When they wake up? And I'll help you with your work and when it's all done, we can play!" That word again. That perfectly good but strange-sounding word.

"I'll go get the checkers." Then she hesitated. "Is it okay?"

"Is it okay for you to get the checkers?" I asked, a little confused.

"No. I mean is it okay with you that I'm not white?" She separated the words, like they were stones she had to step onto, for getting her across something she didn't want to fall into. And her question surprised me, because all I'd been thinking was that here was somebody else who knew what it felt like to lose your mama. I studied her hard then, realizing that this wasn't some white child Aunt Mee was taking care of, but a very light-skinned black child. The face waited, all full of hope, with the eyebrows held high and the eyes wide and the mouth just waiting to break into a smile.

"Of course I don't mind," I said. And that was true. Because it didn't matter to me that there were some folks in our town who were against the black people. Mama had never been, nor Aunt Bett, nor Roy-Ellis, and that's what I grew up with—knowing that you treat all folks the same.

"You kin to Aunt Mee?" I asked.

"Yes," she smiled and the dimples carved themselves into her cheeks once again. "She's my grandmama." She lifted her shoulders in a hopeful shrug, and then she held out one arm and ran her hand over the brown-sugar/cream-colored skin. "Grandmama says I'm a throwback to some white folks who were in our family a long time ago."

I didn't know what throwback meant, so I said, "Run on then and get the game, and we'll get all the work done so we can play." And just like that, she turned and ran off into the tall weeds. The scurrying sounds died away, and then there was only the hot silence of early afternoon, and the sun shining down on the clean sheets, and me thinking that, at last, maybe I had found me a true and loyal friend of my very own. Somebody who knew what it was like to lose your mama.

I was washing up the lunch dishes when I heard a soft knock on the back screen door. "That you, Savannah?" I called.

"It's me!" came the reply.

"Well, come on in." I heard the squeak of the hinges, and in a moment, I saw her coming across the back porch almost on tiptoes.

"Hi," I said, and she froze to a stop.

"Can I come in?" she whispered.

"Of course."

She came into the kitchen ever so slowly, looking all around.

I kept on washing the dishes while Savannah crept

around, peering into the dining room and looking back at the porch, as if something unexpected might jump out at her, and she needed to be sure of a way of escape. What a strange little thing she was, creeping around on her long, thin legs and with her shoulders hunched up around her neck. I just kept washing dishes, but I was smiling because there was no way *not* to smile. Finally, after she had looked all around, she whispered, "You wanta play?"

"There's work to do first," I said, and it startled me, the way I sounded just exactly like Aunt Bett.

"Okay. What do you want me to do?" I gave her a damp rag and asked her to wipe down the table. Then I had her finish drying the dishes while I folded the clothes that had come out of the dryer.

"What you hang out clothes on the line for, if you all got an electric dryer?" she asked.

"I always hang out the sheets," I explained. "Because the sunshine makes them smell so nice and fresh."

"We hang out all our things, 'cause we don't have a dryer," Savannah said with a toss of her head that said she didn't mind. Then she added, "When can I see the children?"

"Soon as they wake up." And right at that moment, as if on cue, Molly appeared in the kitchen doorway, wearing only her panties and with her face in the deep pout that was her usual after-nap expression.

"A-h-h-h!" Savannah breathed.

"Molly, this is Savannah," I said. Molly put her thumb deep into her mouth and scowled. "Savannah, this is Molly." Savannah's face was wreathed in a smile, with her dimples all deep and shadowy.

"Hello, Molly," she said. "I'm glad to meet you." Incredibly, Molly's thumb came out of her mouth, and she smiled and walked toward Savannah, with her arms held up! Savannah put down the towel and picked Molly up. Molly wrapped her legs around Savannah's narrow waist and she put her head down on Savannah's shoulder.

"Why, I never!" I said, still not quite believing what I was seeing.

"Children always like me," Savannah said. "But I don't know why." She started swinging ever so slowly back and forth, giving Molly what was really like a sideways rocking. When Little Ellis waked up, Savannah liked him just as well, but he didn't take right to her, the way Molly did. Instead, he clutched me and just stared and stared at her.

"It's okay," she said, with Molly still wrapped around her. She whispered, "I like little girls best anyway!" We had a good time that afternoon. We fixed a whole platter of vanilla wafers with peanut butter on them, and I found some cake sprinkles in the cabinet and sprinkled them on top of the peanut butter. We all had milk to drink, and we ate that whole plate of cookies, while Savannah told us a wonderful story about a rabbit that outsmarts a fox. We laughed until our stomachs ached. Afterward, I wiped all the peanut butter off Molly and Little Ellis while Savannah washed and dried the plate and glasses. Then we played checkers, with Molly sitting in Savannah's lap and Little Ellis sitting in mine. We played three whole games— Savannah won two of them—and we all had some Kool-Aid. Then, while Molly and Little Ellis and Savannah watched cartoons, I started getting supper ready.

I heard Roy-Ellis holler, "I'm home!" and all of a sudden, Savannah came just flying through the kitchen, her going so fast she was like a little blur as she went through the door and across the back porch. She didn't even stop to get her checkers.

"Who was that?" Roy-Ellis asked as he came into the kitchen and reached into the refrigerator for a cold beer.

"That's Savannah," I explained. "Aunt Mee's grand-daughter."

"Timid little thing, isn't she?"

"She's really nice," I said.

Savannah came back the next afternoon, but her eyes were wide and darting.

"Who was that man?"

"Roy-Ellis. My stepdaddy. You shouldn't be afraid of him," I explained. "He's a good man."

"He scared me," she confessed. "I don't much like meeting new folks."

"But you liked meeting me . . . and Molly and Little Ellis," I argued.

"That's different," she argued back, and I decided not to press her about it. And now that Savannah knew to listen for Roy-Ellis's truck, she always hurried away before he came in. But not running real fast, like before. And she always said, "Bye!" when she headed out onto the back porch. On Friday, she told me that she couldn't come on Saturday if Roy-Ellis was home. And she could never come on Sundays.

"Why?" I asked.

" 'Cause Grandmama makes me keep the Sabbath."

"Huh?"

"We go to church, and afterward, I'm not allowed to play and we can't do any work. Grandmama even makes Sunday dinner on Saturday so she won't have to cook. I'm not allowed to do anything except sit on the porch and read the Bible." I thought of our Sunday afternoons after church, and a big Sunday dinner at Aunt Bett's, after which we could come home and do just about anything we wanted.

"Why's Aunt Mee like that?" I asked.

"Dunno," Savannah said. "But that's the way she is."

"Couldn't you *sneak* over here Sunday afternoons?"

Savannah's eyes grew wide and she shook her head. "That would be a sin," she said, simply.

"Oh."

Savannah bit her lip and frowned. "We have to keep the Sabbath *holy*. That's what she says."

"Well, we can play a little on Saturdays, because Roy-Ellis works a lot of overtime."

"Okay."

So on Saturday, I guess Savannah must have looked to see if Roy-Ellis's truck was gone, and it was. She came up the back steps whistling. "Hi, Dove," she started. "Can you come out in the yard and talk with my grandmama a little minute? I'll watch out for Molly and Little Ellis." So Savannah went on into the living room, and I went out into the backyard, where Aunt Mee was waiting.

"Hi, Aunt Mee," I said. "What you need?"

She kind of tilted her shoulders back and forth and looked at her shoes before she spoke. "I just wanted to tell you not to let Savannah wear out her welcome, is all."

"Oh, she won't," I laughed. "She helps me, especially with Molly and Little Ellis."

"She always did love little ones," Aunt Mee confessed. "But she's timid about Roy-Ellis."

"I know."

"And I didn't want him to get his feelings hurt about that."

"It doesn't hurt his feelings. He knows Savannah's a little timid."

"She is," Aunt Mee said. "She is that, sure enough. Well, I better get on back home. I got things to take care of."

"Does it make things hard on you for Savannah to spend time over here?" I asked.

Aunt Mee laughed. "Goodness, no! You ought to see her just flying through her chores, so she came come over here and play with Molly and Little Ellis." Then she added, "And I'm glad she has you for a friend. She doesn't make friends very easy."

During that first week of summer vacation, Aunt Bett called and wanted to know why we didn't come down to her house very often, and I told her about Savannah and how much I enjoyed her company.

"Well, you do as you please," Aunt Bett said. "But just remember that we're right here and we're family and you're always welcome."

"Yessm."

"Well, I'm bringing you all some summer things today, so if there's anything you want me to do at your house, just let me know."

So that afternoon, Aunt Bett came driving up with her

whole backseat filled with clean, carefully folded clothes for us to wear during the summer. And goodness knows, Molly and Little Ellis were certainly needing new clothes, because they had outgrown almost all the things Aunt Bett had loaned to us a few months earlier.

"This must be Savannah," Aunt Bett said.

"Aunt Bett, this is Savannah, and Savannah, this is our Aunt Bett." And I was surprised as could be when Savannah smiled a big smile and did a little curtsy! That just charmed Aunt Bett no end, and she laughed out loud.

"Where do you come from?" Aunt Bett asked.

"I'm Aunt Mee's grandbaby," Savannah answered easily. "I'm staying with her while my mama's folks get things all straightened out about who all's going to take care of me."

"Well," Aunt Bett said with a little frown. "Come on, you two, and help me unload these things, but be careful now—don't you be dropping these good, clean clothes on the ground."

"Yessm," we answered right together. And we carefully carried armloads of fresh-smelling, ironed clothes inside. Aunt Bett herself carried the Sunday dresses for Molly and me that were all starched and on hangers.

When we got into the bedroom, Aunt Bett said to Savannah, "Honey, I sure am thirsty. Would you mind getting me a little glass of water?"

"Yessm!" Savannah chirped. Then she frowned. "I mean, no ma'am. I don't mind." And she scampered off to the kitchen.

Aunt Bett turned to me and whispered, "Does Roy-Ellis know there's a . . . *black* child coming over here while he's gone?"

"Yessm."

"Well, what did he say?"

I thought for a moment. "He said she's a timid little thing," I reported.

Aunt Bett worried her bottom lip between her teeth. "Well, don't you let her go snooping into things," she whispered.

"She's a good girl, Aunt Bett," I whispered back. And then I added, "Her mama raised her right." Aunt Bett cast a curious glance at me and opened her mouth to say something, but right then, Savannah came back into the bedroom, carrying Aunt Bett's glass of water so carefully and with her eyes locked on it intently, so it wouldn't get spilled. When she gave it to Aunt Bett, she smiled again.

"Well, I thank you, Savannah," Aunt Bett said, glancing at me. Then she drank the water right down and handed the glass back. Savannah studied the glass as if its being empty was a very mysterious thing.

"You're welcome," she said, and Aunt Bett looked at Savannah's face for a long moment before she said, "Well, you certainly do have good manners, I can say that much."

Savannah grinned. "Yessm!" she yelped. "My mama sure raised me right!"

Aunt Bett and I didn't look at each other.

After Aunt Bett left, Savannah helped me put all those nice clothes away in the drawers. Aunt Bett had hung all the hanging clothes right away, but there was underwear and socks and T-shirts for Molly and Little Ellis to put into the drawers, and Savannah helped me until every single piece was where it belonged. Then she opened the closet door and looked longingly at all the Sunday dresses Aunt Bett had fixed up for Molly and me.

"I wish I had me so many nice dresses," Savannah whispered, almost as if she didn't want me to hear her.

"I'd let you borrow some, but Aunt Bett has to have them back, and if any of them got torn or anything like that, I'd be in big trouble!"

"Well, Grandmama's making me some new dresses anyway," Savannah said. "Just not this many. And besides, I'll probably be going to live with somebody else in Mama's family pretty soon." I felt my heart lunge in my chest.

"You're going away?" My voice must have held all the heartache I was feeling, because how could I not have this beautiful friend in my life forever?

"I know," Savannah said simply. "I don't want to go, but Grandmama says she's too old to take care of me all the time, so some of Mama's other kin folks have to help out."

I reached out and hugged Savannah then. She felt small and thin in my arms and a little stiff too, as if maybe she wasn't used to getting hugged. When I let her go, I saw that she had tears in her eyes.

So it seemed like I turned into Aunt Bett in a flash. "Well, we just have to get through this the best we can," I announced, and Savannah brightened at the confident sound my voice made. It even comforted me as well, and made me able to pretend that everything would be all right. And I never said a thing to Savannah, but I remembered that promise I'd made to myself not to love anybody again, and knew that I'd broken it. Even though I meant to keep it. So my heart was hurting again, and I had no one to blame for it except myself.

When Roy-Ellis came home from work—sending Savannah in her usual flight out the back door—he went right into the bedroom, and while I was getting ready to serve his supper, I heard the shower start up. Then he came into the kitchen wearing jeans, his cowboy shirt and boots, and carrying his cowboy hat. He glanced at me a little anxiously, I thought, and started in on his canned spaghetti in a hurry. Then he downed the last of his coffee, wiped his mouth with the back of his hand and stood up.

"Dove, honey—I just can't sit home every single night. I ain't cut out for it. So do you mind if I go out? I mean, you won't be scared or nothing, will you?"

"I was never scared when you and Mama went out," I said, and I kind of stumbled over the words, because just for a moment, I halfway expected Mama to come out of the bedroom, all dressed up and ready to go with him. "Besides," I went on, "I'm older than I was then. So it's okay." Too, I thought about how I could see the porch light on Aunt Mee's house, and that was a comfort, for some reason.

"Good!" he said, grinning in a way I hadn't seen him do in a long time. So I knew he was heading out for Across the Line.

"Who're you going with?" I asked, and my own words were a complete surprise to me.

"Nobody," he said too quickly. "Just nobody . . . somebody . . . alone."

And before I could say another word, he was gone, and only the good smell of his cologne remained. The house seemed so strangely quiet all at once, and when I was bathing Molly and Little Ellis and getting them into bed, it was like the silence was so loud, I could almost hear it. I read for a while, and when I got sleepy, I made sure the door was locked and the porch light was on before I went to bed. Real late, I heard Roy-Ellis come home. He tripped on that same front step, but he didn't say a word, and the next morning, Aunt Bett came by for us children and we all went to church. She didn't ask about Roy-Ellis, and I didn't volunteer anything. She wouldn't like knowing that Roy-Ellis had started in to honky-tonking again, but I didn't mind it one little bit. Roy-Ellis worked so hard all the time, coming home and swallowing down whatever I had fixed for supper, then going right to bed. And too, he'd been awfully good to Mama when she started getting sick. And he was a good provider for us, and me and Molly not even his own children. But there was one thing I thought about: What if Roy-Ellis met somebody he wanted to marry! I mean, Roy-Ellis was a fine-looking man, and he was still pretty young. When Mama died, I always figured he'd spend the rest of his life taking care of us. But maybe that wouldn't happen. Even my own mama found somebody else after my daddy left us. And if that happened with Roy-Ellis, what on earth would become of me and Molly and Little Ellis?

I wanted to talk to Savannah about it, but I couldn't. Because maybe it would have hurt her feelings. She was without a mother or a father, and had to be shifted back and forth among her relatives. If Roy-Ellis found somebody else to love, maybe he wouldn't want us anymore, and we didn't have a big family to be shifted around to.

We just had Aunt Bett.

Chapter Six

ROY-ELLIS was ever so much happier, once he got started honky-tonking again, and also, he'd put a big dent in most of the bills, so he didn't have to work so many extra shifts. He'd already been back to Across the Line two Saturday nights in a row, and he didn't seem to have met anybody special, so I forgot to worry about that. Besides, when he would get all dressed up to go out, he looked so fine and handsome, I was truly proud he was my stepdaddy.

But then there came a very late Saturday night in June when the ringing of the phone startled me out of sleep.

"Hello?" I almost whispered because Aunt Mee had let Savannah stay late at our house, and we'd been watching a movie on television about a man who kept calling a lady and not saying a word, just breathing into the phone. Savannah was so scared after that, I had to take our flashlight and walk halfway through the woods with her so she could get home. She ran the rest of the way, while I shined the light on her, and then I heard her call "Okay! I'm safe!" when she reached Aunt Mee's porch.

"Hello?" I said again.

"Hey, Dove?" Roy-Ellis's voice, loud and clear. Then someone with a high voice giggling, and a muffled sound. Roy-Ellis putting his hand over the receiver?

"Yessir?"

"Dove, honey . . ." the muffled sound again and Roy-Ellis saying, "Be quiet just a minute, darling."

Darling?

Then Roy-Ellis coming back on the line and saying, "Honey, you think it will be okay if I don't come home tonight? I mean, would you be scared or anything?"

I looked at the clock. Almost 5 A.M.

"No, Roy-Ellis, I wouldn't be afraid."

"Good. Now listen to me a little minute—just don't say anything to Bett about this. It will be our secret—yours and mine. Okay?"

"Okay, Roy-Ellis."

"So I'll see you all tomorrow evening, okay?"

"Okay."

"Go to church with Bett, but don't say anything. You know how she worries over nothing."

"Okay."

I hung up the phone and went back to bed.

Darling?

Uh-oh!

The next morning, we were ready when Aunt Bett came for us, and she didn't even notice that Roy-Ellis's truck was gone. Church was good, with lots of singing and a sermon that didn't last too long. When Aunt Bett dropped us back at home, she noticed about the truck.

"Where's Roy-Ellis?" she asked.

"Maybe they called him in for an extra shift," I suggested, trying hard not to lie. Because a promise is a promise.

"Well, goodness knows, you all need the extra money. You call me if you need me," she commanded.

"Yessm. Thanks."

"And be sure to take off your church clothes right away

and hang them up."

"Yessm."

After I got us all changed and hung up the good clothes, I made tuna sandwiches and sliced tomatoes for our lunch, and then I read four picture books to Little Ellis and Molly before I put them down for their naps. While they were resting, I sat in the porch swing, reading *A Tree Grows in Brooklyn* again. But once in a while, I'd put the book down and look out across the dry-grass field on the other side of our road, with not another soul in sight, and I'd wonder what it felt like to live in a real city and have all those people around and things going on all the time. Darlene said something like that to me one time. She said, "This is such a dead little town. I sure do wish I could go some-place exciting!"

Aunt Bett had overheard her and she said, "It's just your age, Darlene. It will pass. Why, when I was your age, I wanted to run away and join the circus." Two of Aunt Bett's youngest children went running by, laughing and whooping. "But look at me now," Aunt Bett laughed. "I'm living right in the middle of my own circus all the time!" She laughed at her own joke, and Darlene and I smiled. But we glanced at each other, because we knew that kind of heart-hungry longing wasn't a joke at all.

I went back to my book. Back to New York City and all the people and things going on. And when Molly and Little Ellis got up, I knew I just had to find something different for us to do. Or that long, lonely Sunday afternoon was going to last forever.

"I've got a surprise for you all," I told them, after they had

91

finished their cookies and milk.

"Prize?" Molly asked.

"SURprise," I repeated.

They were already wearing pants and shirts, so I put on their shoes and socks and sat them on the couch.

"Stay there," I commanded. I got a brown paper bag out of the pantry and in it I put an old sheet, the rest of the bag of cookies, an unopened quart carton of orange juice, and some of Molly and Little Ellis's favorite storybooks. And we all set off down the road. Past other little gray houses like ours, with clotheslines in the backyards and one with an old car up on concrete blocks. Past the flour mill, quiet and deserted because of it being Sunday and nobody at work, and then along the dirt road all the way to the Waynesboro Highway. As soon as we reached that, we could see the big brick schoolhouse.

"The playground!" Molly chirped.

But Little Ellis had begun to whimper, because it was a long way to walk, and his legs were little. So for the rest of the way, I carried Little Ellis on my hip and held the grocery bag in my other hand, with Molly holding on to the bag, as well. It was the next best thing to me holding her hand, I thought.

We put the bag in the shade of a big tree, so our orange juice wouldn't get warmed up. And then we started playing. We rode the seesaw, with Molly and Little Ellis on one end and me on the other. I had to sit pretty close to the middle for our weights to balance, but we laughed and had a good time anyway. Next, they wanted to go on the round-and-round—I really don't know what it was called, but that's what Molly called it. It had a round base that was mounted up on some kind of a pole, and had metal bars for hanging on to. I put Molly and Little Ellis on and made sure they were holding tight, and then I pushed and ran until it was going fast, and I hopped on and stretched out on my back, so that I could see the rich, green leaves on the trees circling round over my head. It was such a wonderful feeling.

After we played for a good, long time—all with that hot summer sun burning down on us—I spread out the sheet in the shade, and we ate cookies and took turns drinking the orange juice. Then I started reading some of the books to Molly and Little Ellis, but I noticed that a brown pickup truck had turned in at the entrance to the school. I wondered maybe if it was someone come to tell us we couldn't be on the playground when school wasn't going on. It just kept on coming toward us so slowly, and there was something about it that made me feel worried. But I didn't know what it was.

I didn't want to frighten Molly and Little Ellis, so I said in my most cheerful voice, "Okay, let's gather up our things and head on back toward home." I had almost everything back in the bag when a strange man got out of the truck.

"You children okay?" he hollered to us.

"Yessir," I yelled back.

"You got a grown-up with you?" The question sounded dangerous, and I was thinking about as hard as I could of what to say. Because Aunt Bett had talked to me several times about being careful around strangers, now that I was getting pretty grown up.

"You'll be getting a woman's figure soon, Dove," she

had said, shaking her head as if that would be a terrible thing. "So you gotta be careful." Maybe I had frowned, or in some way shown my confusion, because Aunt Bett added in a whisper, "Men." She said the word as if it made a bad taste in her mouth. And now here was a stranger—a man—and him asking if we were alone at the playground.

"You got a grown-up with you?" he repeated, and my scalp went all prickly.

"Our daddy's coming for us any minute," I said. I had the sheet folded across my arm, and I lifted it a little and looked at my arm, as if I had a watch on.

"Oh yes—he'll be here any minute now." And strangely, I almost believed it myself. Almost could see Roy-Ellis's truck coming and Roy-Ellis, big and strong and wearing his cowboy boots and hat, walking up and standing beside us and taking care of us.

The man stared for a long time, and then he said, "Okay. You all want a ride?"

"Nosir . . . No." I changed from my good manners. He got back into his truck, but he took a while to drive away. We stayed right where we were. But I wondered if maybe he would be parked somewhere down the highway, in a place where he would be able to see us walking back home, and then he would know I'd lied—that nobody was coming for us.

All I could seem to think about was our own safe little gray house, and how I wished we were there and not out in a wide open playground with nothing near but a deserted school building.

I had to get us home where we would be safe. But how? *Don't worry, Mama. I'll take good care of Molly and Little*

Ellis. Right at that moment, a huge flock of noisy, black crows flew over our heads and landed in the trees above us. They seemed to tilt their heads and look down at us with black eyes that were lost against their black feathers. Then all at once, they started cawing, over and over again, to each other or to me—I didn't know which. So I just stood still and listened.

"*Caw! Caw!*" they said. And in an instant I knew what they were saying.

"*Caw! Caw!*"

Run! Run!

I handed the storybooks to Molly.

"You carry these. They're not heavy."

I picked Little Ellis up, got him settled on my hip, and said, "We'll go home a better way. C'mon, Molly. Hurry!"

"Not such a long way?" Molly's mouth was in a pout.

"Yes," I lied, not wanting to get her all upset. Because I would not take us all back along the highway, when maybe there was a strange man in a brown truck who would see us and know we didn't have any big, strong daddy coming for us. *Run!* The crows had said. And I meant to do just that. We reached the highway and went in the opposite direction from the way we had come.

"Wrong way!" Molly announced.

"No, Molly. This is the right way. Trust me! Hurry!" Maybe she sensed my fear, because she didn't pull against me again. We went on down the highway—fast—in the wrong direction, until I saw a house across the highway. We crossed over, went through the side yard of the house, and came to a thick stand of trees.

"This is the way," I said, more to give myself confidence than to comfort Molly, and we all stepped into the thick woods. It was slow going, with Molly's shoe coming off and briars catching our clothes, and Little Ellis feeling as heavy as a sack full of bricks. I got Molly's shoe back on, untangled us from the briars, and shifted Little Ellis to my right hip. The muscles in my left arm were quivering from tiredness.

Forward! That's what I kept saying silently. And crazily, I remembered the T-shirt I borrowed at Aunt Bett's on Easter Sunday afternoon. *Forward! Forward!* I thought again, *Mama's big girl!*

On and on, until through the trees off to my right, I could see yet another house. I thought we'd probably gone far enough to cut over and find our dirt road, but far, far away from where it met the highway we'd crossed and also maybe far away from a brown pickup truck that was waiting.

"This way," I said to Molly, and I heard her sniffle.

"What's wrong?" I said, but I was thinking, *What's wrong, besides the fact that maybe I've gotten us lost, and you're hot and tired and scratched by briars, and we don't know where home is, and there's a strange man around somewhere?*

"Go home!" Molly fairly shrieked, and I had to work hard to stop myself from screaming those same words. Instead, I said, "That's what we're doing, Molly," with a rough sound to my voice. I heaved Little Ellis upward from my hip and almost yanked Molly along as I trudged off toward the house I saw through the trees. All of a sudden a dog was barking—so loud and so close! We froze, right where we were.

"Who's out there?" A man's voice. Angry. I opened my mouth, but nothing came out. Little Ellis pressed his face into the side of my neck, and Molly stepped behind me, her arms wrapped around my legs.

"Who's out there?" Louder. Angrier.

"Children, sir!" I yelled back.

"Children?" Still loud. Still angry. "Well, get outta here!"

"Yessir!" I yelled.

"You don't get out, I'll turn the dog loose."

"We're going!" I fairly screamed.

Little Ellis had begun sobbing against my neck, and I moved slowly across the side yard, with Molly still behind me, and as we passed, I saw the man—no shirt, leaning on the back porch banisters. Red face. Big white belly.

"Go on!" he yelled, and I sprinted forward, dragging Molly along. When I thought that we were far enough away from the angry man and his big dog, I stopped and tried to put Little Ellis down for a moment. But he hung on to me in all kinds of ways, and trying to unwrap him was like trying to get rid of a kudzu vine. Little Ellis and I wound up on the ground in a heap, and Molly piled right on top of us.

"It's okay. It's okay," I tried to croon to them. But I was trying hard not to cry. Because Little Ellis was so heavy and Molly was so scared, and I still wasn't sure of where we were. I finally got us all calmed down and sat up, and I found that I was looking through more brambles and trees . . . but through them, I could see a dirt road. Our road? Yes! And for the first time in what seemed like forever, I knew how to get us home.

Our little gray house never looked better than when we came up the steps. We were tired and scratched and hungry, and when we got inside, my first thought was to call Aunt Bett and tell her what happened. But then I would have to tell her that Roy-Ellis wasn't home—hadn't been home. Before I could think it all through, the phone rang. It was Aunt Bett.

"Where's Roy-Ellis?"

"Uh . . . he's gone to bed real early," I said, wanting instead to cry and tell her how scared we had all been. "He's awful tired from working so hard," I added, so now there was no doubt about it. I had lied. Twice. Sure enough!

"And where have you all been all afternoon?" Aunt Bett went on. "I've been calling and calling. Are you all right? I've worried myself half to death!"

"I'm sorry, Aunt Bett. We just went for a walk, is all." Maybe I'd lied flat out about Roy-Ellis, but that didn't mean I had to keep on lying. And after all, we certainly had been for a walk!

"Well, just so you're all okay," Aunt Bett muttered.

"Yessm."

"And did you all change out of your church clothes before you went for a walk?"

"Yessm."

After I got off the phone, I tried so hard to settle myself down, if only for Molly and Little Ellis's sake. But I knew I had to tell someone—anyone—about what happened. It was just bothering me too bad to keep it to myself, but I had to find a way to talk about it without letting Molly and Little Ellis know how scared I'd been. Of course, I wanted most of all to tell Aunt Bett, but I couldn't do that. Not without breaking my word to Roy-Ellis. So who else could I tell? Who could I trust?

Savannah!

But it was a Sunday, and I couldn't talk to her on a Sunday, because all she could do on the *Sabbath* was read the Bible and think about God, even after supper. All the way to bedtime. But I had to find a way—and I did! I got my Bible and led Molly and Little Ellis through the dried weeds under the old pecan trees—toward Aunt Mee's house. As we got closer, I could make out Savannah sitting in a rocking chair on the front porch, with her head bent down and her eyes on the pages of the Bible in her lap. Toward the back of the house, I could hear dishes rattling. Then Molly and Little Ellis and I came—bold as brass!— across Aunt Mee's immaculately swept front yard. Not a blade of grass to blemish its pure, clean surface! Savannah glanced up at us, and then she jerked her head toward the screened door, where Aunt Mee might appear at any moment. Then she bent her head obediently back down to the Bible lying open in her lap. But under her dark brows, her warm, brown eyes were watching us. We came up the steps, and I shushed Molly and Little Ellis, settling them at the end of the porch.

"Now you two be quiet!" I whispered, and I glared at them just a little bit, to let them know how important this was. Savannah was still watching me from beneath her strong-looking eyebrows. I sat down in the rocking chair beside her and flipped my Bible open. The first words I saw were: "Behold, a King shall reign in righteousness, and princes shall rule in judgment." It was Isaiah 32:1. So I read them aloud: "Behold!" I said to Savannah, and she jumped and glanced at the screen door again. "A King shall reign in righteousness, and princes shall rule in judgment. And behold!" I repeated. "A man—a stranger—scared us at the playground today," I continued, in a voice that sounded like I was reading right out of the Bible.

Savannah looked a bit startled for a moment, and then she read back to me, "And the anger of the Lord was hot against Israel; and He said, 'Because that this people hath transgressed my covenant which I commanded their fathers, and have not hearkened unto my voice . . .' and saideth unto them, *'What man?'*"

I flipped a few more pages, and wound up in Jeremiah, and I read aloud: "The voice thereof shall go like a serpent; for they shall march with an army, and come against her with axes, as hewers of wood . . . And thereof, I don't know what man. I telleth thee, he werth a stranger! A scary stranger!"

Aunt Mee loomed large at the screen door to the porch.

"Whatchu children doing?" she demanded.

Savannah and I locked eyes.

"Reading the Bible to each other," Savannah said.

Aunt Mee glanced sharply back and forth between us, and once again, Savannah and I locked eyes. The silence seemed to last forever, while Aunt Mee made her decision about whether we were *observing the Sabbath.*

"Well . . ." she finally growled, "make sure you stay with the Bible."

"Yessm!" Savannah and I said together, and as soon as

she went back inside, we both started flipping through the pages, to try and find a way to say what we needed to say, without dishonoring the Sabbath Day. Savannah read first: "Where there is no vision, the people perish; but he that keepeth the law, happy is he," and right afterward, she said in the same tone, "What man frighteneth thee . . . uh . . . you?" Her eyebrows shot up in expectation. Molly and Little Ellis looked at us as if we were crazy. I flipped the pages again and wound up at Ezekiel, chapter five, verse two: "Thou shalt burn with fire a third part in the midst of the city, when the days of the siege are fulfilled . . ." Then, in the same tone, I said: "A man appeareth at the playground and asketh, 'Have ye-all an adult with ye?'"

Savannah's eyes grew wide, and then she looked down at the Bible in her lap. "What saith ye?"

"I saith . . ." I started. "Yea!"

"Yea . . . yes?" she said. "You meaneth you *lieth?*"

I flipped through some more pages, even though I had started feeling something stinging me behind my eyes. This time, I came to John 16:13, and the printing on those pages was all in red. That meant Jesus Himself was talking. But I took a deep breath and started in: "Howbeit when he, the Spirit of truth is come, he will guide you into all truth . . ." I stumbled to a stop, my breath all choked inside of me, and then I confessed, "Yea, I *lieth!*" Savannah was absolutely silent, but when I finally looked up at her, she had tears in her eyes. She leaned toward me, holding out her hand.

"Don't cry," she whispered.

And I grabbed her hand and held it tight. Such a small hand! Almost like Molly's, but oh, so warm and so welcome. Aunt Mee came to the door again.

"You children better come on inside," she said. "After-noon sun's going to make it too hot out here for you."

"I better take Molly and Little Ellis on home," I said.

"You all are welcome to come on inside," Aunt Mee continued. "But Savannah has to stay with reading her Bible."

"Thanks, but we better go now."

And as I led Molly and Little Ellis through the trees, I made another vow: I would never, ever tell a lie again. Just like loving folks, it hurt too much.

While I bathed Little Ellis and Molly and got them into their pajamas, I made another firm and final decision: I would tell Roy-Ellis about the man in the truck. Just as soon as he came home. The thought of having Roy-Ellis back in the house made me smile. But even though I listened for the sound of Roy-Ellis closing the door to his truck and his footsteps coming across the porch for the whole night, he didn't come home. A few times, I thought I heard something, but it turned out to be nothing except me wishing so hard. Finally, a little bit of daylight came, and Roy-Ellis still was nowhere to be seen. But just after I got into the kitchen to fix Molly and Little Ellis's breakfast, I heard someone on the back porch.

"Roy-Ellis?" I called.

"It's me," Savannah whispered.

"It's way too early!" I said, hoping to take her attention away from my thinking she was Roy-Ellis. Because him being gone was a secret, even from Savannah. But then I thought about it and realized that I'd promised not to tell

Aunt Bett—but I sure hadn't promised anything about not telling Savannah!

"Now tell me about that man scaring you," Savannah said, frowning.

"Listen, Savannah," I started, and the words poured out of me in a mighty flood. "That man doesn't matter. What *does* matter is this: Roy-Ellis hasn't come home, and I don't know where he is, and I promised him I wouldn't tell Aunt Bett, and I'm scared! Suppose he's been in an accident or something?" I tried to keep my voice low, so Molly and Little Ellis wouldn't hear me. Savannah stared right into my eyes the whole time I talked, with her frown growing bigger every minute. "Now don't you say a word about this to Aunt Mee," I cautioned her. "She'd probably tell Aunt Bett and then I would have broken my word."

"Grandmama says that if someone says I shouldn't tell her something, that's the very thing I should do," Savannah said.

"Please, Savannah!" I cried. She studied me for a long moment and then said: "Okay. But sometime or other, you've got to tell your Aunt Bett."

"All right," I agreed. "If he isn't home by tonight, I'll tell her. And don't tell Aunt Mee!" I urged once again.

"I have to go do my chores now," Savannah said, but as she turned to leave, she stopped and looked back at me.

"I'm here," she said simply.

Molly and Little Ellis didn't say anything about Roy-Ellis not being there, because he always left for work before they were awake anyway, and mostly, he got home after they were in bed. But I kept wondering what had happened to him. Maybe he was going to turn out like my own daddy and run off with another woman and never come back again!

When I thought of Aunt Bett, I also thought of what would happen if I broke down and told her about Roy-Ellis being gone. But I told Roy-Ellis it would be our secret, and I meant to keep my word. I had also told Savannah that if he didn't come home by that night, I would tell Aunt Bett. So I still had that one day left to keep my word to Roy-Ellis.

In the afternoon, Savannah came over and we took Little Ellis and Molly on a long walk, but not back around that park where the man scared me so bad. We just walked along a little country dirt road, all of us holding hands, and I kept pretending we'd see Roy-Ellis's truck in the yard when we got back. But it still wasn't there.

"You better talk to your Aunt Bett," Savannah said. "You better tell her about Roy-Ellis being gone." With that, Savannah squeezed my hand and went around the house to go home. I knew Savannah was right, and I was going to call Aunt Bett just as soon as I got Molly and Little Ellis some cold water to drink, after our long walk.

But when I got into the kitchen, everything went out of my mind—because there were two coffee mugs sitting on the table, and I felt all the hairs come up on the back of my neck. Was it the stranger? Was he in the house? Because I knew good and well that the last thing I'd done that morning before we left was to wipe off the oilcloth tablecloth, and there hadn't been a single thing left on that table. I went back through the living room and into our room and looked under the double bed Molly and Little Ellis shared.

And under my cot. Nothing. I went into the bathroom and pulled back the shower curtain. Nothing. I looked in the hall closet. Still nothing. The door to Roy-Ellis's room was closed. I reached out and turned the knob, and the door swung open by itself, like it always did.

Somebody was sleeping in Roy-Ellis's bed, and it sure wasn't Roy-Ellis. Because he didn't have long blond hair! I closed the door without a sound and went and sat at the kitchen table and stared at the coffee mugs for a few minutes. Then I went into the living room and called Aunt Bett. In only a couple of minutes, she came driving up in a shower of gravel and dust. I went out onto the porch and put my finger to my lips. Because Molly and Little Ellis didn't know a thing about somebody being in Roy-Ellis's bed.

Without a word, Aunt Bett and I went through the living room and into the kitchen. I saw Aunt Bett notice the two coffee mugs on the table. Then we walked across the back hall and to the door of Roy-Ellis's room.

Aunt Bett silently waved me back, turned the knob, and once again the door swung open. I glimpsed the same lumpy bedcovers and the long, blond hair spread out across the pillow. Aunt Bett looked for a long time, with her eyes wide and her lips in a grim line. Then she eased the door shut, grabbed my hand, and pulled me into the living room.

"Go pack up some things for you and the little ones," she whispered. "Just enough for tonight and tomorrow. Hurry!" I gathered together our things and when I came back into the living room, Aunt Bett had turned off the TV and was ushering Molly and Little Ellis onto the porch.

When I shut the door, I saw a note taped to it. In big, angry letters, it said: *Have you gone crazy? How DARE you put your harlot in my dead sister's bed?*

We all piled into Aunt Bett's car and drove away in another shower of gravel and dust. "Not a word about this to any of the children, Dove," she warned me, and I could tell that she was trying to make her voice sound soft, so as not to upset Molly and Little Ellis. "Not even to Darlene. You hear me?"

"Yessm." Then I added, "What's a h-a-r-l-o-t?"

"Lord have mercy!" she whispered viciously. So I didn't ask again.

Aunt Bett wouldn't let me or Darlene help her get supper ready. She stormed around the kitchen, slamming pots and pans, and once, Darlene and I—from our own safe place in the hallway peeking around the doorway—saw Aunt Bett throw a wooden spoon all the way across the kitchen. Darlene looked at me with the strangest kind of face I had ever seen.

"What's she so mad about?" Darlene whispered. I think I would probably have told her right then and there, despite Aunt Bett's warning, except that I wasn't so sure myself.

"What's a h-a-r-l-o-t?" I whispered back. But Darlene shrugged her shoulders. "I don't know." Aunt Bett drained the boiled potatoes and threw the colander into the sink *hard,* and while she mashed and mashed the potatoes, she yelled things like:

"Gather not my soul with sinners, nor my life with bloody men!" And . . .

"Fret not thyself because of evildoers, neither be thou

envious against the workers of iniquity! For they shall soon be cut down like the grass, and wither as the green herb!" And . . .

"The arms of the wicked shall be broken: but the lord upholdeth the righteous!" And at the last . . .

"God shall destroy thee for ever, He shall take thee away, and pluck thee out of thy dwelling place, and root thee out of the land of the living!"

Why, it was simply magnificent, the way she roared out the terrible words—especially *pluck!* and *root thee out!* and I made myself a promise, right then and there, that I would memorize more of the Bible, so that if I ever got as mad as Aunt Bett was, I could roar out great, wonderful, terrible words like that! Darlene and I tiptoed back into the living room and sat with the silent children. Our eyes went wide every time another stream of holy words erupted and another spoon or pan or something went *smack* against the sink or the wall or the floor. But gradually, the noise got less, and the sounds finally were only those of someone working in a kitchen to fix supper. Once things got that quiet, Darlene and I tiptocd into the dining room and set the table. Then we went back into the living room and waited. Finally, Aunt Bett came through the swinging door, and we all jumped a little, but she was simply carrying two big bowls that she put down on the table very gently. She didn't look at any of us. The next time, she carried in a big platter of ground beef patties and a smaller platter of sliced tomatoes. These, she placed on the table equally as gently.

"Darlene, will you and Dove please get the extra chairs? All you children come on to the table." When Darlene and

I went into the kitchen to get the chairs, we could hardly believe our eyes! There were blobs of mashed potatoes on the refrigerator door and strange-looking green smears on the floor. The dented colander rested crazily in the sink, and a whole bunch of cooking spoons were scattered around the floor. We got the kitchen chairs and took them into the dining room, where Aunt Bett and the children were all sitting silently, staring at their empty plates, and we sat down too.

"I'll say the blessing," Aunt Bett whispered. We held hands and bowed our heads, but I expect that all of us were ready to bolt out of the way at any minute, if we needed to.

"Bless this food to our bodies and us to Thy service. Amen."

Why, her voice was the sweetest-sounding I've ever heard, and we all started passing around the platters and bowls and serving ourselves. Those were the most whipped-up potatoes I ever saw, but they were certainly nice and fluffy. When the bowl of English peas came around, we were all surprised—because the peas were all whipped to death, as well. None of us dared to refuse a serving, but we waited for someone else to taste that strange-looking mess. When the bowl of whipped peas got to Aunt Bett, she put a big spoonful on her plate and didn't even seem to notice what kind of shape those peas were in. She put a forkful in her mouth and her face never changed. She remained quiet and cool, and somehow carved out of a strong, very, very cold piece of stone.

While I ate, I wondered what to do. Maybe Roy-Ellis didn't have a thing in this world to do with whoever was sleeping in his bed. Maybe Roy-Ellis was sick somewhere or had an accident. How long should I wait until I told Aunt Bett about him being gone for so long? Well, at least until she didn't look so rigid, that was for sure. Then, just as we were finishing up our supper, there came a quiet knock on the front door. Aunt Bett's head flew up and red streaks started coming up the side of her neck.

"Children, go into the bedroom."

She didn't have to say it twice. We cleared the room like maybe there was a bomb going to explode any minute! Even the little ones must have just felt that something dangerous was getting ready to happen. When we were all in the bedroom, we heard Aunt Bett call out in a dead-sounding voice, "Come in."

Darlene and I opened the bedroom door just a tiny bit and watched through the narrow crack as Roy-Ellis came into the room. I was so glad to see him safe and sound, I almost ran to him. But then I remembered about someone being in his bed. And besides, Roy-Ellis was walking like he was crawling on his knees.

"How dare you!" Aunt Bett's voice was low, almost like a growl.

"Bett, please," Roy-Ellis's voice was hoarse. "Please listen. She ain't no har-let."

"Har*lot*!" Aunt Bett corrected him, her voice rising. Darlene and I glanced at each other and shrugged our shoulders.

"Okay—she ain't no har*lot*, Bett. She's my *wife*."

I guess in all this world there has never been such a silence as that one. It just went on and on, with Roy-Ellis standing with his hands held out, palms up, and Aunt Bett with her face as white as those beaten-up potatoes, and her eyes and hanging-open mouth just three dark circles in her face. Darlene and I were frozen in place, and we couldn't even shut that little crack in the door because I guess we both felt that the least little thing could make the whole picture of what was happening begin to crack and crumble, and finally it—and we—would be nothing but a pile of dust. Finally, after ever so long, Aunt Bett let out her breath and turned her face away.

"Your *wife?*" she breathed.

Roy-Ellis let his hands drop to his side.

"Yes."

"But what about . . . ?"

"I loved her with all my heart. You know that. But . . ."

"But what?" Aunt Bett whispered.

"Until death do us part. Even in *your* church, Bett, a man can take another wife when he's lost the one he had."

"But . . . so soon?"

"Bett, I've tried to show proper respect." Roy-Ellis looked down at his boots. "I will always show the proper respect," he added. Then he brightened. "Bett, why don't you and the children come on and meet her," he said. "You'll like her. She's young, but she's the sweetest little thing you've ever seen."

"I . . ." Aunt Bett didn't seem to know what to say.

"Come on, Bett," Roy-Ellis coaxed. "Come on and see for yourself."

Aunt Bett was struggling with herself, I could tell. Because she'd start to stand up and then plop right back down in her chair. Maybe the struggle was between being mad at Roy-Ellis and wanting to check out his new wife for herself.

"You need to talk to your children first," she said at last. So Darlene and I closed the door without a sound and ran and sat on the beds beside the children. Aunt Bett opened the door.

"My children come on out here. Roy-Ellis's children, stay put."

As Aunt Bett's children filed out of the room, she said, "Darlene, you and Cassandra get into the kitchen and help me clean up. It's a mess, and I won't have that."

"But . . ." Darlene started to say something, probably about how Aunt Bett herself was the one who had made the mess.

"Don't you talk back to me," Aunt Bett warned. So Darlene closed her mouth and followed Aunt Bett into the kitchen. Roy-Ellis came into the bedroom where Molly and Little Ellis and I were waiting and stood before us, with his hands deep in his pockets. He cleared his throat.

"I loved you all's mama more than anything in this world," he started and cleared his throat again. "And when she started getting so sick, she made me promise I'd take good care of you. And I always will."

Molly said, "Mama go to Jesus."

"Yeah, honey. I know." Once again, Roy-Ellis cleared his throat.

"I met Crystal at Across the Line, and I fell in love with her. And I talked to your mama about her."

"You did *what?*" My voice sounded a lot like Aunt Bett's. "You met her while Mama was still alive?"

"No, Dove. No, honey. I know your mama's gone, but I still talk to her because I still love her. I always will."

"Oh."

"But seems to me your mama would say that if she wasn't around to take care of you all and me and to love us all, she would want some kind, loving person to do that for her. That's Crystal."

"That's her name?" I asked.

"Yes," Roy-Ellis said in the softest voice I ever heard him use. "And I want you all to come home with me now and meet her. You'll like her. I promise."

"Okay!" Molly hopped down off the bed and took Roy-Ellis's hand. I got Little Ellis and we followed them out of the bedroom.

"Bett? You ready?" Roy-Ellis called, and Aunt Bett came out of the kitchen, taking off her apron and pausing before the mirror in the dining room to pat her hair into place.

"I still don't know how I feel about all this, Roy-Ellis," she said. "I just don't know how I feel. You and this . . . woman . . . get married in a church?"

"Justice of the Peace," Roy-Ellis admitted. "But it's legal, Bett."

"I know. I know," she muttered. So we rode with Aunt Bett and followed Roy-Ellis's truck down the road to our very own house. A house with a strange woman in it.

When we went into the house, everything felt completely different. Even though it all looked the same, except for those two mugs I expected were still sitting on the kitchen table. But it all felt so different. Aunt Bett stood by the front door, like maybe she would need to leave in a hurry. Roy-Ellis grinned and motioned to us to stay where we were. Still grinning, he backed into the hallway and hollered over his shoulder, "Crystal? Sugar? Come on out here for a little minute."

Well, at least he hadn't called her darling. That was my mama's word, and I didn't like him using it for anybody else.

"Come on, sugar," he called again. Then he looked toward the bedroom, and his face broke into the biggest grin of all.

"Here she comes!" he announced joyously.

A slender, short girl with long blond hair came out, tying the belt of a pink terry cloth robe. Yes, just a *girl!* About my height and my size, but a little bit older than me. With electric blue eyes and a soft mouth. Roy-Ellis clamped his strong arm around her shoulders and hugged her to him. Her head bounced against him, right about at the level of his heart.

"Bett, this here is Crystal. Sugar, this is Bett."

"Hi," Crystal said, smiling shyly and waving her fingers at Aunt Bett.

"How do you do," Aunt Bett said in a flat voice, separating the words like beads on a string. And she didn't make it a question at all. Just words you say to be polite but that you don't mean. But Aunt Bett wasn't a lady who meant to lose all her manners—at least not in front of a stranger—so she smiled. But only a tight little upturn at the corners of her mouth. Not a real smile, one that would have come from her eyes as well. And she held her nostrils kind of pinched together, like something smelled a little bit bad. But then, all of a sudden, Aunt Bett couldn't hold it in any longer.

"My Lord, Roy-Ellis! She's a *child!*" Her voice sounded

like a hissing cat.

"Well, I told you she was young," Roy-Ellis tried to defend himself, grinning even more.

"How old are you?" Aunt Bett asked Crystal point-blank. Squinting her eyes and tilting her head to the side.

"I'm eighteen," Crystal answered, glancing up at Roy-Ellis.

"And, Crystal," Roy-Ellis said, "these are my children."

Crystal's eyes grew wide and that soft little mouth fell open.

"Your *children?*"

"Yeah, sugar."

"Roy-Ellis! You didn't tell me you had children!"

Aunt Bett's eyebrows shot up almost to the top of her head.

"Well, everything between us happened so fast, sugar." Roy-Ellis tried to make an excuse. And I don't think Roy-Ellis meant to fool Crystal at all. I think that maybe once he got to looking into those electric blue eyes, he forgot he had children at all.

But Crystal broke into a big laugh and her eyes sparkled.

"Children!" she laughed, and her delight was right there for all of us to see.

"Well, introduce us, sweetie," she said, taking Roy-Ellis's hand and coming toward us. Molly ducked behind me.

"This is Dove."

The blue eyes were almost level with my own.

"What a beautiful name," she breathed. "Hello, Dove." The small hand with perfectly manicured nails reached out, and I took that hand in mine. It was surprisingly warm and soft.

"And hiding behind Dove is Molly."

"Hi, Molly," Crystal cooed, but she didn't try to make Molly come out.

"And this is Little Ellis." Roy-Ellis's voice took on a prideful sound.

Crystal kneeled down in front of Little Ellis and cupped one of those small, warm hands under his chin.

"Hi, sweet baby."

Aunt Bett cleared her throat. "I better get on home," she said. "The children made a terrible mess of my kitchen tonight." Aunt Bett shot a glance at me that said: Not a word! And I nodded a silent yessm.

"Thanks for coming," Crystal said, standing up and holding out her hand. Aunt Bett took hold of the tips of Crystal's fingers.

"I'm just down the road, if you all need me," Aunt Bett said. Then she shot a final, fierce glance at me as she left.

The rest of that unusual evening was strangely usual. I bathed Molly and Little Ellis and put them to bed. Then I sat at the kitchen table, writing in my notebooks, while Roy-Ellis and Crystal sat on the couch in the living room, watching TV and holding hands. Sometimes they said things to each other, but I didn't hear what they said. When I was done with my writing, I went out onto the back porch and put a load of clothes into the washing machine, like I usually did.

"P-s-s-t!"

The sound came from the bushes along the side of the porch, and I saw Savannah's face wreathed in a big smile.

"I'm glad Roy-Ellis got home safe and sound," she said. And when I went to answer her, she suddenly disappeared. Behind me, Crystal had come out on the porch.

"Thanks, Dove," she said. "I'll put the clothes in the dryer first thing in the morning and fold them when they're done."

"Sheets get dried on the clothesline," I said. And then I looked at her, at that pretty girl, and I wondered how on earth I could ever—in a million years—think of her as my new mama. But she must have been able to see what I was thinking, because she said, "I won't try to take your mama's place. I know how much you all loved her. And still do. But I'll tell you this: All my life, what I wanted most in this world was sisters and brothers, and I never had any. Until now. So maybe if you all just think of me as a big sister, it will feel better."

"Thanks, Crystal," I managed to mumble. "We all just need some time, I guess." But what she said about being a big sister certainly did make me feel better. I glanced once again into those lovely eyes. "It'll be okay."

Several times during that night, I heard Crystal giggle, far down the hall and behind the closed door of Roy-Ellis's room. After a while, I decided that Crystal must be the most ticklish person who ever lived.

And I smiled and went back to sleep.

Chapter Seven

THE next morning, as soon as I went into the kitchen, I heard Savannah's *p-s-s-t!* from the bushes. I went out onto the back porch.

"What are you doing here so early?" I whispered.

"I wanta know what's going on around here," Savannah answered. "Where was Roy-Ellis all that time you were worried about him, and most of all, who's that strange girl I saw in you all's kitchen yesterday evening?"

"You aren't going to believe it!" I whispered back. Then I reached around and closed the kitchen door so nobody could hear us. Savannah came up onto the back steps and I went out and sat down beside her.

"So who is she?" Savannah insisted.

"She's Roy-Ellis's new wife!"

"What?"

"Yes. He's gone and gotten married."

"His *wife?*" Seemed like now it was Savannah's turn to sound like Aunt Bett. "But she doesn't look any older than you!"

"She's a little bit older, but not much," I agreed. "But you know, she seems right nice. I hope you'll come over on Saturday and meet her."

"I don't know about that," Savannah whispered.

"Please, Savannah!"

"I'll try," she said. And then she added, "Do you have to call her 'Mama'?"

"No. She said we could be more like sisters to each other."

"Well, that's good. I wouldn't ever want to call any other woman 'Mama' except for my real one. It's a special word."

"Yes."

We both stood up and just looked at each other for a long moment.

"You just never do know what's going to happen, do you?" Savannah's question didn't seem to need an answer. She waved her hand at me and walked off under the pecan trees, and I went back into the kitchen to fix Molly and Little Ellis's breakfast. But after they had eaten and we'd all gotten dressed, I wasn't sure about whether I should wake Crystal up or not. I mean, maybe she had a job she should be going to. I'd heard Roy-Ellis leave for work before good daylight, and I just didn't know what to do. So I called Aunt Bett.

"I'm wondering if I should wake Crystal up," I said.

"Why, I really don't know what to tell you, Dove," she said finally. "Does Crystal have a job?"

"I don't know," I admitted. "Maybe I should wake her up and ask."

"Roy-Ellis has already gone to work, and she's still in bed?" I could hear a slight note of disapproval in Aunt Bett's question.

"Yessm."

"Well, since we don't really know what to do, let's just stick with how we've been doing things before *she* ever came around." Again, a note of disapproval.

"Yessm."

"Besides," she added. "The children don't even know her, so I wouldn't be in a hurry to wake her up." Aunt Bett added a little *humph*. Definitely disapproval this time.

"Yessm."

"Why don't you get Molly and Little Ellis and come on down to my house for a little while?"

"Yessm."

"But leave her a note so she'll know you all are all right."

"Yessm."

While Molly and Little Ellis ate their cereal, I wrote a note to Crystal.

"Dear Crystal," I started, in my very best handwriting. "I don't know if you work, so I hope it's okay for you to sleep late. I have taken Molly and Little Ellis down to visit with Aunt Bett." I added the phone number and started to sign it, "Love, Dove." But I didn't. For one thing, I hate the way those words rhyme. Makes it sound like a silly joke. And too, I didn't love Crystal. I didn't even know her, even though she seemed to be nice. But no matter how nice she turned out to be, I wasn't going to love her—ever! Finally, I just signed my name. While Molly and Little Ellis got themselves dressed, I washed the dishes and wiped off the table. Still no Crystal. So if she did have a job to go to, she was going to be late, sure enough. Still, I didn't think it was my place to wake her up.

When we came walking up to Aunt Bett's, she was standing out on the porch, waiting for us.

"Take the children inside and then you come back out here," she ordered. I wondered if maybe she was going to tell me she was sorry for blaming the mess in her kitchen last night on her own children like she did in front of Roy-Ellis and Crystal. But when I came back out on the porch, she was leaning against the porch post, looking out across the empty field and with her arms crossed over each other. Nothing in that to say she was sorry.

"You learn anything else about *her?*" she asked. I thought for a long moment.

"She's going to put the clothes in the dryer this morning," I said. "And she says she wants to be more like a big sister than a mama."

"Humph!" Aunt Bett muttered. "Might as well be, since she's only a few years older than you all." I didn't say anything, but I was thinking that Crystal was about fifteen or so years older than Little Ellis, and I didn't think that was just "a few."

"And I hope to Heavens she doesn't dry those clothes on high heat," Aunt Bett added. "That will wear them out faster than anything."

"Oh," I suddenly remembered. "She's awful ticklish."

"Ticklish?" Aunt Bett asked, surprised.

"Yessm."

"How do you know that? Did she tell you?"

"No ma'am. Just I heard her doing a lot of giggling. After we all went to bed."

"Lord have mercy!" Aunt Bett put her hand over her heart.

Then, "Lord have mercy!" she said again.

It was almost eleven o'clock when Crystal finally called.

With a frosty voice, Aunt Bett told her how to find her house, and Crystal said she would come down just as soon as she had a shower. When Aunt Bett hung up the phone, she muttered "Sleeping half the day away!"

under her breath.

When Crystal finally came, she was wearing a pink T-shirt and the shortest shorts I've ever seen anybody wear. She was all pink and good-smelling, and she had her long, blond hair in a ponytail and tied with a ribbon. Aunt Bett surveyed the short shorts, and her nostrils flared out a bit, but she held her tongue.

After Crystal had been introduced to all Aunt Bett's children, we went into the kitchen and Aunt Bett poured coffee for herself and Crystal. She didn't pour anything for me, so I took that to mean Aunt Bett wanted some private time with Crystal. I hoped Aunt Bett would try to be polite, because I was thinking about how Crystal hadn't tried to coax Molly out from behind me and how she had cupped Little Ellis's chin, and her little, warm hand.

After a long, long time, they came out of the kitchen, and Aunt Bett's mouth looked a little more relaxed, or something like that. When Crystal was ready to leave, she said to Molly and Little Ellis, "You all want to come on home with me?" Molly and Little Ellis looked at me.

"It's okay," I assured them. Then Aunt Bett said, "Dove, honey, why don't you stay here for a while and help me and Darlene with some big loads of laundry?"

I saw Aunt Bett and Crystal glance at each other. "Give Crystal here a chance to get to know the children."

"Yessm."

"And give you a chance to do something other than taking care of them all the time," Aunt Bett added. And I thought that was funny, because I'd whole lot rather take care of Molly and Little Ellis than to help Aunt Bett and Darlene with laundry. But I didn't say anything. Maybe it was a good idea to let Crystal and Molly and Little Ellis get to know each other.

So I stayed at Aunt Bett's house almost the whole day, and after we got all that laundry done, Aunt Bett gave me and Darlene some change, and we walked all the way into town and bought us some Popsicles. It was late in the afternoon when we came back, and I went on home to see how things had gone with Crystal and the little ones.

I didn't even get into our front yard when I could hear Molly and Little Ellis shrieking from inside the house. I raced across the yard, leaped up the steps, and threw open the door. Crystal was on the couch, with Little Ellis and Molly sitting on her stomach, and she was tickling and tickling them, while they shrieked and yelped and laughed and gasped for air.

When Crystal saw me, she stopped tickling them and lifted first Little Ellis and then Molly off her stomach and stood them on the floor. Crystal's hair was hanging in her face and her cheeks were bright pink.

"Oh, Dove," she started out, and I was surprised to see that she was close to crying.

"What's wrong?"

"I'm so glad you're home! I didn't know how hard it is to take care of children!" She swept her hand around the room. Toys and books were everywhere, and soft drink cans on the coffee table—one of them spilled—and the slipcovers on the chair halfway pulled off. Molly and Little Ellis stared up at me. Their cheeks were as red as Crystal's.

"What happened?" I asked.

"We played," Crystal answered simply.

"You played?"

"We played," she repeated. "All day long, we played."

"All day long?"

"Yes. This whole long day," Crystal said, and there was a tone in her voice that added, *Isn't that what you're supposed to do with children?* "And I haven't gotten the laundry done or the lunch dishes washed or tried to fix anything for supper. And Roy-Ellis will be home soon! How on earth did you do it, Dove?"

"Do what?"

"Everything. Do just everything *and* take care of the children?"

"I don't know, Crystal," I answered honestly. "I just did it." Then I got to thinking about Crystal believing she was supposed to play with them all day long, so I asked, "What did you all do today? Can you tell me every little bit?"

Crystal heaved a sigh and started counting on her fingers: "Well, we got home from Aunt Bett's; we played hide-and-seek; we played dolls . . ." Crystal glanced at Molly. "And then we played trucks." Molly and Little Ellis climbed up in the wrecked-slipcover chair and sat quietly, watching us and listening to Crystal.

"Then we played tea-party, and we ate lunch, and we played hide-and-seek some more, and then we played 'tickle,' and then you came home." Crystal sniffed and rubbed her forehead.

"What about naps?"

"Naps?"

We looked over at Molly and Little Ellis. They were sound asleep in the chair, flung over each other like poor, dead kittens.

"Oh, Crystal," I breathed. "What a day you've had!" She sighed and nodded, picking up the soft drink cans and trying to push the hair out of her face.

"I'll help you," I whispered, so as not to wake up the children. I picked up toys while Crystal washed the lunch dishes. Together, Crystal and I carried Little Ellis and Molly into their room and put them on the bed. Then we straightened the slipcovers.

The living room looked right nice, and so did the kitchen. I looked at the clock. Almost time for Roy-Ellis. So I said to Crystal, "You go fix yourself up a little. I'll get supper started." She gave me a look of complete gratitude, and when she had gone into the bedroom, I smiled as I started making grilled cheese sandwiches and tomato soup. Poor Crystal. Poor Molly and Little Ellis. Well, I would have to write down their schedule for her; that's all it would take to fix things. Just write it all down, including nap-time and television time and reading time. And I would make sure Crystal knew Molly and Little Ellis were content to play in their own room and not have somebody entertain or play with them all the time. And that she could tell them what they were to do, and they would do it.

Poor Crystal!

When Roy-Ellis got home from work, he hugged Crystal and whirled her around and laughed. And she sure did look pretty, wearing a fresh blue blouse and with her hair fixed and her lipstick on. Then Roy-Ellis patted my head before he went into the bathroom and took a shower. He came out of the bedroom a little later wearing clean clothes and smelling of soap and aftershave.

"You all going out?" I asked, when I saw how cleaned-up Roy-Ellis was.

"Nope. Don't think so," he answered. "I just want to keep my little bride happy." Crystal smiled and blushed.

"Come on to supper, honey," she said.

But when Roy-Ellis saw what was on the table, he said, "Tomato soup and grilled cheese? Shucks, Crystal—Dove here can cook *that*."

Crystal put her hand on her hip and looked Roy-Ellis straight in the eye. "Dove here *did* cook that."

Roy-Ellis turned red and mumbled something we couldn't figure out, and he sat down at the table and ate his supper, without another word of complaint. And that evening, while Roy-Ellis and Crystal sat on the couch, holding hands and watching television, I sat at the table and wrote out a schedule for Crystal. And then I wrote in my notebook and for the first time, I didn't write about Mama. I wrote about Crystal and the first day she took care of children.

The next morning, I was surprised to find Savannah sitting on our back steps. And once again, I was struck by how little and quiet she seemed to be, sitting there with her chin resting in her hands.

"Hi, Savannah," I said, and when she turned her face toward me, I could tell that something was terribly wrong.

"What is it?" I whispered.

She heaved a deep sigh and said, "I'm going away this morning."

"Going away? Going away to *where?*"

"To my Aunt Vera's. In Atlanta. I'm gonna live with her for a while."

I sat down on the steps beside Savannah and pulled her head onto my shoulder.

"I will miss you!" I whispered.

"Maybe we could write letters to each other," she whispered back.

"It won't be the same as seeing you every day," I said, trying to keep my voice steady and already trying not to think about how much I would miss her. Miss everything about her.

"But at least it would be *something*," she said. I felt myself beginning to cave in, somewhere near my stomach, and I knew that if I started crying, it would break Savannah's heart—and mine, as well.

"We'll write!" I said the words enthusiastically, as if that was the most wonderful suggestion anyone had ever made to me. "That's perfect!" Savannah seemed to brighten a little, and once again, I was comforted by my own words in some strange way. I hugged her tight, and I thought my heart would surely break, but I managed to smile. I *had* to smile. For her. And for me.

Savannah!

Chapter Eight

THAT afternoon, I took Molly and Little Ellis on a long walk, because Crystal said she wanted to cook a special supper for Roy-Ellis, and she always got nervous when anyone was around to watch her trying to cook. Of course, taking that walk without Savannah along was hard, but while we walked, I simply pretended that she was right there beside me, and once, I was almost positive that I heard her laugh.

When we all came back home, the first thing I asked was, "What's that smells so good?"

Crystal laughed. "That's the only thing I know how to cook," she said. "Fried chicken!"

Well, I sure wondered what was going to happen when Roy-Ellis got home and found *that* on the table. He finally came home from work, and—as usual now—went in and took a shower and put on clean clothes before he came to the table. When he saw the big platter piled high with golden brown chicken, he went a little pale and stared at Crystal for a moment. But he said not a single word, drank two beers, and ate three pieces of chicken. While Crystal cleaned up the kitchen, I bathed Molly and Little Ellis and put them to bed. Then, as usual, Crystal and Roy-Ellis sat on the couch, holding hands and sometimes resting their heads on one another and watching television. I sat at the table, writing in my notebook. That time, I wrote about Savannah, and it helped me to feel better.

"You doing homework in the summertime?" Roy-Ellis asked from the living room.

"Not really. I just like writing about things."

"Well, okay then. Just don't forget to have you some fun once in a while," he said.

The next night, when Roy-Ellis came home, he was carrying two big bags of groceries. I was standing at the stove, stirring the macaroni and cheese, and Crystal was emptying canned applesauce into a bowl.

"I thought maybe we could try some new things," he said to Crystal. "You aren't frying more chicken for tonight, are you?"

"No," Crystal answered. "But if that's what you want, I can fix it for you."

Roy-Ellis swallowed and peered into the pot I was stirring. "Macaroni and cheese is good!" He was obviously relieved and began unloading groceries onto the counter. Hot dogs, a big package—"Family Size"—of ground beef, a package of eight pork chops, a big bag of rice, a bag of potatoes, another bag of frozen green beans, and two six-packs of beer.

"Beer's mine," he said. "Rest of it's for cooking." Crystal looked at everything he had brought, and then she picked up the package of pork chops and frowned at it.

"I don't know what to do with this," she mumbled, looking at me.

"Me neither," I admitted. We both looked at Roy-Ellis.

"Ask Bett," he said simply.

As if Aunt Bett could hear what Roy-Ellis said, the phone rang right at that instant. Roy-Ellis answered it.

"Sure, Bett. That'll be nice. Looking forward to it. Okay. Bye." He hung up the phone.

"Bett?" Crystal asked.

"Yeah. She's bringing us some cornbread Saturday morning."

"Oh," Crystal breathed, and she glanced around at the piled-high trash can and the dishes in the sink, and the sticky fingerprints Molly had left on the cabinet door. But I just looked at Crystal and smiled and nodded.

When the dishes were done, Crystal and I said not a

word, but I took the kitchen trash can and emptied it into the big can on the back porch, while Crystal started scrubbing the fingerprints off the cabinet.

"Dove?" Roy-Ellis called from the living room. "Would you bring me a beer, sweetie?" I took him his beer, and then I pushed the other bottles in the refrigerator all the way to the back and piled the packages of pork chops and hot dogs in front of them. Crystal scrubbed down the sink, and I wiped off the table.

"Crystal?" Roy-Ellis called. "You gonna come keep me company? I'm getting awful lonesome in here all by myself."

"In a minute, honey," Crystal sang back to him.

"You go on," I urged. "I'll finish up." I was glad to be able to help Crystal, because I certainly knew what it felt like to have Aunt Bett glancing around our house, this way and that, and—without saying a single word—maybe letting us know that we weren't doing our housekeeping right. Crystal sat with Roy-Ellis on the couch, with her head on his shoulder. And the reflected light from the television swept back and forth across their contented faces. The last thing I did in the kitchen was to put two clean, folded dish towels on the towel holder over the sink. And that little kitchen sure did look pretty and shiny when I turned out the light and went into the dining room to write in my notebook.

"Homework during the summer, Dove?" Roy-Ellis called to me, like maybe he'd forgotten asking that before.

"Nosir, just something I like doing," I called back.

"Well, don't forget what I said about having you a

little fun, honey."

"Yessir."

The next morning, Crystal came out of the bedroom with pink curlers in her hair, and as soon as we'd all finished our cereal, I settled Molly and Little Ellis in the living room with their coloring books and crayons, and Crystal and I did the dishes, dried and put them away, wiped down the table and the sink, and nodded at each other. Why, that kitchen was absolutely spotless! And for drying the dishes, I had used another towel and hung it on the back porch, so as to leave the two pretty ones still clean and dry.

It was one of Roy-Ellis's rare days off, and he went outside to work on the clutch on his truck. Crystal combed out her pretty hair and put it into a neat ponytail, and I sat down at the dining table to write in my notebook. Crystal paced around a little, wiping invisible dust off the coffee table and straightening the slipcovers, even though they weren't messed up one bit. She sauntered back into the dining room.

"*More* work, Dove?" she asked, trying not to look toward the porch, where—any minute!—Aunt Bett could arrive.

"No, not really," I answered, putting down my pen. Because I was mostly too nervous to write anyway—what with wondering if Aunt Bett would think we were doing a good job of housekeeping.

"Not really?" Crystal asked.

"I'm writing a story," I said.

"You are? Why that's wonderful!" Crystal was truly happy about that. And I knew what was coming next and dreaded it.

"What's it about?"

I hesitated.

"Mostly, it's about my mama," I said. But I quickly added, "I've already written one story about you, too. And one about Savannah."

"Oh?" She turned bright red. "You've written a story about *me?*" But before we could say another word, there she was—Aunt Bett—knocking lightly on the screen door, peering in as if she were already looking the place over, and with that kind of a plastic smile she could sometimes get on her face.

"Oh, Lord have mercy on us!" Crystal whimpered.

"Come on in, Aunt Bett," I hollered, nodding at Crystal. *It'll be okay.*

Aunt Bett opened the squeaky screen door and came in hesitantly, carrying a big aluminum pan all wrapped in foil—the cornbread. Her sweet, well-meaning ticket into our house. When I saw her, all I could think about was mean old Michelle making fun of her, and so I ran to her and gave her a big hug.

"Dove?" she said, struggling a little against my hearty hug. I loosened up on her and stood back. Aunt Bett blushed and waved the back of her hand at me. Crystal was still standing in the dining room, as stiff as a statue. I grabbed Aunt Bett's hand and pulled her into the dining room, but it was like dragging a wagon full of rocks.

"Look who's here!" I chirped to Crystal, as if we hadn't been expecting Aunt Bett at all, and we hadn't been scrubbing things half to death.

"Hi, Aunt Bett!" Crystal's voice was way too bright.

And the next thing Crystal said was, "Roy-Ellis brought home some nice pork chops, and me and Dove . . ." She shot a strange glance at me. "Why, we just don't know how to fix them. How to cook them." Aunt Bett brightened on the spot. She thrust the pan of cornbread at me and almost sprinted toward the kitchen, with me and Crystal right behind her, smiling to each other and making okay! signs with our fingers.

"Show me those pork chops," she ordered. "And start some water to boiling. And do you have rice? And some fresh tomatoes? And onions? Get me a dutch oven."

Why I never saw anything like that in my whole life. Aunt Bett came alive, right in front of my eyes. Lost all her timid ways and her plastic smile and got to be a real person again. Crystal got the pork chops out of the refrigerator, I dug around in the cabinets and found the dutch oven, and I got that big bag of rice Roy-Ellis had brought home.

"Tomatoes!" Aunt Bett demanded.

"Onions!" she ordered. Then, right out of the blue, she said to Crystal, "I hope you don't dry clothes on the high setting." Crystal was taken completely by surprise.

"No ma'am," she finally said. "Mama said that wears clothes out too fast."

"Good," Aunt Bett pronounced. Then, "Apron!" she commanded.

And when everything was assembled, and Aunt Bett had one of my mama's skinny little aprons tied across the front of her vast waist, she began showing us what to do with those pork chops. By the time she was done, there was a wonderful-smelling pork chop and rice casserole simmering away. "Now just let it cook nice and slow." We all stood there in front of the stove, looking at the dutch oven with that heavy lid on it, and maybe we were thinking the same thing: It had something in it that we had all made, together.

"Would you like a cup of coffee, Aunt Bett?" Crystal floated the words out into the steamy air.

"That would be nice," Aunt Bett said. "And I'll stay long enough to look at the casserole and see when it's ready to finish cooking with the lid off." Aunt Bett sat down at the kitchen table, fanning herself with her hand and with her cheeks bright red, like they always got when she was cooking. I sat down too, while Crystal made Aunt Bett's cup of instant coffee. Crystal put the cup in front of Aunt Bett and a glass of milk in front of me, and then she sat down with us, with her own glass of milk. Aunt Bett and I both looked at Crystal's glass of milk, and somehow, I was wishing Crystal had made herself a cup of coffee. But it was too late. Aunt Bett was studying Crystal's face, like she was looking for something familiar in it. Like she was trying to see Crystal as another child in the family. But of course, there wasn't anything for her to see—no eyebrows like Aunt Bett's own mama, no slant of a jaw to remind Aunt Bett of herself. Nothing in which she could see a trace of what she would call *us*. She let her eyes drop. And what came down over that table with us sitting at it was . . . just a big, fat *nothing*. Crystal and Aunt Bett were both studying the oil-cloth tablecloth, and at last, so did I, looking at the printed-on little green teapots and faded pink flowers.

"How old are you really?" Aunt Bett asked so low that I almost didn't hear her.

"Ma'am?" Crystal frowned.

"I said how old are you *really*." Aunt Bett was still studying the printed figures on the tablecloth, tracing the edges of one with her finger.

"Old enough to be legally married," Crystal said.

Aunt Bett looked up at Crystal and waited.

"I'm seventeen," Crystal said, at last.

"You're just a child," Aunt Bett stated, her voice gone softer. Because if there was anything Aunt Bett couldn't resist, it was a child. Any child. Even a child who had no resemblance to any kinfolk of ours.

"Well, yessm, I guess that's right." The screen door to the front porch squeaked open, and Roy-Ellis's booming voice came rolling into the silent kitchen.

"Whooo-eee! Something sure smells good in here!" And when Roy-Ellis loomed in the kitchen doorway with grease all over his T-shirt and hands, we all looked at him.

"What's going on?" he grinned.

"Oh, Aunt Bett's helping me and Dove fix some good pork chops," Crystal sputtered.

"Good!" Roy-Ellis boomed. "Bett here is the best cook in the world!"

"Crystal will learn, Roy-Ellis. You just give her some time." Bett's face was dead serious. "Don't you be impatient with her," she warned.

"I won't," Roy-Ellis's voice was just as serious as Aunt Bett's had been. "I promise."

"You've always been a good man," she said. Then she must have remembered about his beer-drinking, because she added, "Mostly."

"Thank you, Bett."

"Well, I better go," she said. "In about forty-five minutes, you can take the lid off and let the rest of the liquid steam off a little bit. And heat up that cornbread in the oven."

We did everything just the way Aunt Bett said, and what a good dinner we had. Even Little Ellis ate everything on his plate and held it out for more. At the last, Roy-Ellis pushed back his chair and patted his stomach.

"That was real good," he pronounced. "If you all can remember what Aunt Bett said to do, I'll bring home more pork chops."

"We can remember," Crystal said. "And how about bringing home some chicken too?"

Roy-Ellis heaved a sigh. "Tell you the truth, I'm not real crazy about chicken." He gave a little shudder.

"But I fixed it the other evening, and you likcd it!" Crystal's voice raised up a little. Roy-Ellis studied his fingernails.

"Naw, sugar. I ate it 'cause I love you."

"Oh!" Crystal breathed.

"I'm sorry," he mumbled.

"No—don't be sorry," Crystal begged. "I just can't believe that you ate something you didn't like . . . for me."

"It's the trucks," Roy-Ellis said. And then he corrected himself. "It's all those chickens in the trucks." Crystal got up, went around the table, hugged Roy-Ellis's neck from behind, and kissed the top of his head, like he was a little boy or something. Roy-Ellis's ears turned red.

"No more chicken," Crystal murmured into his hair.

I put Molly and Little Ellis down for their naps while

Crystal started doing the dishes. When I went back in the kitchen to help her, Roy-Ellis was drying the dishes. Crystal had her hands in the soapy water and was resting her head against Roy-Ellis's strong arm, and they were laughing together. So I went back to writing on my story about Mama. I was just at the place in her story where Daddy had run off and Roy-Ellis took to coming around. I thought about what Aunt Bett had said about him, and I decided she wouldn't mind if I used her words. So I wrote, "Roy-Ellis has always been a good man. Mostly."

After the dishes were done, Roy-Ellis came into the dining room, where I was writing in my notebook. I covered the page with my arm.

"Dove, me and Crystal want to go out this evening. You'll be okay?"

"Sure," I said. "You all going dancing?"

"Yep, if you don't mind staying with Molly and Little Ellis."

"That's fine with me," I said. In a while, I heard the shower start up and then Crystal was giggling again in the bedroom. I liked hearing that. I guess I could have felt resentful, because of Crystal being so young and pretty . . . and full of good health, when my poor little mama was *gone*, but somehow or other, those feelings just didn't come. Maybe I was grateful that Roy-Ellis wasn't going to dump me and Molly off on Aunt Bett and move away with Crystal and his own son, Little Ellis. Whatever the reason, I did like hearing Crystal laugh.

After a while, Roy-Ellis came out of the bedroom wearing his cowboy outfit and smelling like cologne. He went to the mirror in the living room and settled his cowboy hat just right.

"You almost ready, Crystal?"

"In a minute, honey," she called from the bedroom. And when she came out, I could hardly believe my eyes! Why, she looked just like a little doll. Under her white cowboy hat, her blond hair was a mass of curls that hung down over the shoulders of a little white jacket that was so short, her whole stomach was showing, and her white shorts started just below her belly button and stopped as soon as possible! She had on some kind of silvery tights and was wearing white cowboy boots with tassels on them.

"Do I look okay?" She twirled around. Still, nobody said a thing. I'd almost forgotten Roy-Ellis was even in the room, until I heard his voice, strong and low.

"Honey, you better go change your clothes," he ordered, and there was something dangerous in his voice. Something I'd never heard in it before.

"What?" Crystal was clearly surprised, and I saw it go all over her. Because she certainly did look so pretty, and I guess she thought Roy-Ellis would be happy with the way she looked.

"I said you better go change your clothes, Crystal. You're my wife now, and I don't want you dancing in that outfit."

"What?" she said again, and I watched the last little bit of that smile just fall right off her face.

"You're not dancing in that outfit," Roy-Ellis's voice was louder.

"What on earth are you talking about? What are you talking about? It's my job."

Her job? I was thinking. *Crystal's job is dancing?*

"Not anymore."

"Roy-Ellis, what on earth are you talking about?" She was getting close to tears.

Molly, Little Ellis, and I were looking back and forth from one to the other.

"Roy-Ellis!" she pleaded. "It's my job!" Then she jutted out her chin and stamped her foot, making the tassels on her boot go to swinging.

"No it isn't!" Roy-Ellis hollered back at her. We all jumped. "We'll find you another job. There's a real nice beauty shop on the back porch. We'll fix that up for you."

"No Roy-Ellis! I'm a dancer!" Crystal turned her back on Roy-Ellis.

"Honey, I can't let you stand up there and dance in front of all those men." Roy-Ellis explained. Then he added, "And you half naked like that." He lurched uncertainly across the room and put his hands on her shoulders.

"Don't cry, sugar," he begged. "You just go put on those jeans I like so much and that pretty pink blouse of yours, and we'll go to Across the Line. But both of us will be customers."

Both be customers? Crystal's job was being a dancer at Across the Line?

Crystal started whimpering, with Roy-Ellis's big hands on her little shoulders starting to pat her just a little bit.

"I can't stand having those men looking at my wife," Roy-Ellis continued, but somehow, Crystal was beyond his words.

At last, she turned and faced him. "You sh-shoulda told me, Roy-Ellis," she stammered. "I'm a dancer! You shoulda told me you were gonna make me stop after we got married."

"But, hon, you can still dance—only not in that outfit and not in front of other men. Go on now and get on some jeans, and then you can dance . . . but only with me." Crystal's face crumpled, and she ran into the bedroom, slamming the door behind her. For the first time, Roy-Ellis looked at us.

"She's gone to change her clothes, I reckon," he said, uncertainly. And he lifted his cowboy hat carefully off his head, sat down in a chair, and slowly turned the hat around and around, by the brim. We all waited like that for long minutes, and then Roy-Ellis went and knocked on the bedroom door. "You almost ready, sugar?" he called.

"No!" came the angry reply.

"Aw, come on, Crystal," he pleaded.

"No!"

"Honey, try and understand . . . please?"

"No!" The back of Roy-Ellis's neck started turning a deep red.

"Crystal?"

"No!"

"Well all right then!" Roy-Ellis shouted, and we all jumped again. "If you won't come, I'm going alone!" He waited for a moment at the door, and when Crystal said nothing, he stomped back through the living room, settled his hat back on his head, and slammed the front door behind him. We heard his truck start up, and the tires squealed and kicked up gravel as he drove away.

Later, I went to the bedroom door and tapped on it lightly. There was no answer, so I guessed Crystal must have cried herself to sleep.

When I woke up, it was full daylight, and the first thing I thought about was that I hadn't heard Roy-Ellis come home. I looked out of the window. His truck was still gone.

Crystal was sitting at the kitchen table with a glass of milk in front of her.

"Roy-Ellis didn't come home?" I asked.

She looked at me with swollen eyes and nodded.

"That's not like him," I said. "That's not like him at all."

"It isn't? Tell me, Dove, did he ever have such a big fuss with . . . your mama?"

It was a hard question for Crystal to ask, and I thought for a few moments before I answered her. Because I'd never heard Mama and Roy-Ellis speak to each other except in soft, gentle ways.

"No. But it still isn't like him." And I truly meant that. Because Roy-Ellis wasn't one to hold on to bad feelings. He liked things to be peaceful. And happy.

"I ran him off!" Crystal moaned, putting both hands around her glass of milk. "But, Dove, I worked so hard to become a dancer. I worked nights in a box factory, to pay for dancing lessons in the daytime. I hardly ever got any sleep. My job at Across the Line was my first dancing job. It means everything to me!"

I didn't know what to say. At last, I offered, "Let's call Aunt Bett." And all of a sudden, I realized it was Sunday morning, and I didn't know if we—me and Molly and Little Ellis—were supposed to go to church with her.

"Let's call Aunt Bett," I repeated. Crystal nodded.

Darlene answered the phone, and I said, "Hi, Darlene—

can I talk to Aunt Bett?"

"Sure, Dove. You all doing okay? I sure do want to meet Crystal."

"I don't know if we're okay or not," I said most truthfully.

"Hold on," Darlene said, and I heard her muffled voice calling, "Mama, it's Dove, for you." And the way Darlene said *Mama* so easily brought surprising tears to my eyes.

"Dove?" Aunt Bett spoke in a way that made my name sound almost like a whisper.

"Yessm?"

"Is everything okay?"

"I don't think so, Aunt Bett," I gulped. "Crystal and Roy-Ellis had a bad fuss last night, and Roy-Ellis stormed out mad, and he hasn't come back."

"That's not like him," Aunt Bett pronounced. "Roy-Ellis may get mad a little quick-like, but he gets over it just as quick. What kind of fuss did they have?" I glanced into the kitchen, where Crystal was sitting, with her hands clenched around the glass of milk and the corners of her mouth turned down.

"I can't say right now," I whispered, thinking that maybe we could get through all this without Aunt Bett finding out that Crystal had been a dancer at a place like Across the Line. "And I don't even know if we're supposed to go to church with you this morning." There was a moment of silence at the other end.

"Is Crystal a churchgoing girl?"

"I don't know. This is the first Sunday I've known her."

"Well, you better ask her then."

"Yessm." I put my hand over the receiver and called to Crystal.

"Crystal? Aunt Bett wants to know if you're a church-going girl." Crystal looked at me with those poor, miserable eyes, like she was trying to figure out what being a churchgoer or not had to do with Roy-Ellis.

" 'Cause we all go to church with Aunt Bett on Sundays," I explained.

"What did she say about Roy-Ellis?" Crystal asked.

"Wait a minute," I called. And into the receiver I asked Aunt Bett, "What do you say about Roy-Ellis?"

"Tell Crystal I think he's on his way home. We can talk about it after church." I relayed the message to Crystal, who seemed to brighten a little.

"Tell Aunt Bett that I am most certainly a churchgoing girl. My mama and daddy went to church every Sunday morning, and I went with them. For my whole life." I repeated what Crystal said.

"Good!" Aunt Bett said, but I was still wondering how we could keep her from finding out about Crystal being a honky-tonk dancer. Somehow, her being a churchgoing girl *and* a honky-tonk dancer didn't seem to fit too well together.

"Well then, it's all settled," Aunt Bett pronounced. "I'll come by and pick you all up at ten-forty-five."

And so that's the way things went. I got myself, Molly, and Little Ellis ready, and then Crystal came out of the bedroom wearing a navy blue dress with a white lace collar and with her hair pulled back into a neat ponytail. Her eyes were still red, but she did look pretty, I thought. Lots prettier than in that outfit that caused all the trouble.

But where was Roy-Ellis?

I really wondered if Aunt Bett's old car was going to be able to hold another person, but Crystal was so tiny, we both managed to fit in the place where I usually sat. I held Molly on my lap, and Crystal held Little Ellis on hers. I did all the introducing of Aunt Bett's brood, and when it came down to telling them who Crystal was, I said, "This is Crystal, my . . . Roy-Ellis's wife."

The cousins all stared at her dumbly, except for Darlene, who smiled warmly and said, "Where's Roy-Ellis's truck?"

"That's enough, Darlene!" Aunt Bett said. "Don't you ask so many questions." Darlene smiled and shrugged her shoulders.

"Sorry," she said.

At church, Crystal seemed to fit right in. She sat between me and Aunt Bett and she even knew the words to most of the hymns without looking at her book. When Aunt Bett noticed that, she leaned backward, looked at me behind Crystal's head, and nodded. Crystal didn't even notice. Once or twice, she touched her eyes with a tissue, but other then that, she was a real brave lady.

After church, we went in to Aunt Bett's house with her. As usual, Aunt Bett made all of us change out of our church clothes right away, and once again, Darlene had to find things out of The Closet for me and Molly and Little Ellis. I waited to see if Aunt Bett made Crystal change her dress, as well. But of course, she didn't. Probably because Crystal's clothes weren't ones Aunt Bett made so many pickles to get and needed back in good condition for passing on down.

Aunt Bett motioned Crystal to go on into the kitchen, and I noticed Aunt Bett looking at Crystal's dress with frank admiration.

"Such fine stitching!" Aunt Bett exclaimed.

"Yessm," Crystal answered. "My mama is a wonder with a needle and thread."

"She made that?"

"Yessm," Crystal answered, and I could see the clear admiration in Aunt Bett's eyes. I could also see her figuring how to get that dress away from Crystal some time down the line, for passing along to her own girls. I wanted so bad to hear what Aunt Bett and Crystal would be saying in the kitchen, but when I heard Aunt Bett say, "Now you tell me exactly what caused such a fuss," I just couldn't stand it. Because there was no telling what Aunt Bett was going to say if she found out that Crystal had been a roadhouse dancer! So I hurried into the bedroom and got me and Molly and Little Ellis out of our good church clothes and into some shirts and pants Darlene had found for us.

"What's going on?" Darlene whispered.

"Crystal and Roy-Ellis had a fuss," I whispered back. "Roy-Ellis stormed out of the house, and he didn't come home last night."

"All night?" Darlene asked, and I nodded.

"That's not like Roy-Ellis," she said. And I nodded again.

After we got our clothes changed, we all went out and sat on the porch, waiting for Aunt Bett and Crystal to get done talking. Nobody said a thing. We just sat and waited for the longest time, and every once in a while, some-body's stomach growled, and we all giggled. Then silence again, until somebody else's stomach growled. After what seemed like hours, Aunt Bett came to the screen door.

"You children get washed up and come on in to dinner." I didn't know whether she meant just her own children or not, so me and Molly and Little Ellis stayed put where we were sitting on the porch steps.

"You all too, Dove," Aunt Bett said. Why, I was sur-prised as could be! Aunt Bett was inviting all of us to Sunday dinner, and Crystal too, even though I was sure Crystal's secret must be out by now. But when we got into the dining room, I was even more surprised. The table was all set and extra chairs from the kitchen already in place. On the table was a big bowl of applesauce and one of green beans cooked with ham, and also a huge platter of hot cornbread. Just the smell of the food made the place under my tongue tickle. Then Crystal came out of the kitchen carrying a big dish of macaroni and cheese, fresh out of the oven. She put the dish on a folded kitchen towel Aunt Bett had put on the table, and Crystal and Aunt Bett looked at each other and *smiled!*

"You children sit down," Aunt Bett commanded, and she pointed to a chair right beside her own. "You sit here by me, Crystal." So we all got settled and took each other's hands, so Aunt Bett could say grace.

"Dear Lord," she began, and I guess we were all praying for a short blessing, we were so hungry. "We thank you for all this good food." Her words were met by the sound of growling stomachs. She looked up for one startled moment, and so did most of us, as well. Then we got back at it.

"We especially thank you for this good macaroni and cheese that your child Crystal has made us from her own sweet mama's recipe." Another chorus of growling stomachs, but this time, no one looked up.

"And we ask you to bless Crystal as she starts her new career." My eyes flew open and met Crystal's. Hers were full of tears, but she smiled and sort of shrugged her shoulders at me, just like I'd seen Darlene do so many times.

"Bless her, Lord, and help her do well at this new—*respectable*—trade." We waited, praying hard for an *amen,* but it wasn't to be. Not yet.

"And bless Crystal and Roy-Ellis's marriage and bring peace to their home. Bless this food to our bodies and us to Thy service. Amen!" We all knew better than to lunge for the food, but we sure made quick work of passing around the green beans and applesauce and cornbread, and we even managed to get in a couple of quick bites before we had to pass our plates to Crystal, who served us her mama's good macaroni and cheese. Then there was only silence and a very serious time of eating. I will have to admit that the macaroni and cheese was the best I ever tasted. And I was so hungry, I forgot to wonder how Aunt Bett got Crystal to agree to stop being a roadhouse dancer.

As soon as Sunday dinner was over, Aunt Bett said, "Crystal, you take Dove and the children and go on home. I'm sure Roy-Ellis will come home soon, if he isn't already there."

"But can't I help clean up?" Crystal offered. Aunt Bett fluttered her hands at Crystal. "Not at all! But fix Roy-Ellis a plate and take it home, for when he comes."

So that's what we did.

146

Chapter Nine

BUT Roy-Ellis didn't come home. We all just sat around and waited, jumping every time we thought we heard his truck, but it was always something else. By late afternoon, Crystal was in constant tears.

"I don't know how he could get *that* mad at me," she sobbed. "Mad enough to stay away all night and now almost all day, too!" When dark started to fall, I called Aunt Bett again.

"Aunt Bett, Roy-Ellis isn't home *yet*."

"He's not?" Aunt Bett was genuinely surprised. "Why, something's wrong, then," she pronounced. Then there was a long hesitation. "I'm going to call the sheriff," she said. "But don't say anything to Crystal. No need to scare her. Just tell her that I said I'll call around to some of Roy-Ellis's friends from the chicken plant, and see if I can find him. This isn't like him," she repeated.

"What did she say?" Crystal asked, after I hung up the phone.

"She's going to call some of the folks he works with at the chicken plant and see if they know where he is."

This news brought fresh sobs from Crystal. "Oh, Dove, I've been his wife only six *days,* and I've run him off already!"

I didn't know what to say to Crystal, so I didn't say anything at all. When it was time for bed, Crystal curled up on the couch, and all throughout that long night, I could see the ghost-white flickering of the television set in the living room and hear Crystal blowing her nose, again and again.

When the phone rang before daylight, I almost thought for a minute that it was the people at the hospital, calling to tell us that Mama was gone. But then I got wide awake in a hurry and went into the living room. Crystal answered it after the second ring.

"Hello?" Crystal looked at me with her red and tired-looking eyes.

"Oh, hi, Ada," Crystal said, brightening a little. Then she frowned.

"What?" And while I stood there watching her, Crystal just sort of folded up and sat down on the floor. Hard.

"What is it?" I whispered, sitting down beside her. But she said not a single word. Just listened for a while longer and then hung up. And her face held something so serious that it almost looked like it was carved in stone.

"Roy-Ellis . . ." Crystal started, and then she rubbed her forehead and swallowed hard. "He's gone," she said simply.

"Gone?" Why, that just didn't make any sense. Roy-Ellis wouldn't be *gone,* for Heaven's sake! He wasn't *that* mad, so why would he be gone? And gone where? That's what I wanted to know. But then when I looked at Crystal again, I knew what kind of *gone* she meant.

"What?" That one word just seemed to take all the breath out of me. And I've never seen anybody's face turn as white as Crystal's, and out of that snowy-white face, her pale mouth was making words, and I heard them like they were coming at me through some kind of a fog in my ears.

"That was Ada. From Across the Line. Where I used to dance," Crystal added, for some reason. "There was an accident just down the road. Roy-Ellis . . ." Crystal didn't finish her sentence. She didn't need to.

"It happened only a few hours after he left. That's what the police say." Crystal's chin shook. "His truck went down into a ravine and nobody could see it from the road. That's why it took so long to find him." I watched Crystal's face getting whiter and whiter. I got the phone and called Aunt Bett.

It was all like some kind of a bad dream, those next few days. Seems like the hours lasted forever but flew by at the same time. Aunt Bett fixing good clothes, once again, for us to wear to church for another funeral, and us all sitting there and me not really sure whether it was Mama's funeral we were at, or . . . Roy-Ellis's. Crystal was all shrunken up around the neck and shoulders, but she didn't cry out loud. Not at church. And Aunt Bett brought us home but Crystal went to the cemetery alone. Just as Roy-Ellis had done for Mama.

Aunt Mee was in our kitchen once again, and all the people from Roy-Ellis's work came and brought food, and when Crystal came home from the cemetery, a man in a dark suit handed her an envelope. She didn't open it. Some of the people there were folks from Across the Line, and I wondered what Aunt Bett would say about that. But she sure surprised me. She was just as nice as could be to those folks she knew good and well worked in the "den of iniquity." She shook their hands and thanked them for coming. All the folks from Aunt Bett's church were nice to them. But before they started to leave, Aunt Bett said, "I hope you'll come to church sometime." And they smiled and murmured "Thanks," but I don't think any of them ever came.

At the last, there was only one person left from Across the Line—a woman I didn't know. A woman with black, curly hair, perfectly arched eyebrows, like what you see on magazine models, and the reddest lips I had ever seen. I'd noticed her watching Crystal, so I figured maybe she wanted to say something about being sorry. But when she finally went and put her hand on Crystal's arm, it was for saying something that surprised Aunt Bett and Crystal and me.

"Crystal?" she started, almost in a whisper.

"Yes," Crystal said. Then, "I'm Crystal," she added, as if to encourage the girl.

"Well, I'm Roberta—from Across the Line." She paused. "Ada said I should stay behind and tell you about . . . Roy-Ellis . . . before the accident."

"Oh," Crystal sighed. "Do you have to do that right now?"

"It's important," Roberta said. "Can we go someplace private?"

"Okay." Crystal sounded so weary. They went into the hallway, but I saw Aunt Bett reach over and straighten the afghan on the back of the couch, so she could try and be close enough to hear what they were saying.

Roberta started: "I'm real new at Across the Line—only started last week—and I didn't know Roy-Ellis was married." Roberta looked down at her shoes, and Aunt Bett sort of drew herself up, like she was bracing to hear something she didn't want to hear.

Roberta went on. "See, he didn't wear a ring, and all I knew was that he was a customer, and he looked pretty unhappy. So I told him . . ." She stammered to a stop.

Crystal turned her head away, like she was scared of what Roberta was going to say.

"So I told him that I'd try to make him feel better." Crystal closed her eyes and so did Aunt Bett. And seeing how Crystal was hurting, Roberta went ahead at breakneck speed.

"All I meant was that I'd keep the beer coming and the peanut dish full and smile and be nice to him." Tears welled up in her eyes, but she jutted out her chin and almost yelled, "I swear to you, that's all I meant!" She took in a couple of quick breaths.

Crystal opened her eyes and looked at Roberta.

"I believe you."

Aunt Bett's eyes snapped open.

"Oh, thank you," Roberta said. "So please let me finish. This is something Ada said you needed to hear."

"Go ahead then," Crystal nodded.

"Well, he musta thought I meant more than beer and peanuts and smiles too, because he says to me, 'I've had too many beers tonight, but I won't let that turn me into more of an ass than I've already been.'

"I was gonna tell him that isn't what I meant, but before I could say a thing, he stood up, fished some bills out of his pocket, and tossed them onto the table. Then he looked right at me and said, 'I got me a sweet little wife waiting for me at home, and that's where I'm going. Gonna tell her I'm sorry.'" Roberta and Crystal were both tearful now.

"Ada said you should know."

"Oh, yes," Crystal breathed. "Thank you."

Roberta turned to go, but then she looked back at Crystal.

"I'm sorry you lost him so soon, but you need to remember how much he loved you. There are lots of women in this world who never get that—not for a single hour of their lives."

After Roberta left, Aunt Bett confessed to Crystal, "I'm sorry I eavesdropped, Crystal. I only did it so I could help you in any way I can."

"It's okay," Crystal whispered.

"He was a good man," Aunt Bett said. Then she smiled at Crystal and added, "Mostly."

Crystal looked startled, and she stared and stared at Aunt Bett's smile, like maybe she'd forgotten what it was like to see anybody smile, after all the sadness we'd been through. Then Crystal's face softened a bit, and she whispered, "Yes. A mostly good man. A *really* mostly good man."

Chapter Ten

How strange it felt for Roy-Ellis to be gone—and never coming back. I just hadn't known how much he filled up our little house with himself—even when he was at work. Why, with just us there, we almost tiptoed around, and we took to whispering instead of talking. The house was that empty.

For a long time, I halfway expected that he would come in the door any minute, clump across the living room and down the hall, turn on the shower, and start singing honky-tonk songs like he usually did. Then he would come out of the bedroom, with his hair still wet and with little grooves in it from his comb, and he would be wearing clean clothes and smell real good from the aftershave lotion he would put on himself. It took a long time before I stopped thinking those things would happen.

Once again, Aunt Bett took to coming over often, and she and Crystal would go in the kitchen and shut the door. But this time, I stood in the hallway with my ear against the door. If Aunt Bett could eavesdrop, then so could I!

Aunt Bett said, "Crystal, I want to talk to you about the children." Her voice was deep and serious.

"What about the children, Bett?"

"I will take them into my home, so you can get on with your life." Aunt Bett said, and once again, I realized how close we were to having nobody in this world, except for Aunt Bett. But maybe that would be all right—I knew we would all be crowded in Aunt Bett's house, but somehow, we could make do. Maybe I could even get me a job after school and in the summers, working in the dime store or something.

But Crystal must have thought about it already, because she said, "Thank you, Bett. That's so good of you. But these children are all I have left of Roy-Ellis, and I mean to be a good mother to them, no matter what. Other than these children, I don't have a life to get on with!"

"I don't know. You're awfully young to be saddled with three children and not even have a husband to help you," Aunt Bett reminded her.

"I can do it, Bett," Crystal reassured her. "I know I can."

"Well, that's more than I could possibly have expected. Are you sure?"

"I'm *sure*," Crystal repeated, and her voice sounded all full of iron. Or something like that. And in a way, I guess I was surprised at Crystal. Maybe we thought she would kind of fall apart after Roy-Ellis died, but she didn't. In fact, she started right in to looking for work in a beauty parlor. And I'll bet Roy-Ellis never even knew that she'd gone to beauty college right out of high school—that she had been a beautician before and hated it so bad that she worked in a box factory until she could start dancing in roadhouses.

It turned out that the envelope someone from Roy-Ellis's work gave to Crystal the day of Roy-Ellis's funeral had $200 in cash in it, and that would hold us until Crystal could get work.

"I have a family to support now, and dancing isn't a good way to have a steady paycheck," Crystal said to me, and I sure do wish Aunt Bett could have heard that. But of course, Aunt Bett just thought that dancing in a roadhouse was terrible anyway, so maybe she wouldn't have understood how hard it was for Crystal to give it up.

"And besides," Crystal added, "it was our arguing about my dancing that made Roy-Ellis so mad that night. So I won't ever dance again. Not ever." And just like happened after Mama died, the world went on, and we went on with it.

I'm not even sure of when things began to feel a little bit all right again, even though Crystal still hadn't found a job. All I know is that one day I went to hang one of Crystal's pretty blouses in her closet and looked down at Roy-Ellis's other pair of boots, where they still stood, like they were waiting for him to put them on, and I knew that the boots were just that: boots. Just things. But I did take his cowboy hat and put it in the top of the closet in mine and Molly's and Little Ellis's room. Because I wanted to keep it for-ever.

When I wrote in my notebooks, I wrote about Roy-Ellis as well. And pretty soon, I wasn't just writing short things about people, but also about how the people were when they were with each other.

While Crystal was looking for a job, she practiced hair-cutting on all of us, and she did a fine job, even with Little Ellis, who didn't like to sit still for such a long time. Why, we'd never had such nice-looking hair before. Then Crystal went to Aunt Bett's house one Saturday morning and gave haircuts to all Aunt Bett's children. Aunt Bett was grateful, but she wasn't one to accept things for free, so when we were ready to leave, Aunt Bett handed three jars of her good pickles to Crystal and me.

"No ma'am!" Crystal said, trying to hand back the jars.

"You have to take them," Aunt Bett pushed the jars back to Crystal.

I was enjoying watching them, but I knew who was going to win. Crystal was simply no match for Aunt Bett's iron will. Come to think of it, nobody was.

"After all you do for us?" Crystal insisted, trying to hand them back again. "All the work of mending and passing along the children's clothes?"

Aunt Bett jutted her chin and pushed the jars back once again. "You're a working woman now, Crystal. Or you soon will be. You have to get used to being paid for your work." Crystal's mouth opened and closed a few times, but finally, she cradled the jars and simply said, "Thank you."

Aunt Bett said, "Crystal, you know, we could fix up that little beauty shop on your back porch, and that way, you

155

could go ahead and start working for yourself. It could use some curtains, even though the air conditioner takes up most of the window. We could make a little flounce or something for the top."

Crystal didn't answer right away, but she glanced over at me and then cleared her throat. "I've found me a job in a salon out at the mall."

"The mall?" we all chorused, for not one of us had ever seen the new mall that had been built just across the state line in South Carolina.

"The mall," Crystal said again.

"You gonna drive that far every morning and back every evening?" Aunt Bett asked, with a deep furrow between her eyebrows.

"Yes, Bett," Crystal answered. "It's not too far."

Well, I could tell Aunt Bett wasn't entirely happy about that, but she didn't say anything else.

"I sure wish I could get me a job in a mall!" Darlene said, with something bleak-sounding in her voice. "Then I could go to work every single day in a place where there are lots of people and things going on all the time." Darlene pointed at the bedroom window. "And have something else to see besides weeds and a dirt road." The more I thought about it, the more I realized that Crystal had made a good decision. Crystal was so young and so pretty, and I hadn't wanted to see her working all day every day in that tiny little beauty parlor on the back porch. Not at all.

On Crystal's first day of work, she couldn't even finish her coffee, because she had a long way to drive to get to work. After she was gone, I started cleaning up the kitchen, but then I left the dishes in the sink and went out onto the back porch. I pushed open the door to the tiny beauty parlor my mama had worked in for so many hours.

"I'm sorry, Mama. I wish you could have worked in a mall, too. Or someplace a little bit bigger and brighter than this. And I'm glad you got to go honky-tonk dancing with Roy-Ellis. I don't care what Aunt Bett says."

When Crystal came home after her first day of work, she was filled with all sorts of exciting things to tell us about. "Why, the mall is huge! It must have thirty or forty stores in it, and everything is all lit up so pretty. And the smells— I can hardly describe them to you! You can smell popcorn and perfume and then a real sweet smell I finally found out was candied apples. And I brought three of them home to you." She opened the white bag she was carrying and gave us each a candied apple. Little Ellis wouldn't try to bite his, but just licked it like a sucker. But Molly and I bit right into ours, and when I tasted it, I almost got dizzy, thinking about how wonderful the mall must be and how I wished I could see it for myself. Then I would have something new and exciting to write in my notebook. But of course, I knew better than to ask Crystal to take us there. For us, the mall had to be work, not play.

But I was sure that the mall was a place where the rich girls in our town could go, and that thought set me to thinking once again about wishing I could be rich and smell of perfumed soap and wear clothes that weren't too short for me. And have smooth skin and no scabs on my too-big knees and socks that stayed up, like they were supposed to. But I knew not to say those things out loud. We were all doing the best we could, and if Crystal had known what I was thinking, she would have gotten her feelings hurt awful bad. And if Aunt Bett knew—goodness!—she would have given me a long, hard lecture about being grateful for what I had and told me to stop committing the sin of coveting. So I kept my mouth shut, but at the same time, I decided that there were some little things I could do to change the way I was feeling. A strange ache in my stomach that didn't have a thing to do with anybody except *me*. And all of a sudden, I knew exactly what Darlene meant about wanting a window that looked out on something besides a dirt road. And I could almost hear Darlene's voice, *One of these days you'll want nothing more in this world than to have some private time, just for yourself.*

The next Monday, I decided I would change some things about the room I shared with Molly and Little Ellis. So Crystal helped me run a clothesline across the room right up against my cot, so I could hang some sheets over it and have me a little space of my very own.

"Why, Dove?" Molly asked, with tears in her eyes. "Me not see you!"

"That's exactly why I'm doing it, Molly!" I said, impatiently. "But I'll still *be* there."

Molly didn't like that, but she knew better than to carry on about it. The first night, she snuffled a bit, but I wouldn't let myself feel guilty. Not one little bit. And by the second night, Molly didn't fuss at all. So I had me a little space of my very own. When I told Darlene about my own space, she came over to see it and got me to help do the same thing for her, in the room she had to share with two of her sisters. Then we decorated our spaces. Darlene's looked so pretty with a little lamp and bedside table, and I got Aunt Bett to lend me a little lace doily so I could fix up my own bedside table. I even moved my stack of precious notebooks to a shelf in the closet so I would have room for some of the things out of my treasure drawer and for a jar of sweet-smelling hand lotion Crystal had given me the money to buy. And when it would be time for me to go to bed, how I did love to turn on my little lamp and pull the sheets across and get into my own cot. Almost like sleeping in a beautiful, white tent out in the middle of the woods.

Crystal never offered to take us to the mall with her, and that was fine with me. It would probably just have showed me a lot of things I didn't have and probably never would have—and people I would never be like. Still, I made up some good stories about it for my notebooks, about a whole other world apart from our little house and Aunt Bett and our little town with only one drugstore in it.

But pretty soon, I got my mind off of those things, a little bit at least. Because one morning when Crystal got up and started getting ready to go to work, I heard her in the bath-room—being sick.

"You okay?" I asked through the door.

"Must've eaten something that didn't agree with me."

Then she was sick every single morning for over a week, and she just wasn't herself at all. Didn't seem to laugh any-more, just picked at her supper, and then went to bed. Maybe she really had a disease or something. I thought about telling Aunt Bett, but something or other stopped me. So finally, I went to see Aunt Mee.

"You all doing okay?" Aunt Mee asked when she saw

me at her door.

"Well, that's what I wanted to ask you about."

"Somebody sick?"

"Crystal is sick almost every single morning," I told her.

"Sick? How is she sick?"

"Sick to her stomach. Every morning."

"H-m-m-m." Aunt Mee pondered about it for a few minutes. Then she asked, "Only in the morning? Never at any other time?"

"That's right."

"How long has Roy-Ellis been gone now?" Aunt Mee asked.

"Almost a month," I answered, suddenly able to see Roy-Ellis all dressed up and with his cowboy hat and boots on but wondering what that had to do with Crystal being sick. I watched Aunt Mee and saw her eyebrows move up on her forehead.

"Your Aunt Bett know about Crystal being sick?"

"No. I haven't told her. Do you know what's wrong with Crystal?"

"H-m-m-m," she said again. "I'm not sure, but if it keeps up, you're going to have to tell your Aunt Bett."

"Yes. I think you're right. Thanks, Aunt Mee. And how is Savannah?" I added. "Do you hear from her?"

"I expect she's doing just fine. Told me before she left that you and her was going to write letters to each other."

"That's right. But I don't know an address for her."

"I'll write it down for you," Aunt Mee said, and she took a used envelope and painstakingly wrote the address on the back of it. I was happy to have Savannah's address, and it certainly did make me feel better that somebody besides me knew about this strange sickness of Crystal's.

Later, I tried to talk to Crystal about her being so sick, but when I brought up the subject, she turned white as a sheet and went into her room and locked the door. Poor Crystal! She stayed quiet as a ghost for two or three days, but she never missed a single day at work, and after that, she seemed to be trying to get her old self back. But that never really happened. Still, she did stop being sick in the mornings, so maybe . . . just maybe . . . she was getting better.

Chapter Eleven

OF course, there was no way for Aunt Bett not to notice that something was wrong with Crystal. I mean, Crystal had become as white as a sheet, and she'd lost weight, so her face was narrow and her eyes in a deep shadow most of the time.

"You seeing a boyfriend?" Aunt Bett asked her after church.

"No, Aunt Bett," she muttered, and her eyes filled up. "I never wanted anybody except for Roy-Ellis," she added.

"Well," Aunt Bett started out, and her voice was soft, because she could see how bad Crystal was hurting. "You're young, honey—and so pretty. The time will come."

"Yessm," was all Crystal said.

As if it wasn't bad enough having Crystal feeling sick and her missing Roy-Ellis so bad, there came a day that same week when everything changed so hard and so fast that ever afterward, I would remember things as "before" and "after." And it started with something as simple as our phone ringing and me answering it, just like I always did.

"Hello?" I said, expecting it to be Aunt Bett asking what we were having for supper, because Crystal was still at work.

But there was no sound, except, I think, for someone breathing.

"Hello?" I tried again.

"Who's this?" A man's voice.

"Dove," I mewed, hating the weak sound of my voice.

"Dove?" The man's voice was softer now.

"Yessir."

"This is your daddy." For a moment, I pictured Roy-Ellis, whole and healthy, standing at a pay phone in the clouds, with a whole line of beautiful angels standing behind him, grinning.

"This is your daddy, Dove," the voice repeated. "Your real daddy," he added.

"Yessir?" I looked at my arms and all the fine, soft hairs on them were standing right on end.

"I heard about your mama," he said. "And now your stepdaddy." The voice went on. "I'm sorry to hear about that."

"Thank you."

"Well, Dove," he hesitated and I guess I thought he was going to say good-bye then. But he took a deep breath and added, "I want to come and get you and Molly and bring you out here to California to live with me." And what flashed in front of my eyes then was Mama's face—the way it looked after my daddy ran off and flat-out left her all alone.

"What about that woman you ran off with?" I asked.

And I was surprised to hear how gruff-like my voice sounded. Made me think of Aunt Bett.

"She's not with me anymore," he said.

"Why not?" I couldn't help myself from asking, and I truly enjoyed the way he hesitated. "Did she run off with somebody else?" I asked, and finally, he said, "Yes."

"Then she just did to you what you did to my mama," I pronounced and took the receiver away from my ear.

"Dove?" The voice was far away and tin-sounding. "Listen, Dove, I had an old friend of mine keep an eye out for you children, to see if you were being taken care of all right, after your mama died."

I put the receiver back to my ear.

"He said he found you all playing all the way over to the school yard and without a single adult around to watch after you."

The man in the truck! The one who asked if we had a grown-up with us!

"And he says that your stepmama's just a child herself, and he doesn't think she's taking very good care of you children. Now that your stepdaddy's gone, as well, I want my two girls to come live with me."

"Maybe you'll change your mind and leave us, like you left Mama," I said. "And what about Little Ellis?" I asked, hating myself right away for asking my real daddy anything.

"He's not mine," my real daddy said. And when I didn't say anything else, he repeated the words: "He's not mine." And I hung up the phone. I didn't slam it down, but I just let the receiver drop back into the cradle. It rang again right away, but I walked into the kitchen and sat down at the table. The phone rang for a very long time before it finally stopped. Molly and Little Ellis were both staring at me. And I knew right then and there that Crystal and us were a family, and we'd got to stay together.

"Eat your supper," I said, and both Molly and Little Ellis went back to spooning SpaghettiOs into their mouths. When Crystal came home, I waited until she got her clothes changed and sat down at the table. Crystal still looked pretty bad, and she seemed to be awful tired. But I knew what it was like to lose somebody you love, and so I knew how bad she was hurting.

"There was a phone call today," I said, trying to make my voice light.

"And?" She mouthed the word around a tiny bite of tuna salad.

"It was my real daddy," I said, and Crystal stared at me.

"What?" she finally managed to croak. "What did he want?"

"He said he wants me and Molly to come out to California and live with him," I said.

"What?" Her eyes widened.

"That's what he said."

"And what did you say?"

"I hung up on him. I think he tried to call back, but I didn't answer the phone." Just then, the phone rang again. Crystal and I locked eyes, and neither one of us made a move. It rang for a long, long time, before it finally stopped. Crystal and I sat at the table, not saying anything, because I guess we just didn't know what to say..

Then we suddenly heard footsteps on the front porch, and someone threw open the living room door. "What on earth is going on?" Aunt Bett was hollering as she came toward the kitchen. "Are you all okay? Is anything wrong? Why don't you answer the phone?"

When she got to the kitchen doorway, Crystal and I were still just sitting there, staring at her. "What on earth? You're both just as white as a sheet! And why don't you answer the phone?" Crystal let out her breath.

"You better sit down, Bett. We've got trouble."

Aunt Bett sat down, folded her hands on the table, and studied Crystal closely.

"Dove, would you please go and watch Molly and Little Ellis? And maybe start getting them ready for bed?"

Why, I was surprised as could be! I knew Crystal was going to tell Aunt Bett about my real daddy calling on the telephone and wanting me and Molly to go live with him. For Heaven's sake! I'm the one that told Crystal herself.

"Please, Dove," Crystal said, because I guess she could see my surprise. And the way Crystal was looking at me, I figured I would do exactly as she asked. But I still didn't understand why. So I started through the kitchen doorway, and Crystal said, "Would you mind shutting the door, please?"

Well, maybe then I did understand a little better. Crystal wouldn't want Little Ellis or Molly overhearing about Molly and me and our real daddy. So I closed the door behind me and started down the hallway. But for some strange reason, I stopped. Then I tiptoed back and put my ear against the door.

I knew I was wrong listening in on what Crystal and Aunt Bett were saying, but on the other hand, I thought it was wrong of them to shut me out of whatever they were talking about. I had every right to be included, and I meant to be—only they wouldn't know it. So I pressed my ear against the door.

"Dove says her daddy called on the phone today."

"What?"

"That's right," Crystal said. "And he told her he wants to take her and Molly to California to live with him."

Not a sound came out of Aunt Bett. At first. Then I heard her breathe out, "Oh, Lord have mercy!"

"Bett, Roy-Ellis never adopted Molly. Not legally. So I'm scared. And I didn't adopt them either."

"I know he didn't," Aunt Bett moaned. "Didn't adopt Dove either, and I worried a little bit about that. But I never thought they'd both . . . pass away . . . before the children got grown."

"Bett, listen to me, please," Crystal said. "Roy-Ellis didn't *have* to adopt Dove."

"What?"

"He didn't have to adopt Dove . . . because she was his own child."

I jerked my ear away from the door, and I almost fell down right there in the hallway.

What? Me? Roy-Ellis was my real daddy? How could that be?

My ears were buzzing and my heart almost knocked itself right out of my chest. But I had to know it all, so I took a couple of deep breaths to calm down a little and put my ear back to the door. Aunt Bett's voice was rising. "I just don't understand what you're saying! Yes, my baby sister dated Roy-Ellis for a while, but then she turned around and married . . . *him*. And she never said a word to me about anything other than being so happy to have found someone so reliable."

"It's true," Crystal said, simply.

"Dove is Roy-Ellis's child?" Aunt Bett asked again.

"Dove is Roy-Ellis's child," Crystal said.

Aunt Bett was quiet for a moment and then she said, "You mean to tell me my baby sister got herself in trouble with Roy-Ellis and then turned around and married another man?"

"Please!" Crystal pleaded. "The children may hear us!"

Aunt Bett let out a big, sad sigh.

Crystal went on: "Roy-Ellis didn't know Dove was his."

"But why not?"

"He just didn't. No one ever told him. But when I went through his papers—I was hoping to find a life insurance policy or something like that—I found a letter Dove's mama wrote to him when she was in the hospital, just before she died. But it was still sealed, so he never opened it. Maybe he was going to wait until later. Or maybe he just couldn't bear to read it. But if he'd read it, he would have known about Dove being his very own child."

"And you opened that letter my sister wrote to Roy-Ellis?" Now Aunt Bett's tone had turned very serious.

"I was looking for insurance papers," Crystal explained. "But I never found any. Just the letter about Dove."

"And what did you do with it?" Aunt Bett demanded.

"I've got it hidden in my drawer," Crystal said.

"Well, I want to see it. I want to see that it's my own sister's handwriting," Aunt Bett demanded. Then she added, "I can just hardly believe any of this! Her my own sister and she kept this from me?"

"In the letter," Crystal offered, "she said the reason she didn't tell him before was that she didn't want him to think he *had* to marry her. Wanted him to marry her just because he wanted to. And I guess that didn't happen until after her first husband ran off."

"Hummmph!" Aunt Bett snarled.

"But, Bett, do you realize what this means?" Crystal pressed. "The *real* father isn't Dove's real father at all. And when he finds that out, he won't take Dove. Only Molly. She's the only one is his own child."

"But . . ." Aunt Bett stumbled along. "Oh, it's too terrible to think about! We can't let him take Molly away!"

"I know," Crystal said. Another long silence.

Little Ellis my honest-to-goodness brother and Molly only my half-sister? Roy-Ellis my very own daddy and I didn't know it! And he didn't know it! And too late now to do anything about it. Me helping him wash his truck, me fixing his supper, me bringing him a cold beer, us helping Little Ellis color some Easter eggs. And us not knowing?

But once I started getting over that big surprise, I thought about Roy-Ellis and what a good man . . . mostly . . . he had been. And I truly liked the idea of him being my daddy. Because that made me be the daughter of a *really* mostly-good man instead of a man that ran off with a blond-headed lady and left my mama all alone and brokenhearted.

"What are we going to do?" Aunt Bett asked.

"I don't know, but we have to find a way to keep *him* from taking Molly away. Why, I don't know how she could get along without Dove." Another long silence.

"He knows where we live," Crystal said. "And he's already called on the phone. We have to figure something out fast!" Another silence, before Crystal went on. "He could show up with court papers anytime he wants, and there wouldn't be a thing we could do about it."

"Can't we hide Molly somewhere?" Aunt Bett asked.

"But if he took us to court, they could make us tell, if we knew."

"If we knew . . ." Aunt Bett repeated.

"But even if we sent her off and hid her somewhere, she would still lose Dove and Little Ellis." Crystal paused and added, "And me. It would break up our family!"

"Maybe you could all hide?" Aunt Bett suggested.

"Maybe we could," Crystal muttered. "We just have to think this through, and we have to do that in a hurry!"

"Well, show me that letter first," Aunt Bett said. I heard the chair scrape, so I ran down the hall and got ready to plop myself onto the couch, like I'd been reading or watching television the whole time. But as soon as I got into the living room, I knew this was something I couldn't pretend I hadn't heard. That would be impossible. So I took a deep breath and went back toward the kitchen. Crystal was coming out of the bedroom with an envelope in her hands. Aunt Bett was still sitting at the table.

"I heard," I said at once to both of them. Why, I was surprised as could be to hear my voice sounding so calm and strong. I was expecting to squeak when I made my confession to them.

"You heard?" Crystal looked at Aunt Bett. But Aunt Bett's eyes were boring into my own.

"You eavesdropped on our conversation?" Aunt Bett demanded.

"Yes ma'am, I did."

"Why, Dove! That isn't like you!" Aunt Bett moaned.

"I'm not a baby, Aunt Bett," I whispered. "And I have a right to know what's going on."

"Well, I never!" Aunt Bett was truly mad, and I kept watching her mouth like any minute all those terrible words out of the Old Testament would come spewing out, but this time, they would be meant for *me*.

But before Aunt Bett could say a word, Crystal spoke up. "Dove's right, Bett. She's not a baby." And to me she said, "I'm sorry. I should have told you and then asked you to be with me while I told Bett."

Aunt Bett's mouth fell open, but she didn't say a word.

"Was Roy-Ellis really my daddy?" I asked, even though I already knew the answer. Because I wanted to hear it said right out and not just words coming through the kitchen door.

"Yes," Crystal said. "Yes, Roy-Ellis was your daddy. That's what your mama said in this letter to him that he never did open." Crystal handed to letter to Aunt Bett, who opened it and stared at the words. "Yes, it's her handwriting," Aunt Bett finally said.

I thought for a moment. "Roy-Ellis never knew."

"That's right," Crystal almost whispered.

"He never knew," I repeated.

Everything felt all strange at our house that evening, even though we all went about doing what we usually did. Aunt Bett went home after hugging all of us and telling Crystal, "It will be okay. We'll find a way." Crystal washed up the dishes while I got Little Ellis and Molly in bed, but after that we sat at the kitchen table together and just thought hard, trying to figure out how to keep Molly with us. A knock at the back door, and Crystal and I both jumped. But when Crystal opened the door, it was Aunt Mee, standing there with a basket of fresh butterbeans.

"I just came over to bring you all some butterbeans, if you can use them," she said, holding out the basket. "My old garden is cranking out more than I can use this year," she added. "You feeling better, Crystal?" she asked carefully.

"Yes, thank you," Crystal said, taking the basket. "And please don't go."

To me, Crystal said, "I think we should tell Aunt Mee about what's going on and ask advice from someone with such a good head. The more folks we got figuring for us, the better."

"Well, I don't know just how good my old head is," Aunt Mee protested. "But if I can help with anything, I will. You all know that."

"Come on and sit down," Crystal swung her arm toward the kitchen table.

Aunt Mee sort of rolled her eyes at the invitation. Because Aunt Mee had lived most of her life in the way things used to be between black people and white people, and in her way of thinking, no black woman would ever sit down at the kitchen table with a white woman. It was different when I was at Aunt Mee's house, because it was *her house,* and I wasn't a grown woman. Yet. And I don't even know how we knew all those things, because they weren't written down anyplace that I knew of. But still, we all knew them.

"Please?" Crystal added.

Aunt Mee relented and walked over to the table. Ever so slowly, she pulled out a chair. But she looked at Crystal and me again before she finally sat down. Even then, she sat at the very edge of the chair, as if she needed to be able to lift off at a moment's notice. Crystal and I approached the table almost on tiptoe, and we sat down on the edge of our chairs, as well. Aunt Mee studied us carefully and then scooted back in her chair a little.

"What on earth is bothering you children?" she asked.

The way she called us both "children" made Crystal and me look at each other in surprise. And when we looked back at Aunt Mee, I guess we both saw her in a new way—Aunt Mee, wisewoman!

Slowly and carefully, Crystal told Aunt Mee everything about what had happened, and Aunt Mee never changed the expression on her face at all, not even when Crystal told her about me being Roy-Ellis's own child. She just sat and listened, like she was drinking in every single word and rolling it around behind those black eyes. When Crystal came to the end, we all just sat there in silence, with Aunt Mee rubbing her thumb on the oilcloth table-cloth, humming under her breath, and wearing three deep creases between her eyes. We sat and sat and sat some more. Finally, Crystal said, "Can I fix you a cup of coffee?" Aunt Mee didn't look up but just nodded her head slowly. So Crystal got up, glanced at me, shrugged her shoulders a little, and put the kettle on the stove. I stayed at the table, watching Aunt Mee. Crystal put a cup of coffee in front of Aunt Mee, and Aunt Mee picked it up and sipped from it, still without speaking. Finally, finally, Aunt Mee finished her coffee and put the cup in the saucer with a little *click.*

"Here's what I can do to help you all out," she announced. "I got me a cousin lives in a little town about fifteen or twenty miles from here. Works for a real rich white lady who's gone almost all the time. You all can go there. My cousin will take you all in."

Crystal and I glanced at each other.

"You still working at the mall?" Aunt Mee asked.

"Well, yes," Crystal said. "Why do you ask?"

"'Cause that little town she lives in is on the other side of the mall—maybe even a little closer to it than you are here. Won't be as long a drive for you, and you won't have to look for another job. Yes!" Aunt Mee suddenly exclaimed. "That will work." Then she added, "But I don't know for how long. Long enough for you all to get things figured out anyways."

Crystal was nodding her head. "And nobody would know," she whispered.

"'Cept for me," Aunt Mee added. "And nobody would think to ask *me.*"

"Yes," Crystal said. "Yes!"

"Got a funny name, though," Aunt Mee said.

"Excuse me?"

"Got a funny name," Aunt Mee said again.

"What's got a funny name? The town?"

"Oh!" Aunt Mee laughed. "Not the town. My cousin." Then she laughed again. "Name's Buzzard."

"Buzzard?" Crystal and I both said at exactly the same time.

We all laughed a little, but we stopped real fast when Aunt Mee said, "Her mama named her that because she said a black woman had to be able to live off what nobody else wanted."

"Lord have mercy!" Crystal breathed. Then she added, "Was it really that way back then?"

Aunt Mee was forthcoming: "Oh yes. It certainly was. Still is, in some little towns. 'Cause the old ways die so slow." Then she looked at me. "But mostly, things are better now. There was a time when you and Savannah couldn't have been good friends. Not really. Well, let me go on home," Aunt Mee said. "I'll talk to Buzzard on the phone tonight and tell her about you all. I'll let you know what she says." Aunt Mee stood up and looked down at the kitchen table, staring and staring at the coffee cup.

"Dear Lord in Heaven!" she exclaimed, grinning. "I guess times certainly are better! I drank me a cup of coffee and me sitting at the very table with white women and never even thought about it!" How Crystal and I had changed from "children" to "women," we didn't know. We just grinned back at Aunt Mee.

We found a way!

The next day, Crystal and I took Molly and Little Ellis and walked down to Aunt Bett's house. We left Molly and Little Ellis playing in the bedroom, under Darlene's watchful eye and went into the kitchen. Crystal got us started. "Bett, Aunt Mee came over last night and I told her what has happened. And I think she can help us find a way."

"What?" Aunt Bett sort of squeaked, as if she had forgotten what we were talking about.

"I think we've found a way," Crystal repeated.

"A way to do what?" Aunt Bett was still staring at me.

"A way for us to stay together."

"How?"

"Well," Crystal started. "Aunt Mee has a cousin who lives in a town not far away, and her cousin keeps house for a real rich lady who's gone most of the time. We can go there, Aunt Mee says."

"Aunt Mee's cousin? What's her name? Where does she live?"

Crystal sighed. "I can't tell you."

"Why on earth not?" Aunt Bett was starting to sound alarmed.

"Because if *he* takes you to court, the judge would make you put your hand on a Bible and you would have to swear to tell what you know." The breath went out of Aunt Bett.

"It's the only way I can see, for now at least," Crystal said. "And, Bett, there's nothing holding me here now." Aunt Bett's mouth dropped open.

"Why, you have everything to keep you here!" Aunt Bett sputtered. "The house you're in and . . ." she swept her arm toward me. "And the children and me to help you!"

"Would you have us stay even if it means losing Molly?" Crystal leveled the question at Aunt Bett. Her words sat in the air for a long time and just wouldn't go away.

"No," Aunt Bett admitted at last. "Not if it means losing Molly."

A long silence then, with all our thoughts kind of fluttering around like little birds looking for a branch to land on. When Crystal finally broke the silence, her voice was strong and calm-sounding. "I can't tell you where we're going," she said. "But I'll be even closer to work than I am now. It'll mean less driving."

"Closer?" Aunt Bett fairly pounced on Crystal's words. "Someplace between here and the mall?"

"No, Bett. And don't try to figure it out," Crystal warned. "You just think about having to put your hand on a Bible and swear to tell the truth." She added, "And make us lose Molly."

Aunt Bett blushed. "You're right, of course."

Aunt Bett looked back and forth between Crystal and me, and I could tell that she was coming to agree with everything Crystal had said. Finally, her lips parted. "Not knowing where you all are? Or what's happening to you?"

Crystal nodded.

"For how long?"

Crystal shrugged her shoulders and shook her head. "I guess I'll have to talk with a lawyer or something. We'll figure it all out."

"And what about clothes?" she asked suddenly. "What about clothes, huh? How you going to put clothes on three growing children, Crystal? You tell me that!" Well, there it was—Aunt Bett's fear had turned into anger, right in front of my eyes. I thought it was probably a good sign, and Crystal was wise enough not to say anything, just yet. So we just were quiet and watched Aunt Bett struggling with herself.

Finally, Crystal said, "I got me a good job, Bett, and you've provided clothes for your own and mine as well. From now on, I can provide for my own."

My own! How beautiful!

Chapter Twelve

BUT oh, it was going to be so hard, saying good-bye to Aunt Bett and never knowing when we would see her again. And I just stood there, looking at her and thinking about how fast everything had changed and about how little it took to throw everything off track.

"You all take all the clothes I loaned you," Aunt Bett whispered. "And find a way to let me know you're okay."

"I'll call from a pay phone every once in a while," Crystal promised. "We'll be all right, Bett."

"Well, go on, then," Aunt Bett said in a gruff-sounding voice. "And God go with you. Let me know what you find out about getting a legal claim to Molly." Aunt Bett swallowed a sob. So we walked away in the dusk, with the porch light from Aunt Bett's house giving us all long, sad shadows that walked ahead of us.

But just as we got close to our house, we could hear a loud knocking. Crystal pulled us into the bushes, and when we peeked out from our hiding place, we could see a sheriff's car parked in our front yard. We ducked back into hiding, not saying a single word. The loud knocking went on for a long time, with a loud shouting of "Hello? Open up! Sheriff's department!"

Molly started whimpering, and I put my hand over her mouth and hugged her to me. Little Ellis never made a sound. Finally, the knocking stopped. We heard heavy footsteps go across our porch and down the steps. A car door opened and closed and an engine started up. Then the sound of tires on gravel and the red taillights growing smaller and smaller. Until they were gone.

"Jesus, help us!" Crystal breathed, and I added, "Amen!"

"Follow me," Crystal ordered, and we did. She led us through the bushes and around to our back porch.

"We mustn't turn on any lights," she warned. Then to me, she said, "Go get Aunt Mee!" I started running across the backyard, while Crystal herded Molly and Little Ellis into our house. Aunt Mee appeared just as soon as I knocked on her door.

"I been waiting and waiting for you all's lights to come on," she fussed. "Been wanting to tell you about what Buzzard had to say."

"Please come on over, Aunt Mee," I begged. "We've got big trouble!" She frowned and followed me down the steps and across the backyard, muttering things I couldn't quite make out.

"Why, your lights are still out!" she exclaimed as we got close to the house.

"Crystal's inside with Molly and Little Ellis," I explained. "But we're scared to turn on the lights. The sheriff's been here."

"Lord, help us!" Aunt Mee muttered. Crystal was waiting for us on the dark back porch.

"Aunt Mee, we gotta leave right away. Tonight!"

"I talked to Buzzard and she says for you all to come right ahead. She didn't expect it to be so fast, I don't think."

"I know," Crystal said. "I'm sorry."

"So what's going on over here? Dove said the sheriff's been around."

"It can only be one thing: He must be trying to serve a warrant so Molly's daddy can get her."

"Lord, help us!" Aunt Mee whispered yet again. "Now let's us think . . . and pray! Where are Molly and Little Ellis?" Aunt Mee finally asked.

"Sitting at the kitchen table," Crystal said. "I told them not to move an inch."

"Okay," Aunt Mee said. "First thing is we gotta get your car around here in the backyard, so you can load it up without anybody seeing. You get as much of your stuff as you can, throw it in the car, and then get out of here. I'll call Buzzard back and tell her you're on your way."

"Yes," Crystal breathed. "Oh thank you!"

"You all get the car," Aunt Mee said in a commanding voice. "I'll take Molly and Little Ellis home with me and keep them quiet. And when you're done, we'll put them in the backseat and you can be off."

We all went into the dark kitchen and found Molly and Little Ellis sitting exactly where Crystal had put them, their eyes wide and faces pale.

"Come on with Aunt Mee, you sweet babies," Aunt Mee crooned. And she led them out of the kitchen, across the porch, and into the dark backyard. Very quietly, Crystal drove the car around back, not putting on the headlights or stepping on the brakes, and in all that darkness, we started gathering up what all we could and throwing it into the open trunk. The whole thing felt like some kind of a terrible dream. I grabbed armloads of all those nice clothes Aunt Bett worked so hard to get us, and Roy-Ellis's hat because I couldn't leave it. I got all my treasures and wrapped them and my hand lotion in a towel and put them in the trunk, and

Molly and Little Ellis's clothes I jammed into a pillowcase. When the car's trunk was full, we shut it without making a sound and got in the car. Crystal didn't turn on the headlights; she just eased the car out onto the road and turned in at Aunt Mee's. I'd already put Molly and Little Ellis's pillows and blankets into the backseat, and Crystal and Aunt Mee got Molly and Little Ellis loaded in. Our most precious cargo loaded in, all safe and sound.

Aunt Mee put a piece of folded-up paper into Crystal's hand.

"Now don't you lose this," she warned. "Just go straight to the mall, like you're going to work. These directions will tell you how to get to Buzzard's from there." Then Aunt Mee suddenly reached out, grabbed Crystal's shoulders, and pulled her into a long, hard hug.

"Jesus go with you," she gulped. And then we were really on our way—to where, we didn't know. Just the quiet hum of the engine and the quiet, gentle sounds of Molly and Little Ellis breathing deep in sleep in the backseat.

So no matter what, we had each other. We were together, and that's all that mattered.

We rode along in silence for a long time, with nothing to see except our headlights on the gray pavement and once in a while, a large, dark shadow—a barn or maybe a house where everybody was sleeping. People who knew what their tomorrow would be like—people who would wake up in a familiar room. I didn't know what Crystal was thinking about, but once I saw her wipe her eyes. So I wondered if maybe Crystal was just as scared as I was about what was happening. Maybe even more scared, because it was a big job she was starting, taking care of a whole family and without Aunt Bett or Aunt Mee to help her out.

"Hey, Crystal?" The sound of my own voice surprised me.

"Yeah, Dove?" Her own voice was sleepy-sounding, like she'd had to come back from some place far away.

"We'll do okay," I said.

"Yeah, Dove."

When we finally reached the mall, I thought it looked like a strange, silent city. The outside was like a fortress, and I could only imagine the circus of lights and stores inside. And I wondered if I would *ever* get to go inside. There wasn't a single car in the big parking lot and all the streetlights made little yellow pools of light on the dark pavement. Crystal stopped the car in one of those light-pools and unfolded the paper Aunt Mee had given her.

"From the mall," Crystal read, "go north on the Waynesboro Highway until you come to the little town of Autry. Turn right onto Main Street. Go through town and watch for a Dairy Queen. Right beyond it, turn right onto Old Quincy Road. Go about five miles and as soon as you cross the bridge at Boggy Creek, watch for a roadside mailbox with a big, white swan painted on it." Crystal frowned. "A swan? Why a swan?" I shrugged my shoulders. I sure didn't know. She continued reading: "Turn in at the driveway and keep going until you get to the house. Buzzard will be expecting you." Crystal sighed and handed the paper to me. "Okay—north on Waynesboro Highway."

We drove all the way around the mall before we found

that highway, and then we had to figure out which way was north. That wasn't easy, because we had no sun to help us know what was east and what was west. Crystal drove real slow, drawing silent little circles with her right hand, while she figured out whether we should turn left or right. But finally, she got it straight in her heart. We turned left and were on our way.

"There's a flashlight under your seat, Dove. Look at the paper and see what we watch for next."

"We're looking for a town called Autry and turning right on Main Street," I answered. And then we drove on in darkness and silence. About ten miles down the highway, we crossed a railroad track, came to a flashing yellow traffic light, and turned right onto Main Street. I'd never heard of Autry before, and it was just as sound asleep as our own little town had been. Still, far ahead of us, we could see a Dairy Queen sign.

"Turn right after the Dairy Queen," I said. "That's supposed to be Old Quincy Road." We turned onto a dirt road, but there was no sign at all to tell us if it was the right one.

"I don't know," Crystal said. "Maybe this is it and maybe it isn't."

"Let's go that five miles and see if we come to a bridge," I suggested. So down that long, quiet road we went, with our headlights blazing onto the clay road and the dried, dead grass on either side. And we did come to a bridge. Of course, we didn't know what creek it was crossing, but we just kept going forward. Suddenly, on the right-hand side of the road, I saw a big metal mailbox with a white swan painted on it.

"This is it! There's the painted swan," I yelled, and

Crystal turned into a little sand-and-gravel driveway. Ahead of us, nothing to be seen. No house, no lights, no sign of anything.

"Where is it?" Crystal's voice was shaky.

"Just keep going," I said, with my heart beating hard and my teeth beginning to chatter. So on and on we drove, on the driveway that seemed to curve around something like a big pasture. There must have been a thousand crickets chirping in the grass, and the night was so hot and humid, Crystal had beads of perspiration running down her temples. And then, through the trees, I saw a glimmer of light.

"There!" I yelled again.

As we came closer, I saw that it was a house bigger than any I had ever seen, bigger, even, than the houses where the rich girls in my town lived. Two-story and made out of red brick, with a brass hanging-down kind of light fixture on the porch, and it blazing out light that turned the wide porch almost into daylight. Crystal pulled up almost to the front steps, and when she turned off the engine, all we could hear were crickets chirping.

"You stay here," Crystal ordered, and then she got out and started up the steps. But before she could even get to the porch, the front door opened and a big, big woman came out. Crystal just froze to the second step, looking up and up and up at this huge woman.

"Buzzard?" Crystal's voice quavered. And this big woman threw wide her arms and scooped Crystal up, just like she was a little doll or something.

"You poor babies!" she boomed, releasing Crystal a little and sweeping her arm toward the car where I sat with my mouth hanging open, and Molly and Little Ellis had waked up and were staring with wide, confused eyes. Maybe I was thinking that this cousin of Aunt Mee's would look a little bit like her, but that sure wasn't the case at all. Because this woman was just as different as could be. For one thing, she was so *big!* And I don't mean fat, either. Just that she was about as tall as Roy-Ellis had been and nearly as broad in the shoulders. Why, she made Aunt Mee seem like a round little peanut! And where Aunt Mee's skin was absolutely black—like black velvet—this woman's was like mahogany. Like the deep sunshine color of the china cabinet in Aunt Bett's dining room.

She put her hand on Crystal's shoulder and didn't say a word, just guided her back to our car, where she looked at me and at Molly and Little Ellis. I kept hoping the corners of her mouth would turn up. Because a smile from this big woman would certainly have felt good. But instead, the corners of her mouth turned down and a deep furrow grew between her eyes.

And if she changed her mind about taking us in, what on earth would we do?

Then, from either side of that deep frown, her eyebrows started lifting up, like two big black wings so strong, I almost expected to see them lift her right up into the air. And the eyes so deep and brown tilted down, like maybe she was going to sneeze or cry or something.

"You poor babies!" she said again, and this time, the words were almost moans, but I felt a big sigh of relief come through me, all the way from the bottom of my feet.

"Come on in! Come on in!" she boomed. "Let's get you all something good to eat and then get these little ones into a nice, soft bed. You don't have to worry about a thing," she assured us, as Crystal and I got Molly and Little Ellis untangled from the pillows and blankets in the backseat. "No ma'am! You don't have to worry about a single thing. 'Cause Buzzard's gonna take good care of you!"

Once we all herded into the house, we found ourselves in a huge hallway, with a ceiling that went up and up into a white, rounded space and going up into it a wide, mahogany stairway, with steps that fanned out like a lady's fold-up fan. To the right, a big parlor with lots of mahogany furniture and a fireplace. Buzzard herded us past that doorway and through a hall at the back, so that we came into a big kitchen that was warm and happy and filled with the smells of something wonderful.

"You all sit right down," Buzzard commanded, and silently, we did as we were told. At the stove, Buzzard spooned something into pretty blue bowls and brought it over to us. The best-smelling vegetable soup. Then she poured glasses of milk for us and put them on the table. Molly grabbed hers up and drank it down, almost in one big gulp.

"Gracious, honey," Buzzard beamed. "You were thirsty. Let me get you some more." While Buzzard went to the refrigerator for the big pitcher of milk, Molly and Little Ellis took up their spoons and started in on the good soup.

"Wait," I whispered. "That's bad manners to start eating before everybody's been served."

"Not tonight it's not bad manners," Buzzard contradicted me. "Tomorrow is plenty of time to think about manners. Tonight, let's just feed some hungry, tired folks here." The last thing Buzzard did was to take a fresh-baked loaf of bread and slice it up and put a big platter of it in the center of the table, and a dish with butter. After that, we didn't say much. Just gobbled up that good soup and that still-warm bread with lots of butter on it.

At the last, Little Ellis let out a good, loud burp that surprised us. Crystal looked at him as if she hadn't noticed a thing. "We sure do thank you for letting us stay here," she said to Buzzard. "We don't mean for it to put you out any, or to cost you anything."

"Put me out?" Buzzard almost snorted. "How could it put me out to help some folks need help as bad as you all?"

"Well, I just want you to know that we sure do appreciate it," Crystal added.

"Tell you what . . ." Buzzard began. "Let's us get these little ones into bed and then we can sit down and talk a little bit."

So Crystal and I scooped up the well-fed, tired little ones and followed Buzzard all the way up that long, curving stairway.

"I put the two little ones together," she said, pushing open the door to a large bedroom with two twin beds and a tall, mahogany cabinet for clothes, and a pretty table in between the beds with a large, blue lamp on it. Buzzard watched while Crystal and I stripped Molly and Little Ellis down to their underwear.

"Bathroom's right there," Buzzard said, indicating yet another door. So Crystal took Molly and Little Ellis into the bathroom while I gathered up their clothes, folded them, and put them on a chair.

"We usually put them into pajamas," I said, not wanting Buzzard to think that we were trashy people who put children to bed in dirty underwear.

"Well, tonight's kind of different," Buzzard said. "Tomorrow is time enough to worry about pajamas and such." Crystal brought Molly and Little Ellis back out of the bathroom.

"Sure is pretty in there," she said to Buzzard. Then we put the children into the two twin beds. But Little Ellis started shaking his head back and forth and pointing to Molly's bed.

"They're used to sleeping in one bed," I said.

"Then let them," Buzzard ordered. "Whatever makes them feel safe and loved is all that matters right now." So we put Little Ellis into bed with Molly, and Crystal said, "Dove, will you stay with them for a little while? They're in a strange place."

"Sure, Crystal," I said, even though I really wanted to go back down to the kitchen and be in on whatever conversation Buzzard and Crystal were going to have.

As they went out into the hallway, I heard Buzzard say, "And I put you and Dove in a room together, if that's okay."

"That's fine," Crystal answered. "That's just fine."

Then I could hear their footsteps going down.

Molly and Little Ellis were "spooning," the way they always did, with Molly curled around Little Ellis, and already, they were close to sleep. But just before she closed her eyes, Molly said, "We go bye-bye?"

"Well, we already *did* go bye-bye, Molly," I explained. "And we will stay here for a while."

"Oh," she breathed. "Okay."

In only a few minutes, Molly and Little Ellis were both sound asleep, and so I went down to the kitchen, where

Crystal and Buzzard were sitting at the table.

"Mee told me mostly about what's been happening to you all," Buzzard said. "And I said I was glad to be of help to you."

"We sure do appreciate it," Crystal said again. I noticed that the soup bowls and platter and glasses had already been cleared away, and I saw them sitting in the sink. So I went over and squirted some soap into the sink and started running water for washing them. At the table, Buzzard and Crystal went silent.

"And what's your name, girl-child?" Buzzard raised her voice so I could hear it over the water running into the sink. But it took me a second to realize she was talking to me.

"Ma'am?"

"I said, what's your name?"

"I'm Dove," I said, intent upon washing the milky glasses first and rinsing them real good.

"Well, Dove, I'm glad to see you know how to do what needs to be done without anybody telling you."

"Yessm," I said, handling those pretty blue bowls so carefully and thinking about how nice it was to wash such pretty things.

They went back to their talking. Crystal said, "Well, I need to find us an apartment, and I'll start looking tomorrow afternoon, soon as I get off work."

"No need to rush yourself," Buzzard said. "The lady who owns this house—the lady I work for—she's not likely to be back for a long time. And besides, she always believes in helping folks out, anyway. So you just take your time. And just how old are you, anyway?"

The way she shot that question at Crystal reminded me

of Aunt Bett, and I had to hide my smile.

"Twenty," Crystal lied easily, and I turned from the sink to look at her. She darted her eyes at me once, and then she stared down at her hands folded on the table.

"Twenty?" Buzzard echoed. "Don't look like no twenty to me."

Crystal didn't say anything else, so finally Buzzard added, "But twenty it is, if that's what you say."

"Thank you," Crystal murmured.

"Well," Buzzard added, "you all are welcome here. Don't be in any hurry."

"Thank you," Crystal said again.

Buzzard got up from the table.

"Why don't you pull you all's car around in the back of the house," Buzzard said. "I'll get the rest of this soup put into the refrigerator, and then me and Dove here will help you get your stuff inside." Crystal went out to do as Buzzard had said, and I finished washing and drying the dishes from our late-night supper. Buzzard put the leftover soup into the refrigerator and the remaining bread in the breadbox. While she put the dishes away, I wiped down the table, scooping bread crumbs into my hand so they wouldn't wind up on the floor.

"Where'd you learn how to do things right?" Buzzard asked.

"From my mama," I said. "And my Aunt Bett."

"Well, they sure did a good job of teaching you," Buzzard said. And that gladdened my heart more than I could say. "And you did a good job of learning," she added.

When Buzzard and I got to the back porch, Crystal had

already unloaded much of our clothes and stuff. Buzzard and I got great armloads and took them upstairs, where for the first time I saw the room Buzzard had fixed up for me and Crystal. And what a beautiful room it was! Right on the other side of the room where Molly and Little Ellis were sleeping, and all decorated in pink. Pink roses wallpaper and pink bedspreads on the twin beds. And a real dresser with an eyelet doily on it and a little stool for sitting on, and a tall bureau with deep drawers. And even a pink lamp on the mahogany table between the beds casting a pink glow over everything.

Buzzard led me to a big closet—so big that we could really walk right into it. Almost as big as Aunt Bett's famous closet. We hung up the clothes Aunt Bett had worked so hard to get for us. The sight of those clothes hanging in such a big, beautiful closet made my eyes sting. Why, I'd bet anything in this world that the rich girls in my school had closets that looked like this one—and beautiful bedrooms, as well—but the sight of all those clothes Aunt Bett worked so hard to get still made my heart feel like it was broken right in two!

"You okay?" Buzzard asked, and I made a mental note right then and there: *Nothing gets by this one!*

"I'm fine," I said.

"Well, here's the bathroom," Buzzard said, not sounding very convinced that I was fine at all. "It opens into this room and to the room where the little ones are sleeping." She reached inside the door and turned on the light. And then I knew why Crystal said something about the bathroom being so pretty when she came out with Molly and Little Ellis. Because it was the most beautiful bathroom I'd ever seen, with everything in pink and blue. Wallpaper with pink swans that had little blue bows around their necks and swam along in little pale blue circles of water. And a big ivory-colored tub with a shower curtain just like the wallpaper. A big pink counter with two pink sinks in it, and maybe as many as ten or fifteen pale blue, fluffy towels all folded and perfectly stacked along the side. On the floor was a small fluffy pink rug.

"You like it?" Buzzard asked, smiling, and once again, I thought, *She never misses a thing!*

"I sure do," I answered.

"Well then, let's go help Crystal. You all need to get some rest. I imagine she has to get up and go to work tomorrow." And that's what we did—Crystal, Buzzard, and I carried the last of our things upstairs.

"I'll go down and lock up and let you all get some sleep now. But do call me if you need anything."

"We will," Crystal said, but I was thinking that if we needed anything, I bet Buzzard would figure that out all by herself. Crystal took a long, hot shower in that pretty bathroom, and I put my bottle of hand lotion onto that real dressing table. When we were ready for bed, we opened both bathroom doors so that we could hear if Molly or Little Ellis needed us during the night, got into our beds, and turned off the lamp. We fell asleep smelling the soft, sweet aroma of soap from the warm bathroom and the tiny glow of a night-light in there that stayed on all night long. So we were safe and sound. *God bless Aunt Mee* was the last thing I remembered of that day.

But right in what felt like the middle of the night, I woke

up with a start.

"My notebooks!" I whispered into the little glow of light coming from the bathroom. And I sat right up in bed. For one little minute, I didn't even know where I was. Where was my bedside table behind the sheets? Oh—far away. And all my notebooks stacked in the closet and left behind. Gone. I leaned back into my pillow, but I felt as if my heart had been ripped right out! How could I have forgotten them? What would happen to them? And worst of all, would somebody maybe read them? I never even thought about our little house—did we rent it? Or did we own it? Because every month Roy-Ellis would make out a check and mail it. But was it for rent—or for a mortgage? If he was paying rent, who did he pay it to? Probably somebody rich enough to buy a house and not live in it. A man from one of those big white houses on the other side of town. Somebody like Michelle's father. All that pain in my chest just flared and roared like a forest fire.

Somebody may read my stories! Maybe laugh at my mama's liking to go honky-tonk dancing with Roy-Ellis! Oh, there had never been such a hurt in my heart before. More even than when my mama died. I stayed awake for a long time, lying in that pretty bed in such a pretty room in a big, beautiful house and yet feeling as if something in me had died and would never be the same again in all eternity. Finally, I got up and went through the bathroom and into the room where Molly and Little Ellis were asleep in the same bed, and I slipped in beside them. They were warm and sweet, like sleeping puppies. Just breathing their perfume made me feel a little bit better. So finally, I fell asleep, but only after I figured out that keeping Molly with

192

us and keeping our little family together was a lot more important than any story I could ever write.

Chapter Thirteen

I WAKED up the next morning hearing Crystal calling to me from our room.

"Dove? Dove? Where are you?" I pushed back the covers, eased myself out of bed so as not to bother Molly and Little Ellis and went through the bathroom toward Crystal's voice.

"Here I am," I said to Crystal. She was sitting up in her bed, rubbing her eyes and looking tired and confused.

"Oh—okay," she sort of moaned. "I've got to get ready for work, and I'm still so tired! I just don't know why I'm so tired!"

"You don't?" Once again, I knew that I sounded just like Aunt Bett. "We threw all our things into the car, we drove for over an hour, unloaded everything, and got just a few hours of sleep. And you don't know why you're tired?"

Crystal managed a smile. "Yes, I guess it was a lot," she admitted.

"Tonight you'll get to bed earlier," I encouraged. "And tomorrow you'll feel lots better."

"Okay. Thanks, Dove."

"It certainly was a lot, Crystal," I offered. "And it still is."

"Yeah, but I can do it." She sounded like she was trying to convince herself even more than me. So while Crystal washed her face, I made up the beds. But then I heard Crystal close the bathroom door and through it, I heard her being sick to her stomach. It was a terrible sound, and I really didn't know what to do—let her alone or go get Buzzard or what. But right at that very moment, Buzzard appeared at our door.

"You all okay?" she asked, with her big body filling up almost the whole doorway.

"I think so," I said, still not sure of what to do. Then, more terrible sounds from the bathroom.

"Crystal sick?" Buzzard demanded, and without waiting for an answer, she stomped over to the bathroom door and banged on it with her fist. "You okay in there?" she hollered.

"Yes," came Crystal's squeaky reply. Then, "Yes," with a stronger sound.

Buzzard stood there for a few minutes, frowning and staring at the door.

"Well, you get dressed and come on downstairs. I'll fix you some weak tea. Do you just fine." It was a final-sounding command, and Buzzard had already gone back downstairs when I heard Crystal moan, "Oh, Lord have mercy!" But I didn't know what she meant by that. I heard the toilet flush and then water running in the sink. And Crystal came out, pressing a blue washcloth to her paper-white face.

"Dove!" I heard Molly call, and I rushed into the other room to get them both into the bathroom, my face burning as I wondered if Little Ellis had wet the bed and how on earth would I be able to tell Buzzard about that! But—thank goodness!—they were both still dry, but in a big hurry to get into the bathroom. Afterward, I took them back to their bed.

"Sit right there," I commanded, and they did, of course. "You okay, Crystal?" I called.

"I'll make it, Dove," she called back. "Just don't know what on earth made me so sick." Then she added, "Listen, you do all you can to make things easy for Buzzard today, and I'm leaving some money here on the table, in case you all go to a grocery store. I don't mean for Buzzard to bear the burden of feeding us. You hear?"

"Yeah, Crystal. I hear." I got Molly and Little Ellis dressed. Their clothes were clean, of course, but pretty wrinkled. Still, it was the best I could do, for now. So we went down that curving staircase—right into a new morning and to Buzzard.

When we got to the kitchen, Crystal was ready to leave for work, but she still looked pretty pale. Buzzard held out a paper bag to Crystal. "This is some lunch I fixed you. But I didn't know you were feeling poorly, so maybe you won't want to eat that apple today. Save it for tomorrow." At the mention of food, Crystal looked a little paler, but she took the bag anyway.

"Thanks, Buzzard." Crystal glanced over at me and Molly and Little Ellis. "Now Dove here knows how to do almost anything needs doing, so you put her to work. And she'll keep Molly and Little Ellis out from under your feet."

"Won't be any trouble, Crystal," Buzzard assured her. "Matter of fact, I'm kind of glad to have me a little company, to tell you the truth. Gets awful lonely out here in the middle of nowhere. Well, you go on now and get yourself to work." Crystal hesitated for a moment, still looking at me, and I could hear the words she didn't say: *Don't let the children cause any trouble. Don't do anything to make Buzzard change her mind about letting us stay a little while.*

I nodded.

After we watched Crystal drive away, Buzzard herded Molly and Little Ellis toward the table.

"I didn't know what you all like for breakfast, so I made some biscuits and sausage. That sound okay?"

"It sounds wonderful," I said. So we all had breakfast together, with me and Molly and Little Ellis eating those wonderful, light biscuits with country sausage in them and drinking milk. Buzzard sat watching us and sipping from a thick, white mug of coffee.

"Well, you all sure do have good appetites," she observed.

"Oh—I meant to tell you," I said. "Crystal left me some money so I can help out with the groceries. We don't mean for you to have to feed us."

"Now where on earth did *that* come from?" Buzzard asked, frowning at me. I felt my face go all hot. Why, Crystal had been gone only a few minutes, and already maybe I'd said something to make Buzzard not want us anymore!

"I just meant that we don't want to make things hard on you," I sputtered.

"Oh, honey," Buzzard almost crooned. "I know what you mean. But it's more you all's own pride than not wanting things to be hard on me." With that pronouncement, she got up from the table, leaving me thinking about what she said. And maybe she was right. We certainly were a prideful bunch, dirt-poor though we were. I thought of Aunt Bett and all her pickles she traded for clothes. Yes, that was pride.

"Well, would you all like a tour of the house and the garden?" Buzzard asked. "Just leave the dishes for now. We'll take care of them later."

"Can I ask you a question?" I ventured.

"Well, sure you can," Buzzard said.

"The lady who owns this house. Where has she gone off to?"

"Well," Buzzard sat back down at the table. "Miz Swan goes to France a lot. She grew up there, and she has another house just outside of Paris."

"Paris . . ." I murmured, because I really couldn't imagine such a place.

"See," Buzzard went on, and I could see that she was warming up to tell us a good story. That way, she was a lot like Aunt Mee. "Mr. Swan came from a real wealthy family, and they're the ones who built this house in the first place. But when he was in France during the war, he met a beautiful French girl. Couldn't bear to leave her behind when he was sent back to the United States, so he married her and brought her home with him."

"That's lovely," I said.

"Oh yes," Buzzard agreed, nodding her head and looking into her cup. "He's been dead many years now, but she still keeps this house, where she came as a bride. Except now that he's gone, she likes to stay in France most of the time."

"Don't you get lonely when she's gone?" I asked.

"A little bit," she admitted, and then she laughed out

loud. "Let me tell you about the funniest thing Miz Swan ever did." She paused and looked around at us, to make sure we were paying attention. When she seemed satisfied that she had a firm hold on center stage, she went on: "When I first come here to work for the Swans—he was still alive back then—Miz Swan said she liked me right well and wanted to hire me. But she didn't like my name. Said it was purely sinful for a Mama to give her girl a name like Buzzard! So she said that if I wanted to work for her, I'd have to call myself Boo-zar. 'Cause she says to me that French people don't say the last sound of words, so we'd just let the 'd' get lost and I'd be Boo-zar. And by golly, that's what she called me from that moment on. Just that easy. And once I got used to it, I guess I liked it better than plain old Buzzard, sure enough!" She looked at us expectantly, waiting for us to let her know we liked her story.

"Which do you like?" I asked. "Because whichever one you like, that's the one we'll use."

"Well, with Miz Swan gone . . . to France, I mean . . . I guess the name my mama gave me is just fine. I'm not fancy-sounding Boo-zar at all. Just plain old Buzzard!" She laughed loudly, and then she surprised me by reaching across the table and patting my hand while Molly and Little Ellis studied us.

"These two little ones always so quiet?" she asked, drawing her brows together.

"Mostly," I said. "I guess they're kind of solemn, but that's the way they are," I explained.

"Solemn, yes," Buzzard said. "But they been through a lot. What all do they like to do?"

"They love watching cartoons," I said. "And having me read to them." I stumbled to a stop, with nothing else to add. "I guess that's about all."

"Well, they're certainly the quietest children I ever saw." Buzzard studied Molly and Little Ellis for another long moment before she suddenly slapped her hand on the table, making all of us jump. "Well, come on! Let's show them the garden! If there's anything that can make little feet want to run and play and help us get some color into those cheeks, it's the garden." Buzzard led us across the back porch and out into the yard. A big expanse of grass, and farther down the yard, a long line of trees. A real little forest that reminded me of the backyard grove we had shared with Aunt Mee. On the other side, lots of azalea bushes and dogwood trees, and at the last, we could see a small pond.

"Used to be there were big white swans in that little duck pool down yonder." Molly and Little Ellis, who, typically, had said nothing at all, grabbed each others' hands and started running toward the pond.

"Wait!" I yelled. "You'll fall in!" I started after them, but Buzzard held me back.

"Shucks, honey," Buzzard laughed. "It isn't deep enough to hurt anybody. Why, Little Ellis could stand up in it and it wouldn't come to more than around his middle. Let those little ones do a bit of running around. Be good for them." So Buzzard and I followed at a nice, slow pace, and when we got to the pond, Little Ellis was throwing pebbles into it and Molly had found a little branch and was drawing it across the water. I got to thinking about how that pond must have looked when Mr. Swan was still alive, with beautiful Mrs. Swan by his side and lovely real swans gliding back and forth.

"I'll bet it was just lovely, with the swans," I said, not even realizing I was going to say anything until I heard my own voice.

"Oh, yes," Buzzard agreed. Then she added, "Did you see the white swan on the mailbox when you all came last night?"

"I sure did. That's how we knew we were in the right place."

"Well, I'm glad you found the Swan Place so easily."

"Swan Place?" I asked.

"That's the name of this house and garden," Buzzard said.

Why, I'd never heard of such a thing in my whole life! A house and garden with its very own name!

"Swan Place," I murmured.

"Swan Place," Buzzard echoed.

When we went back into the house, Buzzard showed us around. Right inside the back door, there was a small room with a big, comfortable reclining rocking chair. Molly and Little Ellis spotted the television and looked up at me.

"Yes, they can watch cartoons in here," Buzzard said, turning on the set and settling Molly and Little Ellis onto the big chair.

"Across the hall there is my room," she said. "You all don't go in there."

"Yessm," I said. Then she showed me the dining room, with a huge, shiny mahogany table and a crystal cabinet just loaded to the hilt with every kind of beautiful plates and glasses you could imagine. "You all don't play in here," she intoned.

"Yessm."

"Then here's the parlor. You all don't play in here either."

"Yessm."

"Well, that's about it—you already know where the kitchen is—except for upstairs. There's your rooms and two other bedrooms. You don't play in either of those. One of them is Miz Swan's very own room and you don't mess around in it."

"Yessm."

"Let's us get those dishes done now, and then we'll make out a shopping list and go into town for some groceries. I didn't know what you all like, so I figured I'd just wait until you got here and you could tell me."

So we washed up the breakfast things, but when we came to Crystal's cup she'd had for her tea, Buzzard put it aside. "I think we'll want to make sure that one gets washed separately," she said. "Just in case whatever made Crystal sick is contagious." Afterward, we sat down at the table and Buzzard gave me a pencil and a piece of paper. "Let's make out a list," she said. "What do you all like to eat?"

"Well, Molly and Little Ellis like SpaghettiOs and peanut butter and jelly sandwiches. And we all like tuna sandwiches." Then I suddenly remembered Aunt Bett's good pork chop and rice recipe. "And I know how to make a real good pork chop casserole."

"Write that all down," Buzzard said. "And put down milk and eggs and bread too. What do you all like for breakfast?"

"Mostly cereal," I said. "But those biscuits you made us this morning were the best I ever tasted."

Buzzard beamed at the compliment. "I *do* make good biscuits, don't I?"

"You sure do."

Then she turned serious on me. "Now when we go to town, to the grocery store, if anybody talks to us, you leave it all to me. And no matter what I say, don't you contradict me."

"Yessm."

"And let's get you and the little ones dressed up a little bit, for going into town."

I wanted to ask her why, but I didn't.

Within a few minutes, I had Molly and Little Ellis and me dressed in some of Aunt Bett's best Sunday clothes, and when we came downstairs, I saw that Buzzard had changed from her faded house dress and into a stiffly starched black dress with a spotless, snow-white collar and cuffs. Buzzard studied us, looking over our somewhat wrinkled clothes—wrinkled because of how fast we'd had to throw everything into the trunk when we left home— just as I was looking over her crisp, black dress.

"We need to iron your clothes a little bit before we go into town," Buzzard announced. So Molly and Little Ellis sat at the kitchen table wearing only their underwear and shoes while Buzzard ironed their clothes on a pull-down ironing board that came right out of the kitchen wall. When she was done, and Molly and Little Ellis's clothes were well-pressed, Buzzard turned to me.

"Give me that blouse for a little minute, and I'll freshen it up for you."

Why, I was so surprised, I couldn't even speak, and my arms took on a mind of their own and flung themselves across my chest. I felt my ears going all hot, and I must have had a terrible look on my face, because Buzzard's mouth fell open.

"Oh!" she sputtered. "I'm sorry if I embarrassed you." I couldn't even speak, and that was probably just as well, because what was ready to fly off my tongue was a loud, ugly way of saying that I wasn't a *child,* for Heaven's sake! At least not a child like Molly or Little Ellis, who didn't mind one little bit to sit around without their shirts.

"Tell you what," Buzzard almost whispered. "You go into the pantry and hand me out your blouse through a crack in the door." That sounded fine to me, and I was glad she'd realized I wasn't a child.

So I went into the pantry, took off my blouse, and passed it to Buzzard through the mostly closed door. Then I stood in that dim, strangely sweet-smelling little pantry, reading the labels on the cans. I still had my arms crossed over each other on my bare chest, and I uncrossed them and looked down at myself. Flat as a pancake. Why, I didn't look a bit different from Molly or Little Ellis, so maybe Buzzard just didn't realize how much older than them I really was.

"Here's your blouse," Buzzard's muffled voice brought my arms right back up over my flat chest as she passed the freshly ironed blouse back to me. The blouse was smooth and still warm from the iron. When I came out of the pantry Buzzard looked us all over once again and pronounced, "Well, now that we're all presentable, let's go."

We followed Buzzard down a little path that ended at a small stone building I hadn't noticed before. When we walked around the side of it, I saw that it was really a low kind of garage—three sides and a roof, but no windows, and the floor was just gravel, right on the ground. And sitting there in all that cool dust and darkness was the biggest, blackest car I had ever seen.

"You all wait until I back it out," Buzzard said. "Don't want you walking through all that gravel and tracking it into the car." So we waited, standing out of the way. Buzzard got into the car—not without groaning about a bad knee—and then she turned the key. A big belch of blue smoke came out of the tailpipe as the engine started. And then the car came slowly, slowly backing out. I guess it was the biggest, strangest-looking car I had ever seen. Huge, actually, and with kind of a strange, square-looking hood.

"Well, come on and get in," Buzzard called to us, and I opened the back door and started getting Molly and Little Ellis inside.

"Don't put your feet on the seats back there," she said, and Molly and Little Ellis both looked at me with wide eyes.

"You do as she says," I reminded them sternly. They looked at each other and then, as they always did, they obeyed. I got into the passenger seat beside Buzzard, and was surprised to find that the car was so big, *my* feet almost didn't touch the floor.

"You ever see a car like this?" Buzzard asked.

"Never in my life," I answered.

"You know why?"

"No."

"'Cause this is what they call an honest-to-goodness

Rolls-Royce auto-mobile!" she chanted. "It's just about the most expensive car in the whole world. This is Miz Swan's car." I thought of the lovely Miz Swan, elderly now, but of how she must have been so young and beautiful, riding around in this very car with Mr. Swan and him so dapper and handsome at the wheel, and of how lucky I was to get to sit right there in Miz Swan's very own seat. Buzzard backed up a little more and then shifted the gears and went *flying* around the side of the house and out in front—all the way down that long driveway we sped, and by the time we reached the mailbox with the big swan painted on it, I'd quit flinching at how close we'd come to some of the trees. She did stop before we entered the main road, and I was ever so glad of that.

"Remind me now," she commanded. "On the way back, we need to get the mail. Will you remember that?"

"I'll remember." So we drove back down that dirt road we'd come in on only the night before—but it felt as if it that had been in another lifetime. Pretty soon, we were coming to the little town of Autry—into the main street right at the Dairy Queen.

"You little ones be good enough," Buzzard tilted her head toward Molly and Little Ellis. "And we'll stop and get us some ice cream when we're on our way back."

"You don't have to promise them things, Buzzard," I said carefully. "They know to mind, without being rewarded for it."

"Well, a little ice cream never hurt a youngun," she said. And I guessed she was right, so I didn't say anything else. In the town, we turned a corner and pulled into a parking space at a Red and White grocery store. It looked a lot like the little grocery store back home, and its perfume was exactly the same, but I really don't know how to say what it was like. Maybe the smells of paper bags and coffee and bread and oranges, all mingled together. Or something like that. We got our grocery cart, and Buzzard picked Little Ellis up and put him in the seat. Molly moved forward, took my hand, and that's how we started our shopping. But I'll say one thing: Buzzard sure didn't shop like Mama and Aunt Bett had taught me to do. Why, most of the time, she didn't even look at the price—just went down our list and tossed lots of stuff into the buggy. That was no way to get the best use out of the money Crystal had given us.

"It's going to be expensive," I said, not even knowing that I was getting ready to say anything at all.

"M-m-m-m?" Buzzard answered in a truly distracted way, because she was putting a big jar of apple jelly and a smaller one of orange marmalade into the cart. "What'd you say?"

"It's going to be expensive," I said again.

"What's going to be expensive?"

"All these fancy things."

"It'll be okay," she assured me. "Don't worry about it."

But I was thinking: *Don't worry about how much every-thing is going to cost? Why, whoever heard of such a thing!* But I didn't say anything else because I figured I'd ask Crystal how to say something to Buzzard that would make her understand. When we got to the fresh fruit sec-tion, Buzzard started piling shiny, red apples into a sack, but right next to the ones she was buying were some that weren't so red, but that were a lot less expensive. I started to say something, but then, once again, decided I'd just wait and talk to Crystal about it.

"Why, *Booz-ar!*" came a shrill voice. "I haven't seen you in a month of Sundays! And who are these adorable young people with you?" A thin white woman came toward us, looking at Molly and Little Ellis and me with open curiosity.

"Morning, Miz White," Buzzard said in a make-believe-cheerful voice. "You're shore nuff looking pretty this morning, if I do say so myself!"

"Why, thank you Booz-ar!" she chirped, and then she asked again, "Who are these lovely young people you have with you?"

"Well, Miz White, these here little ones are Molly and Little Ellis." Molly retreated behind my skirt.

"And this young lady here is Miss Dove." Buzzard stopped, but Miz White leaned forward and looked at me with her eyebrows high up on her forehead.

"These are the late Mr. Swan's great-nieces and great-nephew," Buzzard said easily, shaking her head and looking so sad. *What?* I was thinking—but I knew not to say anything. But why would Buzzard tell such a lie about us? But just in that moment, I got it figured out: She had to have something to say when folks asked, and this was the best story she could think of. I met Miz White's eyes and smiled.

"How do you do?" I said, extending my hand and taking her cold, thin one into it.

"Nice to meet you," Miz White murmured. "I didn't know Mr. Swan had any kinfolk at all," she said. Then, "Well, this is certainly nice. Is Miz Swan planning on returning home soon?"

"Oh, you know Miz Swan," Buzzard offered. "She'll come home when she's good and ready. But in the meantime, these children's parents are traveling as well, and so the children are staying with me. And there's another sister—she's older and has a fine job."

"I see," Miz White said, and I knew exactly that look in her face: She couldn't wait to get somewhere and see somebody else and tell them the newest news. Why, we wouldn't even get back home before our news would be all over town. I knew about that because it's that way in all little towns, no matter where they are. That's what my mama told me, and I believed her, mostly because I'd seen it happen myself.

"Will their stay be an extended one?" Miz White asked, with her pointy little nose just twitching.

"I expect so," Buzzard said.

"Long enough for Dove here to come to school?"

"Maybe," Buzzard offered. "Why Miz White, I'd forgotten all about you being on the school board," she added. Miz White lifted her head almost regally.

"Why yes, we'll need to know if we're to be honored by having the late Mr. Swan's very own great-niece in our school!"

"Yessm," Buzzard smiled again. "We'll let you know just as soon as these children's parents make up their minds about it."

Miz White cast one long, last look at us, and I could see approval in her eyes. The thin hand came out and we shook hands once again. "Bye-bye, you sweet little ones," she chattered to Little Ellis and to Molly. Then she looked into our buggy, seeing what we'd bought, I guess, and moved along to the big display of oranges.

Buzzard went back to putting those shiny, red apples into the sack, and as soon as Miz White had moved right on out of the fresh fruit section, she said to me: "You did just fine." And I don't know why, but having Miz White think I was related, even remotely, to the fabulous Swans was one of the nicest feelings I've ever had.

When we'd gotten everything on the list—and some things that weren't on it at all, like that orange marmalade—we went into the checkout line. I took the money Crystal had given to me and handed it to Buzzard.

"You don't have to do that," Buzzard said, frowning.

"Crystal told me to do it, so I have to," I explained. And Buzzard took the money. Then she noticed Molly and Little Ellis looking at the candy bars.

"Is it okay for me to buy some for them?" Buzzard asked me.

"I think so," I answered, trying to hide the big glow I felt inside of me. Miz White thought I was kin to the fabulous Swans, and Buzzard had asked *me* if it was okay for Molly and Little Ellis to have some candy. That was the very first time I knew I truly liked Buzzard. But in some strange way I couldn't understand, I knew that it wouldn't be the last time I felt that way about her.

We loaded our groceries into Miz Swan's big car and got Molly and Little Ellis settled in the backseat.

"Remember not to put your feet on the seat," Buzzard reminded them, and it certainly made me think of Aunt Bett's always telling us to be sure to change our good clothes.

"I think I know why you told Miz White we were Mr.

Swan's relatives," I said, as Buzzard backed the car out of the parking space. She cut her eyes at me and didn't say a thing, so I went on: "It's so folks in town won't go around asking questions about us," I suggested.

"That's about right," Buzzard said. "You're from a little town, and you know what it's like."

"Sure do. Everybody knows everybody else's business, all the time."

"Well, it's a little easier, what with us living so far out of town. But school's going to start soon, and if you all are still here, you'll have to be awful careful to remember what I've told everybody."

"I'm sure I can do that," I said. "Why, you sounded so convincing back there, I almost started believing it myself!"

My compliment made her smile a little. "Good," she said. "I *better* be convincing!"

We were getting close to the Dairy Queen. "You all want ice cream?" she asked. "It's mighty close to lunch time, but I said we'd stop, and I'm ready to do it."

"I think the candy will be enough," I told her, glancing into the backseat where Molly and Little Ellis were sitting quietly and in perfect obedience to Buzzard's command about keeping their feet off the seat. They were both looking at me, but I couldn't see any disappointment in their faces at all. "Yes," I concluded. "The candy will be enough."

When we got back to the big mailbox with the white swan painted on it, I reminded Buzzard about us getting the mail, so she stopped the car, got out, and opened the box. She came back to the car with a big pile and put it in my lap.

"Hold onto this, will you, Dove?"

"Sure," I said. "Can I look at it?"

"I guess so," Buzzard said kind of suspicious-like, as she shot us up the long drive to the house. Almost every single thing was addressed to Mrs. John Jerome Swan—except for some envelopes from a law firm, which were addressed to Buzzard herself. I wondered what kind of business she had with a lawyer, but it wouldn't be polite to pry. So I didn't.

We had a good lunch of peanut butter and jelly sandwiches—Buzzard made hers with that expensive orange marmalade—and big bowls of cream of tomato soup. After we washed up the dishes, I told Buzzard it was time for Molly and Little Ellis to have their naps.

"Good!" she said enthusiastically. " 'Cause it's time for my soap opera." Then she added, "What do you do while they're asleep?"

"I usually write in my . . ." I stumbled to a halt.

"You usually write what?" she urged, but my throat had gone tight on me and I had trouble saying anything.

"What's wrong?" she asked, all concerned and wearing a frown—but with a soft something in her eyes. I swallowed hard.

"I was going to say that I usually write in my notebooks," I charged forward. "But I forgot them when we had to leave home so fast."

"That all?" Buzzard was relieved.

"All?" I yelped! "All? Those were my stories. About my mama and Roy-Ellis and Crystal and Aunt Mee and Savannah!"

"Savannah?" Buzzard said. "Who's Savannah?"

"She's Aunt Mee's granddaughter—and my best friend," I said, feeling my throat trying to tighten up.

"Well, honey," she crooned. "I wish you'd said something to me about wanting new notebooks while we were in town."

"I don't want new ones," I argued. "I want my old ones, but they're . . . gone."

"Maybe so," she agreed. "But you can get new notebooks and write all your stories again. Probably be better for having written them twice." Why, I'd never thought of such a thing. I started searching back through my mind, and yes, Buzzard was right. I *could* write them again. I could remember almost every single word!

"Do you really think I could write them again?" Somehow, I wanted her to reassure me—tell me that she guaranteed it was possible.

"Sure you can. Wrote 'em the first time, didn't you?"

"I did that."

"Then next time we go to town, we'll get you new notebooks," she said.

"Until then . . . do you maybe have some paper I can borrow?" I asked, suddenly filled with a burning resolve to write all of my stories again. Only better.

"Let's go see what we can find," Buzzard said. So we went together into the parlor, to a big cherry desk. Buzzard opened the top right-hand drawer, and there were great stacks of creamy-white paper, with a kind of texture to the pages like I'd never seen on paper before. She lifted out a handful of the papers.

"Think this will be enough?" she asked.

The paper in my hands felt heavy and rich—and at the

top of each page were scrolled initials M.E.S.

"What's that mean?" I asked.

Buzzard looked at the pages and smiled. "Mary Elizabeth Swan," she said, almost dreamily. "Miz Swan's very own personal, pure linen stationery."

"Won't she mind me using it?" I hated the thought that one of these days, the elegant, elderly Miz Swan would come home from France and wonder who used so much of her beautiful paper!

"She won't mind," Buzzard assured me. "She doesn't write many letters anymore. Now here's you a pen, as well. Are you all set now?"

"Yes. Oh yes."

I got Molly and Little Ellis into their bed for a good nap and then tiptoed downstairs. The television was on in the little room off the back hallway, and the soap opera had a young man and young woman who were having a fuss with each other. "You don't love him," the young man said. "You love me." "No, Dan," said the woman. "That's always been your imagination. Only your imagination!" When I peeked further into the room, I could see that Buzzard was in the recliner chair—but she was sound asleep. I went into the kitchen, where that stack of beautiful, cream-colored paper was waiting, and I started right in to writing a story called "Mr. and Mrs. Swan and the House They Lived in Together." There would be plenty of time later to remember all my other stories and get them onto paper again, but first of all, I wanted to write this one.

Why, I could have spent the entire rest of that day writing the story of Mr. and Mrs. Swan—that big house so quiet and peaceful and the kitchen filled with the sweet smell of all that fruit Buzzard had bought and put into a big bowl in the middle of the table. And the way the pen felt on that fine paper was something I hadn't expected. Made me feel that every single word I was putting down was fine, indeed!

But after a long time, Buzzard came into the kitchen, with her face all soft from her good nap and her eyes a little cloudy.

"You doing okay?" she asked.

"Oh, yes!" I breathed. "Thanks for letting me use this beautiful paper."

"Might as well," was all she said. A little later, Molly and Little Ellis waked up from their naps, and their cheeks were pink and they were well rested. We all had some milk and ginger snap cookies—another expensive thing Buzzard had bought at the store. But oh, they were so good! Then Buzzard started all of us in to doing the housework. She got a whole drawer full of real sterling silver tableware out of the buffet in the dining room, sat Molly and Little Ellis down at the table, gave them some soft rags, and set a jar of silver polish between them.

"Here's how you do this," she said, and they were both watching her intently.

"You put just a little bit of this stuff on the rag—just a little, mind you—and you rub the silver until it shines." She demonstrated for them, and on a spoon that I couldn't see how it could be any shinier than it already was. But when she finished and showed the spoon to Molly and Little Ellis, their eyes went wide and Molly smiled.

"Do it just that way," Buzzard said. Then, "Now, Dove, you come with me."

I followed her to the pantry and she gave me another soft rag and a bottle of red-colored furniture polish. "I'm going to trust you to do all the furniture in the parlor," she announced, and she made it sound like she'd given me something very, very special to do. We went into the parlor together and she showed me just how much of the polish to put onto the rag and how to polish all that beautiful mahogany furniture until it gleamed. The furniture polish had such a lovely aroma to it—like something magnificent and old and very precious, and the furniture was beautiful indeed. Down the hallway, I heard the vacuum cleaner start up, so I guess Buzzard was cleaning up somewhere else. That's the way we spent most of the afternoon, and when we were done, Buzzard inspected the silver and showed Molly and Little Ellis a few places where they hadn't wiped off all the silver cream. Then she came into the parlor and looked at the furniture.

"You're a good learner, Dove," she said. And that pleased me mightily!

Then we all went outside, and Buzzard showed Molly and Little Ellis how to get some of the ground ready for begonia plants she wanted to put in. And I walked down to the little pond and stood there for a long time, imagining all the beautiful, white swans that used to sail across it—back when Mr. and Mrs. Swan were young and beautiful and so much in love.

The last thing we did that day was to make Aunt Bett's pork chop casserole, and when it was simmering away on the stove, I heard Crystal's car come up in the back of the house.

"Crystal's home," I called. Molly and Little Ellis came

out of the little room where they had been watching television, and when Crystal came in the back door, we were all waiting for her.

"Goodness, what's going on?" she asked. She looked tired, but her face wasn't that awful, pale color anymore.

"We're just glad you're home," I said. "We've almost got supper ready. Did you have a good day at work?"

"Sure did," Crystal laughed, digging into her smock pocket and coming out with a whole handful of dollar bills and some change. "Tips were just great!" Then she frowned, "Buzzard, did Dove remember to give you grocery money?"

"She sure did," Buzzard said. "But wasn't any need of it."

"Oh yes, there certainly was," Crystal argued back. And from out of the handful of bills, she pulled out three dollars.

"You put this away toward the next time you have to buy groceries," she said, thrusting the bills at Buzzard.

"No need," Buzzard said softly, but she took the bills anyway, after she got a good look at Crystal's determined face.

"And were the little ones good for you?" she asked me.

"Good as gold."

"And it wasn't too much for you, having our family around all day?" she questioned Buzzard.

"Not at all," Buzzard beamed. "Matter of fact, they did lots of good work for me. Saved my old hands and back a little."

"Well, that's good," Crystal said. "Let me run upstairs and change my clothes before supper," she said.

When Crystal came back downstairs, wearing blue jeans and with her hair in a ponytail, she looked almost like a little girl herself. But one with something tired-looking around the eyes. Buzzard and I had the table all set and a big platter of Aunt Bett's pork chop casserole in the middle of it, and white rolls with real butter and big glasses of lemonade—because Buzzard said it was dangerous to drink milk when you ate pork. I remembered that we'd had milk with our sausage and biscuits for breakfast, but I didn't say anything about that.

"Not good for you," Buzzard declared. "Won't have you all getting sick." So lemonade it was, and we all ate and ate and didn't say much, we were enjoying that casserole so much. And right when supper was over, we heard a low roll of thunder and the lights flickered.

"Storm coming," Buzzard declared, getting up from the table, going to the pantry, and coming back with a big kerosene lantern.

"Sometimes we lose our power for a little while," she said, putting a package of matches on the table, right beside the lantern. And sure enough, right at that moment, another low roll of thunder came, and the lights flickered once again and then went out.

Such darkness! But then we heard the scratch of a match and a little light put to the wick of the lamp, and in only a moment, there was a pool of warm, yellow light all over the table where we were sitting together. I looked around at Buzzard and Crystal and Molly and Little Ellis, and they were all leaning into the pool of light. And behind every one of them nothing but darkness.

I don't know why, but I liked that ever so much. Us all

huddled around the light, together and safe, while the thunder muttered and the wind came up. A few flashes of lightning lit the kitchen windows and the door to the back porch, but we didn't really seem to care.

"We need a good storm. It'll bring rain to water your begonias," Buzzard said to Molly and Little Ellis. "Help them make pretty flowers."

"Buzzard showed Molly and Little Ellis how to get the ground ready for new plants today," I explained to Crystal.

"That was good of you," Crystal said.

"No trouble," Buzzard muttered. "Just wish you folks would stop thanking me all the time, is all."

Her words surprised Crystal. "But we *should* thank you," Crystal argued. "Look what you've done! Taken us all in when we had nowhere to go and had to run to keep Molly with us." She stopped and clapped her hand over her mouth. But Molly was resting her cheek on her arms and watching the flame in the lamp.

"Be careful," Buzzard whispered. Outside, the soft, warm rain started falling, sending the curtains lifting out from the window and putting a sweet perfume through the kitchen. We all just sat together, nobody saying much of anything. But we were content.

Buzzard was right: The storm didn't last long, and within a few minutes, the lights came back on and the big refrigerator began its purring sounds.

"See?" Buzzard blew out the flame in the lamp.

Crystal said, "Buzzard and Dove, do you mind if I don't help with cleaning up tonight? I'm just so tired, I want to go to bed early. But I'll help next time, okay? And tomorrow, I'll start in to finding us an attorney."

"I know one that's good," Buzzard said, and I was thinking about those letters that had come in the mail to Buzzard that day. "You just work on getting some good rest, and we'll get all the rest figured out."

"I'll be feeling better tomorrow—I promise," Crystal said.

Buzzard and I cleared the table and did up the dishes, and when we were through, Buzzard said, "I'm right tired myself tonight, Dove. So can you get Molly and Little Ellis to bed?" I thought that was kind of a strange thing for her to say, but later on, I figured that maybe it was because we were getting ourselves all twined around each other— but in a real nice way.

"Sure. You go on to bed. We'll be just fine." So Buzzard made sure all the doors were locked, and I took Molly and Little Ellis upstairs. I didn't want to give them a tub bath, because I was afraid we'd disturb Crystal, but I gave them sponge baths and got them into clean pajamas and read them another three stories before I went back downstairs and sat at the kitchen table once again, enjoying the story of Mr. and Mrs. Swan.

It was pretty late when I turned out the lights and went upstairs to bed. And lying there in that beautiful room, with Crystal breathing so sweet and steady, I thought long and hard about the first day of our new lives. About Mr. and Miz Swan and what Buzzard told Miz White, and about Molly and Little Ellis learning how to plant seeds, and about that heavy, fine paper I was writing on, and at the last, about how nice it was to be in a beautiful bedroom high up in that solid house, with all the sounds of the country-side around me. Crickets chirping, and somewhere far off—probably down at the pond—a big old frog adding his deep sound to the night. So that was the way our very first day at the Swan Place turned out, and when I finally fell asleep, I was thinking of two beautiful white swans gliding across the pond, swimming back and forth, back and forth—and with their graceful necks bowed and twined together.

Chapter Fourteen

I SLEPT deeper and sweeter than I ever had in my whole life, but I still heard when Molly called to me, so I took her to the bathroom and then crawled back into that warm, safe bed and went right back into a deep, dreamless sleep. But when first light was coming in the window, I awoke to a strange sound. A choking kind of sound. Somebody being sick.

I raised up on my elbow and saw that the bathroom door was closed and Crystal's bed was empty. She was sick again. I put my head back down on the pillow, and at the last, I put the pillow over my head. Because I was afraid that if I heard much more of that, I'd get sick myself. But after a while, the terrible sounds stopped, and a few minutes later, I heard the bathroom door open.

"You okay?" I asked.

"Oh sure," Crystal said lightly. "Must have eaten something that didn't agree with me, is all." I took the pillow off of my head and looked at her. She was smiling to beat the band and starting to get dressed. But her face had that same pasty look she'd had the morning before.

"Are you sure?" I questioned her.

"Of course I'm sure," she smiled at me again. "I gotta get ready for work."

"Okay," I said. "If you're sure. I better go get Little Ellis up before he wets the bed."

"Dove," Crystal's voice stopped me. "You did real good yesterday. I hope it will all go that smooth today."

"Oh, it will," I promised. "You just have a good day at work and don't worry yourself. Maybe that's what making you sick—you're worrying so much."

"Yeah. Maybe," Crystal said.

When Molly and Little Ellis and I started down the stairs, I could smell that good, warm-flour smell of fresh biscuits coming from the kitchen. Buzzard was at the sink, and I guess Crystal had already left for work. In the middle of the table was a whole platter of hot biscuits, with butter and jelly to go on them. And glasses of milk.

"Oh, you made your good biscuits again!" I said to Buzzard.

"Sure doesn't take much to please you all," she grumbled, but I saw her smile.

Molly and Little Ellis and I ate three whole biscuits apiece, while Buzzard sat near us, sipping her coffee and watching us with a relish she tried to hide. When it was time to do up the dishes, I noticed Crystal's teacup sitting at the side of the sink.

"Crystal was sick again this morning," I told Buzzard. "You think we better wash her cup separately?"

"Don't think so," Buzzard said. "Think what she's got, we can't catch from her."

"We can't?"

"We can't," she repeated. And then she wouldn't say anything else.

I made up my mind right then and there that I was going to tell Crystal she should see a doctor, but it was Saturday, and so she had had to leave extra early, what with it being the busiest day at the salon. But I would say something to her when she came home. Maybe a doctor could give her some medicine so that she wouldn't have to be sick every single morning.

Later, while I was washing up our breakfast dishes, Buzzard got a big broom out of the pantry and leaned it up against the sink. She started untying her apron. "I have to go into town for a few things," she said. "Would you sweep off the back porch real good for me while I'm gone?"

"Sure."

"And maybe wipe out the rocking chairs too—make sure they're nice and clean?"

"Sure. What's going on?" Because Buzzard's voice had such a serious sound in it.

"Circle of Jesus," she answered easily, as if I should know what that meant.

"Circle of Jesus?"

Buzzard had picked up her purse and was starting for the back door.

"What's a Circle of Jesus?" I raised my voice so she would be sure to hear me. Because I couldn't stand for her to leave before I knew what it was.

"Circle of Jesus is kind of like a club—women who are in my Sunday School class." She smiled. "We've been meeting like this for so many years, I don't even know how long it's been. On this back porch when the weather's nice. We study up for Sunday's lesson. Read the Bible together. Gossip a little bit, maybe."

"Oh."

"And pray," she added.

I finished drying the dishes, rubbing the dish cloth in a circular motion in the middle of each plate and thinking: *Circle of Jesus. Circle of Jesus.* When I'd put the last dish away, I took the broom, swept off the big back porch just as Buzzard had asked me to do, and then wiped out each of the wooden rocking chairs. Eight of them altogether. And the whole time, I kept thinking, *Circle of Jesus! What a lovely sounding thing!* Then I got to thinking about Miz Swan and wondering where she went to church—whenever she was home, of course. I'd need to ask Buzzard about that, because I meant to keep Aunt Bett's good example to me and Molly and Little Ellis going strong. But Crystal—Sunday was her one and only day off, so I wouldn't try to make her get up early. That just didn't seem right. I heard the big car pulling into the garage, so I went out and helped Buzzard carry in the brown bags from the grocery store. The bag I carried had a big bunch of green grapes right up in the top, and they smelled so sweet and good and cold on that hot summer morning. Down in the bottom of the bag there must have been a cantaloupe, because I could smell that sweet perfumy aroma as well. And Buzzard was carrying a basket of ripe peaches whose aroma made my mouth water. When we got to the porch, Buzzard looked around it carefully. "Looks real nice," she said.

"Thanks." I didn't add that I wasn't used to having anybody to thank me for just doing the things I should be doing anyway. In the kitchen, we unloaded the sacks. Six cans of tuna—the expensive kind. The grapes and cantaloupe, a head of lettuce, and another big bag of apples.

"I got extra apples," Buzzard said. "In case you and Molly and Little Ellis wanted some."

"What are you going to make?"

"Some special tuna salad, with chopped apples and pecans in it, this fruit, all clean and chilled, some of my famous homemade white rolls, and for dessert, pecan pie."

"For the Circle of Jesus?" I asked.

"Oh yes—those ladies sure do enjoy their food! Me too," she added, patting her stomach. "But I need you to get out from under my feet a little while, so why don't you take Molly and Little Ellis outside? Isn't good for them to stay cooped up in the house all the time." While I was helping Molly and Little Ellis get their shoes on, I could hear Buzzard working in the kitchen, and I never heard such flurry going on before—except for that time when Aunt Bett got so mad at Roy-Ellis. But these weren't mad sounds at all. Just busy kitchen sounds. Chopping and stirring and the oven door opening and closing.

Later, Buzzard came out onto the porch, carrying a platter of sandwiches and with a cloth folded over her arm.

"You all sit down here on the steps and eat your lunch," she said. "Way too hot in that kitchen for you." Well, it may have been hot as the dickens in that kitchen, but the smells that were coming out of it made my stomach rumble.

"What's that smells so good?" I asked Buzzard.

"My good, homemade yeast rolls," she waggled her

head a little, to let me know that she was proud of those rolls. "I always make 'em for Circle of Jesus. Why, if I ever *didn't,* I expect those good sisters would cause a riot or something! Now you all eat your sandwiches, and I'll save out a few rolls for you to have, but not until after the meeting is over."

"Can I come to the meeting?" I asked. "After I get Molly and Little Ellis down for their naps?"

Buzzard frowned. "I don't think so. We don't usually have guests at our meetings. But when it's over, I'll let you come out and meet all the sisters."

Later, I had just finished reading a third story to Molly and Little Ellis and settled them down for their naps upstairs when I heard a truck driving around to the back of the house. From the window, I watched as it slowly rolled to a stop just outside the door to the back porch. The back of the truck had three big, wooden rocking chairs in it and three of the biggest women I've ever seen in my life were sitting in them. When the truck stopped, they got up and, moaning a little, they got down out of the back and went to the passenger side of the cab. Two of them hovered around for a minute or two, while the other one stepped back into the shade of a pecan tree and fanned herself with a cardboard fan like they have in church. When the other two backed away in perfect formation from the truck, I saw that there was a little bitty, very old, very bent woman riding on their strong black arms, just like she was sitting in a swing. Then the driver's door opened, and yet another woman emerged. She was every bit as big as the other three, and as I watched them moving toward the back porch, I was thinking that in all my life, I'd never seen such finely dressed folks.

Two of the women were wearing identical dresses: pink with white lace collars and white stockings and shoes. Of the other two, one was wearing a pale-green-and-white checked dress and the other a pale lavender. And the little bitty old lady they were carrying on their arms had on a buttercup-yellow dress that was so small, it could almost have fit Molly. They all wore snowy white gloves and hats with little nose-veils on them. I watched them moving toward the back porch until I couldn't see them from the window any longer.

Chapter Fifteen

I'LL say one thing: I did try very hard and for a long time not to go spy on the Circle of Jesus folks, but in the end, I did it anyway. Maybe it happened because the bedroom was so hot. I'm not sure. All I know is that I turned on the fan, aimed it at where Molly and Little Ellis were sleeping, and tiptoed down the stairs. In the hallway, I could hear the voices from the back porch, but I couldn't make out the words. I peeked into the kitchen, where the dishes and glasses from the lunch were stacked by the sink.

Good! I thought. *I'll wash the dishes, and that will keep me from spying!* So I put the dishes into a sink full of warm, soapy water, and I was careful not to let anything clatter loud enough for Buzzard to hear it and maybe make me go back upstairs until the meeting was over. After all the dishes were washed, dried, and put away, I washed and dried all the glasses and polished them until they gleamed.

When Buzzard suddenly came into the kitchen, I jumped—like she'd caught me doing something wrong.

"What a nice thing for you to do!" she said in surprise.

"The Circle of Jesus meeting over?" I asked, realizing that I was truly disappointed that I had resisted the urge to spy.

"Time for dessert," Buzzard answered, getting out some pretty cake plates and putting a big piece of pecan pie on each one. Then she put a scoop of vanilla ice cream on top of each slice.

"Want me to help you take it out?" I offered, just bursting with curiosity about the women.

"No, thank you," Buzzard said. "I'll call to you when we get done, so you can come meet my sisters."

"Sisters?"

"In the Circle of Jesus, we're all sisters," she explained. And that's the very minute I decided that I *would* spy! Because once again, it was the only way I'd find anything out. So when Buzzard had taken the last dessert plate out to the porch, I tiptoed down the hallway and slipped into Buzzard's room, which was right up against the back porch. Her window was already open, so I sat down on the floor and listened. At first, all I heard were forks clattering against the dessert plates, but then somebody moaned a happy "M-m-m-m! You sure enough outdid yourself with this fine dessert, Sister Feed-My-Sheep!"

Sister Feed-My-Sheep?

"Why, thank you, Sister." It was Buzzard's voice, sure enough, but what on earth was somebody doing calling her by that strange name?

"I expect we better try to wake Sister Blood-of-the-

Lamb," said another voice. "Else her ice cream will get all melted."

Sister Blood-of-the-Lamb?

A rumble of murmurs, and I lifted myself up a little and peered through the very bottom of the window. I couldn't see very much because two of the rocking chairs had their backs to the window, and both of those chairs—like all of the others, except for the chair of the very old, very small lady—were filled by massive bodies. But then, one of the chairs tilted forward a little, and across the circle I could see the little old lady, all crumpled up and folded in on herself. Just like Molly and Little Ellis if they fell asleep before I could get them into bed. And her pretty little hat had slid forward so far over her face that the hat was all I could see.

"Sister Blood-of-the-Lamb?" Another woman leaned forward and tried to wake up the old lady. And the women sitting on either side of her were patting her tiny hands.

"Oh, Jesus! Take me home!" came the shrill squeak, and the old lady lifted up, looked up, her eyes cloudy and confused. "Did Jesus come?" she asked no one in particular.

"He *always* comes where two or three are gathered together in His name," said Buzzard in a gentle voice. "But did the Second Coming happen while you were taking a nap? No. Not yet."

One of the other women said, "We just wanted you to eat your dessert before all the ice cream melts."

"Ice cream?" The same shrill, not-quite-awake sound. "Where's ice cream?" Oh-so-willing hands fetched the slice of pecan pie and passed it to her.

"We through praying?" she asked, before she would

take a single bite. And satisfied with the nodding heads, she cut right into the slice of pie and stuffed a big bite into her tiny mouth.

"Praise the Lord!" somebody said.

"Amen!" somebody else said.

And right then and there, I knew for sure that I truly liked the Sisters of the Circle of Jesus, even though I didn't know a single one of them or understand why they all had such strange names.

So they all just enjoyed their good desserts and they talked and nodded their heads and every few minutes, somebody would say, "Well, praise the Lord!" and they would all murmur "Amen!" But then, every once in a while, they would all lower their voices and lean forward in their rocking chairs, making that circle even smaller and tighter and talk so low that I couldn't understand a word they said. When I saw Buzzard get up and start gathering up all the dessert plates, I ran on tiptoe back down the hall, went into the kitchen, and started running water in the sink. And I wasn't a moment too soon, either, because in only a few seconds, Buzzard came in, carrying plates, and one of the sisters was carrying some, as well. One of the women in a pink dress.

"Well, thank you, Dove!" Buzzard said. "You've got the wash-water all fixed. And doesn't a single one of these plates even need scraping!"

The woman added, "That pie was so good, I wanted to lick my plate! Awful hard for me not to do it!"

Buzzard looked so pleased at that. "You liked my pecan pie that much?"

"I sure did," the woman murmured. Then, "And who's

your good helper here?"

"Oh, this is Dove. I told you all how her family is staying with me." I turned from the sink and smiled at the woman. And at the same time, I was thinking that maybe they were talking about us when they had all leaned forward in such a tight circle and talked so very low.

"Dove," Buzzard said, "This is Sister All-Forgiving."

Sister All-Forgiving? What kind of a name was that?

The woman smiled broadly at me, showing dazzling white teeth, and before I could dry my hand and hold it out to her and say "How do you do?" she had wrapped me up in a big hug that took me completely by surprise! A hug that crushed my nose into her strong shoulder and mashed my shoulders right into the sides of my neck. When she let me go, she and Buzzard both laughed.

"Come on," Buzzard said. "Let's go introduce you to the rest of the sisters. Molly and Little Ellis still asleep?"

"Yes," I gulped, wondering if I was going to get bear-hugged by all those other big, strong women. Such a thought even made me forget to ask how Sister All-Forgiving came by such a strange name.

When Buzzard led me out onto the porch, the women stopped talking all at once and looked at me with faces that were like whispered question marks.

"Sisters, this is Dove I told you about." The hats bobbed as all of the women nodded their heads at me. Except for the real old child-sized sister, who had fallen asleep again, with her hat tilted down over her face. Buzzard took a deep breath. "Dove, these are the Sisters of the Circle of Jesus," she announced in an important-sounding voice. Starting with the other woman who had on a pink dress just like

Sister All-Forgiving, Buzzard said, "This is Sister Living-Word." And I looked into the open and friendly face identical to Sister All-Forgiving's.

Twins!

"How do you do?" I said uncertainly, hoping she wouldn't jump up and crush-hug me. To my relief, she just smiled and said, "I'm doing just fine." Next to Sister Living-Word was the one who wore the pretty green-and-white checked dress. "This is Sister Lamb-of-God," Buzzard introduced her, and that time, I forgot to wonder about yet another strange name. She smiled and we nodded our heads to each other.

Next to Sister Lamb-of-God was the woman in the lavender dress, "And this is Sister Baptized-by-John." I smiled and nodded my head, but my eyes had already moved to the sleeping, child-sized lady. Buzzard lowered her voice: "And this is our beloved Sister Blood-of-the-Lamb. She's having a little nap right now."

"You sure do have a pretty name," said Sister Baptized-by-John—or maybe it was Sister Lamb-of-God. I wasn't sure.

"Thank you," I said, and then, for some strange reason, I told them about my *real* name, and that was something I hadn't even told Savannah—or Crystal: "My full, real name is Mourning Dove," I offered. "But most folks just know me by 'Dove'—and at school . . ." My mind briefly fluttered to Miss Madison. "I'm registered as M. Dove Johnson."

"Why'd your mama name you that?" asked Buzzard, and I knew—but of course, I had never said anything about it—about why Buzzard's mama gave her such a name!

"She liked mourning doves the best of any bird in the whole world," I said. "She said that they sing the saddest, sweetest kind of song."

"And in the Bible, it's a dove from Heaven that says, 'This is my beloved son, in whom I am well pleased.'" added Sister Lamb-of-God—or maybe it was Sister Baptized-by-John. "We're glad to meet you, Dove," she added. Then, almost as if on signal, the women started stirring around, gathering their purses, and touching cheeks as they said good-bye to each other. They awakened Sister Blood-of-the-Lamb, whose eyes blinked in a confused way just under the edge of her tilted-down hat.

"Jesus come?" she asked the same question. I guess that maybe she asked it every time she got waked up.

"Jesus always comes when we gather in His name," Buzzard said again, and this time, Sister Blood-of-the-Lamb simply said "Oh," but in what I thought sounded like a disappointed voice. But the little old woman wasn't paying any attention to Buzzard. She was staring right at me.

"I'm Dove," I volunteered, because something in her eyes made me know what she was wondering.

"Dove," she repeated.

"Let me help you," Sister Living-Word said. Or maybe it was Sister All-Forgiving, because I'd already forgotten which was which, they looked so much alike. So whoever she was, she reached out and lifted that little Sister Blood-of-the-Lamb out of her chair, just like she was lifting a child. The same two women who had carried her in had crossed their arms to make a sort of seat, and the other one plunked that little woman right on them. They all started moving toward the back door, but then Sister Blood-of-the-Lamb said something real low, and they all stopped, turned around, and looked right at me.

"She wants to know who you are," one of them said.

"I'm Dove," I repeated, and the little old woman gazed at me for a long moment before she nodded her head. The women all went out into the yard, got themselves all settled in the truck, and drove away. I could hardly wait to start asking Buzzard questions! But before I could say a word, I heard Molly crying. She always got cranky if she slept too long, and of course, I'd been so caught up in the Circle of Jesus goings-on that I had not awakened her soon enough. So it took me a little while of sitting with her and rocking her in my arms before she calmed down. Little Ellis never got cranky, no matter what, and while I soothed Molly, he sat and watched us with sleep-swollen eyes in his usual solemn way. When we got down to the kitchen, Buzzard had fixed bowls of ice cream for all of us, and with the kitchen still feeling so hot, it was most welcome.

While we were eating and Buzzard was putting the remaining pecan pie in the refrigerator, I got started right in to asking about the Circle of Jesus.

"How come you all have such strange-sounding names?" was my first question.

Buzzard came and sat down with us, a big glass of iced tea in front of her.

"Well, we started the Circle close to forty years ago," she said. "And we all took special names for the Circle—kind of like I've heard nuns do. Only we got to pick out our own."

"You can have any name you like?"

"Sure. Long as it's something out of the Bible."

"How came you to pick 'Sister Feed-My-Sheep'?" was my next question, and the minute I asked it, I knew I had touched on something truly serious about Buzzard. She waited a long moment before she answered:

"I'd been hearing those words in my mind for years and years—ever since I was just a little thing," she explained. "So when I picked my Circle name, that's what I picked."

"Where is that in the Bible?" I asked.

"The Gospel According to John," she answered, and the way she let those words roll out so gentle and slow, it was like she kissed each word as she said it. And she continued in the same way as she told the story out of the Bible: "Jesus was talking to Simon and Peter and He'd already asked him twice if Peter loved Him. And poor old Peter had answered yes twice before. But Jesus asked one more time, and when Peter had assured Him, Jesus said, 'Feed . . . my . . . sheep.' It just stuck with me all these years. Why, I'll bet I wasn't more than four or five years old the first time I heard that, and it was always like the words had been written just for me." The whole time Buzzard was answering my question, I was watching her as she watched Molly and Little Ellis spooning cold ice cream into their mouths. All of a sudden, I understood why Buzzard would do such a big favor for us, taking us in when we had nowhere to run to!

"You're feeding us!" I yelped. Molly and Little Ellis both jumped a little, at the sudden loudness of my voice. But Buzzard just studied my face and slowly nodded.

"There's more to feeding folks than just giving them food," she said finally. "But I sure do like the giving food part. Why, early mornings when I'm making up a pan full of biscuits, and I know how much you all enjoy them—it's the most wonderful feeling! And speaking of food, we'll all have us the rest of that good cold tuna salad for supper tonight. And some of my yeast rolls."

"That sounds good," I said, but at the same time I was wondering what name I would give myself, if I ever got to be in a group like the Circle of Jesus. And like a flash, I thought about seeing Jesus in Aunt Bett's church, and my mama dancing along beside him. So I knew right then and there that my name would be Sister Up-from-the-Grave-He-Arose. I smiled at the thought of it.

Buzzard must have been thinking about the Sisters of the Circle of Jesus again, because she added, "We used to have a Sister In-My-Father's-House, but she's in her Father's house now." She was just as solemn-sounding as she could be, and I don't know why on earth it struck me as so funny! Maybe it was because I was thinking of myself as Sister Up-from-the-Grave-He-Arose. Or something. I almost laughed out loud! But I stopped myself and tried to make my face as serious as Buzzard's. Then Buzzard nodded her head up and down a few times and added, "We used to have a Sister Sweet-By-and-By. . . ." I waited, knowing what was probably coming and trying to prepare myself for it. "But she's in the sweet by and by now." I had to bite the inside of my lip to stop myself from laughing. But I sure didn't fool Buzzard for a minute.

"You think that's funny?" she asked in a terrible whisper.

"No," I lied, suddenly afraid of her anger. Crystal had asked me to keep things as nice as possible, so Buzzard would let us stay, and here I had gone and maybe messed up everything for us! I looked down at the tablecloth. Buzzard was as still as a statue, and I could feel my eyes being drawn to hers. Finally, I couldn't stop them from rising.

But what I saw in her face wasn't anger at all. It was . . . a sad kind of love, maybe.

"I'm sorry." The words fell out of my mouth, and I didn't even know they were there.

"And I forgive you," she said right away. "Mostly because it's the first time I've ever seen you come close to laughing. Two whole days you've been here. . . . ." She paused and let her eyes sweep over Molly and Little Ellis and me. "Two whole days and not a single laugh."

"I never thought about that," I said. And that was the honest-to-goodness truth. "Maybe we're just all solemn folks," I added.

When Crystal came home, I wanted to tell her about the Sisters of the Circle of Jesus, but somehow, I knew I couldn't tell it the way it really was. For one thing, I couldn't remember all those strange names, except for Sister Blood-of-the-Lamb, that tiny old lady. And too, Crystal looked to me as if she was carrying around all she could handle. All day long, while she'd been at work, cutting, shampooing, curling, and drying people's hair, I'd been having a good time. It didn't seem fair. So I made up my mind right then and there that I would start trying to make things as easy for Crystal as I could. And that meant not telling her about how much fun I was having.

"I called Aunt Bett today," Crystal said. "She says she hasn't heard anything else, and Aunt Mee is watching to see if the sheriff comes back to our house, but she says she hasn't seen anything like that."

"Let's go ahead and call Miz Swan's lawyer," Buzzard suggested. "Might take us a little while before we can get an appointment anyway."

"Yes," Crystal agreed. "Please," she added.

"But on the other hand," Buzzard mused. "If one of these children is really his own flesh-and-blood child, I guess the best lawyer in the world isn't going to be able to do much."

"Oh." Crystal's voice sounded like all the air going out of a balloon. "Well then, let's just wait a little bit," she finally suggested. "If that's all right."

"That's all right," Buzzard agreed.

I'd had so much fun on Saturday, it was Sunday morning before I realized that we needed to find somewhere to go to church. When I came downstairs, Buzzard was taking biscuits out of the oven, and I poured glasses of milk for me and Molly and Little Ellis. Then I got up my courage to ask Buzzard about church.

"Buzzard, where does Miz Swan go to church? When she's here, I mean?"

"Why you asking?"

"I just wondered," I said.

"Oh, Miz Swan goes to a big Episcopal church over in Augusta," Buzzard answered. "A long drive."

"Well then, can we go to church with you? Me and Molly and Little Ellis, I mean. I think Crystal should get to sleep late on Sundays, but I know Aunt Bett would want us to go to church."

Buzzard paused for a moment. "That would be fine,"

she said. "But I sing in the choir, so you'd have to sit without me."

"That's okay."

"Don't know as there's ever been any white folks in our church," Buzzard added.

"Is it okay?" I asked, feeling a little uncomfortable.

"I expect so." But she didn't sound very convinced. "Just that it's never come up before." We were quiet for a while, with me thinking of Aunt Bett's church and wondering how folks would have acted if three black people came to the services there. But I couldn't figure out how it would have been.

"Of course, it's okay," Buzzard said, nodding her head. "Of course it is!"

So I got Molly, Little Ellis, and me all dressed and ready to go. We were real quiet, so as not to wake Crystal up. Then we went and sat on the back porch steps to wait for Buzzard. And when she finally came out, she sure did look fine. She was wearing a navy blue dress with a wide white collar and a white hat with a veil, and white gloves and black patent leather shoes and pocketbook.

"You sure do look nice," I said.

"You all look right nice yourselves," she said. "Let's us get going now. We're running kinda late." We got ourselves loaded into Miz Swan's big car, with Buzzard once again reminding Molly and Little Ellis not to put their feet on the seat.

"I'm glad Miz Swan lets you use her car while she's gone," I said.

Buzzard laughed. "Tell you the truth, Miz Swan lets me do about whatever I please." She laughed again. I didn't know what was so funny about it, but I decided not to ask. After only a mile or so, Buzzard slowed the car and turned right onto a red clay road. Then she stepped down on the accelerator and the big car roared ahead.

"Gotta hurry," she said. "We're late."

When we turned onto yet another unpaved road, even narrower than the one we had been on, I saw the church— a small, white church with a tin roof and a steeple almost bigger than the church itself. But Buzzard must have been right about us being late, because there wasn't a soul outside of the church. We went up the steps and through the wide-open doors, and Buzzard patted the back pew.

"Right here," she said.

"But what about Molly and Little Ellis?"

"What about them?"

"Don't they go to Sunday School?"

"Sunday School during church services?" Buzzard sounded truly surprised.

"Yes. That's the way at Aunt Bett's church," I explained.

"Not that way here," Buzzard said, and before I could say another word, she hurried away. So we settled ourselves onto the hard bench, with me wondering how Molly and Little Ellis would act, sitting through a long service. But soon, I forgot to worry about that because I got to looking around at the people. The men all wore dark suits, and the women were all dressed up just as much as Buzzard, with hats and gloves.

But I also noticed that Buzzard was right again: We were the only white people in the church, and I noticed a few people glancing at us and then nudging other folks, who turned and glanced at us themselves. The glances were quick and polite, and one older man even nodded his head at us. From somewhere up front, piano music started playing something real sweet and sad sounding, and people let out a low moan and started swaying to the music. Some of them swayed front-to-back, and some swayed side-to-side. It was truly interesting, because where there were front-to-back and side-to-side folks sitting beside each other, it was almost like they were doing a dance that could make them bump smack into each other at any minute. A side door opened and the choir came into the room. The people clapped and the choir people smiled and nodded. Buzzard was the third to come in, and she sure looked nice. And I thought I saw one of the Sisters of the Circle of Jesus, but I couldn't be sure. The choir was made up of more people than were in the pews, and I soon found out how silly I'd been to worry that Molly and Little Ellis might not be able to sit still—because in only a little while, *nobody* was sitting still! When the choir started out on another slow, sad-sounding song, some of the people stood up, put their heads back, and held their hands palms-up toward the underside of that high tin roof. The choir rocked oh-so-slowly back and forth, back and forth from side to side like they were all connected to each other, and the song went on and on, like a sad vine that grew and twined around, in and among all the people.

Finally, it wound itself down, and in front of where we were sitting, two women still stood with their eyes closed. They were both crying, though they made not a sound. The final notes on the piano lingered around a little and then started another song, this one faster and lots happier-sounding, and when the choir joined in, their voices were so strong, I almost thought they would break the glass in the open windows. All the people were swaying and clapping and the choir members swaying together again, only much faster, and clapping their hands. Some people got up and went into the aisle and hugged each other and sang and danced around. The music and the singing and the clapping went on and on, until I thought for sure that tin roof high above our heads would surely fly right off! And then it all stopped, but the people were still saying things like "Praise the Lord!" and "Hallelujah!" And one lady said "Sweet Jesus!" over and over again.

When the preacher came out, I thought things would get real quiet, like at Aunt Bett's church, but they didn't. That preacher just sort of jumped into the rhythm that song had left hanging in the air, like his big voice was making the sound of the piano and the choir. Because he got into kind of a singsong talking that was just like the way a poem goes clippity-clopping along, and oh, how the people loved it! They hollered things to him almost all the time, like "Amen!" and "Praise Jesus!" I guess I never saw so much happiness gathered under one roof in my whole life. I looked down at Molly and Little Ellis, and their mouths were hanging open. But their eyes were bright and happy, so I knew they were enjoying every single minute. I wasn't all too sure what the sermon was about, but the way that preacher used all those strong words and the way the people echoed them back to him was just . . . wonderful! He marched back and forth, waved his arms, and even stomped his feet a few times. Maybe me and Molly and Little Ellis weren't showing how much we liked it—at least not like all the other folks—but we enjoyed it almost to death! Finally, he yelled his last *"Amen!"* and sank into his chair, taking out a big white handkerchief and wiping his streaming face. I could hardly believe that we'd been sitting there for almost two whole hours.

"Potty!" Molly whispered to me, so while the choir started up again, I took Molly and Little Ellis outside, and we walked around the building, looking for a bathroom. We found one just inside the back door, and when we came out, church was over and people were standing around in little clumps under the shade of the trees, talking and laughing together.

"Well, how did you all like it?" Buzzard had come out right behind us.

"It was wonderful!" I said most truthfully.

"Good! Let's introduce you all to some folks." We sure met lots of people that day, and they were all so nice to us. I recognized some of the Sisters of the Circle of Jesus, but I couldn't remember their right Circle names. The only one I didn't forget was Sister Blood-of-the-Lamb.

"Is Sister Blood-of-the-Lamb here?"

"She's around here somewhere," Buzzard said, looking around. "Oh, there she is." Buzzard waved her hand to where Sister Blood-of-the-Lamb was sitting in the shade in a folding chair. She was sound asleep, with her head drooped down onto her shoulder and her tiny hands curled in her lap. But while I was watching her, all of a sudden she opened her eyes, lifted her head, and looked right at me.

"Dove." I couldn't hear her voice, but I knew what she had said, and goose bumps popped up on my arms. We looked and looked at each other, and the strangest feeling came over me. Maybe like all the edges of what I call *me*—whatever makes me Dove and simply myself—disappeared for one bright second, and something like a light went right through me! Not a light you could see with your eyes but one you could only feel in your heart. Why, it lasted for only a second, but it almost took my breath away! And the whole time of that strange feeling, Sister Blood-of-the-Lamb's eyes never left mine.

Afterward, I wanted so bad to tell somebody—anybody—about what had happened to me, but I couldn't. It didn't make any sense at all, and besides, I knew I couldn't say it right, no matter how hard I tried.

When we got home from church, Crystal was sitting out on the back porch shelling butterbeans. She was wearing white shorts and a pretty pink blouse, and she had her hair in a ponytail tied with a pink ribbon. Why, I'd almost forgotten how very pretty she was! She smiled at us, and I could tell that she was feeling much better. Still, her eyes were a little bit swollen, so I knew she'd been crying. *Poor Crystal!* I thought. And I wished and wished I could do something to make her feel better. But no matter how hard I thought, there just didn't seem to be anything I could do. We were stuck, pure and simple! And if Buzzard couldn't get Miz Swan's lawyer to help us, all of our being stuck away from home would be for nothing!

Chapter Sixteen

I GUESS that first week we were with Buzzard kind of set things up for how it would be for us all. We had a routine and got to feeling pretty comfortable around each other. Of course, I knew that Crystal was still fretting about finding us a place of our own to live, but every time she said anything about it, Buzzard just soothed her and said she shouldn't be worried about that, right now.

We went to the grocery store in town again first thing on Monday morning, while it was still pretty cool, and Buzzard kept her word about getting me more notebooks. After we got our groceries, we went into a little dime store, and Buzzard got me two new notebooks and a whole box of new pencils. The lady who waited on us eyed us with interest. "These the late Mr. Swan's kinfolk?" she asked Buzzard.

"Oh yes," Buzzard answered. "They're staying at the Swan Place for a little while."

"Miz Swan coming home to see them?"

"Oh, I don't know," Buzzard murmured. "She does about what she pleases, you know."

"Seems to me she'd want to come home to spend some time with them," the woman offered. "Them being Mr. Swan's very own kinfolk."

"Well, they're kin all right, but real distant, you know. Besides, Miz Swan's got some business going on in France that is keeping her there longer than usual, this time." When we were out of the store, Buzzard said to me, "Now every single time we have to tell that story, I want you to listen real good and hard. Because when school starts, you'll have to have it down pat."

"I will," I promised.

So I had me some nice notebooks to write in again, but in my secret heart, I wished I could have kept using Miz

Swan's beautiful, fine paper. I wouldn't have asked Buzzard for more of it for anything in this whole world, but that didn't keep me from wanting it.

I went back to trying to recreate all the stories I had lost—stories about Mama and Aunt Bett and Savannah, and they all came back, but much clearer than the first time, even. The more I wrote, the more I realized that I shouldn't be writing about people separately but maybe write a story where I let them all come together, just to see what would happen. Like wondering what it would have been like if Aunt Bett had known the elegant Miz Swan. And I'll bet you anything, Aunt Bett would have found a way to talk her out of some good clothes! Or what if the two of them had been faithful friends since childhood and Aunt Bett had come to Mr. Swan's funeral. I wondered what Aunt Bett would have said, to try and make Miz Swan feel better. So I started writing a make-believe story about that, and it was ever so much fun.

One day I asked Buzzard, "Where is Mr. Swan buried?" Because I was at the part of that story where Aunt Bett would have been at his funeral.

"How come you to ask such a thing?" Buzzard wanted to know.

"I don't know. I just wondered." I muttered. Then I added, "I thought I'd like to put some flowers on his grave, or something. I've pretended to be his great-niece long enough that I almost feel it's true."

"Well, you can't put flowers on his grave," she said. "Because he was cremated."

"Cremated?" I'd never heard of such a thing.

"It's when the . . . body . . . gets made into ashes, instead

245

of being buried in the ground," she explained. "And he wanted his ashes scattered in the Savannah River, so that's where they went."

"Oh." That was so strange, thinking of the dapper Mr. Swan being nowhere on this earth where anyone could go and visit him. But I did like the idea of his ashes going into the Savannah River.

That last week of summer, Buzzard loaded us all into the car, but when I asked where we were going, she just shook her head and smiled. "You'll see." And that was all she would say. When we got to town, Buzzard parked the car in a shady spot, and we all got out. She took my elbow and guided me into a little department store, with Molly and Little Ellis trailing behind us.

"Those clothes you brought with you aren't right for wearing to school," she pronounced. "So let's us find you some new things."

"*Buy* clothes?" I couldn't imagine such a thing. For as long as I could remember, I'd never had a dress bought right in a real store and with me being first-in-line for wearing it! But even though that thought was completely delicious, I couldn't really comprehend it.

"Why, we can't afford clothes that come from a *store,*" I sputtered, once again sounding like Aunt Bett. And suddenly, I wished Aunt Bett was there with me, to help me persuade Buzzard of the terrible expense . . . the sheer folly . . . of store-bought clothes.

"Well, you're not going to school in outgrown clothes, Dove, and that's all there is to it," Buzzard fumed. "Do you want people to say bad things about the late Mr. Swan and about that sweet Miz Swan?"

"What?"

"We have to think of their reputations in this town," Buzzard went on. "If you go around dressed like a raga-muffin, they'll say Miz Swan isn't doing right by Mr. Swan's kinfolk!"

"Oh."

"When we're out at the Swan Place, it doesn't much matter how any of us dress, because we're way out in the country," Buzzard went on. "But haven't you noticed that I make you all put on your Sunday clothes whenever we come to town?"

"Well, sure—but is that why?"

"It is, indeed," Buzzard said. "Even before we went to the grocery store that very first time, I'd already thought about what I was going to tell folks, and that meant you all had to dress like children who had somebody fine—like Miz Swan—to care about them and take good care of them."

"Oh."

Well, Aunt Bett, I was thinking, *I guess store-bought clothes is what it will have to be. For Miz Swan and what people think about her in this town.*

And I'll say one thing about Buzzard: She sure knew how to shop. It was just a little country town kind of department store, but she flew around, picking out this and that and the other—socks and skirts and blouses, under-wear and sweaters, and just about everything you could think of. She kept saying things like "How about this blouse? You like it?" And "Do you like this sweater in blue or in green?" But I didn't know what to say. All I knew was the skirts weren't too short for me and nobody had ever before worn them! Oh, it did cost a lot of money! But Buzzard made out a check and she didn't even bat an eyelid about it. And when we left that store, we were carrying three bags—my all-new clothes. Back home, she helped me hang all those beautiful new clothes in the closet, and she took my outgrown clothes off the hangers and folded them carefully.

"What are you going to do with the old things?" I asked her, suddenly aware that they should go back to Aunt Bett for passing down to her younger girls.

"I'll just fold them up and put them in a box in the attic," Buzzard said. "You all stay here long enough, maybe Molly can get some use out of them, one of these days." So that felt fine to me. Aunt Bett would like it if Molly could use them too. But I sure wondered how Buzzard could think that we might have to stay long enough for Molly to grow that much!

Crystal was fretful as the first day of school approached.

"You sure you don't mind taking care of Molly and Little Ellis while Dove is at school?" she questioned Buzzard.

"Oh, they're no trouble," Buzzard assured her. "They're just as good as gold."

"If we were still at home, they could go to Aunt Bett's until Dove gets off."

"Well, I'll just be their new Aunt Bett," Buzzard said. And so it was all settled.

On that last night before school started, I waked up a couple of times and went to look in the closet, trying to decide what to wear the first day. But I couldn't make up my mind until the next morning. And instead of me getting Molly and Little Ellis up, Buzzard did it herself, and while Crystal was getting dressed to go to work, I finally made my choice of clothes: a blue-and-green plaid skirt with a white blouse and a green sweater, even though the weather was still far too warm for me to need a sweater. It was pretty, and so I wore it. I had on brand-new socks, too, and Buzzard had polished my shoes so they looked real nice.

When I came out of the bathroom, Crystal was standing sideways at the dresser, looking into the mirror and running her hand over her stomach. She jumped when she saw me watching her.

"You look real pretty, Dove," she said. "But I still hate Buzzard spending so much money on clothes. She probably doesn't make much, being a maid."

"I told you about Miz Swan's reputation and how important it is to Buzzard," I reminded Crystal. "So maybe there's other money for doing something like that. An allowance or something."

"Maybe."

When Crystal and I got down to the kitchen, Molly and Little Ellis were already sitting at the table eating Buzzard's good biscuits. They were wearing good clothes, and Buzzard herself was wearing a black dress and a hat.

She saw us staring at her.

"Well, what are you two looking at?" she asked.

"You're so dressed up!" I said.

"We're taking you to school this first morning," Buzzard said. "Have to get you all registered properly. From then on, Crystal can drop you off in the mornings and you can ride the bus home, afternoons."

"Oh." And all of a sudden, I thought about my school records. I didn't have them! They were still at my old school.

"What about my records?" I asked, glancing at Crystal.

But Buzzard answered for her. "I already thought about that, and I can get you into school without them. I figured you all wouldn't have had time to get them or give them a school to forward them to. Besides, that would let somebody know for sure where you all ran off to."

"How are you going to do it?" Crystal asked.

Buzzard smiled and sipped her coffee. "Don't worry about it. I'll get it done."

To me, she gave the now-familiar order: "No matter what I say, don't you dispute it!"

"Yessm."

Molly, Little Ellis, Buzzard, and I went driving off in Miz Swan's big car, and when we got to the school, Buzzard adjusted her hat and checked her face in the rearview mirror. Then we all got out. Molly and Little Ellis held Buzzard's hands and we walked up the walkway toward the big brick building. All around, children of all ages and sizes were running and playing around and finally going inside. Some girls about my age came by in a little clump, laughing and talking and waving their hands around. Made me think of the rich girls in my old school. But what a difference it was—because now, I had nice clothes and hand lotion for my elbows and knees, and even a little purse to hang from my shoulder, for carrying around my tissues and pencils. The girls glanced at me and then at each other, so I knew their mamas had told them that Mr. Swan's great-niece was starting school and they were to be nice to me. They all smiled at me warmly and then passed on by.

When we got inside, Buzzard ushered us into the office, put Molly and Little Ellis in chairs, and told them to stay put. We approached the desk, where a harried-looking lady was trying to do paperwork and answer the phone, all at the same time. In the hallway a bell rang so loud that Buzzard and I both jumped. The woman didn't seem to notice the bell at all. She just kept shuffling papers.

Buzzard cleared her throat, and the woman looked up at us.

"Yes?" she asked, pushing her glasses up on her nose.

"This is Miss Dove Johnson," Buzzard said importantly. "She is the late Mr. Swan's great-niece, and she will be going to school here until . . . well, we aren't sure."

"Do you have her records?" the woman asked, opening a drawer and taking out a form.

"Her records have been lost," Buzzard said simply.

"Lost?"

"Yes. They were lost while her parents were packing up for their extended stay in the Orient."

That Buzzard! I was thinking with admiration.

"Well, what was the name of her last school?"

Uh-oh!

Buzzard frowned for a moment.

"George Washington School."

"Where?" the woman asked.

"Goodness, I don't know," Buzzard said. "Listen, I know we don't have any records, but if you will just get one of the teachers to ask Dove a few questions, she will find out this young lady is very smart."

Me? Smart? Me? A young lady?

"She writes stories almost all the time and figures her numbers well too. When we go to the grocery store, she can add up all our purchases right in her head, without even using a pencil and paper."

"Well, it would be highly irregular for us to accept her without records," the woman frowned.

"You can ask Miz White," Buzzard retorted.

"Miz White? Miz White from the school board?" Her eyebrows shot up.

"Yes. Miz White has met Dove personally and said that the school would be honored . . ." Buzzard repeated the word and emphasized it, "*honored* to have the great-niece of the late Mr. Swan attending this school."

"Oh," the woman behind the desk looked startled, but then she started filling out the form anyway. As she scribbled away furiously, Buzzard cut her eyes at me and slowly winked one of them.

When the form was completed, the woman reached back into the drawer and took out a blank sheet of paper. She wrote on it for several minutes, but I couldn't read her handwriting, what with it being upside down to me. When she was done, she folded the form and the letter together and put them into an envelope, which she sealed.

"Please take this to Room 14, Dove," the woman at the desk thrust the form at me. "And we are honored—" she glanced at Buzzard—"to have you attending our school."

I took the form and started to walk away, but Buzzard called me back loudly.

"Wait! You need lunch money," she said, raising her

voice so the woman at the desk could hear easily. And while I watched, Buzzard opened her purse and took out a whole twenty-dollar bill! I tried to keep my eyes from going wide, but I just couldn't believe Buzzard was giving me that much money—just for lunch!

"Take it," Buzzard ordered, still speaking loudly. "Miz Swan told me exactly how much money the great-niece of her beloved late husband should have for pocket money every few days."

Buzzard glanced at the woman, who was watching us intently.

"Thank you." I lifted the bill from Buzzard's fingers.

Buzzard motioned to Molly and Little Ellis, and I bent down and hugged them. "You be as good as gold for Buzzard, you hear?" They nodded. "And when I come home this afternoon, I'll tell you all about my day at school."

Then I headed down the hall, to find Room 14.

Chapter Seventeen

THE minute I walked along the hallway, I thought of Francie in *A Tree Grows in Brooklyn*, and how she got to go to a much nicer school and enjoyed it so much. Because the hall floors were polished to a high gleam and the knobs on the classroom doors were clean and shiny, and the whole place had the perfume of something *fine* about it. A waxy, sweet, very clean smell. Even the brass numerals on the doors were shining, and when I found number 14, it gleamed like a sunrise! Through the glass in the upper part of the door, I could see a lady with light gray hair standing before the class. She was wearing a cherry-red suit and had big glasses hanging down, held on by an around-the-neck string that was completely covered with rhinestones. She was smiling and talking, with her happy-looking face turning back and forth, back and forth from side to side—just like the old oscillating table fan Aunt Bett used in her kitchen in the summertime.

Before I could knock, she saw me through the glass, smiled even bigger, and motioned for me to come in. I took a deep breath and went into the room. Inside were five perfectly straight rows of desks, almost every one of them holding a child with hands folded on the desktop and ankles crossed.

"Come on in, dear," the teacher said. I moved toward her, feeling that my legs were made of stiff wood. The eyes of all the others in the classroom were locked onto me. I handed the envelope to the teacher. She put on her glasses so that the rhinestone strings made two shiny loops on either side of her face. I backed up a few steps and looked out at the students, meeting curious eyes and a few shy smiles. Everybody had on nice, new clothes—like mine—except for a girl sitting far in the back of the classroom. Her dress was faded and worn-looking, and the ribbon in her hair was wrinkled. While I watched, she pulled at her dress, trying to get it to cover her knees. But she gave me the sweetest smile of all. I smiled back, and just for a little moment, I got confused. Couldn't tell whether I was the "me" who was standing there in front of a whole roomful of strangers or the "me" who was like that girl on the back row—wearing a faded dress and trying to hide my knees under a too-short skirt. The teacher finished reading, took off her glasses, studied me hard, and then fairly beamed at me.

"Well!" she sputtered. "Welcome, Dove!" She came toward me and put her hand, ever so gentle-like, on my shoulder.

"Class, this is Dove Johnson, who's going to be in our class." The passive eyes and the sweet smile from the back row. I felt my face beginning to burn.

"And I'd like you to know," the teacher said, glancing at me a little uneasily, "that Dove's great-uncle was our beloved Mr. Swan, who so generously provided all the funds to build our town's public library—the Swan Memorial Library."

Then, "Welcome, Dove," she repeated. "I'm Miss Gray, and I'll be your teacher. Now let's find you a desk." Every single seat in the row next to the big windows was filled, but Miss Gray guided me to the front desk, where a freckle-faced boy was sitting.

"Simon, please move to the vacant desk in the third row," she asked in a soft voice. "I don't want you sitting next to Paul anyway. You'll both get into trouble." Simon looked at me without showing any anger or resentment at all.

"Yessm," he murmured, gathering his things and moving out of the seat.

"All right, Dove," Miss Gray said to me. "This is your desk. Please be seated."

Oh, I was ever so glad to be able to sit down—to get away from standing in the front of the room with every-body looking at me. Now, sitting down, I thought that I probably looked pretty much like everybody else. I glanced over at Simon, and he was already looking at me.

I smiled at him a little, to kind of let him know that my taking his desk hadn't been my idea at all. But then I looked away so fast, I didn't get to tell if he smiled back. Miss Gray seemed to be real nice, and the first thing, after we said the pledge of allegiance to the flag, was that she got two pretty-big-sized boys to help her get all our textbooks passed out to us. But I watched and saw her take the newest-looking books in each stack and put them aside. Then, when everything was passed out, she put that stack on my desk. I felt my ears burning, but I just pretended to look over all the books. And there it was: that wonderful thrill of new books with all kinds of things in them that I didn't know—but that I certainly would learn.

The English book was the most interesting, of course. It had stories and poems in it and grammar lessons about things I'd never heard of. Gerunds, for instance. The morning went by so fast that I was surprised when Miss Gray said, "Well, it's time for lunch. Mandy, would you and Rachel show Dove where the lunchroom is? And will you please be sure that she gets everything she wants?"

Mandy, who was plump and red-haired, and Rachel, who was as delicate and small as a little doll, came over to my desk while the rest of the class filed out of the room. Miss Gray introduced them to me.

"Dove, this is Mandy, whose father is an attorney. As a matter of fact, he's Miz Swan's very own attorney." Miss Gray puffed herself up a little, and Mandy turned bright pink and smiled. It was a good smile, not a proud one.

"And this is Rachel, whose grandmother is on the school board."

"Is your grandmother's name Miz White?" I asked.

"Why yes," Rachel said, obviously pleased.

But I was thinking I sure better be careful—*anything I told Rachel would go right back to Miz White!* And that was too bad, because I already liked Rachel—liked her frank brown eyes and square-cut bangs.

"Well, run along to lunch then," Miss Gray chirped, herding us out of the room and into the hallway.

When we got our lunches, I held out the twenty-dollar bill Buzzard had given me. The lady stared at it without saying a word.

"I can't make change for such a large bill," she said. "You ought to know that."

"Oh."

Mandy and Rachel were staring at the bill. I didn't know what to do.

"I'll pay for hers," Rachel spoke up, passing along some one-dollar bills to the cashier.

"Thanks," I muttered, putting the big bill back into my purse. "I'll get this changed somewhere and pay you back tomorrow."

"No need," Rachel said. "Let's just call this your treat on your first day in a new school." When we sat down, Rachel said, "My mama said for me to ask you about Miz Swan's house."

"What about it?"

"Some folks in town say that her maid . . . Buzzard . . . has just *ruined* all of the furniture and everything, what with Miz Swan being in France so long and nobody around to check on Buzzard's work . . . or even to see if she's working at all."

Why, I was so surprised, I hardly knew what to say!

"Rachel!" Mandy exclaimed in surprise. "That's a terrible thing to say about somebody!"

"Buzzard isn't a somebody at all," Rachel insisted. "She's a maid, for Heaven's sake!"

"That doesn't matter one little bit," Mandy insisted.

"I'll bet you it's true!" Rachel said. "You're just taking Buzzard's side 'cause your daddy's Miz Swan's lawyer!"

Mandy clamped her teeth together and turned a bright red. "I'm not supposed to talk about my daddy's clients," she whispered.

I stepped in. "Buzzard takes real good care of everything. It's all so clean and nice, and I get to help too. I do all the dusting of the beautiful furniture in the parlor."

Rachel stared at me. "*You* dust the furniture? She makes you do her work?" she breathed, as if she couldn't imagine such a thing.

"No, she doesn't *make* me do anything," I protested. "I like doing it."

"I can hardly believe it," Rachel said. "Miz Swan's maid letting Mr. Swan's very own niece help with the housework!"

"Stop, Rachel!" Mandy said in a whisper. "Just stop!"

"Great-niece," I corrected Rachel. And all of a sudden, it dawned upon me that these girls were like the rich girls back in my old school, except for one very important fact—this time, they accepted me as one of them. But that was just because they thought I was the late Mr. Swan's great-niece. I guess those important thoughts settled me down, sure enough! Neither Mandy nor Rachel asked anything else about Buzzard, but they did want to know what the house was like on the inside and how did it feel to live so far outside of town. Those were questions I could handle, and I was pleasantly surprised, because I was afraid I'd be asked other things not so easy to answer, like: Where was I born? Why were my parents traveling and where? And what was my older sister like and where did she work? So while I finished my ice cream, I told them everything I could think of about that beautiful house and about the pond down at the bottom of the garden that used to have real swans swimming around in it. And I told them, most truthfully, that I liked living way out in the country. When we went back to class, we stopped in the bathroom, and while Rachel was in the stall and Mandy and I were already washing our hands, Mandy whispered to me, "Don't think too hard of Rachel. She's really nice, but sometimes she starts sounding just like her mama!"

"Is your daddy really Miz Swan's lawyer?" I asked.

"Yes," Mandy said. "And I can't talk about that."

"Okay," I said.

After school, I told Miss Gray, "I'm supposed to ride the bus home, but I'm not sure which bus I am to take."

"Most of the children in this class live in town, so I don't know which bus you're supposed to take, either. Let's go down to the office and find out," Miss Gray said. So she went with me all the way back to the office, and we found out that I was supposed to take Bus #3.

The bus had only seven or eight children on it, almost all of them much younger than me and living out in the countryside. I sat right in the front, so I could be sure to show the driver where to stop. At the first stop, four of the children—all with the whitest-blond hair I've ever seen—got off and went walking down a dirt road. At the next stop, two more did the same thing. And when I looked behind me, there was only one child left on the bus: that girl from my very own class. The one who wore a dress too small for her. She met my eyes and gave me that same sweet smile she'd given that morning. I waved my fingers at her and saw her turn absolutely beet-red! I would have gone back to sit and talk with her, but we were getting close to the Swan-painted mailbox, so I had to point it out to the driver.

When the bus pulled away, the girl stared at me through the dusty back window, and I watched until I couldn't make out her face any longer.

"And how was school?" Buzzard asked as soon as I came into the house.

"Fine. Except the lunchroom lady said she didn't have change for a twenty-dollar bill."

"Then how'd you eat?"

"A nice girl named Rachel paid for my lunch for me," I said. "And she's Miz White's very own granddaughter."

Buzzard frowned hard. "Then you gotta be careful what you tell her, Dove. Be better if you don't say anything more to her than needs be. Anything you say to her, she will tell her grandmama."

"I already thought of that." And for some reason, I thought about telling Buzzard about what people in town were saying about her probably not taking good care of Miz Swan's house. But I didn't. It felt too much like what Michelle had said about Aunt Bett that time. My mama used to say, "There are some things better not said." And this was one of them, I was sure.

"And I met another girl named Mandy," I said. "Her daddy is Miz Swan's lawyer."

Buzzard looked up at me sharply. "She doesn't talk about her daddy's business, does she?" Buzzard's voice was almost like a low growl.

"No," I answered. "Rachel and I both kind of tried to get her to talk about his work, but Mandy was real firm about not saying anything about what he does."

"That's good," Buzzard said in a relieved-sounding whisper. I wondered what that was all about, but I didn't ask. I simply went upstairs, changed out of my good school clothes, and hung them in the closet. I put on my old shorts and a shirt that was a little too short for me and went back downstairs to help fix supper.

"I like all the girls at school that I've met so far," I explained. "But they only like me because they think I'm Mr. Swan's great-niece."

"O-h-h-h." Buzzard drew the word out.

"And there's one girl I really want to get to know, but I don't think the others like her. She rides on the same bus I take, and she stays on it after I get off at the mailbox."

Buzzard's eyebrows shot up. "I know who that is— that's Sharon, old Miss Rebecca's grandchild. Well, I don't know Sharon right well, but she seems real nice. I do wonder why the other girls wouldn't like her?"

"Because she's poor and wears worn-out clothes and her dresses are too little for her, and she's not kin to somebody rich or famous in the town," I spewed the words forth with a poisoned kind of feeling I hadn't even known was there. Buzzard looked at me in surprise.

"I'm sorry," I muttered.

"Don't have to be," Buzzard said. "You're probably right."

"Well, it's a lot harder than I thought it would be—pretending to be Mr. Swan's great-niece," I explained. "It's hard to have people being nice to me just for that."

"Well, I'm right glad to see you've got a level head on your shoulders." Buzzard beamed. "Folks who go around pretending to be more important than they really are, why they're only trying to persuade *themselves*." I thought for a moment about that and decided that Buzzard was absolutely right! How strange that I couldn't have figured it out on my own!

The next day, Crystal started driving me to school, and as I came into the building, Rachel and Mandy came running up to me.

"That your sister driving you?" they asked.

"Uh—yes."

"She's so pretty!" they chorused. "Where does she work?"

"At the mall."

"Is she married?"

"She was," I chose my words carefully. "But now she's a widow. Her husband was killed in a terrible automobile accident."

Rachel and Mandy clucked their tongues at Crystal's misfortune. But I could see in Rachel's eyes the very same glitter I saw in Miz White's the day Buzzard introduced us at the grocery store. She couldn't wait to spread that juicy tidbit around. I thought right then and there that I was awful glad the Swan Place was way outside of town. I wouldn't want to live so close to other people and have them talking about every single thing I said or did. Mandy wouldn't do that, of course. But I knew good and well that Rachel *would*.

At lunch, Rachel and Mandy sat with me again, and Mandy started asking more questions about Crystal.

"What does she do at the mall?" they asked.

"She works in a beauty . . . a salon," I remembered to say. Then, before they could ask any more questions, I asked one of my own.

"Does Sharon ever eat lunch in the lunchroom?"

"Who?"

"Sharon," I repeated. "She's in our class. Sits at the back."

"Oh, *her*," Rachel almost spat the word. "No, she can't afford to pay for lunch. She brings lunch from home."

"Please, Rachel," Mandy protested in a whisper.

"And what a lunch!" Rachel went right ahead, and Mandy turned a deep pink. Rachel giggled and covered her mouth, while Mandy just got redder and redder.

"What?" I asked.

"Strange things—cold sweet potatoes and biscuits with syrup in them," Rachel said. "And a jar with nothing but *water* in it."

"Where does she eat?" I asked.

"Who cares?" Rachel almost snarled. "And why do you want to know anyway?"

I shrugged my shoulders. "I just wondered."

I was ever so glad when Rachel stopped talking about Sharon. Mandy glanced at me a couple of times, and I could tell by her eyes that she was apologizing for

Rachel's bad manners.

When I got on the bus that afternoon, I saw Sharon sitting all the way in the back, so I passed by the front seats and headed toward her. But when she saw me coming, she turned bright red and looked ready to cry. I stopped in my tracks, and she turned her face away from me. Well, I guess I could understand that. Back at home, I would have felt pretty much the same way if any of the rich girls had tried to make friends with me. So I turned and went back to the front seat, feeling pretty bad about embarrassing her like that, but wishing I could find a way to talk with her.

So I decided I would talk to Buzzard about it.

"Well, honey, I 'spect she just wants to be left alone," Buzzard concluded, after I'd explained it all to her.

"I just want to be friends with her," I complained. "I wouldn't laugh at her or be mean or stuck up, at all!"

"Well, let's just see what happens," Buzzard added. "But something you ought to know is this: Sometimes, the harder you push for something that isn't meant to be, the unhappier you'll make yourself. If Sharon's meant to be your friend, then it will happen. But if she isn't meant to be your friend, nothing you do will make it happen."

I thought about Savannah right away and how we became friends almost from the very first moment we met. Savannah was surely someone who was meant to be my friend, and I didn't have to do a thing to make her like me. And I wondered for a little moment about how Savannah would have felt about me if I'd lived in this big beautiful house when I met her. Would she have liked me, if she thought I was Mr. Swan's great-niece?

I took Buzzard's advice and didn't try to force myself

on Sharon, ever again.

Chapter Eighteen

AND that's the way things stayed all through the fall. I liked school, and I also liked getting my homework done fast, so I could write in my notebooks. The only thing I didn't really like was eating lunch with Mandy and Rachel every day. Because they both stared at me too hard, and Rachel asked all kinds of personal questions, like what was my favorite food and how did I like having a big sister who was so pretty.

I asked Buzzard if I could just take a sandwich to school every day, so I could find me a place to be alone and peaceful, but she said a growing girl like me needed a good, hot lunch, especially since cold weather would be coming soon. So I just tried to keep on taking things one day at a time, like Aunt Bett always said to do.

But right in the middle of November things changed for us again, and not in a way I could possibly have imagined. Crystal was washing up supper dishes while I wiped off Molly and Little Ellis's face and hands. Buzzard was taking clothes out of the dryer, shaking them out and folding them or putting them right onto hangers. She always said that made the ironing easier. But that day, Buzzard shook out one of Crystal's work dresses—the ones she wore under her beauty parlor smock—and said in a low voice, "You done popped off buttons on all your work dresses. Same button on every one of them. At the waistline."

As Buzzard spoke, Crystal washed the dishes slower and slower, and finally, she stopped. Just stood there watching water running into the sink.

"Dove?" Buzzard said. "Why don't you go take Molly and Ellis upstairs for a little while?" So that's how I knew Buzzard and Crystal needed to talk in private. But I'd sure gotten myself into the habit of listening in on conversations that were supposed to be private. I guess it was a dishonest thing to do, but it's the only way I ever found out important things I should have been included in, right from the start. So I sent Molly and Little Ellis on upstairs, to pick out what books they wanted me to read to them. I hovered right at the kitchen door. Buzzard was saying, "You eating too much? Or maybe it's something else."

"It's something else," Crystal answered in a strong, clear voice. For a long moment, nobody said anything, but then Crystal added, "A baby is what it is."

"I figured as much," Buzzard said. But my mind was whirling away with all kinds of questions. *A baby? How could Crystal get herself a baby?* And all in that little moment, I remembered Molly and Little Ellis and how pink and warm and tiny they were and how their baby heads would kind of bob around when I held them on my shoulder. *A baby!* I wanted to hear more, so I leaned close to the door.

Silence.

Not a single sound of anything you expect to hear in a kitchen that has two women in it. No dishes rattling, no pot lids going on and off. And not a single word spoken. Molly and Little Ellis were standing at the top of the stairs, watching me, so I finally went up and read them three stories. But the whole time, my mind was just racing. What would become of us if Crystal had a baby? How would we ever get our very own apartment? What would happen if

Miz Swan came back and made us all leave?

Once Molly and Little Ellis settled down, I tiptoed back downstairs and stood once again at the kitchen door. This time, there was plenty of talking going on.

"We sure got ourselves some kind of problem now," Buzzard was saying in a low, huffy-sounding voice.

"I know," Crystal admitted. "But I want you to know one thing: When we left home and came here, it wasn't because of this. It was to protect Molly."

"You had morning sickness the very first morning you all were here," Buzzard reminded her.

"I know," Crystal admitted.

"You knew you were with child!"

"I thought as much, but it isn't why we came."

"It was the first thing I suspected," Buzzard said. "Healthy young woman like yourself, it would take something like that to make you get sick so fast and then get over it so fast. And sick only in the morning, first thing."

"I don't know much about this kind of thing," Crystal moaned. "I'm so sorry, Buzzard. I'm so sorry."

"No need to apologize to *me,*" Buzzard sounded surprised. "One you should apologize to is yourself."

"Why? This is Roy-Ellis's baby. I haven't been with another man." Crystal sounded close to tears when she added, "But what am I gonna do? I'm not even eighteen, and I'm gonna have four children to take care of!"

"Told me you was twenty!" Buzzard fumed. "And Dove isn't a child anymore. She can be such a big help."

"I know."

"We'll just have to find a way, is all," Buzzard said. "That's what women in my family have always done. Just find a way to handle it."

"Handle what?" Crystal sniffed.

"Whatever comes."

"But where will we live?" Crystal was crying openly.

"Why, *here!*" Buzzard sounded surprised. "You all can stay right here."

"But what about Miz Swan? She won't want to come home to a house full of children . . . and a baby, even."

"I had a letter from her just the other day," Buzzard said. "And maybe she's decided to live in France all the time."

Well, that was hard for me to believe! Because every single time we got the mail, I held it while we went up the driveway, and looked at it. And there had never been a letter from France!

"She would stay there and still keep this house?" Crystal asked. "And you taking care of it?"

"Miz Swan does whatever she pleases," Buzzard said with finality. "She's right fond of me, you know. And of this house. So we're okay."

"Well, if you say so," Crystal admitted.

"I say so," Buzzard added. Then she said, "Let's get Dove in here on this. She's big enough, you know." Through the door, I could see Crystal nod.

"No need," I said, walking into the kitchen bold as brass.

"You been listening at the door?" Buzzard growled at me.

"Yes, I have," I said. "It's the only way I ever get included in what's going on." That was a truthful statement, and I didn't feel one bit ashamed of saying it.

"So you know about . . . everything," Crystal asked.

"Yes. And I agree with Buzzard. We'll find a way."

Buzzard said, "Well, pretty soon, we'll have to have a story about this baby that's going to come. Same as the story we have about you all being Mr. Swan's great-nieces and nephew." I sat down at the table with Buzzard and Crystal and we all stared at the center of the table, as if maybe we could find an answer sitting right there.

"Dove, you like to make up stories," Buzzard said. "Think of what kind of story could be made up about this little baby not having a daddy."

"Why, the truth, of course," I said immediately. "Roy-Ellis is this baby's daddy, and he was killed in an accident." Crystal and Buzzard looked at each other in surprise.

"That's what we'll do!" Buzzard said. "We'll tell the truth for once! That'll be something new."

So things settled down a little, and we just moved forward, like we always did. Buzzard moved the buttons on Crystal's work dresses, and even later, when Crystal couldn't button the dresses at all, her beauty parlor smock still covered the gaps. Nobody said anything else about finding an attorney to help us about Molly, and we just finished out the fall in our little routines.

Christmas was kind of hard, because all I could do was think about Aunt Bett. Seemed to me that I could almost smell all our freshly-scrubbed cousins, and I could imagine Aunt Bett's house with a Christmas tree in it and all those many stockings hung up and waiting for Christmas candy. Buzzard and I had gotten a few Santa Claus things for Molly and Little Ellis, and Crystal gave me more new notebooks and I gave her a poem I had written about babies. But I guess that was a mistake, because she cried when she read it.

On the first day of school after Christmas, I stopped to get the mail on my way up the driveway, and there was the usual stuff—an electricity bill, a postcard giving $2.00 off on an oil change at a garage in town. But underneath those, there was a large, thick manila envelope addressed to Buzzard. The return address was Aunt Mee!

It was a long, long driveway, but I ran the whole way. When I got inside, I called out, "Buzzard? Where are you?" Her answer came from far down the hall, and when I got to the little television room, Molly and Little Ellis were sitting on the floor, watching cartoons, and Buzzard was in the recliner, reading. I thrust the mail at her.

"The big one's from Aunt Mee. Open it, please, and see if there's a letter in there for me from Savannah."

"Who's this Savannah?" Buzzard asked as she started trying to tear the envelope open.

"You ought to know," I said. "She's one of your relatives."

"One of mine?"

"Yes. Savannah is Aunt Mee's granddaughter. I already told you that before, and how come you don't know about her?"

Buzzard went on pulling at the tape on the envelope. "It's complicated," she said, and at first, I thought she meant the way the envelope was put together. But then she went on: "We got us such a spread-out family, don't any of us really know all about each other." At last, the envelope tore open, and three separate envelopes fell out. The first one was addressed to Crystal—in Aunt Bett's handwriting.

The second was addressed to Buzzard—in Aunt Mee's handwriting. And the third was addressed to me, from Savannah! I tore it open, right away:

Dear Dove,
    I'm so sorry you all had to move away. Has the bad man found you all and Molly? I am so worried about you, and I miss you very very much. Will I ever get to see you again? Will you write to me? Send your letter to Aunt Mee—but she says that you must not put a return address on the envelope—and she'll send it on to me. Please?

Love,
Savannah

I looked up. Buzzard was reading her letter from Aunt Mee and frowning.

"Soon as Crystal gets home, we got to give her this letter from you all's Aunt Bett," Buzzard pronounced.

"What does Aunt Mee's letter say?"

"She says your Aunt Bett's letter will explain what's been happening."

"Happening?"

"That's all she says. We'll have to wait until Crystal gets home." From Buzzard's tone of voice, I knew there was no use in arguing with her. But Crystal was awfully late getting home that day, and when she came in the back door, she was limping.

"What's the matter?" Buzzard asked, pulling out a chair from the kitchen table and guiding Crystal into it.

"Gotta put my feet up," Crystal said. I pulled another

chair out and Buzzard and I lifted Crystal's legs, to put her feet in it. But when we saw Crystal's ankles, we both flinched. They were all puffed out—probably about twice as big around as they were supposed to be.

"You're holding fluid," Buzzard pronounced.

"Yeah," Crystal answered. "I went to a clinic near the mall when I got off work because I was worried about how swollen my ankles were. The nurse said I had to cut out all my salt and try to keep my feet up as much as possible."

Buzzard touched a finger to Crystal's ankle, pushing into the flesh a little "That's not gonna be easy, in your profession."

"I know." Crystal reached for her purse and fumbled around in it, finally coming up with a big white plastic bottle. "And they gave me some vitamins to take and wanted to know which hospital I was going to, to have the baby."

"Don't need a hospital," Buzzard said. "Got the best midwife in the world living down the road just a couple of miles."

"Midwife?"

"Yes. Best one in the world. Now you go to that clinic so they can keep an eye on you and check your blood pressure and give you more vitamins, but when this baby gets ready to come, we'll get Miss Rebecca from down the road to bring it into this world." Crystal didn't argue—just heaved a deep sigh and rubbed her hand over her swollen stomach. With just a few minutes of having her feet up, her ankles already looked better.

"The place for you, anytime you're sitting, is in that reclining chair of mine," Buzzard said. "And I'll scramble up some eggs for you—without any salt in them, 'cause Dove and I fixed some ham slices for tonight's supper, and you sure can't eat anything that salty."

Then, Buzzard and I both remembered about Aunt Bett's letter at the same time. Buzzard got it and handed it to Crystal.

"What's this?" Crystal asked wearily.

"From your Aunt Bett."

Crystal looked from one of us to the other. "Came in an envelope from Mee, this afternoon."

Opening the letter with shaking fingers, Crystal started reading silently. "Please read it out loud," I begged.

"Okay—it says:

Dear Crystal,

I will give this to Aunt Mee, and she will send it on to you all, wherever you are. You were so right! *He* came to your house again, and a sheriff with him! And when he couldn't find anybody, they came to my house. I was so glad that I really didn't know where you all had gone, because he challenged me right then and there to put my hand on my own Bible and swear it. And I did. So they didn't even have to take me into court for that! The sheriff wanted to do more, but *he* said he knew if I would swear it on a Bible, I was telling the truth. He said he was bound and deter-mined to find his girls, Dove and Molly, and have them with him. I asked him what his wife thought of that, and he hemmed and hawed around and finally said they weren't together anymore. "Did you leave her *too?*" I asked him. Oh, I tried so hard not to say "too," but I couldn't help myself, I was so mad! He hemmed and hawed around some more and finally he said yes. Well, that made me mad as fire! So I said, "Well, I've got some news for you, you stinking . . ." Well, I had to stop there a little minute and ask God to put a big, strong angel in charge of my tongue! And I guess He did, because I changed it and said, "I've got some news for you too. Maybe you're not the daddy you think you are."

"What do you mean by that?" he said. And I said, "Maybe your daughters aren't yours. Maybe you're not the only one who did wrong." I wish you could have seen his face! I was trying awful hard not to enjoy seeing his pain. But after what all he did to my sweet sister, running off and leaving her to raise the children alone, I'm afraid that I did enjoy seeing it. Just a bit. And he just turned and walked away. He hasn't been back, and that was over a month ago. I waited until now to tell you, because I wanted to see if he was going to make trouble again. But I haven't heard another thing. I swear to you, Crystal, when I told him about maybe him not being the daddy he thought he was, I only meant Dove, like that deathbed letter of my sister's said. But when I saw he took it to mean Molly too, I didn't correct him. Maybe that big old angel sitting on my tongue stopped me. I don't know. But I think maybe *he* won't bother you all anymore. When we're sure, maybe you all can come home. I miss you all so much.

Love,
Bett

By the time Crystal finished reading Aunt Bett's letter, she was crying. "Oh, maybe Molly's safe now!" she whispered. And then she started crying even harder. "But I can't go back. Not like I am!" Once again, her hand stroked her stomach.

"Why not?" I argued.

"I can't let Bett know," Crystal pronounced. "This baby will be coming too soon for me and Roy-Ellis to have been married. Aunt Bett will know we didn't . . . wait . . . till we were married."

Now, I didn't know all the details about what happens between a man and a woman that makes a baby, but I did know how folks felt about mothers who got a baby before they were married good and proper. So maybe it was getting a little clearer to me.

"And how much *too soon?*" Buzzard asked. Crystal glanced at me and blushed. "A week," she finally said, and Buzzard laughed in the softest kind of way.

"Wouldn't nobody notice a little thing like that," Buzzard assured her, and then she laughed again and shook her head.

"Well, Aunt Bett *might* notice," Crystal insisted. "And she would never forgive me." I was so surprised when I heard myself saying, "She forgave my mama. My mama got *me* when she wasn't married to Roy-Ellis." Then I remembered my mama again and how she worked all the time in that little bitty shop Roy-Ellis had made for her. And how hard Aunt Bett tried to help us out with clothes.

"Well, you all just don't be in any hurry to make up your minds," Buzzard said to Crystal. "Main thing is to wait until we're sure about Molly's daddy and sure that this baby that's coming is all right."

"Yes," Crystal said, and then Buzzard added, "I think maybe it's time for you all to talk to your Aunt Bett on the phone."

"But that's so expensive," Crystal protested.

"I already told you all not to worry about that," Buzzard said.

"Well, all right then. But I'm not going to tell her about the baby."

"That's up to you," Buzzard said.

So Crystal called Aunt Bett long distance, and they talked for a long time. And like she'd planned, Crystal put Aunt Bett off. "Well, we really still aren't sure, as you know. And it's better to wait and see if *he* comes back. And too, Dove's real happy in her new school."

Aunt Bett said something else, and Crystal answered, "Oh, they're just fine. They have a big garden to play in, and they like Buzzard real well." Then silence. Crystal glanced up at me and bit her bottom lip. "Of *course* we still need you, Bett! Please don't talk like that. It breaks my heart." Crystal was close to tears. I held out my hand for the receiver, afraid Crystal would get so upset that she'd blurt out something about the baby.

"Hi, Aunt Bett!" I said, as cheerfully as possible. "We sure have missed you!"

"Oh, have you really?" Aunt Bett's voice softened right away.

"We sure have. And I'm so glad that maybe nobody's going to try to take Molly away. But we have to be sure about that. And I think God put a very special angel in charge of your tongue. I sure do thank Him for it!"

"Thank you, Dove. Thank you. Now what are you all doing for clothes?"

At that point, I went right into lying like a fool. Lying so much and so convincingly that Crystal and Buzzard both stared at me with their mouths hanging open. I told Aunt Bett that some of Buzzard's relatives had only one girl and no other children, and she was older than me, so I could have all her clothes. I told her that even her shoes got passed down to me, and that she was growing so fast, she didn't have a bit of time to wear shoes out, so they were like new. I told her that other relatives had children just a little older than Molly and Little Ellis for handing down the clothes, and that we all had more than we knew what to do with. And then, I stopped lying when I said, "And I'm still trying to make me a friend."

"You are?" Aunt Bett said. "What's her name?"

"Sharon," I said. "She's timid, but I think you'd like her."

"Well, tell me about this Buzzard—good Heavens, what a name!" Aunt Bett went on. "I didn't even know that Aunt Mee had relatives I'd never heard of."

I glanced at Buzzard. "She's real nice," I said. "And she makes such good biscuits too. She makes them for us every single morning."

"Better than my biscuits?" Aunt Bett asked, and I was thinking, *Uh oh! I think I've stepped on Aunt Bett's toes!*

"Just exactly like your biscuits, Aunt Bett," I said in a hurry. "Why, if I had to tell which were better, yours or Buzzard's, I wouldn't be able to say." I winked at Buzzard, and she nodded and smiled. She understood exactly why I had to say that.

"Well, thank you, Dove. Now let me talk to Crystal again, please."

"Yessm." I handed the receiver back to Crystal, who really didn't want to take it.

"Yes?" Then a long, long silence while Aunt Bett talked, probably urging and urging us to come back home. Finally, Crystal rolled her eyes. "Aunt Bett, Dove and I will write you a letter tomorrow, I promise. This is awful expensive, talking long distance, and I don't want to run up Buzzard's phone bill. Yes. We'll just wait and be sure! Okay. Bye-bye now."

When she hung up, Crystal heaved a sigh. "I don't know if we can go back—ever. Maybe it's not safe! Maybe *he* will wait until we come back and then find out about Molly and take her away. Too, it's better to wait and see about this baby. Then we'll know lots more than we know now."

Buzzard was studying Crystal with a deep frown. "And suppose you take this baby and Dove and Molly and Little Ellis and go back, then who do you think is gonna take care of that baby while you work?"

Crystal's mouth fell open a little, as if she hadn't thought of such a thing. "Why," she sputtered, "Dove here can do it, can't you, Dove?"

"Yes." That's what my mouth said, but my heart was pounding.

"Well, who's gonna take care of it while Dove's in school?"

"Aunt Bett?" Crystal suggested in a whisper.

"You gonna load another child onto that good woman, seeing as how she has so many of her own? And was helping out with Molly and Little Ellis?" What a bleak, accusing question it was! We all just sat there in a little circle full of horrible thoughts.

"Or . . ." Buzzard began again. "Maybe Dove would have to drop out of school to take care of *all* the little ones while you work." Crystal and I stared at each other in astonishment. *Me?* I was thinking. *Drop out of school? Not be like the girl in* A Tree Grows in Brooklyn? *Not have things better than Mama had them?*

"Oh, Dove," Crystal breathed. "I would never let that happen!"

Buzzard nodded her head up and down slowly, and the frown was gone. But those awful words were still hanging in the air, and I couldn't bear them!

Crystal was still staring at me with a stricken look on her face, and Buzzard said to her in kind of a gruff voice, "And have you taken your vitamins?"

"I took them," Crystal said.

"Good. We want a healthy baby."

The next morning, when Crystal dropped me off at school, Rachel and Mandy were waiting for me once again. And they hovered on either side of me as we went into the building. After lunch, I excused myself from them and walked around outside, looking for Sharon. But when I found her sitting beneath a tree, her glance told me without any doubt that she wanted me to leave her alone. I wanted so bad to tell her that I knew what it felt like to have clothes too little for you and to have the other girls not like you because you're poor, but I just didn't know how.

When lunch was over and I was on my way back to

class, I overheard Miss Gray and another teacher talking in low voices in the hallway: "I really hoped she would get off on the right foot with . . . the right group of girls," Miss Gray was saying. "I just can't understand why she seems to be trying to take up with Sharon, of all people!"

And the other teacher said, "Well, you know that Mr. Swan was always a big defender of the weak and downtrodden. He never did join any of the town organizations like the Kiwanis Club, the way most men of *station* do. Just hung around with all the poor folks he could find. Seems to me Dove is an apple that hasn't fallen far from Mr. Swan's tree."

And when I heard that, I smiled. Because what I meant to do was be the best of whatever the wonderful Swans had been—but not to give up being myself, not even if I could have been the most popular girl in this whole world!

Chapter Nineteen

A LITTLE later on, Crystal had to work fewer hours because of her ankles, but she kept her appointments at the clinic near the mall and took her vitamins like she was supposed to. And around the beginning of February, Buzzard said it was time for Crystal to meet Miss Rebecca, the midwife. So Buzzard called her on the phone, and the next Saturday morning, Miss Rebecca came up the driveway riding a bicycle. I was sweeping off the porch when she came up the steps, the skinniest lady I've ever seen in my life, but with a face to behold! The kindest, most loving face I think I've ever seen.

"Good morning," she said to me. "I'm Miss Rebecca,

and I'm here to see Buzzard and Crystal."

"Yes ma'am. I'm Dove. I'm in Sharon's class at school."

"Oh, that's nice," Miss Rebecca said, looking at me in a new way. "Sharon doesn't make many friends, I'm afraid."

"I'd be friends with her, except she gets too embarrassed to let me talk with her."

"Well, she kind of likes to keep to herself," Miss Rebecca said, and she turned as red as Sharon had.

Miss Rebecca was at our house for a very long time. Buzzard, Crystal, and Miss Rebecca sat in the dining room, talking real low for about an hour. I watched cartoons with Molly and Little Ellis, and this time, I didn't try to hear what they were saying. I'd heard some things about how babies come into the world, and I didn't want to know any more. Buzzard came to the door of the little room where we were watching television.

"Dove, Crystal and Miss Rebecca have to go upstairs for a while. I want you to be sure you keep Molly and Little Ellis downstairs until I say otherwise."

"Yessm." But I was wondering why they had to go upstairs. What was going to happen? Was Crystal's baby going to come right away? Buzzard worked around in the kitchen for a while, and I kept Molly and Little Ellis downstairs, just like she told me to do, and after about thirty minutes, Crystal and Miss Rebecca came back downstairs.

Crystal's face was red as fire. They went into the kitchen and the three of them talked again. I heard only one thing that was said, and it was when Miss Rebecca said that the baby was going to be a big one. I shuddered. "But that's okay," she went on. "Delivered a twelve-pounder one time, I did."

"Whoo-eee!" Buzzard responded. "Mama okay?"

"Mama okay," Miss Rebecca confirmed.

By then, the weather had turned too cold for the Sisters of the Circle of Jesus to meet on the back porch, and Buzzard told me that they met in a Sunday School room at the church in the wintertime.

"Why don't you just use the living room?" I asked.

"What?" Buzzard snorted at me. "Use Miz Swan's very own living room?" The tone of her voice told me that it was an impossible idea.

"I don't think she would mind."

"Listen, Dove," she started out in a patient voice. "Who all do you think the sisters are?"

"What do you mean?"

"I mean that other than one of them, they were all maids to white folks. A couple of them still *are*. Like me," she added. "And maids don't sit in white folks' living rooms."

"Oh." But I was remembering that time when Aunt Mee sat down at the kitchen table with Crystal and me, and how surprised she was to realize what she'd done. Of course, Crystal and I didn't think a single thing of it, but Aunt Mee was pretty old. And she probably thought all the old rules were still around. And . . . maybe they were, in a way that I didn't understand.

On the first day of March, in the middle of a cold and windy night, Crystal waked me up by shaking my shoulder hard.

"Dove, wake up. Go get Buzzard. I think the baby's coming." That was all she had to say. I flew down the stairs and into Buzzard's room, where she was a big, snoring lump under all her down comforters.

"Wake up!" I yelled. "Crystal says the baby's coming!"

Buzzard groaned and turned over. "We don't have to rush, Dove. First babies always take their own sweet time. Tell Crystal to time the pains, and I'll call Miss Rebecca when they're five minutes apart and steady." Why, I could hardly believe it! Buzzard was going to go back to sleep! I ran back upstairs. Crystal was sitting on the side of her bed, shaking a little in the chill of the room.

"Buzzard says to time your pains and when they're five minutes apart, she'll call Miss Rebecca," I said breathlessly.

"But I'm sitting in something all *wet!*" she wailed.

Wet? I ran back downstairs.

"Buzzard, you gotta get up. Crystal says she's sitting in something all wet!"

At that, Buzzard threw back the covers and sat up. "Get me my wool robe out of the closet," she said. "And help me find my shoes." When I tried to follow Buzzard into Crystal's room, she stopped me. "You go downstairs and put the kettle on to boil," she ordered. "The big kettle." I did as Buzzard said, and I don't know why, but turning on the lights in the kitchen and being there while it was still dark as midnight outside and knowing something pretty miraculous was getting ready to happen, right under our very roof, was something very nice. Something I was sure I would want to write into one of my stories.

As soon as I had the kettle going, I walked over to the window and looked out to where the light coming out of the kitchen lit up some of the big trees in the back garden.

And there was something there, as well. Maybe the spirits of Mr. and Mrs. Swan walking around in all that fine, chill March wind.

When Buzzard came downstairs, she went and got dressed, right down to her heavy boots. Then she called Miss Rebecca on the phone.

"Yes, the bag of waters have broken," she said. "No, you'll not ride that bicycle all the way here in this cold weather. I'll come get you. About fifteen minutes okay? I'm worried about a dry birth, you know," she added.

"That kettle boiling yet?" she asked as she came into the kitchen.

"Yes. What do you need hot water for?" Buzzard studied me for a moment before she smiled and said, "A cup of instant coffee to tide me over until we can get a real pot going."

Buzzard and Miss Rebecca stayed upstairs with Crystal almost the whole day long. I kept Molly and Little Ellis downstairs, and once in a while, I would go to the foot of the stairs and listen. Not a sound. Not a single sound. Once, Buzzard called to me to bring up coffee for her and Miss Rebecca, and I did—but Buzzard met me at the top of the stairs, took the cups, and motioned with her head for me to go down again. But before I could get all the way back downstairs, I heard a moan. A long, deep moan!

As that day went on, I thought back to how that first moan had startled me, because there were lots more, each one louder than the last. On and on and on they went, and finally, in late afternoon, I heard the first scream. Made me want to scream, myself! Molly and Little Ellis heard the scream too and looked at me with large, frightened eyes.

"It's okay," I tried to soothe them. "That's the kind of sounds a woman makes when she's having a baby." Why, I spoke with such authority and calmness, but in truth, I'd never been around a woman having a baby before in my life. Because Molly and Little Ellis were both born in the hospital, and I hadn't even been allowed to go along at all, either time.

When Buzzard came downstairs again, I didn't ask if the baby had come. I knew it hadn't, not with Crystal still screaming and crying. Buzzard had deep furrows in between her eyebrows when she went to the phone and dialed a number. I couldn't hear what she said, but when she turned to go back upstairs, those furrows on her forehead weren't quite so deep. Had she called a doctor? Was something terribly wrong?

But I got my answer to that in about half an hour, when the back door opened, and the Sisters of the Circle of Jesus filed into the kitchen, with two of them carrying Sister Blood-of-the-Lamb, just like always. They nodded their heads at me, took off their coats, seated themselves around the kitchen table, and took out their Bibles. I didn't even ask them if they wanted some coffee, but I went ahead and started a fresh pot for them while I watched them carefully. But they didn't do much of anything, that I could see. They didn't even open their Bibles—just put their hands on them, shut their eyes, and bowed their heads. No one said a single word. Just a big circle of big women, sitting around a table together. Then, after a few minutes, little Sister Blood-of-the-Lamb reached out her hands to the sisters on either side of her, and soon, all of them were holding hands, but they still kept their heads bowed.

I tiptoed around, getting the cups ready—then another scream from upstairs, the first since the sisters had arrived, pierced the air throughout the house. The sisters all flinched at that terrible sound, glanced up at each other for a moment, and then bowed their heads again. Sister Blood-of-the-Lamb started praying out loud, her words all strewn about with deep, soft moans and whispered "Help her, Jesus!" and "Please bring forth this, Your little child." Their sounds—their prayers—were almost like music.

I got the coffee poured into the cups, quietly put the sugar bowl and cream pitcher on the table, and then I placed steaming mugs of good coffee close to each sister. But not a one of them even looked up. And they stayed just like that for what seemed like hours. Then the strangest thing happened: All of a sudden, I could *feel* their prayers! Like that whole big kitchen was full of invisible butter-flies, just flitting around and heading upward! That lasted for a long time, and when I stopped feeling all those butterfly-prayers, I looked and saw that Sister Blood-of-the-Lamb had fallen asleep with her head on her hands and her hands on the Bible.

When it was time for Molly and Little Ellis to have their supper, I made some peanut butter and jelly sandwiches in that room full of prayers, and Molly and Little Ellis ate them in front of the television. Then I got two spare quilts out of the closet and spread them out on the floor of the little room where the television was and put them to bed in their clothes. For pillows, I found some bath towels and rolled them up to go under their heads.

"Now, as a special treat, I'll let you fall asleep watching

television," I said to them. So I turned on the television and turned it up loud enough that maybe they wouldn't hear so much of what was coming from upstairs. I sat down in Buzzard's chair, and finally, I must have fallen asleep because suddenly there was a new sound coming from upstairs. A baby crying! And from the kitchen, loud choruses of "Thank you, Jesus!" From all the way upstairs, I could hear Buzzard and Miss Rebecca laughing, and that was a precious thing to hear. From Crystal, I heard not a single word.

When I went into the kitchen, the Sisters of the Circle of Jesus were all putting on their coats and getting ready to leave. Their faces were a wonder to behold! They were all covered in sweat and smiles.

"Can I fix you all something to eat?" I asked. Seemed rude to send them out without anything, after all the hard work they'd done.

"No, thank you," one of them answered. "We'll be going home now."

After they all got their coats on and buttoned them up good and tight, they waked up Sister Blood-of-the-Lamb and got her into her child-sized coat, and all the while, she was saying, "Jesus come while I was asleep?" Then two of the sisters lifted her into their arms and carried her out of the house.

After they left, I cleaned up the still-full cups of cold coffee and put on a fresh pot. Buzzard and Miss Rebecca came down just as the coffee was done, and I gave a steaming mug to each one.

"Whoo-eee!" Miss Rebecca said as she slumped into one of the kitchen chairs. "That was a *big* baby sure enough! I've seen three-month-olds that aren't that big.

And she just didn't want to come out into this world!"

"She?" I asked, and Buzzard and Miss Rebecca looked at each other and smiled.

"Nice, healthy little girl," Buzzard said. "Or I should say—a nice, healthy, *big* girl!"

A girl! Another sister for me! Well, a half-sister, anyway.

"Circle of Jesus folks did some powerful praying, Buzzard," I said.

"Yes, Lord," Buzzard whispered happily. "When those sisters get to praying *hard,* we can sure come into some miracles!" They had both drained their cups, so Buzzard said, "Come on, Miss Rebecca, and I'll drive you home. You must be pretty wore out."

I sat at the kitchen table, waiting for Buzzard to come back. I sat so still, but I didn't really know why. Just that everything felt all fragile and maybe ready to fall apart. When I heard Buzzard pulling Miz Swan's big car around back, I poured yet another cup of coffee.

"Getting awful cold out there," Buzzard said as she came into the kitchen, took off her coat, and shivered a little. "I better sleep in your bed tonight, so I'll be near to Crystal and the baby. Make sure they stay toasty warm."

"Is Crystal gonna be okay?" I asked, still hearing those screams in my ears.

"Oh, sure. She'll be just fine. That's just what a woman has to go through to bring a child into this world. 'Specially one that big. Where are Molly and Little Ellis?"

"They're asleep on the floor in the little room," I answered.

Then I asked, "Buzzard, do you think it's possible to *feel* prayers?"

"Sure," she answered easily. "I can always tell when somebody's praying."

"I mean more than that," I ventured. "I mean *feel* them kind of fluttering around a room. Like tiny little butterflies that you can't see, but you can feel their wings."

Buzzard studied me for a moment. "Did that happen to you while the sisters were praying?"

"It did."

"Well, I told you they pray some powerful prayers, Dove. So yes, I suppose it's possible to feel them. 'Specially when they're so filled with love."

And the next words that fell out of my mouth were as big a surprise to me as they were to Buzzard. "I don't want to become a woman," I said.

"Don't want to become a woman? What kind of talk is that?"

"I just don't, that's all. I don't want to have a baby."

"Well, maybe you won't," she said so simply. "I never did."

"Why?"

"Never wanted to mess around with men. Besides, my life has been sweet and wonderful with Mr. and Mrs. Swan." She put her mug down a little hard on the top of the table, and I took that to mean I'd asked enough questions for one night.

"Dove, I gotta go to bed. Why don't you get another quilt and sleep in the reclining chair tonight. It's real comfortable. Sometimes—before you all came—I'd fall asleep in it and stay there all night long."

"That's fine," I said. "Tell Crystal I said I'm happy the baby's here."

"You can tell her yourself . . . tomorrow."

The next morning, I was still sound asleep when Buzzard tiptoed into the little room and touched my shoulder. "You wanta see the baby?" she whispered, so as not to wake up Molly and Little Ellis.

"Oh! Yes!"

We went so quietly up the stairs, and at the top, Buzzard looked at me and put her fingers over her lips. Then she slowly opened the door to mine and Crystal's room. The only light was coming from the bathroom, and all I could see of Crystal was a lump under the covers. Buzzard led me to a bassinette that was standing close to the bathroom door and stood there beaming. I looked—and in that sweet almost-darkness was a little face. A sleeping face. A baby girl with blond hair just like Crystal's and tiny, ruby-red lips. And while I stood there looking at her, the lips pursed and made a sucking sound for a few moments before they relaxed again. I looked at Buzzard and nodded. She grinned as big as if she was the mama of that little baby. Then we tiptoed back out of the room.

"Where'd you get the bassinette?" I asked when we got into the kitchen.

"Out of the attic," she answered. "Sure did take some good cleaning, though, I tell you. Thirty years' worth of dust is an awful lot."

"Whose bassinette was it?" I wondered out loud.

"It's an awful sad story—you sure you want to hear it?"

"I . . . I guess so," I said.

"There was a time when Miz Swan was expecting a little baby, and she had gotten together all kinds of the nicest things you could ever imagine—that bassinette and clothes and toys and blankets, and maybe a hundred diapers!" Buzzard raised her eyebrows, a signal to me to show appreciation for all that expensive stuff.

"Goodness!" I said.

Buzzard nodded and went on: "But that little baby came way too early. Tiniest little thing you could imagine. No bigger than a doll. A little boy it was, and he didn't live."

"He didn't?"

Buzzard closed her eyes and shook her head. "Like to have broken Miz Swan's heart. And she never wanted to try to have another one."

"That was going to be his bassinette?"

"Yes. And I've been washing a few of the diapers and clothes a little at a time. They were all put into a trunk and it never opened, from that very day. Until I found out Crystal was going to have a baby that could use those things."

"That certainly is a sad story," I said, wondering how things like that could happen. That beautiful Mr. and Mrs. Swan, and them so much in love. Things like that shouldn't happen. They just shouldn't, that's all. Buzzard set about making the breakfast biscuits, and I sat at the table, watching her and wondering about that poor little baby that was born too soon.

Around midmorning, we heard the baby starting to fuss, and then it started crying, sure enough. Buzzard went up the stairs and stayed for a very long time. But the baby never stopped crying. Not a single time. Finally, Buzzard came down the stairs with the baby nestled in the crook of her arm. It was all beet-red and making such loud cries, you wouldn't think a little baby could have that much noise in her.

Buzzard looked at me with strangely hollow eyes. "She won't feed it, Dove," she said, above the crying. "I never heard of such a thing! A mama who won't feed her own child? I've got to call Miss Rebecca." And before I knew what was happening, Buzzard just *plunked* that little baby right into my arms! Why, I was so surprised, I couldn't say a word. I just held her and started kind of rocking back and forth with her and all of a sudden, she got to studying my face, and she stopped crying. Molly and Little Ellis were watching me, so I sort of leaned down just a little so they could see the baby. But I kept rocking back and forth.

Buzzard was on the phone, and when all that wailing stopped, she turned around and studied me real close.

"Yes, I can hear you now," she said. "Wait and let me get a pencil." She fumbled around in the drawer and pulled out a stub of a pencil and started writing on the back of an envelope. "That's the doctor's name? Okay. I'll call him right now. Yes, I do understand her milk won't come in at all, unless she lets the baby nurse. But she just won't!"

"How'd you get her to stop crying?" Buzzard asked, dialing the phone again.

"I don't know," I said truthfully. "I just sort of rocked her a little and she stopped."

"Well thank the good Lord for that!" Buzzard exclaimed. "This here's gonna be a doctor can tell us what kind of canned milk to get for this poor little thing." Then someone in the doctor's office must have answered, and Buzzard started telling them that we had a baby less than one day old whose mama "couldn't feed it." I knew why she changed the "wouldn't" to "couldn't." She was embarrassed.

"Uh-huh . . . uh-huh," she grunted into the phone, all the while writing something down on the envelope. "Thank you so much. Yes, I'll bring the baby in if she doesn't hold the milk down." She hung up the phone and studied the envelope.

"Listen, Dove, I gotta go to the store and get some canned milk for this little thing." My heart absolutely skipped a beat! Was she going to leave me all alone with that tiny little girl and her hungry?

"It'll be okay," Buzzard assured me. "If she gets to crying again, you just put your little finger in her mouth and let her suck on it. I'll hurry as fast as I can." And before I could think another thought, she had thrown on her coat and headed toward the garage, running. So there we were: me and Molly and Little Ellis and this baby. And Crystal.

"Now you all come on and sit down," I directed, heading for the little room and the big recliner that would make me feel lots safer about holding the baby. Molly and Little Ellis sat down on their quilts on the floor, but they stayed turned toward me and the baby, while cartoons played on, without any sense to them, seemed to me. The baby had fallen asleep again, and I was awful glad. I just didn't know what I'd do if she kept screaming the whole time! I held her so still and easy and watched her. Under her paper-thin eyelids, I could see her eyes moving back and forth, and she kind of fluttered in her sleep a little. And that tiny mouth would lift up on one side in a crooked grin, showing all her pink gums. I fell in love with her, right then and there. So all my vows about never loving any-body again went right out the window, once again.

"Molly, would you please turn down the sound on the TV a little?" I whispered, and Molly did as I asked, except that she turned the dial the wrong way the first time, and all that blaring cartoon-music filled the room. In my arms, the baby jumped, flung out her arms, and started crying!

"Sowwy," Molly muttered.

"That's okay, honey," I assured her. She'd done the best she knew how to do. But now I had my hands full, sure enough. The baby wailed and wailed, turning so red, I thought for sure she'd explode right there in my arms! I held out my little finger and moved it to the baby's mouth. She whimpered and breathed funny and then she fairly *latched* onto my finger. Why, she was so strong, it sur-prised me, and I had to kind of pull my finger back to keep it from going right on down her throat!

Molly and Little Ellis stared at me with wide eyes. The baby sucked and sucked on my finger, and even when there wasn't anything for her to eat coming from it, she seemed to be comforted. I sat real still and held my finger right where it was, and it was the strangest feeling I've ever had, my finger in that warm, strong, sucking mouth! We stayed that way a long time, and finally, she fell back to sleep again. I sat real still, just listening and listening for Buzzard's car. At long last, I heard it!

"I'm back," came Buzzard's call from the kitchen, and I could hear her putting down a paper bag of groceries onto the table. "You okay?"

Well, I wasn't about to yell back and wake up the baby again, so I whispered to Molly, "Go tell Buzzard we're okay." And she did.

"I'll have this bottle sterilized and some warmed-up milk in it in just a minute," Buzzard called. I sat still and held my breath. In a few minutes, Buzzard came into the little room carrying a baby bottle. The baby was still sleeping and sucking on my finger every once in a while.

"You just pull your finger out, and I'll poke this rubber nipple in, and let's us hope for the best!" It was hard to get my finger out of the baby's mouth, she had such a grip on it! And the minute it was gone, her face turned all red and crinkled up, and she started struggling. But Buzzard poked that rubber nipple into her mouth and she got serious, sure enough!

"Keep it tilted up so she doesn't swallow a lot of air," Buzzard instructed. So I did, and I watched her sucking and swallowing, sucking and swallowing. Then she'd stop for a little moment and breathe so deep and steady-like. And wake up a little and go right back at it. By the time the bottle was about half empty, she had gone all soft and heavy in my arms, breathing slow and steady and waking up every once in a while to suck some more. Buzzard stayed right by my side the whole time, and when at last the baby turned loose of the nipple, we looked at each other and smiled. Sleeping in my arms, she got another one of her crooked, one-side-only smiles, and I could see milk puddles around her gums. I don't know why, but it was something so sweet to see, I almost got tears in my eyes. Maybe that she had been so unhappy and hungry, and now, Buzzard and I had made her full and contented.

"She was certainly one hungry little baby!" Buzzard crooned, running her finger over the baby's head.

"Now we gotta burp her," she said, and she lifted the baby out of my arms, tossed her up onto that big shoulder, and started gently patting her back. "Dove, you tiptoe upstairs and bring that little bassinette down here," Buzzard said. "And don't you wake Crystal. She needs her rest." I went up the stairs as quietly as possible and pushed open the bedroom door. The room was in shadow, because of the heavy curtains still being closed. I glanced over at Crystal's bed. She was lying there with her eyes wide open!

"You okay?" I asked, and I noticed the face that she had turned toward me was something like I've never seen before. Swollen and pasty-looking. Why, right away, I got a remembrance of Crystal's pretty face topped by the cowboy hat with her lips all shiny and red. It was hard for me to believe it was the same person.

"You okay?" I repeated.

"I guess so," came the muttered reply. "What are you doing?"

"Buzzard said for me to come up here and get the bassinette so we can use it downstairs for the baby. We gave her a bottle," I added and then thought maybe I'd said the wrong thing.

"Okay," Crystal replied.

"Crystal, what's the baby's name? What name you gonna give her?" I asked.

"Dunno," came the flat reply. "Can't think."

"You okay, Crystal?" I asked once more, wanting her to sit up and smile and be who she used to be. Ask for her beautiful little baby, take that little girl into her arms. But that didn't happen. She didn't even answer me.

"When you gonna give her a name, Crystal?" I tried again.

"You name her," came the astonishing reply!

"Me? Me give her a name?"

"Yes. Name her whatever you like, but go on now and let me rest."

I got the bassinette and carried it back downstairs in something like a dream. Me! Getting to name that little baby! I went right into the kitchen, where Buzzard had a whole lot of baby bottles lined up and ready to go into the boiling water and the baby cradled, sleeping, in the crook of her arm.

"Crystal says for me to name the baby!" I said. Buzzard stared at me for a long moment.

"She said *you're* to name her?" she asked.

"That's what she said."

"Well then, I guess that's what you'll do." Buzzard put the baby into the bassinette, covered her up with a soft blanket, and went back to working with the baby bottles. I thought for a long time, watching Buzzard and watching the baby, because getting her the perfectly right name was so important. Then I got an idea!

"What's Miz Swan's full name again?"

"What?" Buzzard asked.

"What's Miz Swan's name—other than Miz Swan, I mean."

Buzzard hesitated before she said, "Mary Elizabeth . . . that's her name." And I was thinking of the beautiful MES initials on that fine stationery.

"I like it," I said. And to be completely truthful, I was thinking about more than the way I had imagined the beautiful, young Miz Swan. I was also thinking that maybe, if we named the baby after her, she wouldn't make us all leave, once she came home from France. If she ever came home from France.

I took a dinner tray up to Crystal at noontime, and Buzzard took one up for supper. But both those trays came back to the kitchen untouched. Buzzard didn't say anything, but I could tell she was worried. So we spent our day taking care of Mary Elizabeth, who took to that bottled milk just fine. Molly and Little Ellis were good about staying indoors and taking their naps in Buzzard's bed— because we didn't want them to disturb Crystal. I read them five whole stories, because they had been so good.

That night, I put Molly and Little Ellis to sleep again on the floor of the little room, and Buzzard and I slept together in her big bed, with Mary Elizabeth's bassinette right beside us, so we could hear her if she gave out with so much as a hiccup. We fed Mary Elizabeth two times during the night, and changed her diaper three times, and when I woke up the next morning, I suddenly remembered that it was Monday! I was supposed to go to school! But everything was so quiet, with Buzzard breathing deeply beside me, and Mary Elizabeth not making a single sound—like Molly and Little Ellis, who were obviously still asleep on the floor of the little room, snuggled down all safe and sound under their blankets. Why, I didn't know what to do—how could I miss school? But how could I *go* to school? I stayed put and tried to think, and then I sort of settled back onto my pillow, listening to all that sweet quiet around me, and finally, I pulled the down comforter up over my head and fell back asleep.

"You missed school!" Buzzard's loud whisper and her hand shaking my shoulder. All around us, everything and everybody still quiet. "You missed school!" Buzzard repeated.

"I can miss one day," I assured her, pulling the comforter off of my head, feeling the chilled air, and not even wanting to think about getting out from under that toasty-warm comforter.

"Well," she finally growled. "I guess you can miss one day. I can write you a note. But tomorrow, you go back!"

"Yessm," I pulled the comforter over my head again and smiled where Buzzard couldn't see me. Because I'd seen her write something before, and she always pulled her brows together and frowned heavily and stuck her pink tongue from between her lips. And to think that she would be writing to my *teacher*, I could imagine that she would have little clear-colored pearls of perspiration on her forehead as well!

Later—but I don't know how much later, I heard talking coming down the hallway from the kitchen. I sat up and looked into the bassinette. It was empty. I threw back the comforter, went through the little room—being careful to step around Molly and Little Ellis, who were still asleep—and down the long hallway to the kitchen.

To my surprise, Crystal was sitting at the kitchen table, dressed for work and with a cup of hot tea in front of her. But her face was pasty white and her hair wasn't done right. And when she tried to drink her tea, her hand was shaking so hard that the tea spilled over into the saucer. Buzzard was at the stove, putting a pan full of biscuits into the oven, and once again, with a sleeping Mary Elizabeth tucked securely into the crook of her arm.

"No ma'am!" Buzzard was fuming in whispers—probably so as not to wake up the baby. "You are *not* going to work today! Have you completely lost your mind?" Buzzard's fury filled the whole kitchen with a different kind of warmth, and I backed away from the door and listened.

"You just had yourself a *baby,* for Heaven's sake!" Buzzard went on. "You're going to have you some good breakfast and then you're going right back to bed!"

Crystal's voice was thin and whiny-sounding: "But I got children depending on me! I gotta go to work!"

"You don't gotta do nothing of the kind!" Buzzard whispered back viciously. "First thing you gotta do . . . at the very least . . . is take this little baby of yours into your arms!" I peeked through the doorway. Buzzard had bumped right up against Crystal and simply but gently rolled Mary Elizabeth right into Crystal's arms. Mary Elizabeth frowned a little and made some unhappy-sounding grunts, but then she went right back to sleep. Crystal looked down at the sleeping face, like she couldn't imagine what this was all about.

"Don't you even want to know her name?" Buzzard fumed. And when Crystal didn't answer, Buzzard whispered hoarsely, "It's Mary Elizabeth. She's Mary Elizabeth and she's your very own child!" With that, Buzzard turned back to the stove. I watched Crystal sitting there holding the baby, looking at her—but Crystal's face was like a blank blackboard in my classroom. A thing that was waiting for somebody to fill it up with words that had some meaning. Then a terrible silence in that kitchen. More terrible, even, than the one when I'd heard Crystal telling Buzzard there was a baby coming. Finally, Buzzard sat down at the table with Crystal, who was still staring at the baby as if she didn't know how on earth a baby had come into this world.

"Crystal, listen to me and listen good," Buzzard started out. "I came into some money . . . quite a lot of money. Now don't ask me anything about it because I'm not gonna tell you. But it's a gracious plenty for us all. And there's more coming."

"She *is* kind of pretty, isn't she?" Crystal asked.

"She sure is," Buzzard agreed. "I'm glad you're taking a little bit of interest in her. You've had me worried."

"She's got my mama's ears," Crystal said.

"And looks like she's got your hair," Buzzard added. "Now did you hear me about the money? Did you hear me?"

"Let's put her in the bassinette, Buzzard," Crystal said. "I think you're right about me going back to bed."

"Eat you some good breakfast first," Buzzard insisted, lifting Mary Elizabeth out of Crystal's arms. "You can't get your strength back unless you eat something."

"Not right now," Crystal said, and without another word, she got up and went back upstairs. I came into the kitchen to see if I could help.

"Dove, get the bassinette for me, and we'll keep Mary Elizabeth right here in this good, warm kitchen with us." But as Buzzard spoke, her eyes were on the staircase, and there was a deep frown between her eyes. When I went to get the bassinette, Molly and Little Ellis were getting awake, so I put out their clothes for them to get into while I took the bassinette back into the kitchen. Buzzard was on the phone.

"Yessir, that'll be fine," she was saying. "Around about four this afternoon. Yes. Thank you."

"What's happening around about four?" I asked.

"Miz Swan's doctor is going to make a house call. Check on Crystal for us."

"Is she really sick? Did having the baby make her sick?"

Just as I asked, Buzzard put Mary Elizabeth into the bassinette, and when I looked at that sweet little baby, I thought it would be a real shame if her coming into the world had made her mama sick. She was so beautiful.

"I don't know," Buzzard said. "But her not eating and not really paying much attention to the baby is something we need to see about."

That afternoon, Miz Swan's doctor made his house call. He was a very tall, slender man with white hair and a tiny little beard that wasn't like most beards at all. This one sat right on the point of his chin and nowhere else. Buzzard took him upstairs, and they were gone for a long time. Mary Elizabeth waked up and I changed her diaper and warmed a bottle of milk for her. But I guess I wasn't quick enough to suit her, because she really got in a few long, loud yelps before it was ready. Just as I was feeding her, Buzzard and the doctor came back downstairs.

"Seems as if this one is healthy," the doctor said. "But as long as I'm here, let me check her over." I started trying to pull the nipple out of her mouth, but it was hard to get it away from her. When I finally did, she went into a flurry of crying and jerking. The doctor smiled and took her out of my arms.

"Would you put a towel or blanket on the table for me?" he asked Buzzard. We had a dryer full of clean blankets that were still warm, and Buzzard folded one and put it on the table so the doctor could give Mary Elizabeth a quick examination. But she never hushed crying the whole time he gently felt her stomach and looked in her ears. He had a little light he shined into her open mouth so he could see her throat, and then he felt around her belly button.

"Baby's fine," he said in a voice loud enough to rise above her crying. "Better give her back that bottle." He wrapped her in the blanket and handed her back to me.

"Make sure Crystal keeps taking those prenatal vitamins, and if her appetite doesn't come back soon, call my office and make an appointment. Right now, I'd say it's just a bad case of baby blues. But let me know if anything changes," he said to Buzzard.

"What are baby blues?" I asked when Buzzard came back from seeing the doctor to the door.

"Some women just get real sad right after they've had a baby," Buzzard said. "Don't know why."

"Will she get over it?"

"I think so." But there was a worried sound in Buzzard's voice that sent shivers down my spine.

"Well, let's get us some supper ready," Buzzard said. "And make me remember to write you a note for school tomorrow. You can ride the bus, since Crystal won't be going in to work yet."

"Can you manage everything without me?" I asked, and as soon as I heard the words, I knew that I wanted her to say "No. No, Dove, I can't manage without you."

"We'll be okay," she said instead.

So the next morning, I started walking down the long driveway and saw the school bus go by, going in the direction of Sharon's house. When I reached the road, I waited on the opposite side from the mailbox for the bus to come back. And that school day felt like it would never end. Most of the time, all I could do was wonder what was happening at home. Was Mary Elizabeth taking her bottle? Were Molly and Little Ellis behaving themselves? Was Crystal going to be able to eat a little bite of her dinner?

That afternoon, I ran the whole length of the driveway and when I got in the door, I could smell something delicious cooking in the kitchen. Buzzard was at the stove, lifting a lid and looking into a boiling pot. Molly and Little Ellis were polishing silver at the kitchen table, and Mary Elizabeth was asleep in her bassinette. It was such a peaceful scene, and it gladdened my heart.

"What're you cooking?" I asked, drawn to the stove by the delicious smell.

"My grandmama's chicken and dumplings," Buzzard said proudly. "I figured that if there was anything in this world that would chirk up Crystal's appetite, this is it."

Sure enough, at suppertime, Crystal came downstairs and ate with us. Well, she didn't eat much, but she sat with us. When Mary Elizabeth started squeaking for her bottle, Crystal seemed not to even hear her. Buzzard watched Crystal closely, and I started to get up and tend to the baby. But Buzzard stopped me. "You sit down, Dove," she said in a low voice. "That's Crystal's baby, and she ought to be the one to tend to her." To Crystal she said, "Don't you hear your baby fussing over there? Aren't you going to tend to her?"

Crystal looked up a little surprised and heaved a deep sigh. "Yes," she said.

But we had to help her after all, because she didn't know how to put on a diaper, and she also didn't know where we kept the pot for warming the bottle. And when we got her all set to feed the baby, she didn't even know to hold the bottle at an angle. We showed her all these things, and at last, she was feeding the baby, who stared at her with great, round eyes. We were all quiet. Buzzard was nodding her head very slowly up and down. And I guess I'm the only one that saw a tear slide down Crystal's face and drip off her chin.

Chapter Twenty

THAT night, I waked up hearing the wind howling outside and something that sounded like sand being thrown against the windows of Buzzard's room. We were all still sleeping downstairs so Crystal could get plenty of rest. When I got out of bed and went toward the window, I could see that Buzzard wasn't in the bed at all. I pulled back the curtains and saw that sleet and rain were coming down hard and fast, already coating the branches of trees outside. But where was Buzzard?

When I got out into the hallway, I could see that the kitchen light was on, and I followed the spill of yellow light until I came into the kitchen and saw Buzzard sitting in the rocking chair, rocking Mary Elizabeth.

"Is something wrong?" I asked, because there was something or other in the slope of Buzzard's shoulders that I hadn't seen before. Buzzard sighed and lifted her chin, but she didn't say anything. I went around and stood in front of her, studying her face.

"Something *is* wrong," I said. "And I think I know what it is—Miz Swan is coming home."

"Miz Swan . . . ?" Buzzard seemed confused. "No. That's not it."

"What is it, then?" I urged her, because whatever was wrong, I had to start thinking how to get it right again. I had to!

"Dove, there's no easy way to tell you this," she started out, and I held my breath. "Crystal's gone."

"Gone? She *died?*"

"No! She didn't die. She left."

"Left for where? And in this kind of weather?"

Buzzard pointed to the kitchen table, where there was a folded piece of paper with my name on it.

"What's this?"

"Crystal was sitting here at the kitchen table, writing this letter to you, when Mary Elizabeth started fussing and I came in here to get her bottles."

I got the note and unfolded it, but my hands were shaking so hard, I could hardly read it:

Dear Dove,
    I'm so sorry. I tried. I really tried. I just can't do this. Everybody will be better off if I go away. I tried to do right, but I got myself into more than I know how to

handle. Please forgive me. I wish you all the best and I will love you forever.

Love,
Crystal

P.S. Please take good care of my baby.

Buzzard stood up and deposited a sleeping Mary Elizabeth into the bassinette. She came and sat down at the kitchen table, and I sat down across from her. We sat there for a long, long time. My head was whirling with all kinds of thoughts: How was I going to be able to take care of Molly and Little Ellis and Mary Elizabeth? Should we go home to Aunt Bett? Should we stay until Miz Swan came back? Should I ask Buzzard to let us stay until we knew better that Molly wouldn't get taken away from us? And when we went back home, how would I find the money to rent us a place to stay? We couldn't ask Aunt Bett to take us in! What was going to become of us?

"I tried to stop her," Buzzard mumbled. "I did everything a body could do to try and stop her. I said that if she walked out on her own child, she didn't even deserve to be called a human being! What a hurtful thing to say to somebody!"

"You had to try," I offered, with most of my mind still wondering what on earth was going to happen to us.

Then we sat again for a long time, in the warm kitchen with all that sleet slapping against the windows and all the children safe and warm. How would I be able to *keep* them safe and warm?

Chapter Twenty-one

UZZARD'S voice came through all the fog in my head. "I'm sorry, Dove," she finally said. "I hated for you to know this."

But I was all caught up in imagining that Molly and Little Ellis and Mary Elizabeth and I were out in all that sleet and freezing rain, walking along a long, lonely road with nothing to eat and no place to go. I could really feel my feet going numb and hear Molly whimpering. And in that terrible imagining, I looked down at Mary Elizabeth and saw that she was blue and still. All of a sudden, something in me exploded.

"How could she?" I didn't even know that's what I was going to say. "How could she?" I repeated, and I started feeling like maybe I was a volcano and something terrible and red and evil was rumbling through me and getting ready to come flying out.

"It isn't fair!" I fairly yelled. "It isn't fair!"

"I know you're hurt, and I don't blame you one little bit," Buzzard said. "But Molly and Little Ellis don't know about this, and we don't want to upset them."

"Upset *them?*" I tried to lower my voice. "What about *me?* Somebody just tell me that! How could Crystal go off and leave Mary Elizabeth for me to raise? How could she do that to me?" I was very close to the most furious tears anybody could ever imagine.

"Maybe because she knows how strong you are," Buzzard answered. And that completely surprised me.

"Me? Strong?" I yelped.

"Well, sure!" Buzzard was frowning at me. "Maybe Crystal knows you better than you know yourself!"

"I don't want to be strong," I confessed, feeling as if all my bones had dissolved or something.

"Like it or not, you are strong," Buzzard said. "Strongest girl I ever knew."

"I said I don't want to be strong," I repeated.

"Okay then," Buzzard suggested. "Why don't you do like Crystal? Just run off and leave it all!"

What?

Incredibly, Buzzard laughed. "I sure do wish you could see your face!"

What?

"No, you won't do that. Couldn't do that if your life depended upon it. Just isn't in you. Listen to me—and hear what I'm telling you—things don't just happen to us. We *choose* them."

"Choose them?" Why, that was the most ridiculous thing I ever heard of in my whole life. "Did I *choose* for Crystal to run off and leave us like this?" I was angry again. Angrier than I'd ever been in my whole life. Oh, how I wished I'd learned some of those Old Testament curses so they could spew out of my mouth and melt the whole world!

"No, of course not," Buzzard said. "But just now, I gave you your chance to run off, just like Crystal did, and you didn't choose to do it. So that means you *do* choose to stay and do whatever has to be done. You will *always* choose that."

Buzzard studied me for a long minute, while I let her words soak in.

"But what's going to happen to us?" I asked finally. Asked *myself*, really, because if there was any solving to be done, I was the one who would do it. Who *could* do it.

"Well! It's time, I reckon!" Buzzard said in a loud voice. I jumped a little.

"What?" I asked. But Buzzard just got up without a word and went into the parlor. Then, just as fast, she came back into the kitchen, carrying the big Bible, and plunked it right down on the table in front of me. When she sat down again, I felt my heart go hard as a rock. What was this all about? Hadn't I had enough surprises already to last me the rest of my whole life? And now Buzzard was getting ready to do something solemn to me! Another surprise!

"Do you know how to keep a secret?" she asked.

"Why?" I asked, and it was a real nasty-sounding, sarcastic word that just fell out of my mouth before I even knew it was there.

"Because I need to tell you something, and it has to stay a secret. Do you understand?"

"I think you've told me enough for one day," I shot back at her, and she looked startled.

"Well, you're hurting real bad, so I won't take offense at that," she said, but her voice bristled anyway. "So I'll ask it again: Do you know how to keep a secret?"

"Yes." She studied me for a long time, narrowing her eyes and pursing her lips. I could almost see her thoughts flying around like startled birds for a few seconds, then calming down, and finally lighting on the branches of a tree that seemed to stand right in the middle of her forehead.

"Put your hand on this Bible," she commanded.

"Why?" I asked, feeling all that anger coming back on me and not knowing why.

"You do as I say!" Buzzard yelled.

"You're not my mother!" I yelled back.

Molly and Little Ellis had waked up and come to the kitchen door. They were standing there staring at us, because they'd never heard Buzzard or me raise our voices before, especially not at each other.

"It's okay," Buzzard tried to croon at Molly and Little Ellis. "Me and Dove just having us a little talk is all. You all go on back to bed now. And cover up nice and warm." Obedient as always, they turned and went out of the kitchen. Buzzard reached across the table, grabbed my hand, put it on the Bible, and before I could move it away, she clamped both of her large, warm hands over mine.

"Now say this," Buzzard whispered. "I swear on the Bible, God's Holy Word . . ."

"Why?" I asked again, feeling some surge of terrible power over her. Because after all, I was the head of my family now!

"Do it!" Buzzard whispered loudly, and with her cheeks shaking. So, head of my family or not, I knew I had to give in.

"Okay, okay. I swear on the Bible, God's Holy Word . . ."

"That I will *never* . . ." Buzzard bark-whispered the word.

"That I will *never* . . ."

"Tell anybody what Buzzard's fixing to tell me."

"Tell anybody what Buzzard's fixing to tell me."

Buzzard gave one big nod of her head. "Do you know

what'll happen to you, if you break your word what you swore to on the Bible?"

"No," I said, but I'd been to church with Aunt Bett often enough to know about breaking your word and what would happen to you if you did.

"You'll burn in everlasting hellfire," she warned in a long, terrible whisper. "You'll go *straight* to hell when you die." And for some reason, even through all my hurting, those words hit me like swords going into my heart, and I could feel blistering flames licking at my ankles.

"I won't break my word!" I said, and almost at once, the flames were gone, and I could feel God's cool, blue breath blowing across my feet. "But if you think you can tell me anything that's going to make me feel better about what's happened, you're crazy as a bedbug!" I added.

"That's the hurt talking again," Buzzard pronounced. "Now just listen to me," she started out again. "You need to know that this house and everything that's in it"—her gaze swept around that good, big kitchen—"is *mine*."

What?

"What about Miz Swan?" I demanded. Because what Buzzard was saying didn't make a bit of sense in this world.

"Let's just leave that subject out of it," Buzzard said, lowering her eyes.

"But how can it be yours, if it's Miz Swan's?"

"I'll explain that later," Buzzard insisted. "I really don't want to tell you about it right now." But I never could stand not knowing things, and besides, I didn't understand what Buzzard's "secret" had to do with anything.

"Tell me," I whispered.

"It'll be one more bad thing for you to hear," she warned.

"I have to know, Buzzard," I said. "And I have to know what who owns this house has to do with anything that's happened to us."

"Okay," Buzzard agreed. "But just you remember I warned you."

"Okay." And I braced myself for the next bad thing I would hear.

"Miz Swan's in France, sure enough, and she won't be coming back. Because she passed away."

"Passed away? Miz Swan's *dead?*" I gulped. Buzzard nodded her head, with her eyes still on me so hard, they almost pinned me to the wall.

"Been dead around two years now. And she left this house to *me*. This is *my* house. And everything that's in it." Crazily, I thought at once about what the people in town were saying about Buzzard maybe not taking good care of *Miz Swan's beautiful things*.

"I don't understand," I said. "Why do you act like she's still alive?"

"Because . . ." Buzzard went on very slowly. "If folks kept getting reminded that a black woman owns this beautiful house, they wouldn't know what to think. It's kind of a game we all play, so they can pretend they don't know the house is mine. We all play our parts, me pretending Miz Swan's still in France and that I'm just her maid, taking care of her house. And all the white folks in town pretend the same thing. It's a way we have of trying to stay comfortable with each other."

All of a sudden, I remembered my story of the young

Mr. and Mrs. Swan and their great love for each other. "She's buried in France?" I asked.

"Not buried," Buzzard said. "She was cremated too, just like Mr. Swan." Her voice tried to choke up, and she cleared her throat. "When she found out she was going to . . . pass on, she made out a will that said she was to be cremated and her ashes put into the Seine River. Guess she figured that since Mr. Swan's ashes went into the Savannah River, maybe their ashes could meet up—somewhere out in the middle of the ocean. Or something like that." Buzzard wiped her eyes and then closed them and tilted her face up toward the ceiling. "In the will, she said exactly this: 'The Swan Place in its entirety and all the furnishings go to my good friend and long companion, Buzzard. She's cleaned it and taken care of it for over forty years, so it's right for her to have it.'" Buzzard blew her nose loudly. "You know, of course, that the Swans didn't have any children. No family at all. No kinfolks. Not a one. Anyway—when Miz Swan made out her will, she had it sent to her attorney here in town, and she suggested this game we all play, because she knew how the old ways of doing things die so hard, 'specially in small towns. So she left me this house and everything in it and a bank account that she'd transferred over into my own name. It has lots of money in it, and I got more from her insurance—but the lawyer takes care of sending that money to me through a bank in far-off New York City. And she left me all her investments too—though I surely don't know what they are—and another lawyer in Salt Lake City, Utah, sends me what he calls dividend checks every single month." When she stopped talking, I just sat there, trying to let it all soak in.

"And, Dove . . ." Buzzard finally went on. "That's how I came up with the idea of pretending you all were the late Mr. Swan's great-nieces and nephew, once I'd made up my mind to help you out. Because when the Great God Almighty let me have all this big house and all this beautiful furniture—and anything anybody could ever need: bed linens and blankets and pots and pans—and plenty of money too—I promised Him I'd try to use it to help His children."

I thought for a moment, "So she isn't coming back."

"That's right." Buzzard echoed me, "She isn't coming back."

"So we don't have to leave?" It was a profound question, so profound that it made my voice tremble.

"That's right. So now, let's just let you get used to what I've told you. I know it's broken your heart for Crystal to run off like she did, and I know you're awful worried about taking care of Mary Elizabeth and Little Ellis and Molly, but I've got plenty of money for us all. So you don't have to worry about that."

While I was sitting there trying to take in everything Buzzard had told me, she stood up and picked up the big Bible. "You just remember that you put your hands on this and *swore!*" she warned one last time. "If and when I decide not to play the game anymore, I'll be more open about this house being my very own." She stomped off to the living room.

So then I had more to think about: How it would feel *not* going back to Aunt Bett's? In one way, it made me feel good that we wouldn't have to pile in on her, and her with such a big family to take care of. But in another way, it felt kind of sad. How could we all live here in this big, beautiful house with Buzzard and have everything in the world we would ever need? And Aunt Bett still making pickles to trade for clothes?

"Hey, Buzzard," I called. "Why didn't you tell any of this to Crystal? If she'd known, maybe she wouldn't have run away!"

"I told Crystal there was plenty of money, and that was all she needed to know," Buzzard said as she came back into the kitchen. "She didn't run off because of money. She ran off because she's nothing but a child herself, and it was all too much for her."

"She tried," I whispered, suddenly wanting to defend Crystal, even though I'd been so mad at her before.

"She sure did that," Buzzard agreed.

"I hope she'll come back," I said, even though I had only meant to think it.

"I wouldn't count on it," Buzzard muttered. "*Hoping* is fine, but we have to deal with what *is*—not what we hope for."

It made sense, what Buzzard said. So what I had to do was deal with the way things really were, right there at that minute. Crystal was gone. Me and Molly and Little Ellis . . . and Mary Elizabeth, too . . . all had to have a home, and Buzzard had said we could stay right where we were, at the Swan Place.

Somehow, I had a vision of Mary Elizabeth being able to grow up in such a beautiful house, maybe even a vision of her as a beautiful young woman, wearing a white dress with ribbons on it and walking around the pond on a golden afternoon.

"I wish the pond still had swans to glide around in it," I said. Buzzard looked at me and frowned. "Where'd they go anyway?" I added.

Buzzard shrugged her shoulders. "Well, the swans got old, and finally one of them died and the next day, so did the other one."

Oh, it was such a sad thing to hear! I could imagine those snowy-white, crumpled bodies floating in the pond, their beautiful, proud necks limp and unfurled.

"Of course, they did have some young, and if they'd survived, we might still have swans in the pond, right to this very day," Buzzard said.

"The babies died too?" It was such a terrible question, I almost couldn't ask it.

"Yes," Buzzard said easily. "Fox got 'em."

I don't know why, but it was one of the worst things I ever heard in all my life. Worse, even, than Crystal being gone and Miz Swan being dead. It was the saddest thing I could hear about and still be able to breathe! The beautiful swan mother and father trying to protect their babies and them getting eaten up by a mean old fox.

And suddenly, I was angry all over again.

"Why'd you tell me *that?*" I hollered at Buzzard, and she looked as surprised as I've ever seen anyone look. "Why'd you tell me something so awful?"

"Why, Dove!" She was completely perplexed, and so was I, but I wouldn't have admitted it for anything. Like there was another big buildup of steam inside of me, and it had to come out and there was only one way—through my mouth. My mean, stupid mouth. And while Buzzard stood there staring at me, what I really wanted to do was reach all the way up to Heaven, grab the great God Almighty, look right into His face and ask Him *Why?* Why mamas and daddies die and why new mamas get so sad they run off and leave their own babies. And why Aunt Bett had to work so hard, trading her pickles to get clothes for her children. And, especially, why He lets foxes eat baby swans!

A big, loud moan—something I didn't even know was there—came out of me, out of some place buried so deep, I couldn't even imagine where it was. Buzzard was still staring at me, and I just sat there like a stupid lump, wondering what on earth was happening to me.

Finally, Buzzard spoke: "It's been a lot on you," she pronounced solemnly. Just as she said that, I thought about Aunt Bett, could almost see all those jars of pickles. Aunt Bett, who didn't know about Mary Elizabeth or about Crystal running off. Why, if Crystal had just stayed around, maybe we could have gone back. Maybe even lived in that same little house all together. But now, with just us left, we'd probably have to crowd into Aunt Bett's house and it already bulging at the seams with children.

"Where do you think Crystal's gone?" I asked Buzzard, all the time still trying to figure out what we must do and asking in a real polite voice, so Buzzard would know that I had gotten myself under control again.

"I don't know. Maybe back to her mama and papa—or maybe just to drive until she doesn't have any more money for gas. Then find a job."

Oh, that sure sounded bleak!

"You know what I think?" Buzzard floated the question into the air. "I think you really need to talk with your Aunt Bett. Let her know what's happened and see what she has to say about it."

Well, it seemed to me that I still needed to do some hard thinking before I made that call. We could stay at the Swan Place, have nice clothes and everything and have people being real nice to me because they thought I was Mr. Swan's great-niece. Or maybe we could go home, if Aunt Bett wanted us. Go back to a school where the other girls were mean to me because I was poor. Go back to wearing hand-me-down dresses.

But then I thought about Miss Madison. *She* liked me, and I could go back to writing with her in her classroom every day at lunch. And what I thought about next was everything I could write about the Swan Place. About Mr. and Miz Swan and their little baby. But I wouldn't let him be born too soon. I would write it so that he lived. And the baby swans, too. No mean foxes to carry them away.

"Dove?" Buzzard's voice intruded. "Just make that phone call and let's see what your Aunt Bett has to say."

Suddenly, it all seemed pretty simple. Either Aunt Bett would ask us to come home, or she wouldn't.

"Should I tell her about Mary Elizabeth?" I asked.

"Might as well," Buzzard sighed. "Might as well."

"I don't know what to say, Buzzard," I confessed. "Should we all stay here with you? I'd like that, except I wouldn't want to keep on pretending to be Mr. Swan's great-niece."

"Well, pretending is what goes with living here. I've already explained that to you." Buzzard reminded me. "Go on now and make that call, Dove. It's late enough that she'll be up and around. You'll figure out what's right for you all to do, just as soon as you hear your Aunt

Bett's voice."

I hoped Buzzard was right about that. I went down the hall, dialed Aunt Bett's number, and while the phone was ringing, I could imagine her house and almost see her face. *And who on earth would be calling this early in the morning?*

"Hello?" Her familiar voice, with just a touch of anxiety in it, made my throat tighten.

"Aunt Bett? It's Dove," I mumbled.

"Dove, honey!" She sounded so happy to be hearing from us. But then her voice lowered. "You all okay?"

"Well . . ."

"What is it?"

"Aunt Bett, we've had some hard things happen to us," I started out, trying to ease into a conversation and not get Aunt Bett all upset.

"What kind of hard things, Dove? Tell me!"

"Crystal ran off, and we don't know where she is," I blurted out.

"What?"

"I said, Crystal ran off, and we don't know where she is."

"Ran off and left you all?" Her voice had such an incredulous tone.

"Yessm," I said. "And that isn't all."

"Lord help us!" Aunt Bett breathed into the phone. And then she was silent and I could feel her anxious waiting coming right through the telephone.

"Yessm. Well, it's like this . . ."

"Spit it out, child!" Aunt Bett whispered.

"Crystal had a baby."

"A baby?" Aunt Bett sounded as if she had never heard of such a thing. Then she added, "You mean Crystal had a baby and she ran off and left the baby too?"

"Yessm. She hadn't been feeling good. She was sad all the time," I explained. "Some folks call it 'baby blues.' "

"Take more than just baby blues to make a mama leave her own child! Oh good Heavens! That poor child!"

"Oh, we're taking good care of her," I hastened to add.

There was a moment of hesitation on the other end, and then Aunt Bett said, "Oh, honey, I didn't mean the baby. I meant Crystal!"

It felt strange to hear Aunt Bett talking of Crystal as a *child,* but maybe that was right. Crystal was a child who tried to do a woman's job. Aunt Bett sighed. "She just took more on herself than she could handle." And then she added, "Well, when are you all coming back home?" So there was the question, right on top of me. "Dove?"

"Please listen, Aunt Bett," I begged. "Buzzard says we can stay here. She's got a big house and plenty of money, and we really like it here." From the other end, a long, long silence. "Aunt Bett?"

"Not come home?" Aunt Bett's voice sounded small and tight. "Not come home to your family?" Now there was a catch in her throat.

"We can't crowd in on you," I tried to explain. "Why, where on earth would you put us?"

"Well, I don't know," Aunt Bett sounded exasperated. "But I'll find a way to make room." Her voice was rising. "You're *family!*" she almost shouted.

"And what about Mary Elizabeth?" I asked.

"Mary who?"

"Crystal's baby. Mary Elizabeth. She's not blood kin to you. Me and Molly and Little Ellis are your nieces and nephew, but Mary Elizabeth isn't."

"Well, what does that matter?" Aunt Bett sounded confused. "If she's with you all, she's part of *your* family and you're part of *mine,* so what does it matter?" And standing there, listening to Aunt Bett, I could almost see the old washing machine on her back porch and all the jars of pickles on the shelves in her kitchen, and the big dining table we all crowded around, and what that kitchen looked like the night she thought Roy-Ellis had put a strange woman in her sister's bed. I felt my eyes fill up.

"Dove?" Her voice was plaintive, almost mewing.

Just then, Buzzard passed by me and motioned for me to cover the phone. "Hold on just a minute, please, Aunt Bett," I said. "Buzzard wants to tell me something." I clamped my hand over the receiver.

Buzzard had her hands on her hips and a scowl on her face. "Did she come right out and ask you all to come home and live with her?"

"Yes," I admitted, feeling my face starting to burn.

"And you would say *no* to your very own kin?"

"But you said we could stay here," I protested.

"Yes, but when your own flesh-and-blood kin wants you, you got to go. She's *family!*" Then Buzzard stomped off down the hall.

"Are you sure, Aunt Bett?" I asked, after Buzzard had gone.

"What on earth do you mean? *Of course,* I'm sure!"

"Yes ma'am," I said, instinctively. "Well, let me get

some things straightened out here, and then I'll call you back and let you know when we're coming. I think we ought to wait a few days, just to see if Crystal comes back," I added hopefully.

"Well, whatever God wills," Aunt Bett said. "In the meantime, I'll start getting things ready here." There was a warm, satisfied sound in her voice. "Oh, and Dove, I meant to tell you that when I cleaned out you all's house—it was rented, you know, and the man who owns it asked me to get your stuff out of it—I found a whole stack of notebooks in your handwriting, and I packed them up with the other stuff that's in my toolshed. I couldn't save much, but I saved those and some of your dishes and pots and pans."

"My notebooks! You found them!" Instantly, Miss Madison's face appeared before me, her eyes serious and pleading.

"I've got them here for you," Aunt Bett said again. "Now you go on and do whatever needs doing, and be sure to thank Buzzard for being so good to you all."

"You're sure it's safe for us to bring Molly back?" A sudden, icy current of fear ran through me.

"Yes, I'm sure," Aunt Bett assured me. "If he'd been going to do anything else, he would already have done it. I expect he was really just snooping around about insurance money, but of course, there wasn't any."

"Oh."

"Well, give Molly and Little Ellis a kiss from me," she said. And then she added, "And to Mary . . . what is her name?"

"Mary Elizabeth," I reminded her.

"Yes. Give Mary Elizabeth a kiss from her Aunt Bett, as well."

Chapter Twenty-two

WHEN I got off the phone with Aunt Bett, I just stood in the hallway for a long time, wondering how things could change so fast—again! I'd felt in my heart that something was going to go wrong, but I never expected it to be that Crystal would run off and leave us all—leave Mary Elizabeth for *me* to take care of! And now, in only the last few minutes, I'd learned that Buzzard herself owned the Swan Place and that we were welcome to stay with her. Except that now, we were going back to Aunt Bett's.

When I finally went into the kitchen, Buzzard was sitting at the table, giving Mary Elizabeth her bottle. I looked at Mary Elizabeth's wispy blond hair against Buzzard's dark arm, and my heart pained me deep inside my chest.

"Aunt Bett said I was to thank you for helping us." The words felt empty and sad. And what on earth was I thinking? I should be happy to be going home. But it all felt so bittersweet! I didn't know what else to say, but my mouth opened and the words that fell out were: "I don't know how I'm going to get us home."

"I'll take you all home," Buzzard said, and I could tell she was trying to speak lightly, just as I had done when Savannah left. Like if she sounded lighthearted, she would *feel* that way. "Been meaning to go see Mee anyways. It's been too long."

"I told Aunt Bett I thought we should wait a little bit. See if Crystal comes back. If that's okay with you."

"Fine with me," Buzzard said in kind of a gruff voice. "Told you all you could stay long as you want." She didn't even look at me. Just kept her eyes locked onto Mary Elizabeth. We stayed quiet and kind of strained for long moments, and then Buzzard seemed to shake off whatever kind of gruffness she was feeling.

"We'll wait awhile, like you said," Buzzard sighed. "And that will give us some time to get you all's things together." At that, she looked down into Mary Elizabeth's round little face, nodded, and said in a singsong kind of voice: "Yes, we'll do just that. Pack up all your things and take you home." Mary Elizabeth had finished her bottle, and Buzzard heaved her up onto her shoulder and patted her back. We finally heard a resounding burp, and Buzzard gave Mary Elizabeth to me. Molly and Little Ellis had come into the kitchen and they stood, one on either side of me. Buzzard looked at us all for a long time.

"Seems like I've gotten used to having children around," she said. "Gonna be an awful lonesome old place when you all are gone."

"If you want children . . . a child . . . around, I know one who'd be awful grateful to have a place where she could live. One place where she could live all the time," I offered. "The way it is now, she gets shuffled around to different relatives all the time." Buzzard was listening closely, with a little scowl on her face, so I continued. "Her mama died and nobody wants to keep her all the time, so she has to keep changing schools and trying to make new friends and everything."

"Who is that?" Buzzard sounded suspicious.

"My friend Savannah. Aunt Mee's granddaughter."

"Humph," Buzzard snorted. But still she gazed at us. "Well, we'll see," she added, finally. "Didn't want to get used to having children around anyway." But by the tone of her voice, I could tell that she was arguing with herself, and I believed with all my heart that it was an argument she was sure to lose. So right then and there, I could imagine Savannah living in that big, beautiful house, with Buzzard and the Sisters of the Circle of Jesus all loving her and taking care of her. It was a wonderful thought!

Well, we found out pretty fast that we really didn't need to wait very long to see if Crystal was going to come back. Because only two days later, there came a postcard . . . from Crystal. The picture on the front of the card was a big magnolia flower, and underneath it was printed, ALABAMA. On the back, Crystal had written:

Dear Dove,

I'm on my way to far-off Las Vegas, where I'm going to get work as a dancer. It's the only thing I know how to do right. You're better than me about children, and that's why I left Mary Elizabeth with you.

Love,
Crystal

And right after her name came little circles and crosses.

"What's that mean?" I asked Buzzard, who was reading over my shoulder.

"It means hugs and kisses," Buzzard said in a flat-sounding voice. And I was thinking that it was a strange thing to add at the end of a card that said she was going off and leaving her very own child.

"I guess that's it," I said. "She's not coming back." Buzzard nodded.

And I don't know why, but all of a sudden, everything started trying to go through my mind all at once. So that for a little moment, I didn't know whether I was the Dove who was Mr. Swan's great-niece and lived in a big beautiful house and had everything I could ever want—or whether I was the Dove who wore dresses that were too short and that the other girls in school looked down on. Then I thought about Miss Madison and how *she* didn't look down on me! And right then and there, it seemed that nothing else mattered. The mean girls at school could say anything about me they wanted to say, and I wouldn't care. And I thought about how our leaving was going to open up a lonely place in Buzzard's heart that Savannah would fill. Suddenly, I wanted to be with Aunt Bett more than anything in the world. I wanted her to tell me everything was going to be all right. Wanted her to make me change out of my Sunday dress. Wanted to know that if anything mean or evil or sad tried to get close to any of us, she would pitch one of her Holy Ghost fits and fight against it and keep it away from us.

Maybe Buzzard could see what was going through my mind, because she just looked at me for a long time. Then she nodded her head and headed down the hall toward the telephone.

After Buzzard got off the phone—and she was on it for

a long time, I called Aunt Bett and told her we'd be coming the next morning.

"Well, come on!" she laughed. "I've had lots of help getting everything ready for you. Come on home!"

And it wasn't long after that before all of the sisters came driving around the back of the house in that same truck, and they lifted Sister Blood-of-the-Lamb down and carried her inside. I followed them into the kitchen where they all sat down around the big table, looking at Buzzard expectantly. Buzzard picked Mary Elizabeth up out of the bassinette and held her in her arms. Then she called to Molly and Little Ellis to come into the kitchen.

"These here little ones . . ." Buzzard motioned to us all, and then she tilted Mary Elizabeth up into almost a sitting position in her arm. "These here little ones are going back to live with their own Aunt Bett," she announced. "And I asked you to come here so that we can pray them to a safe trip and happy lives. And to pray for their Aunt Bett, who is getting ready to open her arms to them."

All around the table, heads nodded and "amens" sounded. Buzzard stepped up and put Mary Elizabeth into the arms of the sister closest to her. "You prayed this little one into the world safely, and now we need to pray again." The sister who was holding Mary Elizabeth crooned into the baby's sleeping face, and then she passed Mary Elizabeth along to the sister beside her. I stood there and watched, while Mary Elizabeth made the rounds of those big, strong, dark arms—except for Sister Blood-of-the-Lamb, who had fallen asleep. Then Buzzard guided Little Ellis and Molly around the table, and each sister put her hands on their heads and asked God to bless them. And when that was done, Buzzard's eyes fell on me.

"And we want God especially to bless Dove here," she intoned, and I felt the tips of my ears going all hot. "This child—this young woman—has more courage than almost anybody I ever met before."

Me? I was thinking. *Me?*

Buzzard went on: "She is faithful to family, and I guess there's nothing as important as that."

Moans and amens again, and then Buzzard said, "Let us pray." They all bowed their heads, but nobody said any prayers out loud, at least not so that you could tell what they were saying, but the murmuring voices filled that kitchen just as surely as the aroma of Buzzard's good biscuits could do. They prayed for a long, long time, and finally, Buzzard whispered, "Amen."

When they were ready to leave, each one of the sisters kissed Mary Elizabeth and put their hands on Molly and Little Ellis's heads, and each and every one of them gave me a big bear hug that almost squashed me. But I didn't mind.

Then they went to wake up Sister Blood-of-the-Lamb, and I waited around, wanting to hear her say "Jesus come while I was asleep?" But this time, the hand on her shoulder didn't wake her up. Then someone shook her shoulder, and another sister reached out and put her fingers on Sister Blood-of-the-Lamb's wrist. We all waited. And in a few minutes the sister looked up at all of us with shining eyes. "This time, Jesus came while she was asleep."

The drive back to our little town from the Swan Place

didn't seem at all as long as when we had driven it before—when Crystal was still with us, and we hadn't added Mary Elizabeth yet. And when Buzzard's big black car pulled up in front of Aunt Bett's house, the cousins came out, and Aunt Bett herself came down the steps, wiping her hands on her apron. There were hugs all around and lots of laughing, and then Buzzard got out of the car with Mary Elizabeth in her arms, and a hush fell over everything. Aunt Bett pressed through the crowd of children and stood right in front of Buzzard, who was holding the sleeping baby.

"Oh, please give her to me," Aunt Bett said, and when Buzzard had handed over the sleeping baby, Aunt Bett cradled her and laughed and went into a whole conversation with her that I couldn't understand one bit. All kinds of baby-words and them chanted in a high, soft voice. And when she got done with that, she looked at all of us and announced, "Oh! God is so good to bring a baby into this house again!"

"Amen," Buzzard said. Then to me she added, "I'm going on over to Mee's house, but I'll stop in and say good-bye before I go on back home." And watching Buzzard get into the big black car and drive out of Aunt Bett's yard, I felt my heart just lurch so hard. But there wasn't time for me to think about it much, for we all started crowding into Aunt Bett's little house.

Why, I never saw such a thing as what had happened to it! There was an extra couch in the living room and a bigger table in the dining room and plenty of chairs to go around it. The boys' room had two big sets of bunk beds and each with a cowboy bedspread, and the girls' room had another two sets, but they were white and each had a ballerina bedspread. In the corner was a beautiful white bassinette with a little lace pillow in it—for Mary Elizabeth.

"Now come on and let me show you the best surprise of all!" Darlene grabbed my hand and pulled me to the back porch. But the porch looked so different, because somebody had walled up part of it and built a partition with a door in it, right on the other side of Aunt Bett's washing machine. Darlene opened the door and I saw that it was a small room with twin beds with pretty yellow bedspreads, and a small bookcase with lamps on either end of it right between the headboards of the beds. Neatly stacked on a shelf on my side of the bookcase were all my notebooks. I glanced at Darlene.

"I didn't look at your notebooks, Dove," she said. "I sure *wanted* to, though!" Aunt Bett had come up behind us, and I heard her take in a sudden breath.

"Darlene!"

"It's all right, Mama," Darlene said hastily. "It's not a sin to be tempted—only a sin to give in to it."

"Well . . ." Aunt Bett muttered, as if she couldn't decide whether to fuss with Darlene or not. But Darlene just kept right on talking: "This is *our* room, Dove—yours and mine—because we're the two oldest. And I remembered how we made ourselves some privacy in our old rooms." She went into the room and pulled on a white curtain that was attached to a long wire and slid it forward as far as the door, making two narrow rooms out of the one.

Aunt Bett said, "Folks at church did all this for us, and they sure had to work hard and fast! They brought in all the extra beds too."

"It's beautiful," I said, and I wanted to hug her, but I knew she would just wave away anything like that. So I just said, "Thank you!"

And later, when I unpacked my suitcase, Aunt Bett admired the beautiful clothes Buzzard had bought for me, and the way her eyes glittered, I knew that she was thinking how far down the line of girls those clothes could go, once I outgrew them—all the way down to Mary Elizabeth herself, I expected.

So that's the way our little family changed all around—with folks leaving it, like Mama and Roy-Ellis and Crystal and Sister Blood-of-the-Lamb, and then other people coming into it, like Buzzard and Mary Elizabeth, and the Sisters of the Circle of Jesus. And at the last, we all finally got mixed in with Aunt Bett's family, and that turned out to be the very best thing of all. Why, there were so many of us, we were like a mighty army! When we'd go to church on Sundays—and Aunt Bett made sure we all went with her, every single one of us—we could practically fill two whole pews, all by ourselves. I always felt so happy seeing us there like that, in two good, strong rows.

Miss Madison was so happy to see me back at school, and we went right back to spending our lunch times writing in her classroom. Eventually, I let her see some of the stories I wrote about Mama and Roy-Ellis and Savannah and Crystal and Mary Elizabeth, and she said that they were "promising," whatever that meant. But it sounded good and made me happy.

When Easter Sunday morning came again, I waked up

before anyone else in the house and went and sat on the front porch and waited for the daylight to come. But it was very different from the Easter before, when I had just lost my mama. I could think about her and not feel all lost and alone. I could remember all the good things about her, especially her singing her honky-tonk songs, and I could think of Buzzard, too, and how she helped us when we had no place to go. And Mary Elizabeth, that wonderful gift Crystal left with us.

In the sleeping house, I knew that Easter clothes for all of us were ready to wear. Buzzard had sent a beautiful "first Easter" dress for Mary Elizabeth, but Aunt Bett was never one to accept charity, so she packed up a box with five jars of her homemade pickles all packed in safely and sent it to Buzzard. The postage probably cost more than Buzzard had paid for the dress, but Aunt Bett wouldn't have it any other way.

The Easter baskets for the little ones were well hidden, a big ham was ready to go into the oven, and it would fill the house with the aroma of ham and cloves while we were at church.

Somehow, we had come right back to where it all started, but I had not come back as the same person who fled into the night with Crystal. I knew for a fact that Aunt Bett had been right, that other Easter Sunday when she told me that I was going to grow up to be a good woman—a strong woman.

So *that* Easter Sunday morning, when I heard a young mockingbird, far off, starting to sing, even before good daylight, I remembered that his song would be wobbly and timid. Mama would have said that he hadn't quite learned his song yet. But even while I sat there on the front porch of a quiet little house that held my big, big, sleeping family, he tried again and again.

And he finally got it right.

Epilogue

S O every year, I watch for the first signs of spring and wait for the flood of memories they will bring.

I walked a road that eventually took me far away from that little town and that happy little house all crammed full of freshly-scrubbed children and jars of pickles, because Miss Madison and I continued writing together for all the years of school I had left, and then she helped me get a scholarship, first to a community college and then to the university itself, where I majored in English.

Buzzard took Savannah in, just as I had known she would do, and when Savannah went off to school, it was to learn how to be a kindergarten teacher. I am surrounded by stories, and she is surrounded by children, and we are both happy.

Because *this* book grew out of all the stories that were written in my notebooks and on Miz Swan's beautiful paper. And at last, I know exactly why Miss Madison said that we should speak in the present tense when talking about a story. Because when someone reads this book, they will be able to hear my mama singing her honky-tonk songs, Roy-Ellis will be enjoying his cold beer, Savannah and I will talk with each other in King-James language on Sunday afternoons, and the Swan Place will always be there. And there *will* be swans gliding across the pond.

These are my stories of losing and of gaining, stories of good people and some who couldn't find a way to be good, but mostly stories about *love*—that incredible gift I fought so hard against. In the end, it was all that mattered.

Center Point Publishing

600 Brooks Road ● PO Box 1
Thorndike ME 04986-0001 USA

(207) 568-3717

US & Canada:
1 800 929-9108